WHO
KILLED
PIET
BAROL?

Richard Mason was born in South Africa in 1978 and brought up in Britain. His debut, *The Drowning People*, won Italy's Cavour Prize for Best First Novel and sold more than a million copies in 28 languages. He has been long listed for the IMPAC Award and written for *Vanity Fair, Vogue*, the London *Times, Guardian, Evening Standard, Tatler, Time Out* and the *New York Times*. His last novel, *History of a Pleasure Seeker*, was an *Oprah* selection, a Lammy award finalist, and shortlisted for the *Sunday Times* award.

With Archbishop Desmond Tutu he founded the Kay Mason Foundation to help South African children reach their full potential. See www.kmf.org.za.

Also by Richard Mason

The Drowning People
Us
The Lighted Rooms
History of a Pleasure Seeker

Items should b
shown below
borrowers m
telephone
barcode
This car
Renew
Fines
incurre
be ch

Lea

WHO KILLED PIET BAROL?

Richard Mason

WEIDENFELD & NICOLSON

First published in Great Britain in 2016
by Weidenfeld & Nicolson
an imprint of the Orion Publishing Group Ltd
Carmelite House, 50 Victoria Embankment
London EC4Y 0DZ

An Hachette UK Company

1 3 5 7 9 10 8 6 4 2

A CIP catalogue record for this book is
available from the British Library.

ISBN (Hardback) 978 1 474 60233 4
ISBN (Export Trade Paperback) 978 1 474 60234 1
ISBN (eBook) 978 1 474 60236 5

Typeset by Input Data Services Ltd, Bridgwater, Somerset

Printed in Great Britain by Clays Ltd, St Ives plc

www.orionbooks.co.uk

To the people of Mthwaku, for welcoming me to their village.
To Cebisa Zono, for sharing certain mysteries.
To Onwaba Nkayi, for allowing me to speak.
And to Benjamin Morse, for following me into the forest.

Dramatis Personae with Pronunciations

Piet Barol (*Peet Ba-Rol*):	A Dutch adventurer, impersonating a French aristocrat
Stacey Barol (*Stay-see Ba-Rol*):	Piet's wife
Arthur Barol (*Ah-tha Ba-Rol*):	Their son
Ntsina Zini (*In-tsee-na Zee-nee*):	A young Xhosa man
Nosakhe Zini (*No-sah-kee Zee-nee*):	Ntsina's grandmother. The witch doctor of Gwadana Village
Sukude Zini (*Soo-koo-day Zee-nee*):	Ntsina's father
Luvo Yako (*Loo-Vo Yah-ko*):	A young Xhosa man; pourer of cocktails
Percy Shabrill (*Per-See Sha-Brill*):	A would-be mining magnate
Dorothy Shabrill (*Do-Ra-Thee Sha-Brill*):	Percy's wife
Esmé Shabrill (*Ez-May Sha-Brill*):	Their daughter
Anella (*A-Nel-A*):	The Chief of Gwadana's second wife
Nonikwe (*No-Nee-Kway*):	Her daughter, born blind

Kagiso (*Ka-Gee-So*):	The chief's son
Litha Jaxa (*Lee-Ta Yack-Sa*):	A resident of Gwadana
Mama Jaxa (*Ma-Ma Yack-Sa*):	His wife
Bela Jaxa (*Bella Yack-Sa*):	Their daughter
Zandile Jaxa (*Zan-Dee-Lay Yack-Sa*):	Their daughter
Lundi (*Loon-Dee*):	A resident of Gwadana
Fezile Khumalo (*Fe-Zee-Lay Koo-Mah-Low*):	A false witch doctor
Atamaraka (Ata-Maracka):	The Queen of Evil
Za-Ha-Rrell (Zah-Hah-Rell):	The King of Evil

Glossary

Sangoma:	Witch doctor
Mlungu:	White person (literally: 'the froth at the top of a wave')
Strange Ones:	White People (literal translation from the isiXhosa)
Mphepho:	A herb burned to summon spirits

CAPE TOWN
SOUTH AFRICA
July, 1914

1

The adventures of his twenties had taught Piet Barol that it is unwise to begin with a lie.

He slipped out of the premises of Barol & Co. and moved discreetly through the crowds, giving no indication of haste but nevertheless moving swiftly. He had taken the precaution of avoiding his creditors' bailiffs, who were at that moment disembarking from the omnibus outside the front entrance. He walked towards the Company Gardens, holding his nerve against desperation.

Piet had told his lie boldly at the Mount Nelson Hotel in Cape Town on a blazing day in 1908. It was an embellishment of an untruth concocted by another – an American woman named Stacey, who was now his wife and the mother of his child. This lady exercised over Piet a dominion no one had achieved before her, for his was an independent spirit. She was seldom from his thoughts, and on this particular morning he could think of nothing else.

It was Stacey who had suggested, moments after their arrival in Africa, that they introduce themselves as the Baron and Baroness Pierre de Barol, and Piet who had upgraded *Baron* to *Vicomte*. He had enjoyed this fiction enormously at the start. His French mother had given him the polished manners of that country and he loved watching Stacey dazzle the credulous audience of colonial Cape Town. She had a genius for mimicry and they spent hours crying with laughter. They laughed so much that for months Piet did not appreciate the price of his enormous lie. He was Dutch, not French, and far from aristocratic. The necessity of devising a fictional past made intimate friendship impossible. His numerous acquaintances knew nothing of his real circumstances and were inclined to be envious or bashful in his presence.

For the first time in his life, he had no true friends.

He walked up Adderly Street, doffing his hat at every store. He was a favourite of the neighbourhood. With the exception of two rival furniture makers, whose business had suffered considerably since his arrival at the Cape Colony, he was well liked by his fellows in the Chamber of Commerce, whose wives had sleepless nights after asking his wife to lunch. It was thought rather good of Piet that he should stand so little on ceremony. More than one competitive masculine spirit had been soothed by Piet's sincere desire to see the best in them. In a land where the aristocrats of Europe had the social sanctity of deities, a French *vicomte* who lunched in public with tradesmen was thought of very well by them.

For several years, while early success bore him on, it had given Piet pleasure to see the ripple of deference that spread out from his wife when she entered a room. Self-confidence had hidden from him the dwindling of his capital. Circumstances now obliged him to confront it. No one, least of all the rich, troubles to pay bills on time to men who give no appearance of needing money. Stacey's deftly delivered tales of her father's railroad fortune, and the Château de Barol on the banks of the Loire River, meant that debts to the Barols did not feature prominently in the consciences of their neighbours. Piet had many more outstanding invoices than he had the energy to pursue. His languid approach to debt collection had solidified into an impassivity that bound him so strongly he often woke in the night, struggling to breathe.

It was unfortunate that those to whom he owed money did not show similar restraint.

He drank an iced coffee in a café and read the papers for an hour, then went back to his shop. He was met by the fragranced air, the impression of delights within, that made Barol & Co. one

4

of the best patronized emporia in the city. Piet had long since had to let his white staff go, since they demanded salaries he could not rise to. But he had made a virtue of necessity, and trained his African employees in the highest traditions of European service. These he had been privileged to observe, as a younger man, in the household of the best hotelier in Europe. When an assistant at Barol & Co. asked a client if they might be of service, and bowed, and made eye contact, and then smiled as they extolled the comfort of a chair or the perfection of a stool, they did so quite as well as any shop assistant anywhere in the world.

For many years, Piet's habit of treating his staff as if they were men and women whose lives were at least as important as his own, a habit that differed sharply from the attitude of all but the rarest white men, had inspired in those who worked for him a passionate devotion that had kept them loyal long after their salary payments ceased to be very regular. It was unfortunate, thought Piet, as he caught the expression on his manager's face, that loyalty cannot feed a large family. She was a descendant of high-born Malays, whose innate nobility set even the richest of his patrons at ease. He knew that losing her would be a loss he might not sustain – not only to his business, but to his spirits. For this reason he made no great hurry to open the envelope she put in his hand, lips pursed, restraining the tears that would have been unacceptable on the shop floor. He took it to his office, a handsome room at the back of the shop, furnished with pieces of which he was especially proud. Every wooden object in it was made to his own design, by the master craftsmen he had been sensible enough to lure from his competitors.

Piet sat at his desk, looking at the envelope. He thought of the child he had made with Stacey, a boy named Arthur who seemed only to walk in dappled sunshine, who had inherited his father's love for the world and all that was in it.

He felt unbearably sad.

Louisa Vermeulen-Sickerts-Longchamps stood in front of a long mirror in her suite at the Mount Nelson Hotel, an expression of intense concentration on her face. The aquiline perfection of her youth had resolved into an adult face of arresting severity. She had lost weight on the voyage, having spent every day in her cabin, expelling all her poor stomach had managed to hold down. This had given her an ethereal quality, complemented by porcelain skin, that was given a jaunty finish by the angle of her hat. When she had settled this to her satisfaction, she picked up the telephone. 'Mr Longchamp's suite.' And then, after a moment: 'Darling, I'm ready for you.'

Louisa had taken care that her new husband's room should be at the furthest extent of the hotel from her own, since Dennis seemed inclined to visit at all hours in his pyjamas. She was not looking forward to the day ahead, though she was resolved to do what she had decided. She went into the connecting bedroom without knocking and for the first time all morning she smiled. Facing the window was a young woman whose springy golden curls were held up by sharp spikes of platinum, set with emeralds.

'You're divinely overdressed,' said Louisa, and kissed her once, sensuously, on the mouth.

'Don't set me off before lunch,' said Myrthe Jansen.

'I need you to be a darling to Dennis. I've an errand to run on my own, and you're the only person who can draw him off me.'

Myrthe smiled. 'It would be such bad form if he made love to your best friend on your honeymoon.' She slipped her arm around Louisa's waist.

'But such a relief,' said Louisa. And they kissed very tenderly.

They sprang apart when the door of the next room received a series of knocks that indicated tremendous *joie de vivre*. Louisa went into her bedroom. She opened the door to find her husband in crisp flannels. Dennis was not conventionally handsome, but his enthusiasm for life rendered him attractive. Throughout his dogged pursuit of her, Louisa had worried that in the end this much devotion and light-heartedness might bore her. In fact, having made room for romantic passion elsewhere, she found the reliability of Dennis' good humour extremely pleasant. He wore exactly what she told him to wear and was inordinately proud of the way crowds parted for her. Louisa knew from her sister Constance that there are husbands who resent an attractive wife. 'Darling,' she said. 'You must take care of poor Myrthe for me. The heat doesn't agree with her.'

The faintest flicker of disappointment passed behind Dennis' eyes like a cloud on a cloudless day. 'I'd rather hoped for lunch with my lady wife,' he said.

'You must do with me for tea. I have a family friend to look up.'

'Let me come with you. I'm brilliant with aunts.'

Louisa had learned to speak plainly with Dennis. 'I need to go alone,' she said. And then, because she was a strictly truthful person in all but the most intimate areas of her life: 'I wish to.'

☙

Mrs Hendricks, who until six minutes before had been its manager, was leaving Barol & Co. as Louisa got out of the Mount Nelson Hotel's Rolls Royce. Louisa noticed the woman's elegance, and the fact that she was in tears. It seemed a strange omen. She collected herself. Louisa Vermeulen-Sickerts-Longchamps was not accustomed to making apologies. She had only said sorry, as a child, with the greatest unwillingness; typically only when compelled to do so by a parent. But she was an honourable person and valued her self-respect. Its maintenance required the payment of a penance. Inside, the scented air and spinning fans caught her off guard; she had not expected such refinements. There was no one on the shop floor. She browsed the chairs and tables, moving towards the four-poster bed in the back recess, for she was unerringly drawn to the best thing in any room.

Louisa had a discerning eye for craftsmanship, which her father had delighted in and trained. She did not think much of the Mount Nelson's wicker furniture, and had supposed that this was all a colony at the end of the earth could offer. She stroked the superb finish on a satinwood bed post and weighed the bother of getting it to Amsterdam, where it would look exceedingly well in her third guest bedroom. Then she turned from the bed. She would delay no longer. She went to the office door, knocked and opened it. Seven people were in the room, each one of them distraught. At their centre stood Piet Barol.

The sight of Louisa Vermeulen-Sickerts gave to Piet's traumatic day the quality of an hallucination. He had not seen her since the night, six and a half years before, on which she had accused him of seducing her mother in front of her entire family. Louisa's particular diffidence; the quick, half-suppressed movements by which she silenced the gesticulating people in front of her and became their sole object of attention. He recognized them from Amsterdam, but they were less hostile than they had been when she was nineteen. With a nod, he dismissed his employees, wondering how many would remain by lunchtime.

'It wasn't hard to find you,' said Louisa. 'I didn't expect it would be.'

Piet looked at her, and many things went through his head. Finally he said: 'Of course the Fates should have sent you, Miss Vermeulen-Sickerts, to be present at my downfall.'

❧

He took her to lunch at a tiny place with a Chinese chef recently off the boat from Shanghai. Louisa's appearance at this crisis heightened its embarrassment so acutely that Piet abandoned himself to the suffering ahead. Almost with relish, he put away all deception and said: 'I might as well tell you, I am ruined. My adventures in this colony have not been a success.'

The Piet Barol of six and a half years before would never have made such an admission. Its promptness was disarming. Louisa quite forgot her own mission and leaned forward. 'Everyone means something different by "ruined". What do you mean?'

'We can barely pay our rent another month. The cook went long ago. Soon my son's nanny will have to follow her. I have no

8

funds to obtain wood of decent quality, and no staff to sell my remaining stock for anything like its true value. I have miscalculated. Trusted rather too much to my own luck.' He looked at her, pugnaciously. 'But then you always thought I would, did you not, Louisa?'

Louisa did not look away. 'I suppose I did, Piet.' It was the first time either of them had used each other's Christian names.

He smiled. He felt no hostility towards her. The wounds she had done him years before seemed like a bruised knee of childhood by comparison with his current feelings. 'I used to listen to you and Constance talking about me. The servants' bathroom window was just above your balcony.'

'Did you really?'

'I did. Night after night. Learned never to eavesdrop. And I never have since. Thank you for that lesson.'

There was an uncomfortable silence. Both ignored the steaming dishes of spiced pork before them. During this silence, Piet's mood fell off a cliff. He was not altogether proud of the way he had conducted himself in Louisa's childhood home, and had many times sought to disentangle the mesh of praise and blame that a neutral judge might accord his actions in Amsterdam.

This was never possible.

'I am sorry,' said Louisa.

'We were young. You didn't like me. I was man enough to bear that.'

But the vicious remarks Louisa had made to her sister about Piet Barol were not what she had crossed the world to repent. 'It's the other thing I meant,' she said.

He was touched beyond words. An intense affection rose through him – for Louisa and her family and the world he had left behind. He accepted her apology and peppered her with questions as they walked back to the Mount Nelson. At its gate he kissed her on her right cheek, then her left, then her right, in the Dutch manner.

Impulsively, she hugged him. 'This is not the moment to lose heart. You are exceptionally talented. You need capital and a capable business manager.'

'I'm afraid money doesn't come when you have ceased to believe in yourself.'

'You cannot have reached quite such a pass, Piet Barol. It would disappoint me tremendously if you had.' She smiled. 'Let me give you the money. Enough to pay your staff for a year and buy decent wood. You can sell me shares. It wouldn't be a loan.'

But Piet, who had seen Louisa have this thought, and struggle to hide it from him all through lunch, raised his hand. He said no in plain terms.

'Well eat with us tomorrow, then, and bring your wife. I am intrigued to know the woman who has tamed you.'

Since his arrival in Cape Town, Piet Barol had spent a great deal of money. An American businessman had provided him with one thousand pounds and advised him to exploit his European glamour. He had followed this counsel and leased lavish premises on Adderley Street. He had also rented a beautiful house in Oranjezicht, with a veranda entwined with bougainvillea and a view of the mountain and the vast plains. These expenses he did not regret. As he waved Louisa goodbye, however, it seemed unwise to have spent so much in the restaurant and bar of the Mount Nelson Hotel.

For a moment he considered going into the hotel. Its pink bricks spoke of certainty. He knew someone would stand him a drink if he claimed to have left his pocketbook behind. But he had seen many men in these early days of the Union of South Africa disguise their imminent ruin from themselves with alcohol, and so hasten it.

He pressed on up the mountain, leaning forward as the gradient rose.

It was two months since the Barols had owned a motor car, and the walk from his shop to his house was wearying. Piet had lost the heedless athleticism of his youth and the challenge of these daily hikes shamed him. When he had completed his climb, he was so ravenous he overindulged in the delicious, fatty curries Arthur's Cape Malay nurse made, and though his thighs were as solid as the mahogany he could no longer afford, there was a ring of fat around his waist that spoiled the cut of his clothes.

The Barols had spent their early capital quickly. That they had spent much of it wisely was entirely to Stacey's credit. Stacey Barol had an instinct for human susceptibility, and even Piet's first, rudimentary chairs had found places in the homes of prominent citizens. In the early days, making workmanlike cabinets, tables and desks with a team of Indian joiners, they had made healthy profits – more than enough to leave them disinclined to economize in their private life.

But as Piet began to understand the possibilities of wood, he had become more reluctant to let each piece go until it was ready. At first his wife had found his artistic standards charming. Now Stacey was alarmed by Piet's perfectionism. She knew what life close to the abyss of the fashionable world was like, and would not permit her son to share this knowledge.

Piet did not know when he had grown lonely. At first it had been merely tiresome to live up to an invention; but he had come to hate the Vicomte de Barol, and to wish earnestly that people knew him as he was. Stacey's company and her wicked wit usually consoled him, but today he missed the confidential support of a friend. He found himself wishing he might spend an evening with Didier Loubat, with whom he had passed many hours of hilarious intimacy in Amsterdam.

Behind the pleasures of the life he and Stacey had made, anxiety had for several months haunted Piet like a malevolent demon. He loved taming wood into the shapes of his imagination. He wished he did not have to sell what resulted; that he could make each piece for the love of the thing itself. But by claiming an aristocrat's privileges without entitlement to them, he had jinxed his good fortune.

He was thoroughly out of sorts by the time his own house came into view, and cursed himself for not having bought the place when the money was flowing. He paused outside the garden, catching his breath.

And at once he was calmed.

The windows were lit with a gentle yellow light. His wife sat on the veranda, her back to him, with a blanket about her shoulders. Stacey had a long neck and the carriage of a ballet dancer. He loved making love to her. He loved being loved by her. He trusted her cleverness and her ability to restore his faith in his own value. He felt, as he opened the garden gate, that if he were granted one dying wish as an old man, it would be to return to this house; to one of these nights with Stacey and Arthur; to see them again, just as they were at this moment. And this allowed his gratitude for the present to warm the icy trickle that ran down his spine when he thought of the future.

Piet had been seen by his son, who betrayed his presence with a whoop of joy and launched himself at Piet from the top of the steps. The child's certainty that his father would always catch him banished Piet's fears. The little boy was nearly six years old and getting heavier. Piet threw him over his back, dangled him upside down by his legs and kissed his tummy, provoking squeals and giggles. As he returned him to the ground, he felt the twinge of pain in his lower back that these acrobatics had begun to inspire. His wife smiled. So many of her friends in Paris had been abandoned by their children's fathers that Piet's delight in Arthur neutralized the exasperation that had been building within her all afternoon. As Arthur clung to his leg and tried to climb it, Piet saw that various bills were scattered on the wicker table. He had no wish to discuss them, but in Stacey's eyes was a look he had learned to recognize.

'Will you bath me, Daddy? Please!' called the child, rescuing his father.

'Very well.' Piet leaned over his wife and kissed her on the lips. 'Later, my darling.'

'But we must go through these tonight. Ignoring them won't pay them.'

'We will.'

He made Arthur's bath last almost an hour, and they splashed so wildly that the floor was soaked. Piet mopped it dry himself. This took a further fifteen minutes. He sat with Arthur while he had his dinner, then tucked him into bed and read him four stories. He did not wish the child to fall asleep, but his voice always soothed him; and soon Arthur's eyes were shut, his oval mouth open, his little head framed by golden curls.

Piet sat watching him for half an hour, filled with love. Then he went outside.

Stacey was still on the veranda. On certain nights, miraculously, the wind dropped. The tempestuous currents that raged between mountain and sea calmed. Tonight was one such. He went and sat by her and took her hand. For a long moment she did not speak. Then she said: 'This is the last time, my darling, my dearest Piet, that we are going to find ourselves in this position.'

'I hope so.'

'It must be so.' Stacey turned to face him. 'You observe my current equanimity.'

'I do.'

'This is not how I felt when I discovered this.' She took from the pile of bills an unpaid customs receipt. 'If you'd only told me you couldn't pay it! Every clever woman has something set aside. But you did not tell me, and you did not pay it and now they've impounded our mahogany.'

'Couldn't you pay it now?'

'I don't have the money now. I am almost in a rage with you.'

'I'm sorry, my darling. Truly I am. I will atone in private as often as you will let me.' He kissed her shoulder and expected her to smile but she did not. There was a softness in her husband that made Stacey reluctant to say critical things to him. She tried to speak without anger. 'You *must* behave like a man of business.'

'You're right. I'll do better. I promise, I'll do better.'

And they went to bed, leaving the bills undiscussed, as they had left them on so many nights; and they slept close against one another as the wind lifted and the house clung to the mountainside.

❧

'Of course, she knows who I really am,' said Piet to Stacey the next morning, conveying Louisa Vermeulen-Sickerts' invitation.

'How inconvenient.'

'I don't want to pretend.'

'You'd better hope no one greets us then.'

No one did greet them as they crossed the Mount Nelson's restaurant. Sitting at a table by the window were two of the best-dressed women Stacey had seen in her life, their glamour offset by the sombre tailoring of the man between them. She was used to being very grand in the Colony, and took for granted her status as an arbiter of style. Now she saw that she looked like the provincial copy of a lady of fashion that she was. She felt a sudden instinctive hatred of the two women. One had a mass of blonde curls, held in place by a brooch set with a huge aquamarine and diamonds. The other was dark, with a severe, strikingly beautiful face of the kind that was beginning to look so well in studio photographs.

'I'm delighted to meet you,' Stacey said, taking Louisa's hand. 'My husband speaks so happily of his time in Amsterdam.'

Dennis insisted on the springbok, though Piet told him it was likely to be tough at this time of year. Myrthe and Louisa ordered kingklip. Stacey, who had not eaten in a restaurant for eight months, ordered a slice of foie gras and the largest of the lobsters thrashing in a silver-mounted tank that the waiter wheeled to them on a trolley. Piet felt grateful to Louisa for the absolution she had given him, and exerted himself to entertain her husband. Dennis was not at all the man he would have thought of for her. In fact, he realized, he had never thought of her as any man's wife. And though her husband sat across from him now, with his weak chin and sparkling eyes, he still struggled to imagine them together.

14

'This kingklip tastes rather like turbot,' said Louisa.

'How I miss the turbot at the Ritz in Paris,' said Stacey.

'Do you know Paris?' asked Dennis.

'My wife was a singer there, at the Opéra Comique,' said Piet swiftly, to divert Stacey from the fantastical narrative she usually gave of her time in the French capital. 'We met on the liner coming here.' It was a relief to begin with the truth.

'Too divine,' said Louisa. 'I do hope you'll give a private concert for us, Mrs Barol. There's a piano in Dennis' suite.'

In the Europe she had left behind, the expression of such a hope would have been an insult intended to wound. Stacey did not know what to make of it, and her stomach tightened. She had suffered in the chorus of the Opéra Comique, surrounded by women who were worldlier, and lovelier, and nastier than she. She knew the traceless ways in which women injure one another, and looked sharply at Louisa, whose glance was penetrating.

'I sing nothing but lullabies now,' she replied prettily. 'I do hope you'll come to tea and meet our son before you go.'

❧

Later that afternoon, Piet said: 'You did very well.'

'You should get some money from her. She's evidently stinking. She gave me her card.'

'I would rather starve.'

The resentment that had been simmering in Stacey since her discovery of the unpaid customs bill overcame her self-control. 'You may starve if you wish. But you will not make me or Arthur starve with you. It is time to throw yourself on Percy Shabrill's mercy.'

'Never.'

Stacey stood up. With a great effort of will she resisted the temptation to make any of the cutting remarks that were tearing through her brain. 'As it happens,' she said, 'I've had a clever idea.'

'Which is?'

'I've done the accounts three times and there's no chance of us getting to Christmas without fifty pounds. We need two hundred pounds to get our wood back and hire new staff.'

'How much do we have left?'

'That's not your affair. It's not enough to liberate our mahogany, but it will get us to Johannesburg.'

He groaned. 'We cannot stoop so low as Percy Shabrill.'

'We can indeed. We are going to get a large order from him, with a fifty per cent deposit to be paid in advance. That house he's been building must be finished. They can't have furnished it yet.'

'They might have.'

'If they have, we must make them repent what they have bought.' She sat down next to him. 'Really, do think Piet. Shabrill's terribly jealous of you. One sees that plainly in those boastful letters he writes. He wants you to respect him as an equal. If he can establish himself as your superior by paying you to work for him, what rapture it will give him.'

'You're a devil woman.'

'On the contrary. I'm your guardian angel. I'll send them a telegram this morning.'

2

Ntsina Zini was choked by Bad Magic. He saw it in the black faces around him; heard it in the white voices barking instructions. Even men who made Ntsina laugh till his stomach ached were sombre here. All the sadness in them was lured to the surface by the Pit.

At its entrance, demons swirled in the orange dust. Spirits shut away before time began. How foolish these white men were to liberate such dangerous prisoners! He thought of the snake-tongued man who had tempted him to Johannesburg with talk of radios and money. To whose temptation he had succumbed – he, Ntsina Zini, of the Gwadanan Zinis, great-grandson of the Great Founder who had led the Gwadanans and their cattles to safety during the Great Slaughter. He had been born in the protection of a powerful Good Magic. And he had thrown it aside.

The elevator that took human beings a thousand feet into the earth at the Crown Mine, Randfontein, was sixteen feet long and six feet wide. Ntsina was a son of the uplands, heir to forests and hills and vast skies. He joined the fifty-five other men crushed together in a stench of breath and bodies with distaste. Behind him a man with a morning erection was pushing it hard into the small of his back. Ntsina's name meant 'Laughing Boy' and he had always honoured it. But confinement in a demons' prison had robbed him of laughter. The dust stole into his mouth and nostrils, bringing the first thirst of the day. It crept into his eyes and ears. He whom the girls had called *Enomntsalane*, Alluring

17

One; whom they had delighted in kissing because his smell was beautiful. More beautiful, thought his grandmother, than his face. He, Ntsina Zini, had not once been clean since his first descent. Physical dirt placed a strain on his soul. So did the facts of his predicament. He had been at the mine two months and six days and had only three shillings in the cowhide pouch around his neck to show for it. In his misery he had bought three bottles of brandy and two nights with a plump Sotho woman whose jolliness was a sham. On the morning after the second of these he had discovered a furious rash on her buttocks and behind her knees and five days later, today, he had woken to incorrigible itchiness in his crotch.

Ntsina could not scratch himself in the mass of bodies, and the itch overwhelmed him. He was ashamed of his amusements. From deep within, his truest self told him to go home. Only forests and cold streams could cleanse him of his defilements. But the owls at night that swooped over the men's hostels, harbingers of doom to those who would die on the morrow, shrieked their veto: How? He had been brought to the Rand at no charge. A third-class train ticket to East London, which was a two-week walk from Gwadana, cost two pounds. Even if he never drank again, never bought a woman's caresses, it would be a year before he had what he needed. As they slipped away from the sky, and the clamour of chisels on rock sank through his ears and into his brain, he knew that even another day was too long. The Good Magic bestowed on him by his birth was no match for the daily drinking in of demons and their dust.

They reached the bottom of the first shaft. Already the men were singing to shield themselves from sorcery. Ntsina had no voice for it. He stepped off the platform and went towards the dark tunnel that led from the cavern. He was afraid of it. Enchantments had been laid in this place. They caused beams to collapse and men to be trapped. They broke legs and arms and heads. He was thinking these grave thoughts when there was a shower of sparks in the darkness. High above, another platform was descending. From its passengers came a collective cry, a cry he would remember until his death sixty-nine years later. Eighty feet above the cave's floor the elevator slowed, and for a moment everyone present held their breath. Then the Good Magic snapped and the cage fell until the rock stopped it.

∽

No sound came from the cage. Not a whimper, though the heads were quite intact and seemed to gasp. Toes and feet and ankles and calves and knees and thighs and groins were red, red flesh and white bone. But chests and arms and hands and faces and ears remained. It took two days to send into the depths another platform chained by metal, and guns to herd the trapped miners onto it. During these two days, Ntsina had time to understand just what his ancestors had done for him. He had been early that morning and on the first transport, kept awake all night by troubled dreams. Usually he was late. When he was late, he was on the second descent. Had his dreams not disturbed him, he would be a mangled mass.

'Thank you to the Great Goddess Ma, and the immortal Amarire, and my own revered ancestors, for troubling me last night and seeing me alert for this day.' He intoned it over and over, so the men close to him stepped away, believing him to be mad. But Ntsina Zini was not mad. He was resolved.

The hostels were locked. He made no attempt to retrieve the second vest and undershorts he owned. With his money in a pouch around his neck he went to the gate, topped with barbed wire; and when the guard said he would let him pass only if he gave him two shillings, Ntsina paid this price and did not once look back, lest thoughts of brandy and radios disturb his conviction.

∽

Ntsina walked until he could walk no more. He had walked through a whole day, and now it was night. He barely noticed when the road became a pavement. He did not see the gaslights

19

on the corners. All that held him was his Thirst. In Gwadana one never walked more than three days without finding water. It was a stream he searched for, and none was here. And then it started to rain, and as it did he found his refuge.

It was a bush that grew in Gwadana, vast and tangled and bright with thirsty flowers. He knew that beyond its thorned branches was a snug hollow, large enough to sleep in if the plant was thriving. As a boy in the forest he had learned many secret sleeping places. He lay on the grass, face to the clouds, and gave gratitude for the rainwater. It washed his caked tongue and slid between the curls on his head. It slipped into his ears and ran down his back and the drops got bigger as the lightning flashed; and he, heir to forest and hills and vast skies, was cleansed. Cleansed of what he had been and seen. It was a warm night and the rain was warm. He took off his shirt and washed himself with it. Now it was pouring, and he pulled his trousers off and wrung them out and watched rivulets of demon dust run from them. He longed for the smoothness of a goatskin. Only goatskin could keep a man dry on a night such as this. Not having one, he accepted he would be wet. He was in the grasp of Good Magic at last.

He thanked his ancestors from the bottom of his heart. Then he retired into the depths of the bush, accepting the scratches and the blood, and was rewarded by a rat-proof resting place in a dome of green leaves that smelled inexpressibly sweet. There was mud on the ground and he laid himself on it. It clung to his skin, and dried, and made him warm, and he slept for eleven hours, diverted by dreams of home.

It was after nine o'clock when Ntsina awoke, and the milkman had long since been and gone. The morning heat swelled gently through the leaves above him. He shifted, and the mud on his back cracked. It was rich, red mud. For a moment he thought he was in Gwadana, but the belch of a goods van told him otherwise. He lay in the bush, thinking. To get home he needed money. Having come all this way, he did not intend, upon further reflection, to return without the hut tax or a radio. This part of the previous day's plan he would modify.

Ntsina emerged from the bush and brushed the dried mud from him. He did it vigorously, rejoicing in the softness it had given his skin. He scratched his crotch methodically. Already his memory of the woman's rash was easing, though the itch remained. He put on his clothes, already half dry. Looking about him, he saw that across the road was the largest homestead he had ever seen.

∾

Dorothy Shabrill stood with her husband at one end of the vast space that would soon be her drawing room. With them was the decorator, Mr Naryshkin, an impossibly good-looking Russian from the Caucasus. Dorothy, a parson's daughter, did not like him. She knew that her aunts in Tunbridge Wells would disapprove of him. And yet, as he and Percy conversed, she did not feel able to hold her own against the combined wishes of her husband and this ghastly man. Dorothy had been sent into a panic by Percy's decision to invite Piet Barol. She had met Piet on the liner that had brought them all from Europe. She recalled having been in ebullient spirits, and talking too confidently of the School for Servants' Children she had come to South Africa to found.

The failure of this institution was a matter of unspeakable shame to Dorothy Shabrill.

'Capital, capital,' Percy was saying. *Dear* Percy. She did love him. He took her hand. 'Mr Naryshkin says the papers and the curtains will be hung in time for the party. Whether the furniture is here depends on the boat from Europe. She left Southampton yesterday. If she doesn't arrive, we'll put them up at the Carlton.' He turned to Mr Naryshkin. 'There'd better be a dining table. We've thirty coming to dinner next week.'

∾

Piet was woken by the sound of a battered Louis Vuitton trunk being dragged into the room. He put his face under a pillow but in the darkness his future pressed down on him unendurably. He lifted his head, rolled over, and said, seeing his wife: 'I wish you'd take that off.'

Stacey was wearing the scarlet dressing gown she had worn at their first meeting. It was now open at two seams and stained with breast milk. She looked at him, hesitated, and let it slip into a puddle at her feet. Piet stood up and went to her. Worry had kept Stacey awake most of the night. It seemed fitting that Piet should atone for the anxiety he had caused her. She liked to make love in the morning, and before she slept, and for the whole of Sunday afternoon.

When they were finished they were no longer angry with one another.

'I'm sorry, my dearest one.' Piet kissed her shoulder. 'Forgive me. Help me.'

'It's your own pride that will destroy us. You must conquer it.'

'I know.'

'The more you let Percy Shabrill demean you, the more he will end up paying us. He's terribly jealous of you. You must make him feel like he has won.'

'It rather looks like he has,' said Piet, bitterly.

Ntsina was still gazing, wonderstruck, at the vast house when its wooden gates swung open and an open-topped Packard nosed through them. It reminded him of the murderous monsters Amariva had loosed on the earth. Sitting in the back was a white woman who looked so unhappy he lost his fear of her.

He spoke three of the six English words he knew. These were: 'I am hungry.'

The sight of a half-naked Kaffir in obvious want brought Dorothy to her senses. She was the luckiest woman alive, as Percy often told her. She had studied the Gospel too imaginatively to share most Europeans' instinctive fear of a black face. She could see at once that this young man was from the countryside. He had not the veneer of city suffering. She could tell he was kind, and the way he hung his head and stood back from her, and then glanced up at her, and looked away again, told her that he had been raised by a good woman.

'Do you speak English?' she asked.

'Thank you, sir,' said Ntsina, employing his remaining three English words.

'Very well. Run inside to the kitchen. Mrs Mafuduka will give you something to eat and something to do.'

The Xhosa chauffeur, observing that Ntsina failed to respond to this instruction, translated it for him. The radiance of Ntsina's smile made Dorothy feel better, and silenced her thoughts on the matter of the decorative scheme to which she had just consented. The chief colour of this scheme was mauve. It was she who had remarked how pretty mauve is, when shown a hand-coloured photograph of the Empress of Russia's boudoir. She had not intended this careless enthusiasm to infiltrate every inch of her house, nor did she agree with Mr Naryshkin about the importance of unifying themes. Nevertheless, she had quite possibly saved a young man's life. This being what Jesus would have done, she felt fortified.

Ntsina, meanwhile, walked into a new world. A gang of men were laying bales of real lawn across the dry orange dust of the Rand. Behind them, twenty others were planting rose bushes along gravel paths. Nature had been sold into slavery. The smell of something foreign, which he did not know was creosote, was heavy on the breeze, drowning the scent of the roses. Only a nose as keen as Ntsina's could have caught the flowers' graceful lingerings beneath the dust and the turpentine. He knocked at a door and was pleased to see that the young woman who came to answer it was both a fellow Xhosa and very pretty. He had a way with pretty girls that made them fond of him and he smiled his most submissive smile.

23

'I am here for Mama Mafuduka,' he said.

With his damp clothes, mud behind his ears, Ntsina Zini provoked interest and sympathy in the Shabrills' kitchen. He was given a cup of strong tea with six full spoons of sugar stirred into it. An entire loaf of bread and a half pound of butter were placed before him. The butter was freshly churned and salty. He had not tasted anything so delicious in many moons, and kept his eyes on his plate to make sure no one stole it. But the Shabrills' servants were not like the men in the mines. The only things taken from him were his damp trousers and vest, which were put near a warm stove and replaced by an outfit of rough but spotless cotton. Ntsina's grandmother was renowned as a laundress and Ntsina knew at once that a woman like his grandmother had washed this shirt. The housekeeper was jovial and fat. 'I am your servant, Mama,' he said. 'With this big house and those sore knees you must need a young man's help. I can carry and lift and I do not shirk duty and I am respectful and I do not drink.'

'Then you are welcome here,' said Mrs Mafuduka. 'Where are you from, brother?'

'From the forest of Gwadana, Mama.'

'Then you must work in the garden.' It was well known that Gwadanans had the Good Magic of growing things. 'The Strange Ones love flowers. It is a small aid to us in our troubles.'

The set of three rooms that Percy Shabrill called 'the servants' wing' had been built to house six adults and a golden retriever. Since the passage of the Natives Land Act the previous year, its occupancy had risen to twenty-seven. Mrs Mafuduka enjoyed Dorothy Shabrill's total trust and found it hard to turn away refugees. By the time most country people reached Johannesburg, they were in bad physical shape. The air of these rooms was far from sweet-smelling. Each had a job, nominal or actual, in the preparation of the Shabrill homestead. The pitiful sum paid them was augmented by a generous provision of wholesome food – to the expense of which Dorothy Shabrill turned a blind eye when brought the provisioners' bills.

Ntsina was almost ashamed, in this company, that his family had not been thrown off their land. It was clearer every day what mischiefs the spirits he had helped liberate had accomplished. How else could one explain such viciousness and greed? He heard stories of white farmers turning on workers they had known since childhood; of old ladies thrown out in the snow, and dead children buried in hedgerows. He knew that wicked spirits had roamed abroad in past ages; his grandmother had told him of the Great Slaughter of the Cattle and of many wars. But it seemed that the mines on the Rand, breaking open the hollow, secret places of the earth, work that he himself had undertaken for the lure of money and a radio, were unleashing Bad Magic in undreamed of quantities. He thought of the sadness in the face of the white woman who had saved him. Perhaps the Strange Ones were also afflicted.

The man whose sleeping blanket Ntsina was assigned to share was the backyard refugee best versed in the ways of Europeans: Luvo Yako, who poured the Shabrills' cocktails. Luvo could write and speak fluent isiXhosa, English, German and Afrikaans, having been educated by German missionaries in the town of Cradock, in the upper valley of the Great Fish River. In the care of his teachers he had grasped the grammars of four languages and learned more than ten thousand irregular verbs. Current circumstances now obliged him to devote his prodigious memory to the alcoholic preferences of the Shabrills' guests.

At their little school in Cradock, with its neat Victorian streets, Luvo's German teachers had stressed the virtues of self-reliance, scholarship and allegiance to the Ten Commandments. He had read every book in the Mission's small library and committed long swathes of Goethe and the Bible to heart.

'How are you, brother?' asked Ntsina.

'I am well,' said Luvo.

But this was a terrible lie.

⟡

The mission school where Luvo had been head boy was eight hours' walk from the farm the Yakos had tilled for six generations. The school was an enclosed world, separated from outside events by a timetable of Teutonic precision. The husband and wife who ran it were so horrified by the Natives Land Act, and its abolition of property rights for non-whites in fourteen fifteenths of the country, that they had sheltered their students as long as possible from knowledge of its existence. This well-meaning decision had the unintended consequence of depriving their pupils' parents of the support of their male offspring at the moment of crisis. When Luvo learned what had happened, he ran most of the way home to discover the cluster of huts in which he had lived since birth occupied by a strange and hostile family. This family, he was told by a neighbour, had handed all their animals to the white farmer who owned the fields the Yakos had sown. They had accepted his terms of servitude: a wage of two pounds a month for the father, with ten shillings per son and five for daughters. Luvo knew in his heart that his father would never accept such iniquity – he who often made one hundred and fifty pounds a year from the judicious breeding of cattles. From farm to farm he went, seeking his family, but he encountered only unknown, distraught faces. Some offered Luvo a meal of mealie pap; others told him, as though it were his fault, that they had nothing to share. At length he found, shivering on the side of the road, surrounded by dying animals (for the evictions had taken place in midwinter, just as the goats were kidding), a distant cousin who told him that his parents had gone to Cradock to find him.

Back Luvo raced, sleeping only when exhaustion crippled him; if not oblivious to the cold, then fortified against it by panic. There are many paths across the mountains to Cradock, and he prayed ceaselessly to God to lead him to his parents and sister.

26

On the seventh day, God did. Luvo found them in a ravine, close to sunset, burying his sister's two-year-old baby; and when his mother saw him, she who had not wept once, who had supported her husband's decision to refuse slavery on any terms, even as she saw that freedom in a stolen land was meaningless; she, whom the village rascals had feared, who had raised her children on the strictest principles, gave way and wailed so loudly that even in that remote place, and at that grave hour, her husband shushed her for fear the police would hear.

'Why are you here?' asked Ntsina, who could tell Luvo came from the Cape.

'Why are any of us here?' asked Luvo, dryly.

The Barols knew the value of a first impression, and did not intend to be seen emerging from a second-class train carriage by the Shabrills. Neither did their current situation permit the financing of two first-class tickets to Johannesburg. They solved this dilemma simply. Piet purchased a single first-class ticket and Stacey dressed to the nines. She had the *demimondaine*'s sense of the value of clothes, and had taken pains to treat her dresses well. As they boarded the train, she made a great show of dropping her ticket on the track. It was an old one and was soon taken by the wind. A chivalrous guard told her not to worry the slightest bit about it.

Thus it was that Percy Shabrill, who had come to the station for the pleasure of being present when Piet saw his Packard for the first time, had no reason to suspect that his guests were not in possession of a substantial private income.

Piet Barol was deeply disturbed by his failure to do better than Percy Shabrill. *Than Percy Shabrill!* Piet knew himself to be cleverer and more discerning than Percy. That these advantages were not reflected in their current circumstances was alarming. Since their parting on the Cape Town docks six and a half years before, having shared a cabin all the way from Europe, Piet had mentally divided by many times Percy's tales of success, unleashed in occasional letters full of typographical errors. Confronted by Percy in the flesh, he saw that Percy *was* rich.

'Shabrill!' he said. 'You look devilishly well.'

＠

Percy took them first to the new house. The last square of lawn had been laid and a picnic set under fully grown oaks he had bought from a farm near Potchefstroom.

'Who has the time to wait for trees to grow? Jolly sight worse than watching paint dry.' He laughed and Dorothy blanched inwardly. She hoped Percy would not shame himself by being over-eager for his guests' approval. She looked across the lawn, where Esmé was approaching.

Esmé was the Shabrills' five-year-old daughter. She was spoiled, and inclined to unlovable displays of temper if thwarted. Dorothy knew firmness was called for, yet she could rarely stop herself from giving her daughter exactly what she wanted. This had begun as an expression of love, but lately fear had entered her motivation – for Esmé had her father's stubborn determination and knew that poor behaviour in public was a powerful weapon against her mother.

'Come sit by Mummy,' said Dorothy.

But Esmé walked straight past her, right up to Stacey, and said in a voice of wonder: 'What a pretty lady.'

As Stacey Barol squeezed Esmé to her, she wondered whether the furniture for the vast and empty mansion behind them had yet been ordered, and did her best to concentrate on the little girl. She was rather a poppet. Esmé had dark curls and a snub nose and bright blue eyes. The adoration in them fortified Stacey. She looked at Esmé's father. It was clear from the look on Percy's face that intimacy with his daughter would be well received. 'When is your birthday, my darling?' she asked. 'I am going to give you a marvellous present.'

'In sixty-eight sleeps I will be six,' said Esmé proudly.

Stacey kissed her all over her face, and handed her back to her nanny. Esmé comported herself like a paragon of childhood virtue – Dorothy had never seen her so acquiescent. A little dagger pierced her heart, its point poisoned with the knowledge that another woman could achieve what she could not.

'You've been so clever with this garden, Mr Shabrill,' said Stacey.

cᴏ

The Barols were relieved to be told that they would be sleeping at the Carlton Hotel, the Shabrills being 'all at sixes and sevens'.

'I won't hear of you paying your bill,' said Percy grandly. And when Piet protested too vigorously, Stacey silenced him with a glance. As soon as they were alone, she undressed and went to bed. She was a great believer in afternoon naps. Piet took a bath. He lay submerged in scalding water, his heart thudding. When he emerged an hour later, he towelled himself dry in the dressing room of their suite. He tried to feel sure of success, but tonight he doubted himself; and another man's doubt can rarely be disguised from a highly competitive male. This Percy Shabrill certainly was. Piet was used to being pleased by his reflection and sought the old remedy. He had a high colour from his bath and his eyes were their magnificent blue. But even when he pulled his shoulders back there was no disguising his changed silhouette, nor the fact that its narrowest point was no longer his waist. He dressed quickly.

The tail suit he put on called him to the other side of his twenties: to a slimmer, more certain self drinking champagne on a star-filled night in Amsterdam. That boy seemed lost to him now. He sucked in his stomach to close the trousers, which had already been let out two full inches. His wife appeared at the door from the bedroom, quite naked. She looked at him for several moments without being seen, an expression on her face that was at first inscrutable and then – at once; intensely – tender. She crossed the room and stood close behind him. Sleep had soothed her feelings.

They looked at one another in the mirror, and Piet put a hand on her thigh and pulled her towards him. She put her arms around his neck. She was wearing a perfume he had given her for their first Christmas together, which she had wisely preserved. Its scent conveyed its expense without being remotely ostentatious.

Piet inhaled deeply.

'We're more than a match for these two,' she said.

3

Standing on the terrace of her gaudy new house, which still smelled of paint and wallpaper glue, Dorothy Shabrill found that her hands were shaking as she watched the Vicomtesse de Barol advance across the porcelain tiles. She looked at Percy, who was making nice to the Chairman of the Stock Exchange. The thought of failing him made her mouth dry. She looked up. In heels, Stacey Barol was four inches taller than she was.

'Vicomtesse, how splendid you look,' Dorothy said.

'Do call me Stacey. And let me call you Dotty. I feel we are to be great friends.'

Luvo Yako, standing at the door and watching for half-full glasses, wondered how much the guest of honour's jewellery was worth and prayed for grace. Stacey was wearing paste diamonds so large no one could disbelieve them. Luvo moved to refill Percy's champagne glass in time to hear him say: 'The government is well on the way to settling the native question once and for all.'

At this point, the only white member of staff, the butler, announced that dinner was served.

The thirty grandees whom Percy had invited to meet the Barols took dinner in a mock Elizabethan dining room, the only room in which Stacey was able to see any trace of furniture.

'I expect you miss France,' said Dorothy Shabrill to Piet as he drew out her chair.

'One misses the food, of course.'

This remark ignited Dorothy's simmering unease about the

menu. Mrs Mafuduka was a superb cook when entrusted with simple, wholesome recipes. Phyllo pastry stuffed with artichokes and foie gras now seemed to be asking too much of her. She felt a cavern of shyness open before her.

Percy Shabrill's own opinion that he 'rubbed along with anyone' had been confirmed by his election to the Rand Club, in whose smoking room the adjective 'sound' was often used of his political views. He had come to South Africa with nothing but an ingenious system for cooling air and had begun by installing cool rooms in large houses and country clubs, taking care to get on drinking terms with their owners. Percy had no ear for a snub, which was a powerful advantage. He also had a plummy English voice that got plummier and plummier each season. Though he sang *God Save the King* whenever he could, Percy was glad to be out of England. He had not excelled at his minor public school. He had loitered outside the gates to advancement in his own country and found that his sort of man was rarely at the front of the line. In South Africa all this changed. *Every* white man with some pluck could take for himself a share of the spoils.

It had taken Percy two years, and the provision of many chilled pink gins, to break into the torrent of money flowing from the gold mines. Cooling their managers' offices had made him rich enough to take a seat at the Rand Club's Long Bar within hailing distance of the alcove where Barney Barnato sat. He rather thought he might make it to Parliament, and was cultivating contacts he could rely on when the moment came.

The prospect of one day telling his pompous older brother Cyril that he was a Member of Parliament was very pleasing to Percy Shabrill. He was a believer in Capital, Empire, and the need for the white races of the Union to settle their differences after the unpleasantness of the Anglo-Boer War. Englishmen and Afrikaners alike were welcome at his table, and he was gratified to have prime specimens of both to exhibit before Piet Barol tonight.

'D'you know,' he said, as his guests took their seats, 'I should like to begin with a toast. To friendship and this marvellous country.'

'To friendship and this marvellous country!'

The cry was lustily taken up by the younger men, who were anxious to win Percy's favour. Their wives were full of compliments and wearing new dresses.

'Your daughter is heaven,' said Stacey, on Percy's right.

'A perfect terror, her nanny tells me, but I'm afraid I agree with you. Perhaps she'll marry your Arthur one day.' Percy drained his glass of white Burgundy and motioned to Luvo to refill it. He felt superb. 'If he can afford her.'

'My mother-in-law will insist on a duchess for him, I'm afraid. So old fashioned!'

Percy did a good line in patriotic plain-speaking and was proud of the way he was conducting himself. He had almost forgotten that he had ever been afraid of beautiful women. 'A British subject is worth any number of foreign duchesses,' he said roguishly. 'I can say that to you, of course, as a fellow Anglo-Saxon.'

Luvo counted the diamonds on Stacey's neck. Before every meal at school the boys had recited the Ten Commandments in English, isiXhosa and German. He heard them now and resolved once again to obey them, though it seemed to his methodical mind that Moses had not considered every situation when applying his blanket ban on theft. He moved up the line of guests, pouring white Burgundy, and as he reached his employer, Percy said: 'Mr Keyter, you have done an excellent job in difficult circumstances. My thanks and admiration.'

Mr Keyter, the National Party's member for Ficksburg, who was used to being the object of toasts at official banquets, favoured Percy with the humble smile he reserved for such occasions. 'It is a white man's country now,' he said, 'and the statute books must reflect that. For the good of all members of our society, whatever their God-given hue.'

'Capital!' cried Percy, who had recently bought a share in a gold mine. Although he had promised himself to delay the introduction of this fact, he could not honour his vow a moment longer. He turned to Stacey and said: 'I've just bought a mine,' rather exaggerating the scale of his purchase. 'I can't tell you the trouble we have with labour. That's why this new act Keyter's lot have brought in is so precisely what the country needs. These Kaffirs don't want to work. They don't value money. If left to themselves, they'd do nothing but beat their women and raise cattle and make war.'

'How tiresome for their women.'

'Indeed. Better separate the men from them entirely. This is the clever thing Keyter's done.'

Stacey nodded, an expression of great interest on her face. In truth, she did not care for political talk. On her right was a portly English gentleman named Merriman, who now spoke.

'My dear Shabrill. That's not quite fair. You forget who laid the railways and dug the mines. Indeed, many natives have a greater trade value than a lazy white, and yet we do not make poor Afrikaners homeless. Nor,' with a jovial bow in the direction of Mr Keyter, 'would we dream of doing such a thing.'

Mr Keyter was too tactful to point out that Englishmen like Mr Merriman had done exactly this barely twelve years before, when, in a bid to win the Anglo–Boer War, they had burned thousands of Afrikaner homesteads and herded their occupants into concentration camps. His own uncle and aunt had been among the unfortunates, six of his cousins had died, and in his youth he had sworn never to break bread with a bloody Englishman. This vow long overturned, his only response was the beatific smile that had won him a reputation for wisdom.

Luvo filled Percy's glass and stepped back. He trained his eye on an imperfection in the panelling. Had anyone looked at him, they would have seen that his carotid artery was throbbing.

'This legislation is not sensible,' said Merriman. 'The natives are exceptionally docile when well governed and fairly treated. In my opinion, it is dangerous to throw them off their land and leave them to roam the countryside.'

'Our land, Mr Merriman!' said one of the young wives.

'Hear hear!' roared Percy. Dorothy glanced at him and he lowered his voice. 'I don't deny that natives, backed by European capital, have accomplished much that is useful. But we must look to the future. A man will not work in a mine for long if he has the least desirable alternative. This Land Act is timely and admirable. In a short period of, admittedly, some little suffering, the native will relinquish his claims to equality and accept his condition.'

'But surely, Mr Shabrill,' said a young woman with pale skin and a sunburned nose, 'the black races are the original occupants of South Africa. It cannot be just to prohibit them from owning land in their own country. Nor to deprive them of land they already occupy in these so-called "white" areas.'

The volume of talk and laughter dipped noticeably. The young woman had recently arrived from England and spoke louder than necessary. She was not three weeks married to a lieutenant of Percy's, whose chances of advancement shrivelled then and there. Percy's father, when challenged, had specialized in freezing stares. Percy essayed one now, but he was on his third glass of white Burgundy and his gaze lacked focus. All his employees fell silent.

'But enough about politics!' exclaimed Dorothy. She rang the bell for the next course to disguise her confusion. She had never enjoyed being the object of attention. When a young man began to talk about race horses, she felt obliged to say something to her neighbour. To her dismay, she found herself introducing the topic she least wanted to speak about. 'I'm so glad the house is finished at last,' she told Piet. 'It has been a monumental effort. So much choosing!'

Piet steeled himself. The moment had come.

'Have you furnished it?' he asked.

'We've a few sofas in the drawing room. Everything else is on the boat from England.' Dorothy fiddled with the rope of medium-sized pearls round her neck. 'We rather went in for mauve. Our decorator is a Russian. He tells me it is the Empress Alexandra's favourite colour.'

The obliteration of Piet's hopes made the room swim. Everyone felt very far away. Watching him, Stacey felt fiercely protective. 'Of course Pierre's ancestors,' she murmured, 'who date to Charlemagne, think the Romanovs rather common.'

~ⅎ~

The idea that the Russian imperial family might be common so disturbed Dorothy Shabrill's confidence in the order of things that she barely registered relief when the phyllo pastry Mrs Mafuduka served was perfect. As she discussed the African heat with Piet, and how pleasant a European autumn would be, her mind enumerated the many instances of mauve to which the Barols would be exposed as they toured the house. She began to harbour violent thoughts about Mr Naryshkin – and then about herself.

Percy, intending to reprimand the sunburned young woman severely, dismissed the servants. Luvo left the dining room and walked down the long passage to the kitchen. He was a person who preferred his own company, or his sister's, to that of most people. The battle of voices coming through the kitchen door was a powerful repellent. He found the overcrowding of the servants' quarters unendurable. On certain nights, when the others were asleep, he crept out of the yard and went to the glade of oaks that Mr Shabrill had bought. He was a devout believer in the Lord Jesus Christ, and thought of the barbarities the Israelites had endured and been saved from. Surely God would not abandon His Bantu in South Africa.

He thought of his sister's baby, and frowned. The child had died on the mountainside in the days after their eviction from their warm, thatched hut. He kept to the side of the house. He felt his chest might explode from the turbulence of his thoughts. Leaning against the fountain made of imported Italian marble, looking up at the clouds, was Ntsina.

'Good evening,' said Luvo.

'Greetings, my brother.'

They stood in silence. Ntsina, feeling awkward, broke it with a question. 'Where is your home?'

'I have no home.' Luvo did not cry, mindful of what was proper for a man. 'I was too late to save my father's house, or my sister's child.' He told Ntsina how he had taken his family to Cradock, to his German teachers, who had offered them employment and the permission it conferred for a black person to reside in a white area. 'The government says natives must work for whites or go to the native locations. But the locations are so crowded there is no land to farm, and no employment to pay the hut tax. It is simply a ruse to force us to work on the mines, as you have done.' As he spoke, the moon came out and the house reappeared and Luvo remembered that he should be on duty, handing round the coffee and cognac. The thought appalled him. 'We must *act*!' He kicked the fountain, impotently. 'Waiting in those stinking rooms will avail us nothing. We must protest.'

'But to who?' asked Ntsina.

'To the King of England. We are British subjects, just as much as the whites. The British let the blacks of the Cape Colony vote. Some of them, at least. It is because we are voteless now that we have no one to speak on our behalf in the Parliament.' He glanced at the house. 'Some of our brothers and sisters have formed a congress. It is named the Native National Congress, though I think *African* National Congress would be better. We are Africans, after all. They want to raise funds to send a delegation to England.'

Ntsina was stirred by what he heard. 'Let me go into the house and steal a treasure,' he said. 'These Strange Ones have stolen so much there is honour in stealing from them. I will do it while they are eating.'

'That would make us as bad as they are. Believe me, I have considered it. But Moses tells us "Thou shalt not steal."'

'Who is Moses?'

'A prophet of the Jews.'

'But we are not Jews. And our needs are pressing.'

37

In their bedroom at the Carlton Hotel, Piet took off his tailcoat and groaned. 'God, I hate this thing.' His shoulders had broadened in his late twenties and the coat no longer fitted as it had once done. He feared Stacey would be angry with him, but instead she was thinking how handsome he was, and remembering how divine his hair smelled when she woke in the morning, curled against his chest.

She went to him and nuzzled his neck. 'We must make them hate what they have bought. That is all.' She tried to put her hands through the waistband of his trousers, but they were too tight to admit access. She moved to stand in front of him, and forced the clasps. 'I love you, Piet Barol,' she said. 'Do as I say and all will be well.'

⤲

Lying under the blanket with Luvo, who seemed to be sleeping, Ntsina was seized by an itch worse than he had ever known. An autocratic itch. A curse sent by Atamaraka, the Queen of Evil. He lay in the dark, oblivious to the snores of his neighbours; wondering how he could lie still all night with such an itch as this. Eventually he could bear it no longer. He slipped his right hand through the uncomfortable *mlungu* underwear Mrs Mafuduka had given him, and scratched so hard he made the skin bleed.

Luvo, who was not asleep, attempted to decode the significance of his blanket-partner's furtive movements. At his boarding school, he had been introduced to masturbation by several of the boys, and had grown used to falling asleep to the gentle rasp of blankets on skin. But he was a fastidious person. He had never been drawn to touch anyone, and when touched himself he had not liked it. He did not at all like the idea that the man with whom he would be sharing a blanket for the foreseeable future might be masturbating beside him.

'What ails you, brother?' he asked at last, in exasperation.

38

The answer was silence and an abrupt cessation of movement under the other half of the blanket. Luvo turned over and closed his eyes, relieved that no vulgar expansion was required. He was afraid of his dreams, but Mr Shabrill was quick to spot a dozing servant and he needed his sleep. Ntsina waited tensely until Luvo's breathing regularized, then scratched again. Each touch was at once relieving and intensifying. He tried to sleep and dreamed of fire flaming in his crotch. Escaping it he kicked Luvo so violently that Luvo sat up and said: 'What is the matter?!'

'I am not well,' said Ntsina. And he told Luvo of the fire in his crotch.

'What you describe sounds like lice,' said Luvo. 'We had two outbreaks at school while I was there. I have never known such itching.'

'What did you do to stop it?'

'Come. I will show you.'

Mrs Mafuduka was a sound sleeper, and Luvo extracted the key to the kitchen door from the pocket of her apron without much trouble. He let Ntsina into the cavernous room and lit a paraffin lamp. Ntsina's smooth, voluptuous buttocks were perfectly lit as he took down his shorts. Luvo did his best not to look. Instead he mixed a concoction of vinegar, carbolic soap, sunflower oil and a few pinches of rosemary, taken from the newly laid vegetable garden. 'You must leave this on for an hour but no longer,' he said. 'And neither of us can sleep in that blanket again until it has been washed with boiling water.'

'Thank you,' said Ntsina. And he added two words that men did not use lightly in Gwadana: *mhlobo wam.* They meant: my friend.

Luvo looked down and left the room.

❧

In the Carlton Hotel's dining room, where she and Stacey were lunching the next day, Dorothy Shabrill was reminded of the occasion in her youth when she had been invited to sit on the library steps with the girls who ruled the roost at St Agatha's Convent School. Barbara Harris had recently had a profound encounter with the Holy Spirit, who had remonstrated with her for her many unkind actions. She had reformed, briefly, and inspired a fashion for piety. This had elevated the social stock of Dorothy Prince, though she could not grasp why. The chance to escape obscurity had been thrilling, but its scale inhibiting. As the head waiter led them to her table, she trailed behind Stacey's skirts, remembering how she had failed to impress the popular girls.

At this moment, Mr Naryshkin emerged from the bar, wearing a suit of radiant whiteness. Dorothy supposed it was gratifying to encounter acquaintances in public – but she wished that the acquaintance was not Mr Naryshkin.

The Russian kissed Dorothy's hand, and when she said 'May I present the Vicomtesse de Barol,' Stacey saw a leap in his bright green eyes that made it plain he scented a potential client. Stacey knew exactly who he was, having done her research the night before with Monsieur Etellin, the Carlton's manager, who had told her that Naryshkin always lunched with them on Tuesdays. She was very gracious to him, but as soon as he had gone she said: 'Who was that odious little man?'

This so encapsulated Dorothy's own thoughts that she found herself, despite a strict upbringing, gossiping unkindly about Mr Naryshkin. Stacey was an enthusiastic audience. As Dorothy recounted the various ways in which Mr Naryshkin had bullied her into violating her aesthetic conscience, Stacey's spirits rose.

Neither Barbara Harris nor Cynthia Carmichael had ever, even at the height of their social toleration, treated Dorothy Shabrill with the mischievous amiability Stacey Barol lavished on her as they ate smoked chicken and drank almost a bottle of Sancerre. Dorothy knew that Percy was occupied showing Piet around his mine, and apart from Mr Naryshkin there was no one in the room she knew, not being as socially adventurous as her husband. This gave her the feeling of freedom inspired by unexpected half holidays in her youth. As she dug viciously into Mr Naryshkin behind his back, inspired by the way Stacey looked at her as she laughed, she felt drawn to confidences. She did not tell Stacey that she hated South Africa, that the incessant cruelties of daily life necessary to be a citizen of the first rank offended the principles of her happy childhood. But she did tell her that she could no longer live in an ugly house. That colonial taste, with its slavish adherence to the British fashions of five years ago, depressed her immeasurably.

Watching Piet at work when his attention was engaged gave Stacey an intense, arousing pleasure. As Dorothy Shabrill spoke, she imagined how she would feel about Piet while he made a house full of furniture for a client wholly under his spell. All the sullen accretion of disappointment and irritation, blended with worry – gone. She enjoyed his carnal attentions in many moods, but when she was delighted with him . . . Oh, that was quite different. 'Now tell me my dear,' she said. 'How much did it all cost?' And Dorothy, with a swish of wine, told her.

❧

As they left, Stacey said: 'Show me the catalogues you chose from.'

Dorothy did so. Mr Naryshkin had pasted into an album of mauve Moroccan leather photographs of each of the pieces the Shabrills had ordered from Hepplewhite's. Dorothy's timidity as she turned the pages made Stacey feel solicitous, even as she prepared to wound. 'Dearest Dotty.' She sounded so friendly. 'What is the point in being rich if one has to have such vulgar things in one's home?'

Dorothy had no answer to this question.

Stacey smiled tenderly, and at this moment she did feel tender. She knew Dorothy was going to do exactly as she wished. 'A lady must know when to overrule her husband.'

❧

'Now Pierre,' Percy was saying, as the Packard slowed at a pair of gates topped with barbed wire, 'I have one mission today, and one mission only. To help you see that men like us belong on the

Rand, where the gold is. Cape Town's for sissies.'

Piet said nothing. Percy poked him good-naturedly in the ribs, as the popular fellows had done at school. Unlike his wife, who had been ignored by her classmates, Percy had been disliked. It made him feel anxious around Piet, who was so obviously a man people warmed to. 'I've a little mine I thought we might look over,' he said.

The chauffeur opened the door. Piet was hit by a torrent of orange dust. He coughed and put his hat over his mouth. 'You've failed at the first hurdle, old fellow. Give me fresh mountain air any day, and damn your money.'

'This is the life of a real man!' Percy banged him on the shoulder.

They were within a high barbed-wire fence. 'Once they've signed on the dotted line,' said Percy, linking arms with Piet, 'a lot of our chaps think of breaking the contract and heading home. We don't stand for that. Hence the gates. Occasionally someone slips out or bribes a guard, but not often. And when he does he has nowhere to go.' They stopped outside a low hut made of tin. Behind it were piles of orange earth, shaped into flat-topped pyramids. Piet had a confused sense of railway tracks and winches and cranes, rising and falling, like monstrous insects draining the sap of the earth. The ancient trees on the perimeter, which had once marked the limits of a farm, loomed like ogres. Men were milling about the mine entrance, shirtless mainly, and even the dust did not blunt their smell. The muscles and sinews on their torsos were finely etched; none had an ounce of fat. 'It's vigorous work,' said Percy, 'but we give them breakfast and dinner.'

'What about lunch?'

'If they want it, they must buy it.'

'How can they shop if they're locked in here?'

'Oh, we have a mine store. A wise man keeps the money close to home.'

Piet had enjoyed graduating to the aristocracy of race. It was a wonderful thing to live in a country in which no white man except the very poorest demeaned himself by hard manual labour. But he was used to the blacks of the Cape, many of whom had once had the vote; who were now domestic servants, street sellers, messenger boys. The men in Percy's compound seethed with the energy of caged animals. They watched Percy pass, their expression unreadable, then turned away as a bell rang.

'Are you man enough to venture into Hell?' Percy beamed with pride.

They went down into the pit.

The chiselling of the rock made Piet want to scream. When the platform stopped, they entered a cavern and a rush of cool air, released from deep in the rock, caught him unawares; brought with it smells of things long left undisturbed. The drill stopped. 'I've seen enough my friend,' he said.

It had not occurred to Percy that Piet might be claustrophobic. He himself was not – 'wouldn't mind spending a night underground, you see if I wouldn't,' as he often said at the Rand Club. This chance was too good to miss. 'Come along.'

Piet looked at the narrow tunnel – two feet shorter than he was, wide enough for two men to pass with barrows – into which Percy was sauntering. He did not fancy it. A white foreman had arrived to greet Percy, and Piet felt himself obliged to go forward. He was not a coward, but he did so unwillingly. His carpenter's eye spelt out every danger. The crossbeam of the second roof support was splintering in three places; had never been strong enough for the weight of so much rock. Everywhere one looked the supports were inadequate, awaiting only the slightest tremor to crumble and collapse. 'How many injuries do you have here?' he asked the foreman.

'Oh, not too bad,' said the officer, conscious of Percy's eye upon him.

Piet bent low and followed Percy. They went into a small cave, and then into a tunnel. And then it was dark all around except for the light of their gas lamps. Piet thought of the three hundred metres of rock that separated him from the world of air and sky.

43

He thought of Stacey and Arthur – gorgeous, adorable Arthur. He loved the boy with a joyful passionate intensity that deepened with occasional periods of distance – when all he could remember was Arthur's smell, and the way he laughed when amused; and he forgot that he could sometimes be a pain and make it impossible to nap on a Sunday afternoon.

'This is a marvellous concern you have here, Shabrill,' called Piet. 'Now let me buy you some lunch. And you, Mr—?'

'Walmer,' said Mr Walmer, the foreman.

'You'll join us too, won't you, Walmer? Tell me how this all works.'

Percy was two bends further on, and went some distance before he realized that his foreman was not following him. He had gone further than he wished, even he who felt no fear, and scampered back with secret relief. When he saw how pale Piet was, his heart soared.

⌒〜

'We can undercut that Russian Jew by twenty per cent and still make a killing,' said Stacey as they dressed.

'It's off, darling. We will not accept money from this man. We will not take the money he makes by such means.'

'You've had a trying day.'

'Shabrill is a monster.' It was a blessing to be alone with his wife at last. 'You should have seen the poor creatures toiling for him. We are not so desperate that we must seek his favour.'

'I'm afraid we are, my darling.'

'There are other ways. We'll go back to Europe.'

'And do what there, might I ask? Should I be a chorus girl again, and you a tutor?'

'Something will come up.'

'My dearest—' Stacey's voice was knife-sharp. 'The time for hoping something will come up is passed. It is sweet of you to care so much about the Kaffirs. But the gold will be mined regardless. I have fixed everything. You need only pluck the ripe fruit.'

She kissed him. 'I'll wager they're having a scrap about it at this moment.'

∽

But Stacey was wrong. Percy Shabrill, while blinded by Mr Naryshkin's eloquence and apparent cordiality with several grand dukes, was aware in his deepest soul that his wife did not care for the furniture she had endorsed. He loved his little woman ferociously. In vain had he implored her, in the dark of a mosquito-laden night, to tell him if there was anything that did not please her. Again and again she had told him that it was all wonderful, she couldn't be happier, not possibly, and he had known in his soul it was a lie.

When Dorothy told him the truth, which was that she wished to send everything back to Hepplewhite's and order a house full of original objects of art by Barol & Co., he took her in his arms. Her timidity made him feel powerful, and power was Percy's drug.

'You women will never cease to astound me, my pussy pie,' he said. 'But you are a rich man's wife now, and you can afford to be capricious.'

The effects of the wine at luncheon were beginning to lift and Dorothy felt a pang of guilt at the cost of sending everything back. Then she considered the emotional toll of living with it, and made an accommodation with her conscience. 'You are my little man,' she said.

'And you are my little wifey.' Percy pulled her towards him and touched his lips tenderly against hers. It was a phrase they used with each other. It was their highest compliment.

They went to the Carlton Hotel, and entered the lounge just too late to hear Piet say: 'Shabrill's the kind of fool who will get more pleasure by paying double.'

∽

They ate dinner and talked and laughed. As soon as the ladies had gone for a stroll in the Conservatory, Piet seized the initiative. 'Now look here, Shabrill. Your wife has got it into her head to

45

send all your furniture back to England and commission the whole house from me. My dear fellow, do not think of it. You have been a huge success in Johannesburg, anyone can see that— But you could not possibly afford it.'

This was exactly the right thing to say. By the time the waiter had filled their brandy glasses for the second time, a bargain had been struck. The sum agreed was so astronomical that Piet had to dig his nails into the flesh of his palms to avoid looking jubilant. 'You'll have to pay up front, Shabrill,' he said. 'In case you're ruined while I make it.'

Percy fancied himself a shrewd negotiator. 'Six hundred pounds now, six hundred on delivery, piece by piece.' And when Piet nodded, as though a great condition had been wrenched from him, his new client, in a gust of spontaneous joy, bellowed: 'God save the king!'

☙

Piet and Stacey Barol occupied room 238 of the Carlton Hotel. Their neighbours in 240 had a night of severely interrupted rest. They were a middle-aged German couple and lay awake in single beds, listening. It was a painful experience for them both. There had been a time when Fritz Bayer had inspired such sounds from Klara. He had not done so, he thought, staring at the ceiling, for eight years at least, not since the night – he smiled, and involuntarily reached his hand beyond the coverlet to touch his wife. Her bed was just too far away. A stiffening in her, a sense of unwillingness that communicated itself in infinite ways, made Fritz withdraw his hand.

On the other side of the wall, Stacey said to Piet: 'Let's go again.'

They went at it hell for leather, with an abandon that reminded them both of the first time they had made love – in another hotel room. Piet's victory over Percy Shabrill – *their* victory – made him feel superb. He stayed hard for four hours and Stacey made full use of him. She did things with her tongue that flooded her husband's head with endorphins. Sensual rapture made them whole after the anxieties of the last six months. As she lowered herself onto Piet, setting his angle with imperceptible movements, Stacey felt a surge of happiness. They could have a cook and a car *and* a chauffeur – at the least, she thought, mentally doing the arithmetic as a glowing orgasm built within her.

'Just . . . there,' she said.

By the time dawn broke and Fritz Bayer, who had not slept a wink, got out of bed, they were spent.

'You shall find me much more responsible in future, my love.' Piet kissed her forehead. She turned on her side. He cuddled up against her, his nose at the back of her neck, where her smell was sweetest. 'I know when I've had a narrow escape.'

❧

Piet went early to the house. It was icy on the Rand, and the air had a thin beauty. The smell of dust was damped by frost. He took a taxi, expecting to find a night watchman on duty, but in fact the house was buzzing with activity. Mrs Mafuduka recognized him and let him in. She would have done so with no one else, but the master's guest of honour must be her own.

Piet walked through the mansion, mentally removing the mauve hangings and papers. Herbert Baker had conceived four substantial rooms on each floor, each open on two sides to a garden, clustered around a magnificent central hall where a double branched staircase rose to another floor, with another four huge rooms. It was monumental but spare. A space waiting for things to happen. Piet began to feel the prickings of an intense, euphoric joy – a bubbling of his purest self that had nothing to do with his rescue from destitution. It was the joy of an artist presented with a blank canvas. He wandered through the empty house as the sun rose. He began to see shadows of the drawings he would make, that would one day become furniture. He resolved then and there to copy nothing.

He was standing in the centre of the upstairs hall, with his eyes closed, when Dorothy Shabrill coughed to announce herself. He turned to her. He felt full of love for her.

'Dotty,' he said. 'When you came on that ship, did you ever imagine what would happen?'

It was the first time Piet had used her first name.

'Nothing I thought would happen happened,' she said.

They spent six hours together. Piet paid such attention to what she said that Dorothy was able to access her own intelligence, too often shut down by shyness. He let her opinions direct the thoughts of his highly creative mind. Together they settled on a subject, inspired by Percy's toast at their first dinner: This Marvellous Country. Furniture inspired by the natural treasures, the fauna and flora, of South Africa.

'Percy will love it,' said Dorothy. 'He wants to go to Parliament.'

When she really had to go, because she had a tea she could not cancel, she went with twenty sheets of sketching paper clasped in her hand, each bearing the wisp of an idea. Piet stumbled into the garden. His head was full of blazing glorious dreams.

The marble terrace announced its owner's wealth in no uncertain terms. Piet was sobered by it. He must honour his promise to Stacey – to make money by being practical. But how? Mahogany was devilish expensive, yet he could not settle for pine. What he needed was wood of distinction – a lot of it, as cheaply as possible. In this vast country there must be what he sought. He sat on a low whitewashed wall, looking at a rose garden being brought into being. A few feet away, a man in his early twenties was removing aphids from newly potted roses, an expression of blissful absorption on his face. He was clearly alive to the natural world. Piet stood up, went down the stairs into the garden, and joined him.

'Good day,' he said. 'My name is Piet Barol.'

'Thank you, madam,' said Ntsina Zini.

The Strange One continued to speak. For the first time Ntsina heard the beauty of the Strange Ones' tongue, because Piet spoke it gently. Ntsina did not feel afraid. He felt curious to know what this person was saying to him. '*Linda apho,*' he said, speaking louder than was necessary – as though extra volume could help the white man comprehend. What he meant was: 'Wait there.'

Luvo was most unwilling to get involved. 'It is better not to understand what the Strange Ones say,' he said. But Ntsina took him to the Strange One, whom they found crouching down on the ground, plucking fat aphids from the plants and squeezing them between his fingers.

'Good morning, sir,' said Luvo. 'My colleague tells me you were speaking to him. I'm afraid he does not understand. I would be honoured to translate.'

'I was telling him my name,' said Piet. 'Which is Piet Barol. And I was asking him his name, and where he comes from.'

A quickfire exchange of isiXhosa ensued, after which Luvo turned to Piet and said: 'His name is Ntsina Zini. He comes from the village of Gwadana, where his grandmother is what the natives call the *sangoma*. In other words' – it pained him to declare such misguided superstitions – 'the witch doctor.'

'Where is this village?'

Luvo consulted Ntsina. 'At the most easterly extent of the Cape, beyond the great forest.'

The words 'great forest' lifted Piet's mood further. 'Are the trees in this forest good and strong?'

When Luvo translated this question, Ntsina's face brightened. He began to talk animatedly. Finally Luvo raised a hand to stop him. 'He says the trees are fine, and have many uses among his people.'

'Who owns this forest?'

A further consultation ensued, during which an air of puzzlement spread over Ntsina's face.

'He says no one can own a forest,' said Luvo.

A forest full of good trees that no one owned: it was the answer to all Piet's troubles. 'How far is it from Cape Town?' he asked, but his mind was already half made up.

'More than one thousand kilometres,' said Luvo.

49

The journey's glamour sizzled. If the wood were free, and of good quality, the cost of transporting it to Cape Town could be borne without compromising his profits too greatly. 'How old are you?' asked Piet.

'I am nineteen,' said Luvo, with dignity.

'Then you are ripe for an adventure. I would like to go to this forest, and for this man to be my guide. You may come too and translate for us. What do you say?'

The route to Gwadana lay through Cradock, and the chance of seeing his parents and sister made Luvo's heart leap. When told of the Strange One's request, Ntsina knew that his ancestors had sent him the means of getting home. Their favour was confirmed when Piet offered to pay him twice what he was currently earning – on condition that he did not tell Mr Shabrill where he was going.

Hands were shaken and plans laid. And that evening, when the Barols embarked on the Cape Town train, Luvo and Ntsina got into a third-class carriage, with provisions packed by Mrs Mafuduka.

'We are being sent on a great mission, my brother,' whispered Ntsina to Luvo in the darkness. 'Our ancestors have saved us for a special purpose.'

'It is the Lord Jesus Christ who has saved us,' said Luvo. 'Say a prayer of thanksgiving to Him with me.'

'I will say my own prayers,' replied Ntsina; but he spoke with great friendliness. And when the young men had completed their devotions, they sat in companionable silence as they left the Rand behind and shot beneath blazing stars towards the Cape.

4

To return to Cape Town with six hundred pounds in his pocket, and the prospect of six hundred more to come made Piet Barol very happy. He paid his most pressing creditors and hired back his senior staff, who were overjoyed to be given work again. Stacey paid three months' rent on their house, took on two new servants and bought herself one delightful hat – which she wore to their farewell luncheon at the Mount Nelson Hotel.

The night before their parting was exquisitely tender. But the next morning, when Piet told Arthur he was going on a business trip, and could not take him, the little boy cried so quietly Piet felt his heart might break. He held his son close to him and buried his nose in his curls. Arthur smelled of childhood and the jasmine oil his mother used in his hair, for its curls were inclined to knots.

'I am going to make us a great fortune,' Piet told him. 'You must look after your mama while I am gone.'

He did not look back as he went down the hill towards the bus station, where he had sent Luvo and Ntsina to purchase tickets. At the bottom he turned. Stacey had taken Arthur indoors and there was no one to wave to. He collected himself and shook free of his sorrow, his spirits responding to the lure of adventure.

The presence of an *mlungu* on the native bus caused a sensation. There was much disquiet, and then exuberant approval when Piet lifted his hat to the ladies. As he prepared to plunge into the crowd of black faces, he felt an unaccustomed shyness. The friendlier people were, the shyer he became, as had sometimes happened when grown-up strangers fussed over him in his boyhood.

Ntsina cleared the front seat for Piet, and was very polite to the young lady he dislodged from this prime position. His grandmother disapproved of the metal beasts that hurtled from one end of the country to the other, at speeds that could not be healthy for a human digestion. He held her in high regard, but now that he was in one he felt the young man's thrill at taking a risk. He knew he was in the grip of a powerful Good Magic again.

'I wish you a pleasant journey, sir,' said Luvo.

'Call me Piet,' said Piet. 'Let there be no sirs between us.'

Luvo began to think more sympathetically of his new employer. He settled at the window seat Ntsina had given him. He found the stink of bodies distasteful. He leaned on his hands, looking out of the window, seeking his own smell. He thought of the rose soap the Shabrills stocked in their guest bathrooms, which Mrs Mafuduka had rationed carefully between the refugees. He had been sorely tempted to take some, but he had not. In his heart he felt a superstitious fear that something would happen before he embraced his mother again. Before he stayed up till dawn with his sister, learning what had happened. He thought of his father and blinked. That his father's many sacrifices should have come to nothing tempted Luvo to the grave sin of bitterness. He turned from it and prayed for the safe carriage of the bus. It had twenty seats and forty-eight people were inside it. Some of the ladies were so large they weighed as much as three or four men.

It was dark when they set out, along the road that leads from Cape Town towards the Eastern Cape. In the seat beside Piet Barol, Ntsina gave thanks to Amarire, the daughter of the Mother of the Universe. His itch had gone. In even this detail, his ancestors had gone to trouble on his behalf. He wondered what the purpose of his life was to be and he looked at the Strange One, who had closed his eyes. He remembered tales of the first Strange Ones, who had appeared hundreds of moon cycles before, and seemed friendly; and in fact brought with them alcohol and guns. His granny had told him all about them. He made a decision then and there to determine, in consultation with Luvo, whether to abscond with the Strange One's money and leave him behind in Cradock, or to take him further as they had promised. The stories the refugees had told him tempted him strongly to steal something from a white man who was foolish enough to sleep in a public bus.

Piet had closed his eyes because he found it embarrassing to sit beside someone he could not speak to. The good manners of his youth had stressed the importance of keeping up a pleasant flow of talk with any person in his immediate vicinity. Since this was not possible with Ntsina, he preferred not to endure a silence. In the dark he became aware of the jolting of the bus. As his bones rattled, he felt that he was being shaken free of the effete and surfeited Vicomte de Barol. He was Piet Barol again.

He started to feel happy.

It was not the euphoria he had experienced in the empty house Herbert Baker had built for Percy Shabrill. It was the solid, dependable happiness that comes from telling the truth. The bus met a piece of tarred road, one of the new projects of the government. The immediate improvement in personal comfort improved Piet's mood further. What an inconvenience it would be, he thought, if there were no blacks to build roads such as these. Roads for everyone to use – European and native alike. Surely it was better to build a road than to chisel stone below three hundred metres of rock. Deep within, he was glad these were not his options. Optimism took hold of him. There was a certain swagger in this impetuous journey that made him think well of himself. He and Stacey had outfoxed Percy. What a joy!

And then the singing started.

A lone voice, pitched as true as a star. Then everyone joined in, as though they had been practising all day – in perfect synchrony and eight harmonic lines. By the time the tune was through once Piet knew it. Back it came, again and again, swirling into different moods, now the men, now the women taking the lead. Ntsina started singing. It shocked Piet that this garden boy should have perfect pitch. He began to feel like an adventurer, leaving for the unknown – as Magellan had done, or Livingstone. Now that Ntsina was safely singing, Piet opened his eyes. To his left, a sheer mountain cliff disappeared to a vast plain. He got a shock, and inched unconsciously away from the window.

'Tell the Strange One not to worry. My ancestors are protecting us,' said Ntsina to Luvo.

❧

They hurtled across plains of farmland in the dark and by the morning were in the Karoo desert, and very bruised. The bus stopped once every ten hours for its passengers to relieve themselves. Many found it impossible to wait that long. Arrangements were made, not all of them successful – with the result that when Piet woke, the assault on his nostrils was as painful as his crushed vertebrae. He wanted water, but they were down to half a flask and he dreaded having to hold in his pee. The desert stretched in every direction, fatally beautiful.

'Teach me how to say "I'm sorry, I don't speak your language,"' said Piet to Luvo.

'*Indilusizi isiXhosa sam sincinci,*' said Luvo.

In the rapid trickle of sounds there was nothing for Piet to cling to. He spoke English and Dutch and French, and could follow German and Spanish. But these sounds were wholly foreign. His attempts to replicate them produced howls of merriment. Everyone was waking. Stale white rolls were shared round. That a Strange One should bother to say anything at all in their language, let alone apologize for not speaking it better, made several of the older people think generously of Piet Barol. A woman in her sixties, observing Luvo's failure to impart to Piet the art of clicking, made him change places with her and put Piet through an intensive vocalization lesson. He had a musician's ear. Once he understood what each of the strange sounds meant, they began to be more distinct. Piet took out a notebook and jotted certain phrases down. He asked how to say 'My name is Piet Barol' and

'Sleep well' and 'This is beautiful'. To see a white man fail so utterly was endearing to the other occupants of the bus, who were used to whites keeping their failures secret if they could.

In this way half a day passed very pleasantly.

Of course the desert heat made the radiator boil over. This led to a long wait in the baking sun. The land had grown stranger. For miles in any direction there was nothing but flat golden plain and scrub. And then, suddenly, a single hill. Some were perfect pyramids. Others had flat tops, as straight as the horizon, as though a celestial gardener had made a topiary of land masses. When the bus continued, Piet was ready for the journey to end – but it did not end. It went on and on, through that afternoon and evening, into another night – at which point the bus broke down again, and everyone on it was very cold. The windows did not close, and the desert wind felt like iron nails drilling into Piet's skull. After five minutes he got out and looked at the engine. He was no mechanic, but he read the resignation in the driver's face.

'We are going to be here for a long time,' said Piet to Luvo. 'Let's find another way.'

Luvo was most unwilling to abandon the bus. He had seen it stop a thousand times in Cradock. He trusted that it could take him to his parents and sister, and did not wish to desert it.

Piet flagged down the first vehicle he saw. It was a small truck, driven by a fertilizer salesman from Humansdorp. This gentleman was glad of some company, and soon he and Piet were ensconced in the cab while Luvo and Ntsina sat on the open back, wrapped in blankets. Piet had taken care that they should have blankets, and had lent Ntsina his own woollen mittens. But he had not once considered giving up his warm place inside for either of them.

'You think you find a nice one,' said Luvo bitterly, his teeth chattering as he shouted over the whistle of the air. 'But they are all the same.'

Watching Piet in the cab, roaring with laughter, Ntsina decided to abscond with all the Strange One's money in Cradock, and leave him to beg his way home. The decision gave him peace, and he lay down on the hard belly of the metal beast. It was numb-ingly cold, but the moon was at her smallest and the stars were magnificent. He cuddled up to Luvo for warmth and the young men lay together, looking up at the vastness above them. A me-teorite shower was pelting through the earth's atmosphere. The heavenly fireworks made Luvo think of the star that had heralded the Saviour's birth. He tried to read hope in the omen, but there were so many flashes of streaking light that instead of peace he thought of war, and shuddered to think what would happen if the great anger of his people, the justifiable and great anger, should ever be visited on the Strange Ones.

⸺

At ten o'clock the next morning, Cradock appeared like a mirage from the great plains. It was civilized and pretty, with a church modelled on St-Martin's-in-the-Fields in London. Johan van der Westhuizen deposited Piet and his two darkies in front of the Victoria Hotel. It was clear from the colonnaded expanse of the veranda that long clean baths would be available within.

Piet had rarely been in better spirits. 'I am sorry I don't speak your language better,' he said to the doorman, in isiXhosa, and was led cordially to the receptionist. 'Come with me,' he said to his companions. But Luvo knew this establishment and its rules.

'No Piet,' he said. 'This place is for Europeans only.'

'We'll see about that.'

Piet went to the desk. The hotel was old fashioned and well ap-pointed. There was a piano and a gramophone player and books and a great wicker electric fan and elephant-ear plants. Piet had total confidence in his ability to hire a room for his employees, and this he wholly intended to do. He did not mind taking a better seat – or, indeed, having a room to himself while making them share – but it did not occur to him to leave them without the opportunity to have a good wash and a good meal and a good sleep.

But Piet was quite unable to persuade the hotel clerk to let a native sleep in a guest room. 'Very well,' he said at last. 'I'll take your largest suite.'

It was wonderfully cheap. The porter led him through the hotel and onto the street behind it. Charming little houses served as the hotel's most luxurious apartments. The one he was given was exceptionally comfortable. When he had tipped the porter, and asked him to return with some ice and a gin and tonic, he went round to the front of the hotel to find Luvo and Ntsina. 'You two can sleep in my sitting room,' he said. 'No one will see you.'

'It's alright,' said Luvo, standing. 'Ntsina may stay with me. My parents live here, in the German Mission.' And then he looked squarely at Piet, who saw that he was angry, and said: 'Sir.'

✀

The Yako family's joy at being unexpectedly reunited created such a commotion that Frau Doktor Ranke, who had been Luvo's teacher, came downstairs. She had a cold, and liked quiet. In truth, she found the presence of Luvo's parents and sister, who had nowhere else to go, draining. She was going to remonstrate with her guests, when she saw that the cause of the commotion was Luvo.

She stood on the stairs, watching him with his parents; remembered his neatness, his attention to detail, the pleasure he took from pleasing others. In thirty years of teaching, he was by far her favourite pupil. With no other had she so relaxed the barrier of formality that should exist between professor and student. It took some time for his mother to let go of him. When she had, Frau Doktor Ranke said: '*Willkommen*, Herr Yako.'

Luvo went to her, bowed and shook her hand. In flawless German he said: 'There are no words to tell you how happy I am to be in this house once again.'

Cake was served. Luvo's mother could not stop crying. Nor would she let go of her son's hand. She was a large woman, and this meant that only she and Luvo could sit on the sofa. Others clustered on chairs. The Rankes' maid brought tea and Luvo's sister Anna helped her, cutting cherry cake as she cried with joy and disbelief, the yellow sponge dissolving into a golden blob and the cherries into bolts of red.

⁓

Piet's pleasure in the appointments of his suite at the Victoria Hotel was spoiled by the rage he had plainly seen in Luvo. He could not think what might have inspired it. He had a capacity for conscience, and exercised it diligently as he ran a hot bath. He had been polite to the ladies on the bus, had not shown – at least he hoped he had not shown, had he? No – any race superiority. He had got them to Cradock quicker than if they had stayed on the bus. They might have been cold on the back of the truck, but he had given them blankets, and tried for a room at the hotel. At the hotel! As he got into the bath – which was deliciously too hot – he asked himself which other white man in the whole country would consider paying for two Kaffirs to stay in a comfortable hotel? He lowered himself in slowly, the scalding water sending goose pimples across his skin. By the time he had submerged his knees he was conscious only of the heat. He turned the cold tap on. The perfect temperature was achieved. He put his head under the water and let out a long bubbled sigh.

In his dressing gown later, listening to the radio, he learned that Germany had declared war on Russia. It made him feel doubly grateful to be in South Africa – a safe distance from a conflagration that could only end terribly for all concerned. He hoped Holland would stay out of the war, but he knew how difficult it is for little countries to resist the bad behaviour of their neighbours.

He walked into the bedroom, thinking of Leiden, where he had been born; and then of Amsterdam, and the family that had changed his life. Egbert Vermeulen-Sickerts would be a young man already. He hoped he would not have to fight.

His bedroom was small but high ceilinged. The walls were a pale ochre to the picture rail, and a lighter shade above. The bed

58

was brass and the lamps beside it shaded in silk. The sheets were divinely clean. He felt a sudden, insuperable weariness. He forgot about Luvo's anger and Holland's troubles and crawled into the sheets, rejoicing in their crispness.

❦

It was late at night before Luvo and his sister were alone. 'How has it been, Basha?' he asked. Basha was their name for each other, its derivation long lost.

'Tell me how *you* have been, Basha,' said Anna. 'And why you have come home.'

Luvo told her about Johannesburg and the Shabrills, his refusal to work on a mine. He told her about the white man who had hired him as translator while Ntsina took him to his village.

'What can a white man want with Ntsina's village?'

'He wants wood, and he does not want to pay for it.'

To both of them, it felt strange to be making small talk. Both had looked forward intensely to seeing one another again. Up to the disasters of the previous year, their bond had been sustaining, unbreakable. Now Anna found, looking at the concern in Luvo's eyes, that she did not want to speak of her feelings, nor tell him the darkness that weighed on her as she cleaned her saviours' house. When Luvo told her of his plans to assist in the creation of a delegation to England, to be on it if possible, she thought it unlikely that he would ever achieve these lofty aims. She had always believed in him, utterly. The fact that she no longer did made her sad.

They held each other tight as they said goodnight. Luvo and Ntsina were to sleep in a classroom of the school.

'Would you not like to have my comfortable bed, my dear brother?' asked Anna.

'I would like it very much,' said Luvo. 'But you having it will please me more.'

He went down the stairs thoughtfully and let himself out of the back door. He went across the road to the school and into the

59

fourth-form classroom where he had left Ntsina with a blanket and a candle an hour before.

But Ntsina was not there.

⌒

Ntsina Zini had no great experience of criminality, beyond the theft of poultry that is the pride of every Gwadanan boy. His family were Gwadanan gentry, used to having, if not the best, then quite enough of everything. Having decided to take the Strange One's money, he had resolved to waste no time. As soon as Luvo left him, he made his way to the Victoria Hotel, trusting in the guidance of his ancestors.

Ntsina's grandmother Nosakhe was a Guardian of the Knowledge and the *sangoma*, or witch doctor, of Gwadana. She had raised him steeped in Bantu mystery. His memories of his own mother had resolved into a sense of her smile, and the feeling of being held against her breasts. Nosakhe was an accomplished ritualist, but she did not over-value rules. She had taught him from an early age that the spirit world can be heard whenever a being takes the trouble to hear.

Outside the hotel was the doorman to whom Piet had spoken in isiXhosa. He recognized Ntsina and they exchanged pleasantries.

'I have a message for my master,' Ntsina told him. 'Where may I find him?'

The doorman led him on arthritic hips around the corner and up a street. He stopped at a whitewashed cottage with a veranda adorned with wrought iron curled into elegant shapes.

'Thank you,' said Ntsina, stepping forward. 'You may go back to your post, Father.'

He made a show of going up to the cottage's door, while the doorman went back down the street. As soon as he had gone, Ntsina went round the side of the house and shinned up a rough brick wall. On the other side was a garden. It was a magical garden, in the shade of a lemon tree. Ntsina had a keen sense of smell, that the fumes and dust of Johannesburg had blunted. As his feet

60

connected with springy turf, his nose fell into a pool of scent.

Ahead was an open window.

His ancestors had opened it for him, Ntsina saw. He felt fortified, sure that he was on the right path. He pushed the window open further. The room beyond it was lit by moonlight. But Xhosa parents do not believe in being too soft on their young ones, and Ntsina's ancestors had set him a challenge. Right under the window was Piet Barol's bed, and Piet Barol was in it.

Ntsina contemplated Piet's sleeping form. At the mines he had slept on a concrete ledge built into a wall, with his boots for a pillow. At the Shabrills' he had lain on the floor of the servants' quarters. Even in Gwadana he used a grass mat. He had never before seen someone in a bed like this. It opened worlds of possibility to him. He stood in the garden, watching Piet, and thinking of his future and his grandmother's comfort. Then he climbed onto the frame, leapt clear of the bed, landed on the floor with the lightness of a panther, and looked about him. None of Piet's possessions were in the room. He opened the door and went into a sitting room. Hanging on a hook was a jacket. In the jacket pocket was a wallet. Ntsina felt charged with life, in tune with the universe. He opened the wallet. Out fell a photograph, of a woman with a long face and a little boy laughing. As he contemplated it, the wallet's owner switched on the light and said: 'Don't steal from me.'

Piet's words meant nothing to Ntsina, but their tone told him that something confident, but also kind, had been said. He was furiously embarrassed. He was standing in the middle of the room, holding the wallet. There was no denying his crime, and the times were not kind to thieving blacks. He stood where he was. He could not even put the wallet down.

'I am sorry I do not speak your language better,' said Piet, in isiXhosa. And added another word he had learned: 'Truly.'

For the first time, Ntsina Zini could understand Piet Barol. It made him stop shaking.

'I will not steal from you again,' he said.

These words meant nothing to Piet, but he understood from the way they were spoken that something honest, but also gentle, had been said.

Piet stepped forward and offered Ntsina his hand. Perhaps, thought Ntsina, his ancestors had brought him here in the middle of the night to make him and the Strange One better friends. He knew, from the way Piet was, that he would not call the police, or make any kind of trouble. Given the magnitude of the trouble he could make if he chose, this was merciful. Ntsina shook Piet's hand and walked past him and out of the front door, bowing his head as he closed it. Piet went back to his bedroom and checked under his pillow, where the bundle of notes he had brought from Cape Town, which infiltrated his dreams, created rocks and obstacles as he tried to find a comfortable way to lie on top of it, was still safe.

❦

Piet woke with the conviction that he had better inspire some loyalty in his guides. The news that Luvo's parents lived in this quaint town with its replica churches and neat gardens gave him confidence. He was good with mothers, and suspected that winning over Luvo's would guarantee the allegiance of her son.

It was not difficult to find the home of the German missionaries. As he knocked at the door, Piet's head was full of his white acquaintances expounding on the dangers of treating Kaffirs too kindly. 'You give an inch, they take a hundred miles,' was often heard in the bar of the Mount Nelson Hotel, and the same thought, more vulgarly expressed, in cheaper dives. But this was not Piet's way. His nature was affectionate and responded to affection. He would much rather be friends with his travelling companions.

A maid admitted Piet to the sitting room. Frau Doktor Ranke came down, and when she found that he was Luvo's new employer she gave him a sharp speech on the subject of racial equality and stressed that Luvo had a fine mind that should not be put to menial work. The fact that her star pupil, in a school founded on temperance principles, should have spent the last year pouring cocktails for a white man in Johannesburg still smarted.

'I have employed him as my translator,' said Piet. 'His English grammar is better than mine. You have educated him superbly.'

'Thank God,' said Miriam Ranke, settling into a chair. 'You are one of us.'

Tea was brought, and Luvo's parents invited to share it. Piet was very respectful to them, bowing his head as he shook hands. Luvo's father was so grateful to Piet for giving his son a job that removed him from the temptations of Johannesburg that he could not look him in the eye. Both he and his wife understood some English – she knew more than he did.

'You must be proud of your son,' said Piet.

Mrs Yako was extremely proud of her son. That morning, she had interrogated him minutely and learned, to her great satisfaction, that he had not defiled any women in Johannesburg. Nor had he permitted a drop of alcohol to cross his lips. 'He is a good boy,' she said.

'Now tell us, Mr Barol. What is your business?' asked Miriam Ranke.

'It is hard to get decent wood at Cape Town,' said Piet. 'Most of the forests have been cut down and replaced with pine, which is too soft for good furniture. And the . . . European situation makes importing difficult.'

At this moment Herr Ranke walked in. 'We have invaded Luxembourg,' he said.

'That wretched little Kaiser!' Miriam leapt to her feet. 'That fat, conceited, belligerent baby. What a dishonour he does his dear grandmother Victoria.'

'She will be rotating today in her grave,' said Herr Ranke, who had an eccentric grasp of English idiom.

∽

The next day, August 3rd, 1914, while Piet bought provisions in the Cradock General Store, Germany declared war on France. The temper flare of the European powers had happened so quickly that Piet had not thought it very serious – until it was. He put a call through to Stacey from the Victoria Hotel, where a line of Germans were being put off by the manager, whose mother was French.

'Are you safe? Should I come home, my darling?'

'You can do us no good here. And less on a troopship. Every French national in the city is enlisting. They would think it most odd if you did not, *mon cher vicomte*. But I love you for asking. Stay out of sight. When you have the wood I will send Mohammed and Ierephaan to start making the furniture. You could set up a workshop there – just for a few months. They say the war cannot last beyond Christmas.'

'I will leave for the forest at once.'

Piet completed his shopping and had it delivered to the hotel. Then he prised Luvo from his family and spoke to him seriously. 'I offended you on the journey from Cape Town,' he said. 'I am sorry. We are to spend a great deal of time in one another's company. It would be much better if we were friends.'

Forty-eight hours with his family had cured Luvo of all grudges. 'I have nothing against you,' he replied, and at that moment this was quite true.

'I caught Ntsina stealing from me. Tell him I understand the temptation. But he will be better rewarded if he serves me faithfully. I don't like to spend my life looking over my shoulder.'

'I will tell him.'

'Then let's go. I have bought us a vehicle.'

❧

It was a picturesque wagon that had caught Piet's fancy at the farmer's market, drawn by a pair of sturdy horses.

'Please let me drive it!' cried Ntsina.

'He asks to drive,' said Luvo to Piet.

'I am always happy to be driven,' said Piet Barol. And they set off out of town, going much more slowly than the mechanical beasts had travelled, and yet moving with purpose. The wagon was heavily loaded, Piet having made many impulsive purchases with the idea of bartering with the natives, but the horses bore its weight without complaint. Luvo, sitting beside Ntsina on the box, said: 'What possessed you to try to steal from him?'

'It was for your fund.'

'Do not steal anything on my behalf. Theft is the first step on the path to wickedness, and there is enough wickedness in the world today without a good fellow like you adding to it.'

Ntsina felt ashamed. 'I told him I would not steal again. I do not think he understood me.'

'I will tell him when the moment is right. But I want you to promise that this will not happen again.' As Head Boy of the Mission School Luvo had often delivered lectures on the dangers of stealing and lying.

'Your Moses is not my Moses!' Ntsina clapped his friend on the back, eyes twinkling. Seeing the look on Luvo's face, he added: 'Very well. I promise.'

They continued the journey in silence, while Piet lay in the shade behind them. The day was radiant, with no trace of winter but the brown, brown grasses. The cold breeze cooling the hot sun, the gentle swaying of the cart, the sense that he had handled an awkward situation with aplomb, produced in Piet Barol a superb sense of well-being. He had always known his life would be full of adventure. All he had not known was what form the adventure would take.

Now he knew.

Just after lunch, making excellent progress as the road wound towards the ocean, they passed the Falls where the High Princess Nomikonto emerged long ago from the Underworld, after braving many perils. Ntsina told Luvo this in reverence. Luvo did not comment. He knew he would have to tackle his friend's superstitions before they parted ways. But he also knew that it is

65

often better, in such undertakings, to bide one's time.

Piet had woken after a long nap, and made them stop while he got out and peered over the steep side of the gorge. The cliff was white beneath the dense green scrub that covered it. Then the rock turned orange, and finally black. The water snaked down it in a narrow band and poured into a muddy basin. Piet had never seen such a thing in his life. He found it wildly glamorous.

'We will be at the forest by nightfall,' said Ntsina. 'We will camp at the edge and set out tomorrow. I'm afraid the Strange One will have to leave his wagon behind.'

'And most of his trinkets,' said Luvo.

The white man's idiocy was comic to them and they laughed without conscience. From miles before they saw the forest Ntsina caught its scent and began to feel uncontainably happy. He had attained his object: his own home. His ancestors had guided him, but he had heeded their guidance. He had refused the slavery of the Rand and yet found the means to acquire the hut tax and a radio. With happy visions of the future, he covered feelings of a different colour, at the centre of which stood his father.

The forest of Gwadana began abruptly in a more or less straight line at the top of a steep hill, and guarded the coastline from outside eyes. The cloudless sky above them was turning purple with approaching sunset. Ntsina knew it would be magnificent. He was proud of the sunsets Gwadana was blessed with. 'We will sleep here tonight, and make the offerings tomorrow morning,' he said.

Piet and Luvo conferred.

'The Strange One says he wants to press on now and sleep in the forest. He does not want to wait.'

'That is not possible. This forest is the sacred home of my ancestors, and the ancestors of every family in our village. We cannot enter it without entertaining them to a feast.'

'I'm sure they won't mind,' said Luvo.

But Ntsina was adamant.

Piet could not wait. He sprang out of the wagon and examined the hillside. He expected to find a cart track, but there was none.

'Why is there no path?' he asked Luvo.

'People do not visit the villagers of Gwadana.'

'Why ever not?'

'There was a difference of opinion, three generations ago. They are not on speaking terms.'

Piet looked at the wagon. 'What will we do with that?'

'We will leave it with the people of Idutywa. For a small fee they will keep it and not use it too often. If you do not pay them well they will use it every day and take money for rides.'

'I want to sleep in the forest tonight.'

'That will not be possible.'

'Of course it is possible. Get the bags.'

A mist began to form over the forest. The green of the trees darkened.

For the first time in the journey Piet showed himself prepared to engage with the basic business of life. He pulled on a pack containing a tent and cooking supplies, and two parcels of groceries. He was seized by the romance of their location. It mattered to him that he should enter the forest on the day he first saw it. He felt it would be a promising omen. When Luvo told him of Ntsina's reservations he was amused. 'That's all rot. Follow me. He can sleep in the wagon if he likes. You and I are men of the wild.'

Piet strode up the hill towards the forest, heavily laden. Luvo looked at Ntsina. He knew Piet was right. It was rot. He did not wish to offend his friend, yet he had a duty to his employer. He weighed the two and chose duty. He went to the truck and put on his pack. In his jacket pocket was a little prayer book his mother had given him as a parting gift. It was one she had owned since childhood. He packed it safely away in the satchel and followed Piet, going quickly to catch up with him.

The mist had settled into thick white cloud.

Ntsina watched them, angry and overruled. He wondered how

to stop them from transgressing in this way. His ancestors had been so generous to him. It broke his heart to enter their forest without making the ritual gifts. Only force would prevent the Strange One from climbing the hill, and the incident of the wallet made it clear to Ntsina that his ancestors did not want him to rob or harm the Strange One. At least, not yet. He watched them, and from nowhere came a declarative thought. It did not feel self-generated, but as though it had been put into his head, fully formed, by some outside presence. It was not in words, and yet its meaning was plain. In brief the message was: 'Stay in the wagon, and do not worry.' It was tremendously calming. He began to see the advantages of his situation. He had the wagon wholly to himself. It was full of food and comfortable blankets. He watched them on the hill, struggling with their packs. The ascent to the forest was steeper than it looked.

There was a low growl of thunder, and a fat raindrop hit the wagon's tarpaulin roof.

◡◠

Neither Piet Barol nor Luvo Yako, the products of urban educations, had great experience as outdoorsmen. Piet had been on two trips with the Officer Training Corps at his high school, both at his father's insistence, and had gracefully avoided the onerous duty of pitching tents. He had watched a salesman in Cape Town show him how simple it was to erect the expensive tent he had bought, but once the bag was open and the poles laid out on the first flat piece of turf they could find, each pole looked approximately like every other one, which was unfortunate because there was a precise sequence to their usage.

'We should go down,' said Luvo at the first drop of rain.

But Piet would not retreat for the sake of a few raindrops. 'There's a booklet somewhere here.' He found the booklet. It had pages of drawings of identical poles, but it turned out that the poles in the bag were not, in fact, identical. The forest was black now. He abandoned the instructions and used his cabinetmaker's eye. This was a much sounder guide. The thunder got louder, the sky darker.

There was a huge flash of lightning.

Ntsina, snug in the wagon at the bottom of the hill, began calling. Luvo heard him. 'We should go down,' he said. But Piet was spurred by this challenge of the elements. He carried on threading the poles into the canvas of the tent as the lightning crackled overhead.

It was as though a giant bathtub had been upturned over them. At once the slope turned into a mudslide. Luvo was the first to go, sliding off his feet and onto his arse. His pack fell open, and the prayer book his mother had given him fell into the mud. The tent's stakes were not driven deep enough, and soon the entire structure fell on Piet, sending him into the quagmire. At which point both his packs opened and all their contents spilled out.

Watching them from the comfort of the wagon below, Ntsina did not stifle a chuckle. This was a much more elegant punishment than any he could have devised. He saw from the expressions on their faces that they were having a row with each other, and closed his eyes. He intended to get as much rest as he could before they returned.

When they did return they were covered in mud, and Piet was in a terrible temper. As they reached the wagon, his rage turned to laughter. He laughed and laughed.

'Tell our friend he was right,' he said. 'We have offended his ancestors. This is no more than we deserve.'

And he took off his sopping clothes and wrapped himself in a blanket and lay on the wagon floor, very grateful for its tarpaulin.

୧ଚ

The next morning, they left the wagon with the villagers of Idutywa and purchased two bottles of brandy. Piet refused to leave the barter goods he had brought behind, and this compelled Luvo to inform him, regretfully, that the Gwadanans did not approve of European junk.

When this was translated for Piet he felt rather excited than otherwise, and began to imagine the stories he would tell in the bar of the Mount Nelson Hotel. The trinkets had, indeed, been cheap, and he relinquished them. Even if they were stolen it would be no great loss. The black men watching saw a cloud pass over the white man's face, and presumed that he was too lazy to contemplate the walk ahead. But in fact Piet was thinking of the fellows at the Mount Nelson, with whom he had sunk cocktails and played tennis, on jovial terms, for six and a half years. Which of them would not return from a European War?

'Tell me what I need to do to get on the good side of his ancestors,' said Piet to Luvo.

The ceremony of propitiation has three objects: to alert the spirits of the Gwadanan ancestors to the arrival of guests in their forest, to invite them to a feast, and to ensure that they leave it in high spirits. This required a quantity of brandy to be poured into the ground at the forest's edge. What is not poured into the ground must go into the mouths of the hosts, with the result that when Ntsina finally invited Piet and Luvo over the threshold of the forest, as was fitting for the great-great-grandson of Gwadana's Great Founder, all three were feeling rather merry.

'Tell him I am grateful to his ancestors for their graciousness,' said Piet.

'The Strange One says thank you,' said Luvo to Ntsina.

'Welcome to the forest of Gwadana,' said Ntsina.

The green ahead was infinitely variegated. Piet's faith in his star soared. Trinkets or no trinkets, he had never yet failed to make people like him when he sincerely tried. He did not doubt that he would succeed now, and that he had useful helpers for the undertaking. That morning, buying brandy, Luvo had taken him aside and told him that Ntsina would never steal from him again. All in all, it was rather better to have got that out of the way at the beginning, than to enter a dark wood without trusting one's companions.

'Shush,' said Ntsina as they passed beneath the canopy. 'It is

Marimba, the Goddess who leads all in singing. The trees sing with Her.'

As Piet stepped into the cool darkness of the canopy floor, moisture pricking his skin, he stopped to listen. Above and all around them, millions upon millions of leaves rustled as warm air rose through them. The more he listened, the more he heard. He could have sworn the forest was almost silent from the road, but in it – listening to it – he heard infinity in the sound of the leaves.

'Follow me,' said Ntsina. 'And I will show you some secrets. Do not be afraid of the leopards.'

This admonition spoiled Luvo's equilibrium. He watched, warily, as Piet and Ntsina strode forward. The smells of the forest were intoxicatingly complex: mud and leaves and fungi and flowers and droppings and bark and pools where fishes leapt through shafts of sunshine. Piet felt drunk on them, but it was a drunkenness that left him energetic, his senses alive. They found a stream and followed it. 'He says that all the little streams lead to one large stream, and that leads all the way to the village,' said Luvo, translating. Ntsina led them into a tunnel of green, lit by green light filtered through the touching leaves above. 'I am going to find you a welcome,' he said.

He left Piet and Luvo by the stream and went off. After months in Johannesburg, taking orders, Ntsina was in a mood to impress the Strange One with his own powers. It required a high degree of skill to find a nest of the stingless bees. Once one had, heroics were possible without grave risk – but he could not listen properly with the others there.

When he was twelve trees distant, they were lost to him. He took in the clearing, focusing on precise details, for there are many clearings in a forest, and one can lose oneself for ever if one does not concentrate. He closed his eyes and said a prayer of thanks to his ancestors for saving him. A wind swept over him, caressing him, and above him the leaves swelled into a deafening chorus: the friendly welcome of a voice stronger than the Universe and older than Time. He abandoned himself to it. Felt the sound, as he cleared the ways for it to reach his soul, make his body tingle. He thought he might drown, felt dizzy, almost wanted to vomit. The trees got louder and louder, and then he opened his eyes, and focused on a single leaf, as his grandmother had taught him, observing what made it unique. And when he had done this to four leaves, creating neural pathways that would release exact memories of this day in the deliriums of dementia sixty years later, he heard the low, consistent, unmistakable hum of the stingless bees.

Like a panther stalking its pray, he followed the sound. His eyes examined in advance every patch of turf his feet touched, lest he disturb a sleeping snake or a colony of ants. He had known the forest since he was a baby, and his nervous system fired the primal powers of hearing, seeing, sensing. His grandmother had taught him that it is possible to be quite safe in a forest. But inattention is the difference between life and death. 'Death, in any case,' she used to say, sitting on the stone slab outside her kitchen hut, 'is the object of Life. Our only lesson is this: to learn how to die.'

The first time she had told him that, when he was aged six, three days after his mother had died, he had turned to Nosakhe and clutched her legs and said: 'Don't ever die, Grandmother. Promise me you will never die.' And she had been so touched, so unexpectedly moved and charmed, that she had not found the strength to answer him.

Ntsina stalked the bees mercilessly, every nerve aflame. It is natural for a young man to take pleasure in treating his friends. Natural, too, that he feels twice the pleasure if he can also impress them. He shouted the names of his companions, and when they appeared, Luvo ill at ease and trying not to show it, he said: 'Watch this.'

Ntsina climbed a few branches, for no conjuror wants to be seen too close, and punched his fist through the bark of the tree. Like a volcano, the bees erupted. Piet cried out. Luvo backed away. Ntsina was covered in black bees. 'Tell the Strange One I have a magic power of taming bees!' shouted Ntsina, and lifted out three huge honeycombs, to howls of hysteria from their owners. He dropped the combs onto Luvo, who caught them with distaste and was revolted by the stickiness of the honey on his hands.

They ate the honeycombs on the far side of a bigger stream. Stingless bees do not like to cross water, and had declined to pursue them. Piet was truly impressed. Ntsina knew this, and swaggered. He was not used to swaggering, but something about the way the white man did it was alluring, and he enjoyed outshining Piet in an act of valour.

Piet had never eaten honey taken from a hive. He had a gift for savouring the present, and while Luvo wondered how he would get the sticky mess off his fingers, and watched warily for snakes, Piet held the honeycomb in both hands (Ntsina had given him the biggest) and consciously sank his teeth into it. The resistance of the wax was irresistibly satisfying, the sweetness beyond it breathtaking – rich, heady, musky, infused with the subtle taste of the Mopani tree in which the honey had been lovingly made.

He ate and ate and ate and ate.

For several seconds, the forest shimmered before him. Then *bam!*, the sugar reached his bloodstream and a surge of invincible energy soared through him. 'Come on!' he cried. He seized his pack, and Luvo's (Luvo had been struggling rather sullenly with it), and stormed away up the stream, in the direction of the Unknown.

They camped in a glade of tall, thin trees. Only one was thick enough for furniture, Piet noted, and it was hollow. They had walked all day through dense forest, and it was very pleasant to throw their packs down and rest their heads upon them. They had strayed some distance from the river, in search of a space big enough for their tent. But the prospect of a further struggle with that piece of unsatisfactory equipment was not enticing to Piet Barol. 'It's a fine night,' he said. 'Yesterday's storm cleared the air. Let's sleep under the trees.'

'That is a sensible idea,' said Ntsina when Luvo had translated it, rather despondently – for he did not wish to seem a coward but had begun to yearn for a dry bed. 'It is foolish to sleep in a tent in a forest.'

'Why? What if it rains?'

'If it rains, the trees will shelter us. But if we are in a tent how can we spot the leopard or the jackal that comes snooping? This is not a pleasure garden.'

Piet lay with his head on his pack. The sickness that comes from gorging on honey until your stomach is stretched to its limits, and then continuing to gorge, is by no means a pleasant sort of sickness. His mind spinning from the sugar, his tongue searching for more of the mysterious, infinitely smooth, semi-solid elixir, given texture by stray pieces of bark or the crunchy body of a dead bee, his insulin levels spiralling, he got a thundering headache and was consumed by a sudden, unconquerable exhaustion.

'Tell Ntsina to lay out a fire,' he said.

There was a small patch of sunlight close by, and he moved to it, and lay down with his face at its centre. He closed his eyes, unaware how many eyes were trained upon his warm, fleshy body, oozing sweat and smells of such deliciousness that insects more than a thousand trees away came to investigate and further away than that an ageing leopard, who was sleeping, twitched his nose and dreamed of an impala kill.

The patch of sunlight faded as soon as Piet fell into a sugar-induced coma, his senses shut down. He was much closer to the hollow tree than the spot Ntsina had chosen, which was judicious-ly equidistant from all obstacles that might preclude a clear line of sight. Piet would not have fallen asleep so easily had he known that the occupant of the hole in the hollow tree was a five-metre-long female rock python who weighed fifteen times what he did. This python had noted with alarm the settling of three strange apes in the clearing of which she was used to being the undisputed sovereign. Each noonday she lay in the sun, warming herself to the point of near-expiration before returning to the tree, coiling round her eggs and incubating them. Her nostrils twitched as one of the apes came closer. He did not smell like a young one, yet only the youngest, least experienced creatures ever ventured near her fortress. The python's tongue flicked. Her four thousand muscles contracted. But the creature outside fell silent, and stopped moving.

'Go and break that big branch up. It will burn nicely,' said Ntsina. And as Luvo approached it warily, for he had never done such a thing before and did not trust his physical strength: 'Check there is not a snake behind it.'

'Stop talking about snakes.' Luvo moved towards the hollow tree, stepping over Piet's recumbent body. The fact that the Strange One was not going to assist in setting up the camp put him in a bad mood. He was not quite careful as he stepped over Piet, and kicked his foot. It produced no response whatever. He skirted the hollow tree, deep evolutionary instincts warning him against advancing further towards a dark space in an unknown forest, and checked the rotting log Ntsina had pointed out. There did not seem to be a snake behind it. He dragged it away from the hollow tree, and the python – who had risen half a metre – lay down again, her temper disturbed. She felt that these apes, knowing so little of the hierarchies of the forest, were sure to do mischief to it – for a forest's order of precedence is sanctioned by Time itself, and is not to be meddled with.

What Luvo did not know was that Ntsina had given him a task he knew would be easy for him to accomplish. In fact, he was giving him the first assignment his grandmother had ever given him: breaking a rotting branch into firewood. At the age of six, it had made him feel tremendously powerful, and that imagination of power had been the first stirring towards the physical strength of his manhood. Luvo kicked the log doubtfully, and it splintered apart with gratifying cracks. He could not but feel proud of the ease with which he had damaged something so seemingly solid. He glanced over at Ntsina, who was watching him. This time he kicked the log as hard as he could, and that was the end of it. He

gathered the pieces and carried them to the middle of the clearing, dragging the jagged edges against Piet's calves, provoking a
twitch but no more.

'I can see you are going to be useful in the forest,' said Ntsina.

There was nothing in life that gave Luvo so much pleasure as
feeling useful. They made the fire and set up camp in companionable silence. Piet had bought a great deal of biltong in Cradock
– squishy, salty, hung kudu meat, dripping fat and deliciousness.
It was a wonderful complement to the honey. They ate a great
deal of it. 'What about wild animals?' said Luvo, as Ntsina drew
the blankets tightly round them.

'Animals do not like human beings. They have learned not to
seek us out.'

This was quite true of many of the more highly sentient animals
– the forest elephants, for example, who had embarked already
on a long diversion to avoid coming anywhere near the creatures
who in their language were signified by a low hum, at a pitch
far beyond human perception, a sound that meant danger and
a callousness that offended the elephants; for elephants, though
turbulent, especially the young bulls, are not callous. It was not
true of the forest's insects, who arrived in great numbers to feast
on the sweet blood of *Homo sapiens.*

Ntsina was oblivious to them, having been taught that he must
offer these tastes of himself as a contribution to the livelihood of
the forest; that to do so hardened a man, and called protection
upon him from larger predators whose bite was far worse.

Luvo hated them. Their noise drove him mad. He tried to pray,
but the little whitewashed church of the mission school seemed
very far away; curiously unreal, irrelevant, in this chapel of trees.

༄

The leopard whose dreams had been disturbed by the far-off scent
of hairy apes moved gingerly out of a cave, having eaten three
bats who had chosen a dangerous perch. The fact offended his
leopardly pride. He had sired eighty-two cubs, been lord of the

territory of a thousand trees. To be dining on bats was a humiliation. He had not caught an impala for three winters. He had almost forgotten their taste – but not the luscious *pluck* as his claw sliced into plump, moist flesh.

He sauntered down the steep stone cliff, the muscles of his haunches flowing with the elegance of old. He could not even get in on kills three days' dead – the hyenas whose grandparents had dreaded him now flaunted his authority and kept him from all but the occasional anus. The anus of a wildebeest is not an appetizing recollection, and his nose twitched. As it did, he caught a different smell – the smell of a fire, but a small one, by no means a conflagration like those so often caused by the fire that came from the sky. And beyond that, an intriguing smell – of moist, fat kudu meat that has been hung in a dark place for a long time (a method of preparation dear to him, who still had the gourmet tastes of the alpha male). And near the kudu meat a baboon – but not a baboon, an ape with no hair, or very little. He turned his path in the direction of the scent and came to a river. He hesitated, because he knew what it was to cross this river. Then he sprung across the water, landing heavily – for his back left leg was lame. The belligerent scent of the male who had replaced the leopard who had replaced him as the lord of a thousand trees confronted him. He ignored it. He was mesmerized by the smell of the hairless apes, for within it was a piece of information his nose could decode with total confidence: they had no idea that he was moving towards them.

                           ⤳

Luvo, watching Ntsina's face, lit by firelight, decided that he was not handsome. His nose was too big, the space between his eyes too large. Luvo had been brought up on European ideals of physical beauty. In all the art the Rankes had shown him, in all the flickering slides showing masterpieces by the great *mlungus* across the sea – Titian in Venice and Renoir in Paris; he knew their names, their dates, their cities – not one face looked like Ntsina's.

77

And yet . . . The strangeness of the forest had an unexpected effect on Luvo: it made him less self-conscious. His companions were fast asleep and would not wake. No one else might possibly see him now. He felt the freedom of solitude, he who had known no worlds but that of farm and school and the Shabrill household, each of which was jammed with people and their observations and their gossiping.

There were parts of Luvo's nature he devoted great energies to keeping beyond the suspicion of any other living being. In this space, lit by this light, with the leaves rustling above him, he was less fearful. He had moved closer to the fire and freed himself of assaulting insects; its heat sharpened his thoughts. He leaned towards Ntsina's sleeping head. Ntsina's smell, as the young ladies of Gwadana knew, was very sweet. Luvo had caught it when they slept side by side on the Shabrills' concrete floor, but he had never allowed himself to luxuriate in it. Tonight he bent down and inhaled at the nape of his friend's neck, and was met by a scent that made every part of him feel grateful to be alive. His erection was instantaneous and solid as a tree root. But what was entrancing about Ntsina's smell was not only the muskiness of a strong man after a day of intense exertion, but a vulnerability, a gentleness, that made Luvo feel light-headed.

He closed his eyes, breathing him in. Felt the blood rush to his head, himself teetering on a cliff he would never jump off. He was careful not to let his nose come into contact with Ntsina's skin, but he ranged up and down his back, and then over his collarbone. And then he opened his eyes and saw a leopard on the other side of the fire, its eyes huge and dazzled.

'Wake brother, wake.' Luvo touched Ntsina's shoulder. Ntsina did not stir so he scratched his neck, and when Ntsina said 'What is wrong?' he replied: 'There is a leopard over there.'

Their visitor had been delighted to discover, on arriving at the clearing, that his quarries were engaged in a pre-mating ritual that was likely to keep their senses fully occupied. Their total vulnerability had inspired him to dally, staring at the fire. He was mesmerized by fire. When lightning struck a dry Mopani tree, as happened almost every time there was a storm, he would climb to the top of the valley, a journey by no means easy for him any longer, simply to sit, back straight, and stare at the flames below. The intensity of the coals enslaved him. He entirely missed the signs that one of the hairless apes had become aware of his presence, and was annoyed to find them both staring at him when he took his eyes from the bright red coals. He would not have made this kind of error even two years ago.

'Close your eyes,' said Ntsina to Luvo. 'I will squeeze your hand when you must open them again. Keep in time with me.'

Ntsina took Luvo's hand. Luvo closed his eyes. It was the most terrifying thing he had ever done. Ntsina's palm pressed into his. Luvo was reminded with alarm that his erection had by no means been entirely anaesthetized by fright. He opened his eyes slowly, as instructed, then closed them when Ntsina pressed again. Nosakhe had always said: 'Keep going. Do not stop. Force them to recognize that you speak to them in their own language. You are saying "I see you. Go well."' She had taught Ntsina the rhythm, the slow blinking that is to all the large cats the sacred greeting of their kind. It is a greeting that cannot lead to bloodshed, at once a truce and a welcome. There is friendliness in it and respect, an acceptance of the order of things.

When the two hairless apes spoke to him in the way of his own kind, the leopard was shocked. He had been having vivid dreams lately, in which nothing was as it should be. Was this one of them? He did not acknowledge the apes. He had never blinked to any creature who did not have a tail and four strong, swift legs. He had a glimpse of the many leopardesses he had mounted over the years, and experienced a pang of regret for the fact that he would never mount one again. Here were two young hairless apes, mating. There was a sentimentality in his nature that the tough life of a pack leader had repressed. He advanced.

'Keep calm. Do as I say,' murmured Ntsina. There was iron assurance in his tone, the focus of a man whose wisdom is being strenuously tested. Luvo was so afraid he forgot even to pray.

The leopard skirted the fire and went to the box that was still half full of oozy, fatty biltong. With a click of his powerful jaws, he lifted the package into his teeth, turned, blinked, and bounded off into the night.

⁓

Piet woke the next morning, feeling light-headed and thirsty. His bones were stiff and he was very cold. Dawn was just breaking and his companions were fast asleep on the other side of the still-smoking fire. He made his way through the forest towards the river. The beauty of a stream in an African forest as dawn breaks is a powerful beauty. Piet sat by the stream, shivering and gathering the courage to wash in the clear, cold waters. There were trees to be had here in any quantity, but none of them would do for the furniture he had in mind. They were too tall and too thin; too focused on reaching the canopy in time to fill a gap left by the death of an ancient. He washed and roused the others. 'Tell him I want to see the trees he has told me of,' said Piet to Luvo. And when the two young men had conversed in isiXhosa for a few moments, Luvo said: 'Then you must keep walking.'

The tree Ntsina Zini intended to show Piet Barol was a tree of which the Gwadanans were very fond: called, in that part of the world, the Furniture Tree, though Strange Ones referred to it as forest mahogany. Its wood was strong and capable of a gorgeous sheen when polished. Mahoganies grew in solitary splendour in several places in the forest. There was one close by, but Ntsina wished the Strange One to employ many young men of his village to transport the wood to the city, and resolved to show him another, on the far side of a steep gorge. He was surprised when Piet, strapping his pack tighter, set off without a murmur of complaint.

The mist was still heavy. As they went they descended into cloud and Luvo, who had not yet recovered from his encounter with the leopard, began to feel afraid. He did not like making his way into a valley he could not see. Nor did he enjoy the thought

80

of lumbering up the other side with his pack. He could think of no reason to delay or change their route, and did his best to keep up, focusing his gaze on the rounded splendour of Ntsina's arse.

The heavy tread of three hairless apes caused a consternation among the creatures who were used to unchallenged possession of the gorge. The snakes were not yet out to bask, but thousands of spiders felt the impact of their treads as their webs shivered; and a hundred and nineteen lost the work of weeks as Piet, Ntsina and Luvo walked through them.

Between two trees, about halfway down, angled slightly to catch the larger flying insects, the golden web of a spider with a livery of yellow and black held its own against the morning breeze and the approaching humans. At its centre, a large female was replenishing her life force from eleven fat, juicy moths that had flown through her clearing in the night. From the edge of her web a much smaller male eyed her, his thoughts on mating. He had not yet mated, and had begun to know that he would not many more times see a moon.

He spun a small web of golden silk and ejaculated onto it. The lady whose eggs he so earnestly desired to fertilize was a capricious lover, and had eaten several unsuccessful suitors – and once, six days before, very nearly himself. It was wiser to be prepared. He sucked the sticky ball of his sperm between two strong pedipalps and advanced.

The web's creator was having a pleasant morning – a reward for the panic of her first few moments of life. It had been a cumbersome process, hauling her heavy body over an eternity of rough ground to reach the edge of the gorge, the siblings who had shared her egg sack in hot, cannibalistic pursuit. She had moved blindly, in terrified haste – for she was not the largest of her sisters, and did not relish their proximity. The Universe had rewarded her with a web spot ideally placed to intercept insects as they descended to the still pools at the gorge's bottom.

The night's yield had been generous, the moths flavoursome. She knew of the presence of males at the outer edges of her web,

81

and tentative tremors this morning told her that one of them had taken his courage in both pedipalps. She was surfeited and had no idea to eat him. She had not yet reproduced, and her carapace tingled with readiness to take her own step in the magnificent currents of creation. She awaited his approach. He stopped. She did not move, and neither did he. She was conscious of his fear, and a part of her thought less of him. She started on another moth, so that he might feel that her attention was elsewhere engaged; and indeed this did set the web trembling again, as he came nearer.

As they passed the web, Ntsina, in the mood for a joke, took Luvo by both shoulders and hurled him towards it. To a human eye, used to the comforts of the town, a golden orb spider presents a terrifying aspect. Ntsina caught Luvo when his nose was six inches from the spider, but the sound Luvo made ricocheted off the walls of the gorge. The terror in it stopped Piet dead, but Ntsina only laughed at them both.

Luvo's fear faded and was replaced by shame; and then anger. He looked at the huge, evil spider, and a desire to take out his feelings on a lower order of being was strong. A little spider was making its way towards the large one. Luvo picked up a stick to smash the web, but as he did so the little spider dashed over the last few inches of golden silk and put his claws into the abdomen of the larger one. The intimacy of the gesture arrested Luvo's violence. He had been raised on the sanctity of all life, and had a flash of the many spider lives he would terminate if he killed this mating pair.

'I am sorry,' said Ntsina. 'I won't play such games.'

'I wouldn't play them with you,' said Luvo, stiffly.

The last of the mist disintegrated. They were closer to the stream than he had feared. All three went more quickly, eager for the water; and once they had found it they drank deeply of it. Piet's many walks up Table Mountain from his shop to his home had prepared him for forest exertions. The others were impressed when he stood first and pressed on. Ntsina followed, thinking that

Piet was an unusual *mlungu* after all – for the *mlungus* he had seen were not much blessed with athletic gifts.

cᴑ

They found the mahogany as the sun reached the midpoint of its journey to the meridian. Its canopy was broad and dense, the shade it offered very sweet on this day that was unusually hot for the depths of winter. Luvo threw himself on the ground beneath it, in a bad temper with the others, but Piet was well pleased. He stripped away the smooth, grey bark revealing tender pink wood beneath. It was even-grained, quite suitable for carving.

Ntsina, watching him, was well pleased too. It would require many men to get this wood to the main road.

As if reading his thoughts, Piet said: 'It's a handsome tree. But how on earth can we get it out of this forest?'

Piet and Ntsina began to talk enthusiastically. Translating for them, Luvo grew tired. He was a perfectionist, and strained to achieve perfect subtlety – a challenging feat in languages as different as isiXhosa and English. Frau Doktor Ranke, who was a great believer in effort, had found that in Luvo's case his challenge was often to try less hard – because she knew his perfectionism to be a burden, having carried a similar one herself. The incident of the spider had embarrassed him, and while he translated another part of Luvo's brain was developing a narrative of self-pity and irritation.

Here he was, risking his life to make a Strange One rich. He would make a few pennies for every pound the Strange One made – hardly enough to assist his own family, let alone contribute to the sending of a delegation to England. This thought began to fill his head, crowding his linguistic efforts towards less conscious realms; and as the others spoke, laying plans to transport the wood, he retreated. Even the man who had proposed the Natives Land Bill had not voted for it when the moment came! The cowardice and injustice of it was galling. A commission had been promised, to 'look into' the fairness of the legislation – but the law had been

83

implemented, in midwinter, before any commission could report; before even a date had been set for that report. He was aware of the English expression 'possession is nine tenths of the law', and knew that white farmers now in possession of the livestock and land that had once belonged to their black neighbours would be most unwilling to relinquish it. He became more and more convinced of the necessity of appealing to the King of England. The Rankes were passionate Anglophiles, and Luvo had been raised in the strictest traditions of Empire. He believed without question that the King-Emperor across the seas would protect the property rights of his dark subjects. So intense was this conviction that when Piet said 'We'll hire strong men, and you can translate,' Luvo said: 'I would only do such a thing for a hundred pounds.'

Few black men in the country had ever asked a white man for a hundred pounds. Piet thought immediately of the warnings about grasping Africans he had heard at the bar of the Mount Nelson Hotel, and was angry that Luvo should exploit their isolation, and the usefulness of his skill, in this manner. 'Let's see about that when the time comes,' he said, resolving to find another translator at the first opportunity and send this impudent young man back to Cradock.

It was the only imperfection in a mood otherwise unsullied. Piet resolved to put it aside and lay back under the shade of the tree. The scene was idyllic, but the idyll wasn't comfortable. Sharp grasses poked his back, insects alighted on his skin, drawn by the intoxicating scent of salt and sweat. From every side, creatures slithered or crawled or wriggled on their daily paths, navigating his body as they would any other obstacle, with the result that after a few minutes he stood up again and said: 'Let's press on.'

They did, in silence; and in that silence Piet made his calculations. The mahogany was of fine quality. He did not see that it could rightly be said to belong to anybody. He would pay for the felling and transport, perhaps even set up a workshop in a convenient town and sit out the European War making beautiful things – and a great deal of money. He had begun to worry in

Cape Town that Fortune, which had always favoured him, had grown tired of him. Now he knew he had won her attention again, and congratulated himself on the pluck he had shown in coming all this way to find his own wood.

⁓

They made camp that night in dense forest, and Piet sought escape from the encroaching cold in the oblivion of sleep. Luvo was wary of closing his eyes, and of being alone with the creatures of the wood.

'Why was the Strange One angry with you?' asked Ntsina.

'Because I asked for more money,' said Luvo. 'And you should too.'

They fell to discussing Strange Ones. Ntsina had learned from his grandmother that they were conceived under the waves, sons of a great living flower that grows in the deepest stretches of the sea. He shared this with Luvo, who wondered what hope there was for the Bantu while such superstitions occupied the place that should belong to Scientific Fact. With an unconscious echo of his grandmother's certainty, Ntsina told Luvo that the Strange Ones with yellow hair are half-human, half-plant. 'Do you not see,' he asked, 'that they look like the maize that grows in the field? I am glad this one is human.'

'Oh, he is human alright,' said Luvo.

He looked at his friend. They had both eaten well and were beginning to feel pleasantly sleepy. It was the tender hour that follows exertions and the satisfaction of physical wants. Perhaps it was the moment, thought Luvo, to talk about God.

'Do you know, brother,' he said, 'I think you are a clever man.' He said so because he was about to demolish Ntsina's conception of the universe, and did not wish him to feel patronized. 'You know many things about this forest, and you are brave.'

No one had ever called Ntsina a clever man. Nosakhe had known, and shown, that repeated iteration could carve deep paths in Ntsina's brain, but he had left quick wit to others and did not step forward in the kraal, to tell outrageous stories, even after his initiation into manhood. He felt proud, and then sorry for the fun he had made of his friend's fears.

'It is you who are clever,' he said. 'And you are also brave. To go beyond the seas to the country called England, to meet their Great King, that is a feat that most would shun through fear.' He promised himself never to frighten Luvo with a spider again.

'Man was made by God,' said Luvo, 'in His own image.' As he spoke, though he believed what he said, he was also conscious of a second, contradictory story in the Book of Genesis, which said that God made Man from the dust of the ground, and breathed into his nostrils the breath of Life. And that in the first version Man and Woman were created at the same time, and in the second Woman was created after Man, from a rib bone taken from his side. He did not share these contradictions, because he did not wish to confuse a new convert. But Luvo was a Biblical literalist, and it caused him much pain.

'Oh no, my friend,' said Ntsina, who was sure of what he said. 'The Universe was created when Time and Nothingness had a child, a spark of Fire, and Fire devoured Nothingness, his mother. Everyone knows that. And Man is the offspring of the Tree of Life, which is a special sort of tree, and terrifying to behold.'

'You are wrong,' said Luvo. 'God made the Universe when His spirit was moving over the face of the waters and He said "Let there be light" and separated the light from the darkness.'

'Do not let us argue,' said Ntsina. 'It all happened long ago.'

On this they could agree, and Luvo tried to silence his fear that Ntsina would not know salvation unless he came to believe what was right, and reminded himself that his friend was young, and so was their friendship, and that miracles might be accomplished with all the time that lay ahead.

❧

While Ntsina slept, though he could not know it, negotiations that concerned him intimately were nearing their close.

They were being conducted by his father, Sukude Zini, whose name meant One Who Makes Clothes From Skins – though behind his back, Sukude's neighbours called him Nukude, which means He Stinks From a Very Far Distance. Sukude was short and immensely strong; in his youth he had wrestled wild boars for sport. Such displays had won him the hand of Ntsina's mother, a direct descendant of the village's Great Founder, and the taking of her family name. These achievements naturally inspired resentment in less fortunate men, but it was not for this reason that Sukude was disliked. It was for something else, a flaw that indeed could only be smelled and not described. It had something to do with the fact that he possessed the only metal lock in Gwadana, and his hut the only steel door.

Eyeing him across the fire, Litha Jaxa was troubled by the thought of consigning his daughter to the care of the Zinis. Litha was the head of the Jaxa clan, one of Gwadana's most prominent families. His daughter Thembela, whom all called Bela, was known to be the best-brought-up and most beautiful girl between the great forest and King William's Town. 'Her bride price is one hundred cows,' he said. 'And six bulls.'

Litha set this astonishing sum half hoping he would be refused. But Sukude said: 'Very well. My son must have the best wife in the village. Are we settled?'

Litha said yes. He had not the strength to turn down an offer so extravagant – especially in such troubled times. As the negotiators drank in celebration, he soothed his conscience with the contemplation of future riches. Sukude was charming, and went home to tell his mother-in-law what he had accomplished on his son's behalf.

Ntsina's grandmother, Nosakhe, had been chosen as a Keeper of the Knowledge by her grandfather Thembinkosi, the village's Great Founder, who had a cool head and an argumentative turn of mind. When, three generations before, a prophesy had spread that the Xhosa had only to sacrifice their cattles and burn their crops to ensure the destruction of the hated English, he had refused to bow to convention and struck out for himself. Thembinkosi was a charismatic man of great sexual stamina and had six devoted wives. These ladies trekked off with him, their children driving his cattle herds. As he passed through village after village, those who also doubted, deep within, that killing their livestock was the best way to defeat the Strange Ones, were inspired to follow him. Perhaps five hundred made it as far as the forest of Gwadana, but when it became plain that their leader intended to enter it, only a hundred and eighty-seven followed him, of which one hundred and eighty-three made it as far as the idyllic bay he found for them on the far side of the forest's narrowest point.

The Great Founder had chosen his quick-witted granddaughter Nosakhe to be the Keeper of this Knowledge, and of a great deal more besides. Nosakhe had hoped to do the same with her daughter Mandisa, but the child was a sweet foolish thing, quite incapable of the discernment required of a *sangoma*.

When Mandisa's fits started Nosakhe had at first entertained hopes that spirits were visiting her daughter – though gradually she had understood that if this were the case, they were wicked spirits. On no account did Nosakhe wish Mandisa to become a vessel for the reincarnation of Za-Ha-Rrell, the King of Evil, which was a grave risk for all those who rarely think for themselves. The day her daughter had a fit that left her unconscious, one part of Nosakhe's brain was convinced that this was final proof she was a dark witch; the other that perhaps a Strange One's medical opinion should be sought. A visit to King William's Town, which had cost a good portion of the Zini family fortune, had resulted in a diagnosis of epilepsy, and packets of expensive white pills. These banished the fits and it became clear to Nosakhe that her daughter was not – and never would be – the vessel of any spirit, good or ill. When Mandisa died – bitten by a snake, while bathing on the rocks with her husband – Nosakhe had felt furious sorrow.

She loved Mandisa's child with all the fierceness in her, and had gone to pains to provide Ntsina with the practical experience he would need if the spirits came calling.

Nosakhe had kept Ntsina away from his father, and was jealous of his love. It was cruel of her, and Sukude sought refuge from the pain of her cruelty by gradually caring less for his son. Privately, he thought the boy effete and sentimental, too much in his grandmother's aura. But she had a witch's power that woman, and he did not dare cross her. So he lived out his life as the prince consort of the village – the necessary man at rituals when only a man could perform the rites, but with very little else to do.

Nosakhe would not permit Sukude to sully her daughter's memory by taking another wife, much less a concubine. In these circumstances, Sukude's thoughts strayed to sex. For years he had had sex thoughts about almost every woman he saw – each had something to focus on as he imagined fucking them. Breasts, bottom, the faint appearance of underarm hair on a woman with a plain face, a big wide nose. But he lacked the courage to take a mistress.

Since his son's departure for the mines, Sukude's desires had focused on one object: the beguiling Bela Jaxa, just entering the first flush of womanhood.

There was a gentle quality in her grandson that made Nosakhe believe Ntsina might be a vessel for Good Magic, if only he could hear it. On each of their journeys into the forest she had taught him to listen. She had waited to send him to the mines until he was well trained, and in truth it was not so much the paying of the hut tax that concerned her. She, Nosakhe Zini, did not doubt her ability to stand up to a British Inspector, should one call, and in any case the forest was thick and full of leopards and there were few safe tracks through it. She had sent Ntsina into the heart of the earth because purity untested is not a strong purity. She did not have total certainty – such as she experienced upon other matters – that her grandson had the qualities required of the next Keeper of the Knowledge, and she wished to be sure. She was too honourable to pretend that personal desire is the same as divine inspiration.

Ntsina's departure was his father's opportunity to execute a plan he had long nursed, and for which he had sought and received the sanction of three *sangomas* in King William's Town. Only by obeying the strictest interpretation of the law of his ancestors could he get his own way with Bela Jaxa, and he was determined to give his mother-in-law no grounds for objection. No one could condemn Ntsina marrying, or his father for beginning the bride price negotiations in his absence. Were the negotiations to be concluded, and should Ntsina fail to return (as so many young men failed to return), then the ceremony might be conducted *in absentia*. This would bring Bela into Sukude's homestead, and under his power. He would have the right to sex her if his son did not do so within three months of the marriage. This explained his haste to agree to her father's bride price, to avoid protracted haggling.

When Sukude told Nosakhe that he had negotiated the marriage of his son to the most desirable young wife for many miles around, Nosakhe knew that Sukude had a dark intention; but he had handled himself so well that she could not thwart him. Instead, she laid a Charm of Return upon the pile of hair and toenail clippings that allowed her to operate on Ntsina's body at a distance, and she woke every morning hopeful that he would enter her hut.

But so far, he had not.

⌒

He was closer, however, than she guessed: barely three days' distance, hacking to pieces a young steenbok he had killed that morning with a hard stone, flung at its head, and then a knife at its throat. Piet watched the twitching animal and felt a pang of regret for all the flesh he had eaten in his life. But he also felt brave, a man in touch with harsh realities; and he made himself look as Ntsina sawed the creature's limbs off, with a sharp knife Piet had bought in Cape Town which nevertheless, though Ntsina was too polite to say so, was a blunt, useless thing by comparison with the knives of Gwadana.

Luvo, having grown up on a farm, knew how to skin a beast,

and applied himself to it with accuracy and skill. It pleased him to show Ntsina that he could handle himself in the wild, and he trimmed the fat with great delicacy. They made a fire and cooked the steenbok over it, watched by many enquiring eyes – for the scent of a steenbok goes a long way in a forest, and many creatures had come to see what they might share.

It was Piet who suggested adding herbs, and Ntsina who found them, hacking his way through the jungle to scare off the hyenas. When he returned, he was carrying several slender mushrooms, tinged with blue – a treat he had learned from the older boys in the village, not from his grandmother. Piet did his best to eat the steenbok, for he was hungry. But it was tough and gamey and smelled of luscious blood and he could not stomach it, used as he was to meat served in restaurants, prepared in kitchens. He thought longingly of the kudu biltong the leopard had stolen. He did not quite believe the story of the leopard, thinking it much more likely that the boys had scoffed the biltong while he slept. He had brought a few tins of soup, but forgotten a tin opener, and did not fancy his chances of opening a can with a knife. Nor would his pride permit him to ask Ntsina for assistance.

So he watched as the young men tucked in, at once hungry and revolted, feeling light-headed and cold. It was a grey, overcast day. For the first time since setting off he felt despondent, and began to see the difficulties of his scheme. The mahogany was of good quality, but situated a long way from anywhere he might make a piece of furniture; and after all he was a white man among darkies, who *in extremis* would cheat him of all they could.

'Why does the Strange One look so sad?' said Ntsina to Luvo.

'I don't know and I don't care.' Luvo had his own grievances. He would have preferred it, he thought, if Piet had not affected equality with them. He would then at least have known what to expect. Piet's friendliness on the bus, however, his insistence that he be addressed as Piet and not as Baas or even Sir, had made Luvo think that he was an *mlungu* like the von Rankes. Piet's total unconcern with domestic duties, his unquestioned sense that it was Ntsina and Luvo who should lay the fires and skin the animals, that he was going beyond the call of duty simply by carrying his own pack, made Luvo resentful. He felt he had been tricked into affection, then shown for a fool.

Sensing the tension in the group, Ntsina thought of the mushrooms. They were used in certain secret ceremonies, and strictly controlled; but the older boys defied official convention and ate them for sport. Ntsina realized, as he ripped the steenbok meat from the bone, that although his name meant 'Laughing Boy' he had not laughed in too long.

'I have something that will cheer us,' he said, and reached for the mushrooms in his pouch.

Luvo was sceptical, and asked many questions which Ntsina refused to answer. All he said was: 'These will not harm you. But you must make your own choice.'

When the fungi were shown to Piet, they looked much more edible than the steenbok. His spirits revived at the prospect of a new anecdote to tell at the bar of the Mount Nelson Hotel.

'Tell the Strange One he should eat no more than three, and chew them well,' said Ntsina.

Luvo hesitated. He had so far been a wholly faithful translator. 'Might they kill a man if he has too many?'

'No, they won't kill. But the consequences can be frightening.'

Ntsina went off for a piss, and Luvo, moved by a rare spirit of vengeance, said: 'He advises you to take ten.'

Piet was chewing them by the time Ntsina returned. They tasted vile. Acrid and bitter, with an undertone of a flavour he had never encountered but would never thereafter forget. There was a challenge in their vileness, and Piet was a man who responded to challenges. He kept his face straight and chewed, and saw that Ntsina was impressed that he should make no complaint. In the forest, Ntsina's expertise had begun to reverse the race superiority Piet had taken as his natural right, and Ntsina's respect had become worth winning. He chewed for three minutes, until Ntsina made a swallowing gesture.

Piet swallowed.

Nothing happened.

Ntsina selected three mushrooms and chewed them too. Luvo refused, having been given too many lectures on the dangers of intoxicants to abandon his principles on so small a provocation.

'We must move away from the meat,' said Ntsina, 'so the animals may have it and leave us alone.'

They resumed their walk through the forest. The bitter cold of the morning had eased, and the trees protected them from the stinging wind. The canopy had kept some of the heat of the day before, and the air was humid and caressing. Ntsina found them a pleasant spot on the banks of a stream.

'Teach me some isiXhosa,' said Piet.

Luvo, unwillingly, guided him through the phrase for 'What a beautiful home'. At first Piet caught the jumble of sounds quite well, but as they went on a certain slackness descended on his jaw, and then his tongue. The sun was glinting through the trees, in a halo of red. The red intensified, began to spread. Piet's hunger lifted, was replaced by a tingling sensation in his limbs. Ntsina smiled at him, and then they both began to laugh. Piet could not say what was funny. Perhaps it was the shape of Ntsina's lip, or the crookedness of his teeth. An insuperable hilarity bubbled from within, and the look on Luvo's face stimulated it. The more disapproving Luvo became, the more Piet and Ntsina laughed, Luvo's disapproval sparking the flint of untapped merriment deep within them.

Piet's head, usually so full of words, became gloriously empty. He who thought so much lost all consciousness of not thinking. The universe began to stretch and billow. His hunger ceased.

Piet had now reached the level of intoxication achieved by the three mushrooms Ntsina had prescribed. Ntsina, in the same place, felt a strong affection for this risk-taking *mlungu* rising through him, an affection like the one he had felt for his dearest boyhood friends when they, too, had sneaked into the forest and hunted for the mushrooms with their slender, blue-tinged stems.

But Piet had not eaten three mushrooms. As his stomach broke them down, their key ingredient raced towards his brain – where it caused glorious mischief. He had rarely drunk to excess and had no experience of the white powders his friends took from tiny golden spoons in the bathrooms of nightclubs. The fabric of the universe began to undulate like curtains billowing in the breeze, and then the breeze became a hurricane and he began to be afraid.

Luvo, watching him, felt a different kind of fear clamp his spine. It was clear that he had unleashed in the Strange One something beyond anyone's capacity to control, and Ntsina's assurances that these mushrooms would not kill had surely, he reflected, been constrained by the number ingested. To his horror, Piet's face twisted from mirth, through mystification into terror, and then tears formed in his eyes.

The sight of an *mlungu* weeping pricked Luvo to the quick, and he began to offer fervent prayers for Piet's recovery. Piet's vulnerability made him see that he did not hate him, that Piet had tried, in his own way, to be kind; and that if he had failed to treat his employees as equals, the roots of his failure were anchored in a wider malaise that was not of his making.

Piet tried to rouse himself, but his strongest efforts resulted in his raising his head barely an inch from the ground. His body had grown unresponsive. Only his mind was alive, and it was flooded by sensation. The trees had lost their shape. Their bark was shimmering. He began to sink into the ground and as he sank certain feelings rose through him, in opposition to the downward movement, and chief among them was love. Love for his wife. Love for his son. Arthur's voice came to him, the flash of sunlight on his golden curls, the weight of his body as he fell asleep against Piet's chest. Piet grasped for this love. It was the only thing he trusted, and as it floated above him, fusing with the red ball of the sun, flooding the clearing with multi-hued light, he felt Ntsina's arm slip round him, after which Luvo's voice, very soothingly, said: 'We have you safe, Piet. This will pass.'

It did not pass. The universe swirled and shifted. Beneath his love for Arthur came scenes from a house in Amsterdam filled with exquisite furniture and all manner of sensual delights. These brought with them the sharp cut of cruelty, as he remembered Louisa Vermeulen-Sickerts' stinging distrust of him, and then this sweetened – for she had crossed the world to say sorry. He sank down and down into the ground, into the shouts and cries, the smell of fields, of Leiden, where he had spent his youth. A grumbling of his father, the heaviness of his tread, his ghastly snores rumbled across the forest. And then – it was this that made him cry – his mother's kindness, the sound of her voice as she sang and told him she loved him, and missed him, and sent him money and forgiveness and a kiss.

Ntsina found a sweet, sharp fruit and squeezed it into Piet's mouth, and the sensation was a jolting joy. Piet drank what he was given, and another, and another, and after an eternity the universe's billowing grew gentler. His descent into the ground slowed and he began to float upwards, towards the light, the sky, the kind expressions of his companions. In this wordless state Piet understood emotion only. The look on Ntsina's face, Luvo's concern, communicated more powerfully than words could have done that they wished him well, that they waited for him in the world he had so recently shared with them. As the bark on the trees began to etch itself into a myriad embroidery, an answering feeling rose within him and solidified as a bond of deep affection and trust.

When Piet could move again, because the drug had subsided, he sat up – but he had no words, and through the trees the sunlight spun radiantly. The sounds of the forest were brighter, and he heard meaning in the squawks and croaks and hisstles and creaks. Two birds were calling to each other. He understood that one was inviting the other to follow, that the second was coyly resisting, with every intention of yielding in the end. Luvo was so glad Piet was going to live that he found in himself all the joy

95

in domestic duties that had made him the Rankes' most beloved pupil. He made comfortable rest places for his friends, and then Piet and Ntsina lay down side by side and stared at the sky.

'I will introduce this man to my ancestors tonight,' said Ntsina to Luvo, a long while later. 'He is prepared for them now.'

They stood and went on, led by Ntsina, whose mortal powers were returning. Piet walked through the forest in silence, his mind still malleable. The hallucinatory power of the mushrooms had subsided with the sweetness of the juice, but his heightened perception remained. He moved slowly, smoothly, almost in a trance. He felt at one with this natural world, a creature descended from apes, and the lifting of language revealed deeper, wordless responses to the rhythms of the forest. He was alive to the scents in the air and the communications of the beasts.

The going by the stream was difficult and rocky. Seeing that Piet was in no state to navigate this terrain, Ntsina led them away from the water and into the network of avenues made by the forest elephants. Nosakhe had taught him their geography, and he found that his sojourn in Johannesburg had not robbed him of the knowledge, and this made him sure that he had escaped the Bad Magic before it was too late. He thought with distant horror of the mines and the falling platform, the shattered bones of the men he had known. These memories had taken on the quality of a nightmare. With every step he felt woken from it.

The *mlungu's* vulnerability, and then his quietness, and Ntsina's own consumption of a potent hallucinogen, had cleansed his feelings towards Piet Barol. The bowing and scraping of the blacks in Johannesburg, which had so injured his dignity and made him sorrowful for them, even as he was grateful for the welcome Mrs Mafuduka had given him, were irrelevant in the forest. With each step they took Ntsina grew more certain that it was time to honour the summons of his ancestors.

There was only one place in which to do it.

They came to the grove of the Ancestor Trees as the sun began to dip. The creeping cold of approaching night was held at bay by the insulation of the leaves. The elephants' paths led to it, for this was their meeting place too.

The trees to which the villagers of Gwadana gave the name *Nin-yanya*, or Ancestor, predated their arrival by two thousand years. They had been alive before the Xhosa became distinct from the Pedi and the Zulu, their reputation as cattle thieves and fine hosts not yet won. The trees had been alive when the great *mlungu* Jesus Christ persuaded the few who had bread and fish to share what they had, and so fed five thousand on the dry plains of Galilee. Their root systems had explored the soft soil of the forest, and then the clay beneath it, and then the fissured rock that was the forest's foundation, throughout the great dramas of Rome, the stabbing of Julius Caesar on the Senate steps. They had grown towards one another and fused, sharing the water and the nectar that could keep weaker ones alive through a harsh season, or restore those struck by lightning and wounded by fire while in Africa wars raged and in Europe men set out on fragile vessels to conquer worlds they described as 'new' – but which were as old as any world. The grove was almost a single being, so bound were its member trees to one another, and yet each was wholly individual. They had grown together from saplings and forged a union without conflict, free from betrayal and viciousness. In their crowns were gardens of fertile soil, several inches deep, dropped over centuries by passing birds. In these gardens earthworms wriggled, grown distinct from those that churned the forest floor. Their branches began thirty feet above the ground, and this refuge from predators made them desirable residences for all sorts of creatures that relished distance from the great cats. Monkeys lived in them, and frogs, and squirrels that had learned to fly between them, leaping from branches and spreading their tails. Beetles toiled diligently and laid their eggs in cracks in the bark; but the wood was impenetrable to them, hard as metal. They were so far from the forest floor that the arrival of three hairless apes caused little consternation.

Piet Barol, entering the grove, experienced a sense of wonder so profound he could only lie down without a word. Observing his prostration, Ntsina felt he had done well to bring his new friend here – to a place no *mlungu* had ever seen. There was a time when trees of this kind had grown in their millions across Africa, but the steady march of *Homo sapiens*, these creatures' consuming desire for wood and space and warfare, had destroyed them. Not these enduring members of an ancient race. These trees had withstood all the vagaries of two thousand years, and found in the villagers of Gwadana humble supplicants, who sensed the inviolability of beings so ancient, and celebrated it. The Great Founder had declared that the spirits of the ancestors who had led him to save his cattles, and his people, resided in the distant canopies of these trees, and it was this fact, after almost an hour of silence, that Ntsina shared with Luvo, who said to Piet: 'The ancestors of the villagers of Gwadana are worshipped here. It is a savage custom, but we must not blame them.'

'These trees are the descendants of the Tree of Life, by his mating with a mortal tree,' said Ntsina. 'They are half-immortal. Tell him so.'

Luvo did, with some embarrassment. Piet bowed his head.

The Gwadanans had built wooden structures on poles, high enough above the floor not to disturb the forest elephants, and to Luvo's joy he saw that he would not spend another night under the starry skies. He found the others' wordlessness, and the lifting of his obligations as translator, profoundly relieving. He left them sitting in silence and swept out the largest hide, braving himself to remove the many spiders he found there. Growing on the edge of the clearing was a bush spangled with purple flowers that reminded him of the trumpets he had seen marching bands play in Cradock. He gathered some and put them in a flask, and surveyed his handiwork with pleasure. The question of what to eat arose. He longed to find something for their dinner, but did not trust himself. When the hide was ready, he saw that a hare had come to investigate their presence, and flung a rock at it, as he had seen Ntsina do, but the stone went wide and the creature leapt away.

Neither Ntsina nor Piet experienced any hunger, and Luvo dared himself to leave the clearing, spurred by the rumbling of his belly. He found water and made porridge from the oatmeal they had brought from Cradock, and offered it to the others who smiled beatifically and shook their heads.

And so they all went into the hide to sleep, side by side, and the rains came, and they were dry, and Luvo gave heartfelt thanks to God. And while the others snored he watched the elephants who arrived as the moon rose, and rubbed their trunks against one another, and mated, and caroused, and for the first time he felt that he was on a glorious adventure.

⌒

When Piet woke the next morning, he had no idea where he was. He had slept so deeply that the journey to consciousness was slow. Above him was thatch, beneath him hard wood. He felt a new man, restored, refilled. He looked to his side and saw his companions, and the flowers Luvo had arranged, and the pleasant proportions of the hide. Slowly a recollection of the day before came to him, formless as a dream. When he moved he half expected his head to ache, as it did when he had drunk too much. But in fact he felt supple and strong.

He emerged from the hide and jumped from the platform. The floor of the forest was springy and took his weight like a mattress. He saw where he was. And that some dreams of the day before had been real. In fact, in resplendent sobriety, the trees that marked an oval shape, their roots criss-crossing the ground, rising ten inches high in certain places, were even more magnificent than they had been in his hallucinations – because they alone, of all he had seen, preserved their scale. In silence he approached one. It was so tall, its proportions so elegant, that from a distance it might have looked slender. Up close, he saw that twenty men could not link arms around it. The bark curved in elegant swirls up the trunks,

99

as though the men who first conceived Rococo pillars in Italian churches had drawn inspiration from them.

A ravenous greed rose within him. He felt delirious at the possibilities of such a wood. An enchanted bed sprung into his head. The first piece he would make. A bed that celebrated the wonders of this land so far from the world he and Percy had known. He would make it all from a single piece of wood. With a tree this size, that would be possible. Not a single join, not a screw. A bed as magnificent as a sculpture carved from a solid marble block. He began to pace, and saw that the trunk's diameter was twenty feet at least. It would be the longest, biggest bed in Johannesburg – how perfect for the man who was paying for it! But for Dotty he would also make it the most beautiful, and for himself.

Over six and a half years in Cape Town, watching others give life to his designs, Piet had learned a great deal; built on the talent for drawing he had brought from Europe. His thirst for knowledge and excitement and challenge had seen him spend hundreds of hours in his workshop presided over by skilled Indian craftsmen, and he had learned something of the mysteries of wood. But he had never truly been tested.

Now a challenge worthy of total acceptance had presented itself, and the means to make a piece of art like no other – which is the essence of a piece of art, that it should be a thing unto itself, he thought, imagining how his fame would spread like a veld fire. With Percy as his salesman, boasting of his new possessions, everyone would see his creations, and everyone would order. It was a calm knowledge, not a hope. He saw that with this wood he could lift himself for ever from the ranks of toiling cabinetmakers who sold their wares to the newly affluent members of Europe's lower middle classes, who had come to South Africa and now had houses to furnish. At last, he could make something with *panache*.

With this came another certainty: that he would make an inordinate amount of money. Enough even to pay these natives for the wood, since they seemed so attached to it.

When Ntsina appeared, he embraced him, grinning widely. He

could not wait, and shouted up to Luvo. When Luvo emerged, rubbing his eyes, Piet put his hand on Ntsina's shoulder and said: 'What must I do to have *these trees*?'

Once it was made plain to Ntsina what Piet was asking, he was not so much offended as amused. 'Tell the Strange One these trees are the homes of my ancestors,' he said to Luvo. 'There can be no talk of his having them.'

The matter-of-factness in Ntsina's tone told Piet that this was not a preamble to negotiation, but a statement of fact. He did not press the point, but neither did he doubt for an instant that he would one day possess these trees. He could, if necessary, pay for new shrines to be built to the villagers' ancestors – shrines closer to home and more convenient for worship. He had a quick imagination and trusted in his powers of persuasion. These conjured for him now a vision of a happy native tribe, delighted with their new shrines and the money they brought with them.

As they ate porridge for breakfast, Piet decided not to trouble Ntsina further with his questions, since Ntsina was a junior man in the village. He would meet the chief and win him round by any means necessary.

cᴏ

At this moment, the chief of the village of Gwadana was also sitting down to breakfast in the large thatched rondavel called the King's Place. The title was a courtesy one, since he was no king, but there also was truth in it – for no man's word held more sway in Gwadana. Once a year he attended the gathering of the princes at King William's Town, and in his youth he had been a strident critic of the many accommodations they had made with the British – who flattered them and gave them the guns that turned long-standing feuds into bloodbaths, while buying railway and telegraph concessions on the cheap.

The chief was not related to Gwadana's Great Founder by blood, since Nosakhe's grandfather had outlived all his male descendants and the idea of a woman chief had not crossed his mind. He was,

101

instead, the son of the first man to join the trek through the forest. The transfer of power, agreed before the Great Founder's death and ratified before every human in the village and all their male cattles, had been public and transparent; its emotional legacy was murkier. The chief had grown up in awe of the Great Founder's granddaughter, Nosakhe. In the days after his circumcision, as he nursed his bleeding member in a lonely forest place, spirits seething round him in his pain, Nosakhe had appeared to him in a dream and banished them. He was grateful to her, but her power also frightened him. For the one person in Gwadana who had ever considered the possibility of a woman as chief was its chief, who knew that Nosakhe Zini had personal capacities he lacked.

From the day of this chief's elevation, he had never been addressed by any other name than his title. This acted as a constant, oppressive reminder of his responsibilities. He had striven to be a good chief, knowing that he would never be a great one, but his speeches against the English at the Council of Princes had not won him friends among the appeasers, and he lacked the courage to continue a lonely fight. In Gwadana itself it was almost possible to believe that the Strange Ones were as unreal, as far-fetched, as their idea that a carpenter had saved the world.

He had sired three sons and assured the succession. He had four wives, a modest number, but each had her own special qualities and he was satisfied – for there are four seasons in the year, and four wives in the bedroom is an elegant sufficiency. In his forty-eighth year, his second wife, Anella, had given birth to a daughter who was blind and had no left hand.

The omen was a terrible one. Even as he beseeched Nosakhe to explain it, he wondered whether it was she who had caused it; whether beneath her dignity there lurked a slow-seething resentment that he should occupy the place of her grandfather. Nosakhe saw this plainly, and because it was partly true she did her best to reassure him. She would never desecrate her grandfather's memory by contravening the settlement he had made, in full possession of his faculties, at the onset of his final illness.

Nosakhe knew at once what must be done to children who are born blind or deformed. They are to be thrown from a cliff, to be eaten by birds. Left alive, they might become vessels for the reincarnation of Za-Ha-Rrell, who first introduced ambition and violence to the world, or Atamaraka, the Queen of Evil. Nosakhe was used to stating harsh truths, for the laws of the ancients are by no means always suited to tender delivery. But the way the chief looked at his wife, and the way Anella looked at the child she had just given birth to – a tiny thing, hideous to all but her parents – these looks were so full of love that she could not bring herself to say what must be said.

Nosakhe was steeped in the Knowledge and had a great store of precedents. She held the silence, her face betraying nothing as she ran through them in her mind. She failed to think of any grounds on which a deformed and blind child might be saved. This failure made her anxious. Her anxiety caused her brain to cloud. This was most unlike her. She lit *mphepho* and breathed its smoke and sank into a deep trance, aware that every eye in the village was upon her; sensitive to the vibrations of their tension. It came to her then that those who are blind are said to have the gift of Farsight, and those who are saved from death are spared for a special purpose. From these two facts she wrought an elegant solution: a child might be saved in such circumstances if she had the gift of seeing the future.

'She must be thrown from the cliff,' she said. 'Unless she has the gift of Farsight. I will call it on her, and we must wait to see if the seed I plant ever grows.'

Anella, sobbing in gratitude and fear, fell to the ground. It was the chief who said: 'How long must we wait, Mother?' He called Nosakhe mother, even though she was but five years older than he.

This was not Nosakhe's decision to make. She left the King's Place and stood under the Tree of Justice, calling for a sign. Eight gulls swooped low overhead. She read this as the verdict of the Goddess Ma and went inside.

'The gift must manifest by her eighth year,' she said.

'And what if she has no such gift when she is eight years old, Mother?'

'Then she must be thrown from the cliffs by the cave of Nomik-honto the first full moon of her ninth year.' There was no more Nosakhe could do than this, but in the ceremony of the planting of the seed of Farsight, she gave all that was best in her.

⌒∾⌒

They called the blind, deformed child Nonikwe, after the hunch-back in the ancient legends who was, despite this, a Blessed One. It was a strange thing for a man with three strapping sons, but nevertheless the truth of it was that the chief came to love this little girl to distraction, and so did his four wives and her strong older brothers. They called her Noni for short, and though she did not grow into a striking beauty, she grew markedly less hid-eous to look at, and wore her deformed arm in a sling made of embroidered linen that hid the absent hand. Her staring eyes frightened the village children, so her mother taught her to keep her eyelids closed. This did not mean that she saw nothing. Her interior world was radiant with colour, and included a map of the village and its homesteads so eerily detailed that she was able to go wherever she wished, almost as other children could.

This facility gave her parents hope. She was a clumsy toddler, but by the age of four she could run around the King's Place, and then around the village, almost as well as those who could see. This made them proud, and dimmed their fears that she might never manifest a gift. Noni developed a reputation for being a person who could find things. Indeed, by knowing the regular movements and eccentricities of those closest to her she was often able to locate a misplaced cattle stock. Each time she did so, word was sent to Nosakhe, who absorbed the information gravely until one day, exasperated at having her afternoon nap disturbed to be told that Noni had found her brother's second-best spear, which all thought lost, she was obliged to remind the chief that finding lost objects, though undoubtedly useful (she had the skill herself), was by no means the same thing as the gift of Farsight.

'Those with Farsight speak of what will happen, before it happens,' she said. 'It grows from within and cannot be taught.' And then, because she saw the anguish this caused Noni's parents: 'Do not worry. She has four more years.'

These four years became three, and then two; and on the morning Piet Barol first glimpsed an Ancestor Tree, Noni was seven years, six months and three days old. Her elders had coaxed all sorts of prophecies from her, in hysterical secrecy lest they turn out to be inaccurate; and they had turned out to be wrong as often as not, and in the end she had begun to cry every time anyone asked her a question about the future, and they saw that their eagerness for the gift to develop was inhibiting it.

Noni herself did not know what her fate was to be should she pass her eighth birthday without demonstrating the gift of Farsight. She sensed the deep love of her family, and its eminence meant that she was elevated above being a figure of fun for the village children. She was a happy child, and a great cuddler. In the absence of sight, her senses of touch and hearing and smell were heightened. She had an ear for the way people spoke, and was capable of isolating the distinct registers of a lie and a truth.

She went with her elder brothers to make sacrifices to their ancestors at the full moon, and was at ease in the forest. It was on one such journey that she stopped them, some distance from the grove of the Ancestor Trees, and said: 'Ntsina of the Zini clan is there, and two strangers. One of them is a Strange One.'

∽

Ntsina had fondly imagined his entry to the village in the company of a white man with the money to buy radios, and had any other person surprised him in the forest he would have been disappointed. But Kagiso the chief's son was the bosom friend of his boyhood, and his older brothers had initiated him into many a young man's mystery.

Kagiso saw Ntsina from beyond the edge of the clearing and felt a pang of joy. Noni was right. Ntsina *was* there. So were two strangers, one of whom was indeed a Strange One. Surely this was a glimmer of Farsight? It doubled his rapture at seeing his friend, and heightened his urgency to return and tell his parents.

To Noni, the Strange One's voice was a blazing colour that sighted people might call 'red' – though 'red' did little justice to the undulating blaze Noni saw. She heard happiness in it as he said 'I am sorry not to speak your language better'. The sounds he made had unfamiliar shapes, but she could understand this sentence – alone of all the sounds the Strange One made. She was used to deference, being the beloved daughter of a chief. She stepped forward boldly and touched the Strange One, and at once the shapeless mass of colour became distinct, resolved itself to her astonishment into the contours of a man. She had been taught that Strange Ones are descended from a star, and the explanation of what a star was had led her to expect a different shape.

Ntsina made the introductions, and Piet felt instinctive sympathy for the little girl with her closed eyes and missing hand. It was not a patronizing sympathy; rather a warmth that added to the richness of the red Noni saw when she sensed him. He crouched beside her and she touched his face, felt a nose sharper than anyone's in Gwadana; and then soft hair, as smooth as grass; quite unlike anything she was used to. This hair made her afraid. She drew back into the protection of her brother.

The chief's children made offerings to their ancestors and Piet watched, observing that one of the vast trees was their focus. Surely one – at least one – in this grove belonged to no village family. When the ceremony was complete, Kagiso said to Ntsina: 'You are to be married.'

The revelation that his bride was Bela of the Jaxa clan made Ntsina feel light-headed, and then ashamed. It was a strict rule that no young man should take a woman to the mating mat before he is twenty-five years old. He thought of the woman whose caresses he had bought with brandy in Johannesburg, who had given him the infernal itch. It made him feel unworthy of Bela, whose reputation for modesty and sweetness was unrivalled.

The men took turns carrying Noni on their shoulders, and she moved happily between her brothers and Ntsina as they walked to the village. She warmed to Luvo, whose gentleness communicated itself to her as a soft, warm turquoise, tinged with a colour that shone like the moon. Piet offered to share the burden, but the touch of his hair made Noni scream; so he did not press it, aware of the importance of getting on with little children if one wishes to win favour in their parents' eyes.

When they stopped for their first rest, Ntsina drew Luvo some way off and took him into his confidence. He felt an urgent need to confess. 'I took a woman to the mating mat,' he said. 'More than once. When I was in Johannesburg.'

'That is a grave sin,' said Luvo.

'How might I be worthy of my bride?'

At last! God had sent him the opportunity to relieve a burdened sinner of the weight of his guilt. 'Eve introduced Evil into the world,' said Luvo, 'when she tempted Adam to eat of the forbidden fruit in the garden of Eden. Did this woman tempt you, brother?'

Ntsina thought of the circumstances of their coupling. They had met in a tavern, and the woman he had bought with brandy had indeed been very friendly to him; had jiggled her breasts when she danced near him, and pushed her bottom against him. 'Yes, she did tempt me,' he said.

'Then pray with me that you be spared from future temptation, and forgiven your sins.' Luvo began to say the Lord's Prayer. Ntsina did not respond, but he did not protest either; and Luvo's certainty that his crime had been forgiven, which shone through him as he said 'Amen', comforted Ntsina. In his own head, he apologized to his ancestors for what he had done, and promised never again to be unworthy of them.

Of Piet, he said to his friends: 'There are good *mlungus* as well as bad. Luvo was raised by some good ones in Cradock, which is a town beyond Butterworth. This *mlungu* has become my friend. You must treat him kindly. His name is Piet Barol.'

Kagiso did treat Piet kindly, and bombarded him with all sorts of questions concerning his early life, so that Luvo grew quite exhausted from all the translating.

⁓

A woman who has a reputation for sweetness must needs have one outlet for the less sweet parts of her nature, and Bela Jaxa's outlet was her older sister Zandile, whom all called Zandi. At twenty-seven, Zandi was old to be unmarried. When Ntsina's father first came to fix a bride price, Zandi had wept with excitement, convinced he had come for her. It was customary in Gwadana for the daughters in a family to be married in order of age. She had dressed her hair with oil and waited patiently, wondering who her bridegroom was to be. All through the negotiations, she had sat in calm anticipation, trusting her father to choose wisely for her. When the knock came, she had risen and faced the door, her head bowed meekly as was proper. They had entered and her father had touched her shoulder – to comfort her, she later thought. For the negotiators had brushed past her and gone into the inner room, in search of her younger sister.

Bela, so sweet with her elders, so beloved of the girls of the village, had always been sharp with Zandi. She had a quick eye and a pointed tongue, and Zandi was clumsy in aspect and affect. Bela maintained the strictest ideals of Xhosa womanhood – meekness, kindness, modesty, beauty. The effort it cost her to be correct in public, never to gossip unkindly or to say a harsh word, meant that bile built within her, and she relieved it by teasing Zandi, and pressing home her advantage when it was clear that her words had wounded.

Bela's perfection of conduct was legendary. She herself found her beauty an obligation as much as an advantage. A girl as beautiful as she was – and she knew the quality of her looks – was a woman beloved of the Great Goddess. Bela was as fat as a pedigree veal calf nourished on wholesome food, and plenty of it, for the Jaxa clan, though poorer than the Zinis, kept a generous table and had a goat once each moon. Her skin was lustrous brown, her breasts at once heavy and pert, perfectly rounded. It was not for nothing that she had entered unawares into Sukude's daydreams, until he could no longer conceive of a life in which he did not have her. Bela's hair was springy and luxuriant, her hands dainty. She did her share of the housework but no more, leaving Zandi to cultivate domestic expertise as a means of standing her ground against her dazzling sister.

It was Zandi who saw the young men approaching from the forest. She knew it was wrong for a groom to visit his bride, and yet also that such transgressions are overlooked by indulgent parents. Ntsina was with the chief's children and—she felt her heart flutter – a Strange One. Was he a government inspector? She had superb long-range vision, though things blurred when she held them in her hand. She could not understand the easiness of the men and called her mother, who drew her away from the window.

Under her father's eye, Bela wrapped a blanket about her shoulders and prepared to meet the man whose children she would bear and whose porridge she would cook until the end of her earthly life. It was in the nature of her beauty never to need preparation. She was as entrancing on waking in the morning, her hair in disarray, as she was when dressed for the most sumptuous festival. Her breasts were bare and she drew the blanket over them, taking care nevertheless to leave enough exposed to make it clear that delights worth having were beneath.

'You may greet him, but no more,' said her father. 'I have always been able to trust you, Bela.'

'You may trust me now,' she said. And walked with light elegance away from him, towards the farmyard gate.

⌒

It was the night after a full moon, and a silvery light blinded the stars. Luvo, Kagiso, Piet and Noni hung back, and Ntsina advanced alone. He knew Bela only from a distance. His father's selection of her made him think more warmly of the old man. This warmth made him happy, for it is hard on a boy to distrust his own father.

Bela was standing behind the gate. The arrangement of her blanket was perfection. The glimpse it offered of her breasts in the moonlight, the way the light shone on her strong, smooth neck, the shadow thrown by her bottom, made Ntsina stop and draw breath. The image of his wife banished all recollection of his joyless romping in Johannesburg. The rash, the itch, the consequences of sex with strangers who give themselves too readily – all this was gone for ever.

The way Bela was standing – the openness and submission of her posture, combined with a rare, fetching dignity – touched Ntsina to the quick. He yearned to protect her. He thought of making children in her, and his cock throbbed, straining against the buttons on his trousers. He did not wish to approach her for the first time unwashed after a day in the forest. He paused, and saw that the moonlight had thrown his silhouette in shadow onto the ground. He hastily put his hands in front of himself.

But Bela had seen the shadow, and felt a tingling over her whole body.

She had never given herself, not the smallest part of herself, not a brushed hand or a touched cheek, to any man. Glances, of course, for the homage of youths was delightful to her. She was especially gifted in the matter of glances, and glanced towards her future husband, lifting her eyes from the ground in a manner that set Ntsina's soul aflame. Despite himself, he advanced. He came within a few feet of her, and she caught his smell on the night breeze, and she, like every other girl in Gwadana, liked it.

'I see you, my soon-to-be husband,' she said.

'I see you, my soon-to-be wife,' said Ntsina. And he bowed and retreated, and then ran back to his friends in a soaring euphoria.

They slept near Bela's homestead, on a piece of flat turf beside the vegetable patch. An elaborate pretence that Bela's parents did not know they were there was maintained, but Zandi came out to offer them potent pink beer that tasted of sour milk. Piet did not care for it, but he understood that it would be a rejection of friendship to refuse it. So he drank two clay bowls' full, and a pleasant, sated kind of drunkenness crept over him. It was clear to him that the woman serving the beer had conflicting feelings about the gorgeous teenager who had retreated to the house as the strangers entered the yard. 'Are they sisters?' he asked Luvo. And when he received his answer he felt that his instincts would be as sure here as they were everywhere else.

The fact that the first person from the village he had met was the chief's son struck Piet Barol as a confirmation of the good graces of the Universe. He exerted himself to be pleasant and succeeded. Kagiso was not often treated as a wise man, a fact that had begun to irk in his twenty-second year. He looked forward to commanding the attention of the council when he reported on this Strange One. Luvo's interpretation had been accurate, but no accuracy could succeed in conveying to Kagiso the city Piet Barol had come from – half a world away, with rivers for streets. He knew the stories of the Strange Ones who had come hundreds of years before, in great sea creatures with many legs, and set the Bantu against one another. Kagiso reminded himself of this knowledge as he and Piet spoke by the fire, draining Luvo's energy as Ntsina stared dreamily at the moon. He had to remind himself, because he could not help liking this *mlungu*, who answered so freely and asked so many questions. Kagiso had not gone to the mines, but he had for a time worked in a timber shop in Butterworth. He had never known a white person display such an unfeigned interest in his family and the circumstances of his village.

The night was bitterly cold, but the fire was warm. A sense of nearing his journey's climax kept Piet awake till dawn. The trees exerted their spell on him. He must have them, and move the villagers' ancestors to different quarters. He asked Kagiso if his father's word was law, and was reassured when Kagiso said yes – for it is easier to persuade one man than every resident of a village. He could not know that Kagiso had said this out of pride, and that it was by no means true. A Xhosa chief is first among equals: a great power but by no means an absolute one.

As he inched closer to the fire, Piet felt sure of victory.

❧

Having secured the hand of the most beautiful woman in Gwadana for his son, Sukude Zini could not wait to organize Ntsina's wedding. This demanded the invitation of the bridegroom. With great fanfare, and a corruptible witness, he had gone to Butterworth and gone inside its post office for fifteen minutes. The witness, whose name was Lundi, was a member of the chief's council and a man whose word could not easily be questioned. Sukude had gone to great lengths to keep secret his clandestine funding of Lundi's adventures in King William's Town, where he was well known at the native taverns and whore houses. They were not known to be friendly, and it was for this reason that Lundi was useful to Sukude.

Lundi swore that he had seen Sukude pay a clerk to write and then send a telegram to his son at the Crown Mine. With it, he said, had gone a postal order for a train ticket – a sum of money Lundi had taken for himself, as the price of his compliance. It was Lundi's duty to travel to King William's Town in a week's time, and from there to send a regretful telegram from the bridegroom, saying that he could not leave his work and suggesting that the wedding take place by proxy.

This telegram was important, for reading was one of Nosakhe's many mysterious powers.

Between Sukude and his mother-in-law a complex respect had established itself over the years, its foundations more solid than they would have been had they felt any affection for one another. Sukude, with his bull strength, was not Nosakhe's first choice for her daughter, but the child had insisted on him and she had not

112

refused. He had been conscious of the honour it did him, a poor farmer, to be raised into the household of the descendants of the Great Founder, and he had done well by them. He had not beaten his wife, nor taken to drink, nor gone whoring in King William's Town when the chief had chosen him to join his delegation to the Council of Princes. Since his wife's death, he had performed the sacred rituals Nosakhe assigned him, and only once half-asked for permission to wed another woman. The look in Nosakhe's eyes on that occasion had given him her final answer. He had now decided to claim his prize in his own way.

Sukude had begun the arrangements for the feast before receiving the telegram explaining that Ntsina could not be present. It would have been suspicious to do otherwise; and the truth of it was that the closer he came to sexing Bela Jaxa, the longer each hour that separated him from having her was. Ntsina must have a marriage feast worthy of his family's deeds. Nosakhe had been saving since the time of Ntsina's initiation into manhood, and now had a sizeable collection of the scraps of paper for which Strange Ones hand over goods of real value. This store was also the family's capital, and Sukude applied himself with focus to the task of giving the most lavish feast in the cheapest possible manner.

It is the golden rule of Xhosa hospitality that no matter how many come, supplies must never run out. Sukude knew every one of the seven hundred and thirty-eight men, women and children of Gwadana; knew who the secret and not-so-secret drinkers were, which wives went crazy at a party, and he drew up a careful provision list. He set six cattles aside, but would slaughter more if the need arose.

Nosakhe had watched these proceedings, and tended daily the pile of hair and toenail clippings in the corner of her hut, willing her grandson home.

⚭

The forest ended as abruptly as it had begun. The stream they were following ran into a river, which became a lagoon as they stepped beyond the trees. Ahead was a cove of miniature perfection. The sky was grey and tinged with salt. The ocean was a deep aquamarine, the beach as round as the moon. On one side rose a steep hill, at the top of which the forest began again. To their left a promontory in the shape of a sleeping whale guarded the harbour against crashing tides.

With pleasure, Piet realized that he had prepared sufficiently well for this moment to be able to say exactly the right thing to his companion: '*Ubuhle obunje.*' Kagiso was touched to the heart to hear these words in his own language – for Piet had said 'What beauty.'

'Tell the Strange One he has one more hill to climb,' said Ntsina to Luvo. 'My homestead has the best view.'

It was true. But the escarpment was so steep Luvo felt like the last portion of the journey took as much resilience as all that had gone before. The hill seemed never to end. The path was slippery with salt. His pack grew heavier with each step, but the men around him were so strong he could not bear to show weakness. Piet was entranced. 'Ask Ntsina when he is to be married,' he said to Luvo. But Luvo pretended not to hear.

At the top of the escarpment the ground levelled abruptly. Ahead was a stately homestead. Ntsina was proud of the perfection of the goat fence, which unlike so many fences of the village ran in straight lines. They went under the gate. Beyond was a cattle kraal, and beyond that latrines and two vegetable gardens. Several round thatched huts were placed in the enclosure, within a few steps of one another; and right at the back, beyond the gardens, was one larger hut, alone at the edge of the cliff.

Ntsina took them to the nearest hut and threw open the door. It was a tidy kitchen. He was calling the word 'Nosakhe'. Piet had no idea what it meant, but he heard joy in Ntsina's tone. Ntsina called and called, going from one hut to another. Then at last he turned to Luvo and said: 'The spirits wish me to greet my father first.' And he went to the lonely hut beyond the vegetable gardens, and knocked.

114

Stupefaction, then ferocious disappointment, then fear: these were the emotions Sukude went through as he raised himself to his full height and greeted his son. Lundi was already in King William's Town. At any moment he might deliver a telegram explaining that Ntsina could not be present for his wedding. He tried to decide what precautions he might take, while he bade Luvo and Piet welcome.

To have a white man incarnated beside his son – a white man who remarked politely how beautiful his house was, and how fine the day was, and asked him how he was, and apologized for his poor pronunciation – brought home to Sukude the strangeness of what was taking place. He knew now that his mother-in-law had cast a spell, not trusting him to ensure Ntsina's return; and that meant that she might never have been deceived by his elaborate preparations. Up to this point in the venture, he had been safely sanctioned by custom. Were it to become clear to anyone, Nosakhe most of all, that he was thieving the love mate of another man, his own son, he knew what the punishment would be.

He felt faint with terror.

He took them into the kitchen hut, but he rarely ventured into Nosakhe's domain and did not know where anything was. Fortunately Ntsina did, and soon they were all drinking the beer that the Sondela family delivered to Nosakhe twice a month, free of charge, in gratitude for her healing of their prize bull and the accident that had befallen Mr Sondela's former business partner at King William's Town.

⟡

Nosakhe was walking along the barnacled rocks that had cut her feet as a girl, until they hardened into a better-fitting boot than any available in the shops of the Strange Ones. She was the kindred of the Sea and she sought the Sea's guidance. There was knowledge in the endless iteration of Her waves. She made a sound the nesting gulls knew as the call of the hairless ape who roamed their cliffs but did them no harm. It was a sound to summon the Goddess

Ma, who knew all about the wicked ways of men. Lundi's account of how he had seen Sukude send a telegram summoning Ntsina had confirmed Nosakhe's worst suspicions of her son-in-law. No man who had actually sent a telegram would go to such lengths to provide a witness to the deed. There was a stupidity in Sukude, a brute deafness to the subtleties of life, that was the chief reason Nosakhe had not wished him to be her daughter's mate. It was this deafness for which she was always on the lookout in Ntsina. She was severe with the boy when he daydreamed and did not hear, being mindful of his parentage. For Nosakhe did not need any Strange One to tell her about the power of heredity: one had only to look at a herd of cattles or a litter of dogs.

Nosakhe kept a dog, the best-trained animal in Gwadana. She called the bitch Atamaraka, or 'Ata'. Nosakhe knew that at some point in her life she would meet the Queen of Evil face to face. Nosakhe's grandfather had told her so on his deathbed. To accustom herself to the use of this frightful name, by using it for a lesser being, was an important preparation for this ordeal. Today, as she called for the dog, whom she loved with all her soul, more straightforwardly, if truth be told, than she loved her grandson – because Ata had long ago reached the perfection of her kind that Ntsina was still grasping for – she knew that Atamaraka might hear.

The waves lashed against her. The dog came to her side and sat, back straight as a leopard's. Ata had a coat of impossible sleekness and a diet better than all but the wealthiest Gwadanans. Nosakhe made the call again, and the gulls rose from the cliffs and began circling, cawing and cawing where they had been silent before.

Nosakhe told Ma she was aware of Atamaraka working within her son-in-law. She acknowledged the logical interpretation of Sukude's deception – that he wished to take Bela to the marriage bed himself. Nosakhe admitted that Atamaraka had forced her into a delicate choice: to expose her son-in-law, and bring shame and ridicule on the family; or to let him go his way, unpunished. The Goddess did not acknowledge Nosakhe beyond the cawing of the gulls, but She reminded Nosakhe that she should trust herself.

Nosakhe knew, because her grandfather had told her, that if she prepared with rigour she would be equal to Atamaraka when the time to meet Her came. She well understood that this might happen after the death of her physical body, and often prayed to be reincarnated as one of the great birds that dived for fishes in the sea. She took from her bag a folded cloth, and opened it, and scattered Ntsina's hair and toenail clippings on the waves. No other *sangoma* would dispose of the means to act on a person at this most vital time. Nosakhe did so to invite the Sea's aid, to show her trust in Ma, to call for the goddess Amarire to join her in what she, a poor mortal, had failed to do on her own: to bring her grandson back in time to prevent his father from committing a capital crime.

She walked over the rocks, waiting for a feeling. And when it came, transmitted by the leaping of a wave, the grace of a whirl-pool, it was one of resolute calmness. She washed her feet in the Sea and climbed the high escarpment. As she reached the top, through the open door to her own kitchen, she saw Ntsina.

In a voice as loud and clear and beautiful as Marimba's herself, Nosakhe lost all her dignity and shouted: 'I am as happy as a BIIIIIG fish swimming in a DEEEEP pool!'

Sukude went to bed as early as he could. He knew he must keep a constant watch for Lundi. He had never been demonstrative with his son, and told himself that Nosakhe had not seen his disappointment. He had blunted it with drunkenness, but as he walked to his hut it overwhelmed him; became self-pity. And then rage. Ntsina had given him a bottle of the brandy Piet had bought in Idutywa, and it was this brandy that lit the fire of his anger. He raged against Nosakhe, who kept him like a zombie, with no outlet for a man's natural needs. He raged against his dimwitted wife, who had stepped over a rock and trodden on a puff adder. He might have managed her. Together they could have made a

117

family, and broken from the evil old woman. At least a wife would give him some protection. He knew the value of women.

He watched and watched for Lundi, until it was dark and the moon had risen over the sea. Lundi was not foolish enough to wander at night through the forest, but he was known as an early riser and Sukude knew he would need to be awake before dawn. One of his little rebellions against Nosakhe was the acquisition of a watch like the ones the poorer sort of Strange Ones wore. He told himself he must wake at the hour of the sea bird, and looked at the clock, and tried to sleep. But he opened his eyes every few minutes until, as dawn was breaking and Lundi was just beginning his ascent of the escarpment with a telegram from Ntsina in his hand, Sukude fell into an insuperable sleep.

5

Nosakhe sent Piet and Luvo to rest as soon as she decently could. She was agog to know the means Ma had employed to bring Ntsina to Gwadana at this vital hour, and she, like Sukude, was perturbed by the presence of a Strange One. She watched Noni step nimbly down the steep path with her brother, trusting wholly in her senses, and asked Ma not to forget her. And also, if the child must be sacrificed, to give her, Nosakhe Zini, the strength to do it quietly, and quickly, with dignity. Nosakhe had never before been compelled to throw a child from a cliff, and though she knew it was a sacred duty, just as much as it was her duty to burn with hot stones the thighs of an adulteress before her execution (which she had done before, twice) she prayed to be excused it.

When the others had gone, she put away the brandy Ntsina had brought with him and got out the special sheep fat he loved, which she had not shared with her guests. Nosakhe had a paraffin stove, as befitted a magician, and it was the work of minutes to melt the sheep fat and fill the hut with a savoury scent so all-compelling in its deliciousness that Ntsina's mouth ran as much as Ata's. Ata loved Ntsina, and had been as glad as her mistress to have him home. Ntsina sat on the floor, watching his grandmother, and the sleek dog curled against him. Nosakhe thought, as she had often thought before, that those parts of her own spirit which could not fit into the body of Nosakhe Zini had taken up residence in Ata. For though she was excited, and talking volubly while she cooked, she was also as peaceful as the dog.

'I set you a great test, my grandson. I sent you to the Under-world to see what you would see.'

'There are many dark spirits there, Grandmother. The Strange Ones are blasting the earth open and setting them free.'

Ntsina told her everything he had seen, except for the woman with the rash behind her knees. He told her how troubled sleep had kept him awake, and made him early that fateful day, and how he had been on the first platform, not the second. And therefore how he had lived, rather than died.

Nosakhe, watching him, was fully replenished by the Great Goddess Ma for all her recent worry. Ntsina's return was a tri-umphant benediction; the ways Ma had spurred him homewards were clear to her. She did not tell him that she had cast a spell for his return, for she knew it would deflate his pride in himself. And pride in himself was the one quality Ntsina had lacked before his departure to Johannesburg. Having him return with so much of it made Nosakhe think well of the spirits, to whom she had done so much honour during her life. She heard all about Luvo's delegation to England, and wondered whether she should fly him there on an eagle wing and save them all a lot of trouble. But she had not yet tried this spell, which is notoriously hard, and she did not wish to seem immodest by flexing her powers after such a great victory.

At length she said: 'Can I trust this Strange One?'

'Yes,' said Ntsina. 'There is good at the depths of his heart. But we must use him too, Mama. The whites have stolen so much, from all those who burned their cattle and made themselves weaker in the moons before. Our ancestors have sent us a white man to make *us* rich.'

'And to help us fight back,' said Nosakhe.

But Ntsina, whose dreaminess she had never quite squeezed from him, was not listening any longer. He was wholly pres-ent at some glorious future moment, when he would give his grandmother a bed as comfortable as the one he had seen the Strange One sleep in at Cradock. He would give her a radio, *and* a bed, *and*, he thought, help make the money for a delegation to England. When he came back to himself, his grandmother was speaking about the princes in derisory terms. 'They must take action, these men. They must join forces.'

'They are too far from one another,' said Ntsina.

'Then they must be summoned to the feast for your marriage.'

Before they went to sleep, Nosakhe took Ntsina's wide face in her calloused hands. The scratch of her skin made him feel safe. She said: 'You have the stirrings of wisdom. You have done well to bring this Strange One here. We must make from him a sum of money bigger than the difference between success and failure for those who seek the protection of the English king. And we must bring our own kings together.'

As she spoke, she had no great faith in the one they called King George the Fifth of Great Britain and Ireland. No word in isiXhosa required the vulgarities of the 'G' sound in English, and Nosakhe knew that few who have ugly names have strong souls. But she also knew that in a great undertaking one must leave no anthill unopened.

༄

Piet woke the next morning in a bare mud hut that smelled of earth and thatch. There were no windows and it was very dark inside. For a moment he did not know where he was, and felt afraid, as though he had woken in a dream. But the seepage of daylight round the hinges of the door, which did not fit snugly in its frame, caught the elegant structure of beams above him and at length he understood that he had ventured far beyond the paths of the white man.

He opened his door to find that morning was well advanced. Beneath him, the ground fell away to blue ocean. He was high enough to see two bays, the grasses emerald green against the blue of the sea. In the field beyond a neat fence, a calf was scratching its ear with its back hoof – a balletic movement at once comic and graceful. He saw that the hut he had slept in was whitewashed, above a band of green paint. Ducks waddled across the lawn, skirting the geese, while chickens pecked thoughtlessly between them.

'Ah my brother! You have woken,' called Ntsina. But he had to find Luvo before he could make plain to Piet that a bath awaited him.

Fresh water had been fetched from the stream by the girls of the village, who left two earthen jars of it outside Nosakhe's gatepost each morning. Piet was presented with a small basin and a jug of warm water, and found himself at a loss. It was bitterly cold. He undressed in the dimness of the hut and stood in the little basin. He had not grown up with indoor plumbing, but had taken his baths as a child in a warm kitchen by a fire, in a receptacle big enough to sit in and deep enough to cover his knees. He poured some of the water into the basin, but it was so small he could not sit in it. Finally he squatted, and soaped himself, using the water as sparingly as he could – but much of it still went on the floor, and rose as steam from the cold hard mud. It was an unsatisfactory experience, and he resolved to better it should he be compelled to spend much more time among the Xhosas. However, he finished cleaner than he had been since leaving Cradock, and cleanliness is a great boon to the human spirit. He left his hut, resolved to be friendly and to face his fears – for it was awkward speaking so little of their language. He was relieved to discover that neither Nosakhe, nor Ntsina, nor the heavyset man of the night before were anywhere to be found. Only Luvo sat in the kitchen, polishing the cauldron, and Piet took the opportunity to eat his fill of mealie meal before turning his attention to a morning of strict grammar. It was time, he felt, to step beyond the rote learning of sounds and see if he could discern the deeper structure of this strange but beautiful tongue.

༄

Nosakhe opened her treasure chest and took from it the wealth of the Zinis. She had not made all of it available to Sukude, but now that Ntsina had come, bearing with him the blessings of the Goddess Ma, she knew that his marriage should be the most splendid feast anyone had given in a generation.

Between the descendants of the followers of the Great Founder, who continued to enjoy the fruits of ancestral wealth, and those of the Xhosa who had obeyed the *sangomas'* instruction and burned their livestock, existed a feud of intense hostility. Nosakhe did not believe in self-indulgence. The prospect of spending her capital only made her happy because she understood its part in the great order. As she held her shell necklace to her throat, she resolved to invite the leaders of the Xhosa beyond the forest's edge, to find out what ailed them, and to assist in their hour of need.

The day of reconciliation was at hand.

She took herself down the hill to the village proper. The chief's household were well apprised of the Strange One's arrival, and the chief listened gravely as Nosakhe told him what must be done. He had risen intending to inform her of the way Noni had foreseen that a Strange One was in the forest, with Ntsina, but he could tell from Nosakhe's manner that she was thinking of other things today, and that this information would be better used when she was calmer.

He acquiesced to her request that the princes be invited, and the date for the wedding was set for two weeks hence.

It was Nosakhe herself who had bade Lundi keep in his pocket his fraudulent telegram. She had not decided what attitude to adopt towards Sukude, and did not wish to be placed in open knowledge of his guilt. The proper punishment for a man caught stealing another's love mate is a slow death, its manner chosen by the injured party. She did not wish Ntsina to have to make such a choice for his own father.

So Sukude burned the telegram, and watched his mother-in-law's face closely, and as the days passed he became more convinced that he had got away with it.

Piet did not delay in making preparations for his meeting with the chief. He spent his first day assiduously, and when he found he could make no sense of Xhosa grammar he set himself the easier task of learning the longest speech he had so far attempted. He wrote the words on a page in his notebook, and above them Luvo wrote the Xhosa translation, and Piet busied himself in fathoming which sound meant what. It took all day, and much of the night; but by the morning of the second day, Piet was ready.

It was Nosakhe who led him, as was proper, down the escarpment to the King's Place. They had waited a day so that the village council might digest the news of a Strange One in their midst and make arrangements to be present. A messenger had asked for the Strange One to be brought at the hour of the eagle, and it was a tribute to the intensity of local curiosity that in a place where time had an imprecise meaning, and was rarely strictly stuck to, all were present.

Piet, Luvo, Sukude and Ntsina followed Nosakhe down the hill, and from a distance many pairs of eyes watched them. Most of the men in the village, and not a few of the adult women, had seen Strange Ones in the flesh. Hardly any of the children had, and it was they who lost control of their curiosity first and pressed towards Piet as he made his way across the beach. Noni led them, but she did not join them in stroking the hair on Piet's arms with wonder. The adults nerved themselves, for it is one thing to see a dangerous creature from afar; quite another to have one in one's hut.

As Piet crossed the beach, he lost all shyness. He was used to the notoriety of celebrity. Kagiso greeted him beyond the fence of his father's homestead and brought him into the yard. Piet had not been presented to the chief's ancestors, and so could not be present in their kraal. The meeting had, accordingly, been moved outside, since the day was fine, and the people were waiting under the Tree of Justice. Piet had taken care to learn from Ntsina the correct mode of address, and had practised the subtle hand movements that indicate polite greeting in this part of the world. To the watching eyes, many of them sceptical, he performed these movements gracelessly; and yet the fact that he made the effort to perform them at all was a point in his favour.

It was on days like these, when life threw unexpected happenings in his way, that the chief of Gwadana felt least equal to his duties. He had questioned his son closely about this Strange One and knew that he had come in search of fine wood, and the labour of strong men to carry it as far as a useable road. He had no idea what to charge for such services and knew that many of his kind had sold their labour and their goods too cheap to those of Piet's kind who were polite enough to ask before taking.

Piet did not wither under the attention. He made the ritual greeting, then said, in tones at once fearfully odd and comprehensible to his audience: 'Good day, Mighty Chief. I have come from Cape Town to do you service.'

It was not the opening anyone expected, and many pairs of eyes met other pairs across the green space.

'You are welcome, Strange One,' said the chief, in his gravest manner. At a prod from Ntsina, Luvo said: 'Welcome, sir.'

Piet was shown to a cowhide stool and waited while the chief's council rather self-consciously went about their daily business, making, truth to tell, rather more of the back and forth of village affairs than was usual. They did not wish the Strange One to feel too special. Piet waited with an expression of polite attention on his face. Luvo, bending low to his ear, whispered an approximate translation of the proceedings. As he listened, Piet thought how enviable were the lives of these natives, despite their inadequate bathing facilities. He stared out across the pretty bay. Far away on the horizon, visible only because the day was bright and clear, was a battle cruiser in full camouflage. He wondered what these primitive people would make of such a sight, and gave thanks for his preservation from this senseless European War.

When his name was called he stood and smiled his warmest smile. 'I have come to bring you good things,' he said. 'I have need of strong men, and good wood. I know I can find both here. Those who assist me will be well rewarded.'

It provoked an uproar. Those in the village, and there were many, who doubted their chief's negotiating skills swarmed round Piet Barol to strike their own bargains with him. The Elders, knowing what was proper, pulled them back, beat them if necessary. 'You must return tomorrow,' said the chief, who knew there were many he should consult with, 'and bring us the full animal' – by which he meant all the details.

'There's no time like the present,' said Piet Barol. But he was silenced by a look from Luvo, who came up to him and said: 'You must never rush the Bantu. Everything must be discussed, and discussed again. If you wish to get your way, you must observe the proper form.'

'Tomorrow then,' said Piet.

'And you must ask only for the tree you first saw, with which you were well satisfied,' said Luvo gravely. 'Even to ask for a tree in the grove of their Ancestors will cause offence.'

'Then you must help me to ask without causing offence. We could build their ancestors shrines elsewhere. Handsome ones.'

'That will not do at all.'

It was clear to Piet that without Luvo's support his task would be far harder. He looked at the young man, thinking of his teachers, and found a better approach. 'It is up to us,' he said, 'to liberate these natives from their superstitions. You must help me in that noble endeavour.'

⤟

When the meeting concluded, Piet repeated the names of everyone he had met – Mzwamadoda, Ntombizodwa, Xolani, and a host of others impossibly hard to pronounce. It was a terrific party trick and made many people, the ladies especially, roar with laughter. After years in Cape Town posing as a French vicomte,

Piet was used to having people fawn over him, and he did not like it. Others' shyness of him made them dull. He hugely enjoyed appearing at a disadvantage.

He made his farewells and jogged up the mountain, feeling strong and alive. He could hardly wait to be alone. He was used to many solitary hours in his workshop and the burden of discourse in a strange tongue with so many strangers induced euphoria at the prospect of solitude.

He walked across the neat green grass of the garden that divided the spaces of the Zinis' goats and geese and sheep and pigs. Dark clouds were rolling in from the sea, made dazzling by the lightning within. The Zinis had an adolescent billy goat, whose fury at being prevented from mounting the nanny goats who called to him from the other side of a fence had led him to spend all day charging it. Piet was just in time to see him break it and leap into the enclosure of the nanny goats. He pretended not to have noticed, and hurried to his hut.

When he opened the door, he saw that it had been made ready for him, in ways that had not been possible the evening before. He had been brought an extra grass mat, which was rolled beside a pan made of a pumpkin, and filled with spring water. A fire had been laid in the centre, in one of the only tin buckets in the entire village of Gwadana. The roof was blackened with soot. He decided to be cold, rather than subject his lungs to smoke in a confined place, and was glad that two extra blankets were also folded on the polished floor. The hut had a strong smell that Piet could not place, and he opened the door and let the sea air in, which took the edge off it.

He rolled the second grass mat out above the first, and lit the lantern on a ledge built into the wall. Its warm, generous light was the perfect complement to the other colours in the space. It cast his shadow huge against the wall, and he looked at himself, so large and strong, and felt certain of victory. He felt that in Luvo, properly managed, he had the strategic insider with whom he would be able to navigate all obstacles.

The thunder roared overhead. Piet felt cosy and at peace. He took from his wallet the photograph of Stacey and Arthur, and looked at them. To his own surprise, he found himself praying.

He prayed for his wife and his son. To be reunited with them. He gave thanks to God for sparing his family from the destruction of families that was going on in Europe. He gave thanks for the commission from Percy, for his discovery of a wood he could truly be worthy of. He reached this point in his prayer after several minutes sitting quite still and staring at the lantern flame, which had blue and black at its centre.

Piet had drawn things since he was a little boy. He had become exceptionally good at capturing an object or a glance and had an instinctive grasp of the telling detail. He thought of the pieces he might make for Percy Shabrill. All the shapes of nature, a portrait of the forest made into chairs and tables and beds. He felt ready to make a work of art, to embrace im-perfection as a means to an end. He reached into his pack and took his sketchbook from it, his concentration heightened by the cold.

For six hours Piet drew, getting up once or twice to stretch his back by pulling on the central pole that supported the roof. Some-times he stood up and danced. The only effort was keeping up with the richness of the detail he saw. Legs, horns, tusks, leaves, flowers, became desks, chairs, console tables, library shelves. He drew the contents of Percy's study till his hands were aching, and kept on. He felt joyful and wildly alive.

When at last he had filled every page of the sketchbook, and most of its unused corners, he put it on his mat and lay with his head on it. He pulled the two blankets over him. He was again conscious of the cold. He understood why there were no windows – the draft would be unbearable on a night like this, with so ill-fitting a door. He felt full of love and affection. He was a man who took great happiness from making others happy, and as he lay in the pitch dark, listening to the gorgeous crash of rain on thatch, the air sweet and earthy, he decided to do something he had not before considered.

'I will be generous to them,' he said aloud, to the darkness.

⤬

The opportunity for generosity presented itself at dawn the next day, when Piet went for a piss and saw that the goats had got out in the night. The adolescent billy goat, having knocked down one fence post, had thrown himself twice as strenuously into gouging a hole in the vegetable-patch fence, through which he was just escorting his lady friends when Piet spotted them. The Zinis' vegetable garden was abundant and well tended. Piet ran at the goats, who panicked and retreated – all save the rambunctious billy goat who had led them there. Watching him capture this animal, and return him to the goat pen, caused Nosakhe to frown. This white man had vigour as well as money. She knew how rare this was, and wondered whether perhaps he had been sent to aid her in a deeper battle than the conquest of cash. What did money purchase, after all, but 'more comfortable couches on which to mate and die'?

'It buys freedom from the British tax inspectors,' said Ntsina, when she put this question to him.

⤬

In the chief's council hut several hours later, Piet Barol made from memory the speech Luvo had written out for him. 'It is good of you to receive me in this warm manner. I know the hard times many are having in this country. I have come with an undertaking that will benefit . . .' He struggled to remember his lines and grasped at sounds. 'Village every family in the.' He grew frustrated with himself, and tried to summon the image of the page on which Luvo had written his speech. Certain words leapt out, and it was these he spoke: 'Furniture wood for I need. Labour will I pay.'

Luvo winced as Piet's word order collapsed, but he was a little – he could not help it; he had judged the Declamation Competition

129

in his final year – just a little bit proud of the Strange One who did such a creditable job despite his inexperience.

Luvo had been raised in a school where sincere effort of any sort was perceived and rewarded. He could not but be moved when Piet, turning to him, made two different click sounds, each with a recognizable thwack, and said: 'May I present my friend Luvo Yako. He is a lynchpin of this organization, since it is through him that we can all speak frankly with one another.'

The chief was so taken aback by this speech, and so moved to be addressed with such inspiring courtesy in his own language, that he said (for he could speak English quite well; he pretended not to for business purposes): 'We will make a business with you.'

It was a measure of Piet Barol's personal charisma that, though the chief acted strictly against custom, for no decision can be made without consultation, no one objected. And there were members of his council who spent their lives objecting.

Piet's was a nature that flowered in the good will of others. He listened with attention while Kagiso explained to him the many virtues of the Furniture Tree, and the fact that they were scattered far and wide in the forest, in places known only to the strong men (he did not mention the women) of his village. As Kagiso talked, Piet's neck ached, for he was leaning close to Luvo, who spoke softly. He was aware that Luvo was translating only a fraction of the number of words Kagiso was using, and this made him sure that he was missing subtlety and nuance. What required no direct translation was Kagiso's willingness, on behalf of the village of Gwadana (for he claimed this prize then and there, in the presence of his father and the council), to undertake his side of the business. 'He says he has many good men, much forest knowledge,' said Luvo to Piet at the end of a torrent of words.

Piet thought of the work that would have to be done before any tree, of any kind, could be made into furniture, and decided not to introduce a topic that would create awkwardness among his new friends. Far better to wait until they knew him better, and to collar the chief alone with his proposal of new shrines, than to ask for an Ancestor Tree and risk sullying the impression he had made.

So he said: 'We will make a plan this afternoon. I will list the tasks to be done. You tell me how many men you can provide, what their skills are, and how much you think is a fair payment.'

The chief looked at his son. His hatred of money was a bristling subject between them. Kagiso looked back, and his face said: Leave Me Be.

His father did leave him be. But it made him angry to be put in his place by a youth barely past his circumcision. He felt the first stirring of the knowledge that he would one day be old. It was because he was a good man, and a devoted father, that he said 'I will leave you with my son, Kagiso. Together you will draw up the plans. In three days, we will meet to discuss terms. Until then, you are an honoured guest of the village of Gwadana. We who thought for ourselves salute you,' with no trace of bitterness.

⌒

Over the next few days, Piet saw that he had been wise to refrain from asking for an Ancestor Tree. He would have caused offence without necessarily getting his way. Far better to let the cheeriness around him forge into friendship, and to ask when the right moment came.

In Gwadana, no one cowered in the presence of a white man – or called him 'Master', as they were obliged to do in other parts of the country. With Luvo at his side, Piet was able to be himself – or at least the version of himself that Luvo judged appropriate, for Luvo's translations were much shorter than Piet's speeches. Often this annoyed him, and he told Luvo to keep up. But he knew that sometimes things are said that are best left untranslated, and his instincts told him that he was thought well of, and this was Piet Barol's ideal atmosphere.

Days of furious effort followed. Those who stood Piet's pace knew the intoxication of being well led. To Ntsina, the active presence of Kagiso, the bosom friend of his youth, the sense that they were taking on the mantle of the village's great deeds from the generation above, made him struggle to sleep at night for the difficulty of waiting for the day to come. Kagiso and Ntsina undertook to find the men to do the jobs that Piet and Luvo listed on pages and pages of notepaper, full of diagrams and Piet's arresting, incomprehensible handwriting.

Piet sent a boy up the hill to collect from Nosakhe a cupful of the brandy he had brought, with which he made an offering to the ancestors of everyone in the room. In isiXhosa, learned from Luvo in the dark hour before dawn, Piet asked for assistance in their endeavour: for them to be given strength when it failed them, and good humour when discord arose among them. 'You can ask to be paid a monthly salary, or you can be paid in shares in the business,' he said. To learn that they might be owners in a business founded in such glamorous circumstances made Ntsina and Kagiso and the boys very happy.

Piet overruled Kagiso and Ntsina, who said they could get the wood out easily enough by taking it to the river and building rafts. 'In the high season it is deep enough for floating,' said Kagiso, seriously. Piet knew that this stream might do for forest mahogany, but it would not be at all practical for a large bed made from a single block of ancient wood. 'We need a road,' he said. 'If we hack through one of the elephant paths, it should be easy enough.'

This road was the subject of a heated argument that evening in the King's Place.

'There must be no tracks between our village and the Strange Ones beyond the forest!' shouted the chief, while his four wives watched and Noni sat under his legs, stroking his knees.

'The Strange One needs a road. He wants to transport all

year round. He cannot be expected to wait until a river fills,' said Kagiso, trying to sound reasonable. He looked at his older brother for support, but his brother sided with their father, and was beside himself with jealousy that Kagiso should have met the Strange One first.

The chief said nothing. At length Kagiso said: 'We need only build a path from the Furniture Tree to the edge of the forest. It wouldn't come close to the village. We can cover up the other end with thorn bush.' He threw himself at his father's feet. 'I *promise* this will work, *Tata*.' Noni touched her brother's head. She wanted to support him, for she understood his yearning. But something deep within, a sense of the brilliance of the Strange One's colouring prevented her.

'I will decide once the princes have visited,' said the chief. 'I must consult with them.'

⎯⎯

In no time at all the wedding was upon them.

Bela was woken by the sound of her four best friends giggling. She opened her eyes to see them at her door, ringing cowbells. They were the most popular maidens in Gwadana, and Bela was their leader. Lurking just beyond them, as she always lurked, was Bela's sister Zandi. She held no cowbell.

Bela hated the cold, but this morning she hardly minded the whip of the wind as she took her clothes off beside the waterfall. Her mother told her to wash her body well, since misfortune flows away with running water. Bela did so, and then everyone was laughing and she was shivering under a blanket and making her way back to the house.

Ideas, borne by the birds, transmuted mysteriously through the great forest they had crossed not more than three times in their lives, had reached Bela and her friends. They had heard of ladies getting married in white satin, with long trailing veils. Thinking of the white satin made Bela's blanket chafe her shoulders, but she bore this cheerfully.

As they gathered on the grass to begin her journey from her parents' homestead to her husband's, her father clipped hairs from the tail of her mother's bridal cow – a descendant of the cow Mama Jaxa had brought with her at their marriage. He gave Bela the longest, whitest one, and kissed her. 'I am transferring you from my care to the care of another family, my dearest child,' he said. 'You must be an obeying wife without asking questions. You must do exactly as you are told, or you will bring shame on us and our clan.'

'I will obey, Father.' Bela bowed her head modestly.

'Once you are married, you are never to enter your new family's kraal, on the lives of all the ancestors. Not until you have brought your first born into the world and he is twelve moons old.'

'I know it, Father.'

'You will do our clan proud.'

'I will, Father.'

What an arrogant bitch, thought Zandi, and looked at the ground.

It was hard on Zandi – both her parents knew it – that they should be marrying her attractive younger sister first, as if to acknowledge that no man would ever claim her. Or sex her. Zandi was a woman of strong natural appetites, and at the age of twenty-seven the strictures of chastity were hard to bear. Ever since catching her first trace of Ntsina's scent she had thought of him as she fell asleep. Sometimes she found herself thinking of the Strange One too. What would it be like . . . ? Zandi could entertain this thought because it was so far-fetched it could be safely held in the chest of fantasies, guarded by porcupine quills, in which she stored treats to lighten the burden of virginity.

Her ancestors had protected Zandi by making her far-sighted, which is not at all the same thing as having the gift of Farsight. She would not see how the women – it was always the women – looked at her as the smooth pink beer flowed and loosened tongues and hearts. She almost missed her sister's sharpness, but on this day, watched by so many, Bela was as sweet as treacle to her, and won much approval for her tact and kindness.

Their mother thought of Zandi's humiliation. It burned her. And yet she knew that her husband had made the only possible decision. With one hundred cattles and six bulls, it would not matter whether any man took Zandi to his wife, saw the virtues of her constancy, her gentleness. What a lucky fellow he would be, thought Mama Jaxa, as she watched Bela set off in a crowd of her attendants, who had Zandi to love him through his life and tend to him in old age.

☙

At the groom's homestead, festivities were well underway. Nosakhe had decided against purchasing any of the goods available from Strange One shops. Everything she served was made by Gwadanans in the old way, and she had bartered her six best cattles, her talents in the matter of several long-running feuds, and the billy goat who had broken her fence, in order to purchase beer and honey and sweet fruits and chairs and plates. She had laid a charm for good weather – these were tricky, and apt to go off in quite the opposite direction from the one intended. But today she had done her work well and it was fine, with no promise of rain. The women wore their finest adornments, and Nosakhe's were finest of all, for her grandfather had commissioned for her the full white regalia of a *sangoma*.

Nosakhe's small victory in the matter of the weather spell did not compensate for a great setback. She had sent messengers to all the princes between Gwadana and King William's Town, bringing glad tidings from the descendants of the Great Founder of Gwadana, and summoning them to a feast. She had also sent good spirits to ripen their minds with thoughts of retaliation against the British. All had accepted, with extravagant words of thanks and praise. They had been invited for the night before, and only as she watched the bride's party approaching did Nosakhe finally admit to herself that none of them would come.

135

It made her furious with them. It was clear – had been growing clearer for years – that her battle with Atamaraka was entering a new and deadlier phase. Of course the Goddess would have closed the chiefs' minds to the idea of patching up old enmities. 'But even a goddess can only tempt, never force,' she said under her breath, hearing the voices rising from below. And she wondered what the Bantu would do if their leaders continued to behave so unworthily.

Bela wore her hair in the oldest hairstyle in the land of the tribes: brushed up into two lobes and held in place by a paste of her mother's concocting. Her attendants stood beside her, and her cousins guarded her. Since she was a little girl she had dreamed of her marriage. She had been prepared for ugliness in her husband, but in truth Ntsina's nose charmed her, and she had caught his smell on the breeze.

As they reached the top of the escarpment, the ladies fell to ululating, making the high-pitched shrieks with which Xhosa women signify momentous events. The chief himself welcomed Bela, and she was not insensible to this honour. It made her annoyed at Zandi's sulky face. 'Twist your mouth into shape,' she said under her breath, as they were shown into the bridal hut.

Bela had not found a moment to use the latrine. Now she must be still and silent as her in-laws inspected her. She wanted badly to urinate but the horror of embarrassing herself kept her bladder controlled. It meant that she was thinking her own thoughts, barely conscious of Sukude as he looked closely at her neck, her hands, her feet, as if inspecting a prized cattle.

Nosakhe, who did not care for housework, was delighted with the gift Ma had given her in this wholesome young woman. 'You will do well, my dear,' she said, and left to attend to the feasting, feeling light of heart.

⟋⟍

Piet Barol had washed his own shirt. He put it on in his hut, by the light of a lantern. No mirror was available, but it did not

136

matter what he looked like to these natives. He put his head out of the door and called Luvo's name at the top of his voice.

Luvo was in Ntsina's hut, helping him dress. Ntsina had asked him to be a member of the groom's party. It was the first time Luvo had ever assisted so prominently at a wedding, and it made him feel manly and grown-up. He had spent all day grinding soft white rock and water into a smooth paste. White was Nosakhe's colour, the colour of a witch doctor, and she had decreed that Ntsina must wear white beneath his leopardskin kaross. Ntsina stood before his friend. They had all drunk a little beer and the sounds of merriment outside filled them with anticipation.

'You are a lucky bastard,' said Kagiso. He was speaking to Ntsina, and he meant that he was lucky to have Bela as his bride. But Luvo, hearing the words, accepted them in secret for himself – for he felt lucky indeed. He plunged his hands into the white paste and began to smear it across Ntsina's chest. Living, as he had from birth, at the top of a hill, Ntsina had never had an ounce of fat. As a boy he had been skinny, his rib cage visible through the stretched skin of his torso. Months in Johannesburg hammering rock had added muscle to his frame, and as Luvo rubbed his chest Ntsina made his muscles stand out, for he was proud of them. Luvo had never before touched another man in this way, and he understood that he would never do it again. To be able to take this pleasure in public, with no thought of censure, even among these superstitious natives, shielded his conscience from the wrath of the Hebrew God. He pressed the paste down Ntsina's navel, across the smooth ridges of his abdominals. Kagiso dipped his hands in it too, and was about to touch Ntsina's back when Luvo, with the impulsive creativity of lust, said: 'Your hands are dirty from the blood of the goat. There must be no red in this.' And since this was true, Kagiso desisted, and Luvo continued his task.

He rubbed the paste across Ntsina's shoulders and down his back, into the hollow curve above his buttocks. He had taken care to strap himself tightly beneath his traditional blanket skirt, and to position his cock between his legs – so that his erection was neither visible nor inhibited. He felt light-headed with pleasure. He took his time over each of Ntsina's arms, careful to get between the indentations of his triceps, and twice when Ntsina wriggled their bodies touched, and Luvo felt his friend's solidity, and stored this with every other detail of the experience to revisit at his leisure.

He was intensely displeased when he heard Piet Barol shout his name, for he had not yet done Ntsina's hands. He ignored the summons, but Piet called louder and louder, and in the end Ntsina said: 'I can do my fingers alone, brother. You had better see what the Strange One wants.'

Luvo took himself to Piet's hut in a towering rage, and was quite discombobulated to be met with radiant affection. 'You are a civilized man, unlike these natives, good natured as they are.' Piet clapped him on the back. He was full of plans. 'Can you in all good conscience, as a Christian, encourage their superstitions?'

The Bible contains many cautions against false belief, and Luvo did not need them listed for him. 'No,' he said, putting away the recollection of Ntsina's taut chest.

'We must teach them how to pray for the souls of their ancestors as we pray for ours – in a church, before a cross.'

'I doubt very much that you will get the trees you want,' said Luvo.

'I might not get them alone. But with you, my friend . . .' Piet hesitated, remembering the many white men who had cautioned him against being too generous with Kaffirs. Then he pressed on, thinking well of himself. 'When we were in the forest, you asked for a hundred pounds. That is a large sum and I did not commit to it. I wanted to see what you were made of.' He put his hand on Luvo's shoulder. 'I can see you are a person of rare quality. If you help me get the wood, I will give you *three* hundred pounds once we have delivered the furniture.'

His words hung between them, glowing in the cold air.

'They will never give you an Ancestor Tree.'

'I will pay them handsomely for it. And I will pay for a church to be built here, as soon as Shabrill has paid us. The desire to pray for one's forebears is a good one, but they must pray in the right way.'

For one brought up with the conviction that there is only one route to Heaven, this was a potent argument. Luvo stopped frowning.

'A man can set himself up for life on three hundred pounds,' Piet went on. 'And take care of his parents, so that they need no longer live in the house of people who are strange to them.'

Luvo said nothing. Had this man been sent by God, to help him care for his family and reach the great English king? Piet looked like a vigorous angel by the light of the lantern; quite unlike the pictures of wicked men in the illustrated manuals on ethics that formed the larger part of the mission school's library. Luvo thought of the Gwadanans. They had been generous hosts, but they would not be saved while they clung to their superstitions. 'One tree,' he said. 'One tree must be enough for you.'

'One tree will be,' said Piet. 'I give you my word.'

꩜

Sukude was one of the three people in the village of Gwadana to possess a mirror, and he contemplated himself in it that evening with sullen satisfaction. He had donned the skin of a handsome leopard he had killed with his own assegai. He was fatter than he had been as a young man, but still strong. He flexed his muscles, thinking petulantly of all that had been denied him by Ntsina's abrupt return. He felt a hatred of his mother-in-law burn his insides. Who was she to forbid a powerful man the satisfaction of his natural wants? He had posed the question many times before, and there was no answer to it.

In the bridal hut, Bela was so conscious of her own good fortune that she felt sympathy for Zandi. While her attendants fetched the ochre, she took her sister's hand and said: 'You will always be an honoured guest in my homestead.'

Zandi looked at her warily. 'You will never ask me here. Once you are married you will forget me.' And then – she could not help it; the truth rose unstoppably from within her – 'everyone will forget me.'

Bela was shocked to see Zandi's tears, for Zandi never cried in her presence, no matter how often she wept alone. She squeezed her hand. 'I think Kagiso likes you. Tonight, when he is drunk, you must give him a sign that you like him too. Just think! He is my husband's best friend. The son of a chief. What glory it would bring on our house if you were to marry him. Even—' for she could not quite stifle the impulse to honesty – 'as his second wife.'

Zandi said nothing. It was typical of Bela to lace her kindness with this sort of poison, and she was angry with herself for crying. Their mother entered the hut. She was splendidly dressed, in blankets of orange wool with bracelets stitched with tinkling shells. She wore across her shoulders the beaded collar her grandmother had worn as a bride, and in her hand she carried a long wooden pipe trimmed in copper. Seeing her daughters together made her very happy; and Mama Jaxa was in any case a cheerful woman. 'How lucky you are, Bela,' she cried, 'to have a new mother whose spells command the weather!'

It took three hours for Bela to be painted red from head to foot, and a further hour for her bridal blankets to be draped to perfection. Her maidens covered themselves in ochre too, and draped their blankets as she waited, contemplating her reflection in the shard of mirror her mother had brought. She was well pleased. Black cloths were wrapped tightly over the young women's heads, and left to hang in front. For the first time Bela felt a tingling of nerves – the nerves of any first lady facing a large audience on the opening night of a great drama.

The door burst open and a little girl put her head round it. 'The cow is being slaughtered!'

෧

As Sukude entered the kraal, watched by all their guests, he scoffed at his mother-in-law in the privacy of his own head. What a jumped-up charlatan! She had failed to see into his soul, for all her gift of Farsight. He sliced into the cow with a knife just behind her horns, the cow that must cry to signal the approval of the ancestors.

The creature submitted without a murmur.

Sukude twisted the knife, his heart rate rising. The cow was clearly alive. He withdrew the knife and drove it in again, savagely. But she made no sound.

As an omen, this was bad indeed. Sukude had never been present at a ritual slaughter at which the cow did not cry, but he knew – everyone knew – that it was an indication of grave displeasure from the ancestors. The laughter in the watching crowd died down. Nosakhe stood rooted to the spot, and Ata the dog began to bark. Sweat dripped from Sukude's brow down his face; his hands were slippery with blood. Perhaps Nosakhe had been fooled, but the ancestors knew his dark heart. He gave the cow a terrible kick, right in her uterus, a kick that held all the force he was capable of.

At last she bleated. It was a plaintive bleat, not at all what was looked for, but at least the cow had not lain silent to be slaughtered. The guests, wanting a party, and too polite to draw attention to this scandal, raised their tankards of beer and shouted. All save Bela's father, whose blood had turned to iced saltwater. Standing at the front, he had been close enough to see that it was not Sukude's knife that had made the cow cry, but his boot; and this brought to the surface many unspoken worries he had about consigning his daughter to this family's care. He was seized by an instinctive, reflex wish to return the hundred cattles and six bulls and to reclaim his darling daughter. But his wife's eyes found his over the clearing that separated the male from the female guests, and in her look was the knowledge that they could not go back now; it would be a scandal that reverberated for generations, leaving both their girls unmarriageable.

The bridegroom appeared, as white as a statue carved from rock. He was flanked by Luvo and Kagiso and several of his closest boyhood friends. Ntsina looked magnificent in his way, thought Piet, envying the young man his splendid physique.

Ntsina was hung with all the beads of the Zinis; they fell in ropes from his neck, gripped his head in a white band edged in blue. The crowd parted, men on one side, ladies on the other. An immense shout went up, and above it the high ululations of the women, which made the gulls on the cliffs far beyond soar skywards.

As Ntsina's procession passed him, Piet pulled Luvo's shoulder. 'Stay with me. I wish to understand.'

Luvo was relieved to be spared the ordeal of sitting beside his friend at the moment of his union to a woman. He hung back. 'The bride will come out soon,' he said. 'They will meet each other on this grass mat.'

'And then go into the kraal? Is that where the ceremony will take place?'

'There is no ceremony in the native tradition. And the bride most certainly will not enter the kraal. She may not enter her husband's kraal until her first child is a year old. It would be considered a grave crime.'

Piet stored all these details, looking forward to the day he might recount his presence at a Xhosa wedding at the Mount Nelson Hotel. The wails from the crowd rose. Five young women appeared, dressed in red blankets, with black headdresses veiling their faces.

'We are not meant to know which one the bride is,' said Luvo.

But in the case of Bela Jaxa, everyone knew.

She was a foot taller than her attendants, and her presence inspired an audible intake of breath from those watching. Her

142

mother felt a delirious pride. A pride that made her eyes fill with tears and obliterated her concerns for Zandi's future, and the troubling omen. She looked at her husband and his glance met hers. Together they contemplated the perfection they had brought into the world.

Jealous male eyes looked at Ntsina, acknowledging his strength but thinking, on the whole, that they had better noses. It was part of Bela's gift that her beauty did not inspire hostility in other women; she was too kind and merry for that.

Piet could see she was a beauty of her type, but he did not, he told himself, care for native women. He thought instead of how he and Stacey had met, and how impulsively they had thrown in their lots with one another. They had known each other hardly longer than these two.

For the time it takes a gull to sweep from the top of the cliffs to catch a silver fish, husband and wife looked at one another.

'I see you, my wife,' said Ntsina.

'I see you, my husband.' And this time there was no maidenly modesty in Bela's glance. She looked right into Ntsina's eyes, taking in the body she now might claim; and even his nose was endearing to her.

'I will take no other wife,' said Ntsina.

'And I no other husband.'

༄

Then the feast *really* started. Store huts were thrown open, revealing vats of pink, frothy beer and sheep fat, already prepared, and loaf upon loaf of bread with the mysterious, smoky flavour of the anthill ovens in which it had been baked. The Jaxas' guests and the Zinis' began singing at full voice – different songs, that clashed and twisted round one another in a glorious competition. Bela's father had brought brandy, crate upon crate of it, and with Nosakhe's permission (for she was known to distrust the goods of the Strange Ones), it was liberally served. The guests drank in a rush and grew drunk as one body. Goatskin bags full of finely

143

ground dagga and tobacco were produced, and the children went from adult to adult filling long, slender-stemmed pipes, which were lit by embers from the fire on which the cow Sukude had slaughtered was roasting.

A village barred by long-standing feuds from discourse with its neighbours must know how to make its own fun, and this the people of Gwadana undoubtedly did.

Noni heard Piet's voice congratulating Ntsina. She had grown up on tales of Strange Ones coming from the depths of the sea to cause havoc in the lands of the tribes, and at once a demonic green seeped into the noise made by the dancers, and she began to be afraid. She called for her brothers, but each was lost in the dancing. She who knew every inch of the village was literally in the dark in this strange homestead at the top of the cliffs, full of adults whose speech was slurred, whose breath rasped heavy in their throats. She began to wail, but no one heard her, and the village children did not approach her, afraid of her closed eyes that saw so much.

Sukude stifled the urge to kick the screaming brat only because she was the daughter of a chief, and the chief was near at hand. He began to find it impossible to live another day without mounting a lovely female. He looked at the dancers. He knew there were women among them he might have, and willingly too; but he also knew how hard it is to keep such a secret. And secret his coupling must be, now that he had lost the only means of taking a woman openly and with honour. Lundi sidled up to him, a cup of brandy in his hand. 'Your son will return to the mines soon enough,' he murmured, reading Sukude's thoughts. 'As long as she is not pregnant . . .' He left the sentence tantalizingly unfinished.

But Sukude doubted that Ntsina would ever return to the mines, since he had a new white friend to make him rich, and in any case the animal in him knew that Bela would be pregnant sooner rather than later. He had done his investigations well and knew she was a virgin. He had looked at her closely as she revealed

144

herself to her husband for the first time, thinking painfully that it should have been *his* eyes she stared into. She was obviously looking forward to her first sexing, and he knew that women who are happy with their husbands conceive quickly. He shook his fist at the clear heavens and the twinkling stars. 'Give me that brandy,' he said, and he took the mug from Lundi's hand and drank its contents in a single gulp that left him full of inward fire.

It did Zandi's spirits no end of good to be bowed to by a handsome Strange One, who then asked her name, and told her his, and said 'It is an honour to meet you on this happy occasion' in her own language. She was not used to being the object of other women's jealousy, but she saw as she hung on Piet's arm that she was. It made her cling tighter, and when he offered to fetch a drink for her she accepted graciously. As Piet was making his way to the hut from which drinks were being dispensed, Zandi said to Luvo: 'Does your Strange One like black girls?'

The question shocked Luvo profoundly. He said, with great severity, that he did not believe so. Piet arrived with the drinks and Luvo declined his. In English, he said: 'Do not be too friendly with the women, or their fathers will compel you to marry them.' This prohibition provoked an abrupt diminution of Piet Barol's friendliness to Zandi, who ignored it and drank her beer down and said: 'Let's dance.'

'She wants to dance with you,' said Luvo, wearily.

So Piet and Zandi danced. He led her in the European dances of his youth, aware that he could have her if he chose. It made him proud that he was not tempted. Stacey had asked only one thing from him on the day, three days after their first meeting, that they had decided to marry. It was physical constancy, and he had always honoured it. He had an opportunity to extricate himself from Zandi when a cry went up, signalling that the cow was ready. Everyone stopped dancing, and all eyes turned again to the bride – for no one might eat until she had taken her first bite.

Bela ate daintily, and cleaned her fingers on the hem of her blanket. A line formed, and more roasted cattle appeared, and in the merry throng Piet went about greeting the people he had met at the public meeting. He had gone to great lengths to remember their names and to master the phrase 'It gives me pleasure to see you again'. The impact of this, on human beings already primed for friendship by alcohol and dagga and the sentimentality that must touch the hardest hearts on witnessing the bonding of a loving pair, was explosive. As the beer flowed, Piet lost his self-doubt and hurled Luvo's brain through torturous gymnastics as he talked nineteen to the dozen with everyone he met.

He was a *huge success*.

As tongues loosened and the moon rose in the sky, more than one person told Piet Barol that he was by far the best of any Strange One they had ever come across. They congratulated him on his way with words – for his Xhosa phrases, though full of errors, were comprehensible and charming. His inadequacies were poetic on this night full of poetry, and the pleasure he took from giving pleasure combined with the Gwadanans' delight in welcoming a guest from the world outside (for one was rare), and soon he was singing their songs and dancing their dances, careful not to favour one lady above any other, but also to dance with Zandi again, for he sensed that her feelings on this evening were complex.

Kagiso found Noni, and she consented to return to the throne of his broad shoulders. For an hour he danced with his sister, and she felt the sea wind in her face, and smelled the sweat of the dancers, and the good humour of their revelry; and again and again there was the golden red of the Strange One's voice, until she climbed down from her brother's back and followed Piet, listening to this man whom everybody made so much of.

It was because she was following him closely that she heard him say something to Luvo that had a different colour altogether, an aquamarine of avarice; and she listened closely to Luvo's reply.

146

'You say it in this way,' said Luvo. '"I wish to purchase an Ancestor Tree, and to build new shrines for your ancestors. Handsome ones, closer to home."'

Spurred by the moonlight and the drinking and the goodwill all around him, Piet looked for the chief, who had retired from the dancing. He was in a superb mood, the kind of mood he had not known for some time; a mood in which people found it very hard to resist giving him exactly what he wanted.

But it was Noni who found her father first. The chief was sitting by a fire, in deep talk with several members of his council, and she rushed blindly at him, running so fast he feared she might fall into the flames.

'I know the Strange One's true purpose here,' she shouted. 'He wishes to buy from us an Ancestor Tree.'

'Nonsense, darling.' The chief hoisted her onto his lap.

'It is not nonsense. In a short time he will come to you and ask for it. He will say "I wish to purchase an Ancestor Tree, and to build new shrines for your ancestors. Handsome ones, closer to home."'

The presence of unimpeachable witnesses to Noni's prophecy made her father's blood pound in his ears. Perhaps the dawning of her gift of Farsight was at hand, and thus the sparing of her life. He sent for his wives and bade them wait. And thus it was that when Piet Barol found the chief, his wives were also present, as well as many of their friends.

'You Xhosa understand how to revel,' Piet said. He was too happy, and a little too drunk, to notice that his audience looked warily at him. Noni's mother closed her eyes and dug her nails deep into the palm of her hands. She prayed with every fibre of her being that her daughter might at last have demonstrated the gift of Farsight. While Piet trotted out all the phrases he had learned, commenting on the beauty of the night, the deliciousness of the food, his own shortcomings in the matter of Xhosa pronunciation, 'which is hard for an *mlungu* with a clumsy tongue,' said Piet, it seemed to her that her ancestors were standing by to assist, if only she could understand their price. At last, murmuring under her breath, she said: 'If you save my child, I will cut off the tip of my little finger.'

At this moment Piet said, 'I wish to purchase an Ancestor Tree, and to build new shrines for your ancestors. Handsome ones, closer to home.'

6

Piet Barol had expected resistance, sincere or as a pretext to financial negotiation. He was taken aback to be greeted with joy. Noni's mother threw her arms to Heaven and burst into tears. Her sister wives began ululating – higher and louder than any lady had ululated so far on this night of celebration. Little Noni was caught by her father and tossed high into the air, and caught again. *En masse* the group carried her straight to Nosakhe. Piet made to follow, but the chief barred his path.

'Say yes,' said Piet.

'It is out of the question,' said the chief, in English.

And he left the white man by the fire and hurried with the others to find Nosakhe.

Their hostess was standing alone at the edge of the cliff, looking out at the moon and trying to divine meaning in the glow of its light on the waves. She was thinking of the cow that had not cried. What did the omen mean? It was clear that the ancestors knew, as well as she did, Sukude's motives in choosing for his son such an appealing bride. She could not be sure whether the silent cattle was an instruction to her, as well as a judgement on him. To bring everything into the open, to enact the punishment the law demanded, meant bringing death into this ritual of thanksgiving. Had this been another family's wedding, it would have been easier to discern right from wrong. Since the wedding was her own grandson's, she found it harder to take a strong line – for she had seen the happiness she would rend asunder if she exposed

Sukude, and compelled Ntsina to decide the manner of his father's death.

When the chief and his wives reached her they were almost incoherent with joy. It took her some time to understand that it was another 'prophecy' of Noni's they had come with, and the distraction irritated her. It must be remembered that many of Nosakhe's tranquil moments over the last seven and a half years had been marred by an over-excited emissary of the chief's clan, claiming that Noni had the gift of Farsight because she had said, correctly, that a bitch would have five puppies.

She listened while many things were said. Kagiso swore that Noni had told him, in the forest, long before they reached the glade of the Ancestor Trees, that they would find Ntsina there with a Strange One. 'Why did you not tell me at the time?' she asked, sceptically.

'I was waiting to tell you until after the feast, Mama.'

'And was there a witness beside you, her own brother?'

'No, Mama. But tonight the ancestors have blessed us with many witnesses.'

'Who are they?'

'We saw it,' said the onlookers.

And they told her what they had seen, and how precisely Noni had predicted what the Strange One would say – right down to the very words.

All this while, Noni stood silent, holding her brother's hand, while words of many colours swirled round her. She had stayed up late, and the passion of the adults, the muchness they made of what she had told them, banished all the shyness she usually felt in Nosakhe's presence. 'I have seen his colours in the way he speaks,' she declared. 'He wants to take the homes of our ancestors.' She paused. The waves crashed. The sounds of feasting and dancing seemed very far away. 'You must kill him,' she said.

It caused a consternation. Nosakhe had never cultivated any sort of intimacy with Noni, in case circumstances should compel her one day to hurl her from the cliffs, to be eaten by vultures. Truth to tell, it was not even the unquestionable corroboration of the witnesses that persuaded her, but the total confidence with which Noni spoke on this strange night, so full of portents. Nosakhe knew that those with the gift of Farsight are given another gift, without which the first is useless: the gift of courage, to speak difficult truths out loud.

'You must kill him!' shouted Noni. She began leaping like a wild thing. Again and again she shouted – until her father, seeing the look on Nosakhe's face, put his hand on the child's shoulder and stilled her.

Noni's dancing introduced to Nosakhe's mind another possibility – which was that Atamaraka had entered the body of this deformed child, to use her for Her own purposes. It was for this reason that deformed children were meant to be destroyed at birth, lest their bodies be used as vessels for dark spirits. She remembered the part she herself had played in commuting Noni's sentence. She wondered (not for the first time), whether she had betrayed her duties as a *sangoma* by allowing sentimentality to guide her.

'Let us kill him tonight,' said Noni's mother.

It was never done for the second wife of a chief to take the lead in a discussion without being called upon, and this development heightened Nosakhe's sense that strange things were unfolding. She thought of her feud with Atamaraka, of the vigour and money of the white man. If indeed he had been sent to aid her, it would explain why the Dark Goddess had gone to such lengths to have him executed. Her own mind felt cloudy. She was used to clarity of feeling, but there were too many patterns in the omens of the evening to reach any certain conclusion.

She looked at Noni's parents, aware that they expected from her, at the least, an acknowledgement that Noni had shown the gift of Farsight. That this gift might be the inspiration of a dark spirit now seemed a strong possibility, and Nosakhe cursed herself for allowing things to reach this pass.

'I must consult the ancestors, and the Great Goddess Ma,' she said at last. 'I can make no pronouncement until I have sought their counsel.'

Watching her, the chief felt a murderous rage – the rage of a man who has lived his life by another person's rules, only to find them repudiated at the moment of crisis.

'She has plainly demonstrated the gift of Farsight,' he said. And this time he did not address Nosakhe as 'Mama'. 'You must absolve her from your sentence. It is you yourself who planted the seed within her, and it has grown. Now she must be let alone.'

Poor man, thought Nosakhe. He has no profound intelligence. How could he possibly make sense of these complex events, blinded as he is by love?

'I do not say that she has not shown this gift,' she replied, choosing her words carefully. 'But I must consult Ma before saying anything else.'

'Kill him! Kill him!' cried Noni. 'No good will come of sheltering him.'

'You have said enough for one evening, my child,' said Nosakhe. 'The Strange One is a guest in my house, and tonight is a marriage feast. He cannot be harmed while he enjoys my hospitality.'

'But—'

'I have spoken, chief. I will speak to Ma as soon as the last guest has gone, and fast for three days. Then you shall have my answer.'

Meanwhile the flames leapt higher and more logs were burned and more beer was poured from its jars and more pipes were filled. Piet was disconcerted to be met by an abrupt refusal, and wondered whether he had been unwise to state his wishes so openly. He could see from the look on Luvo's face that his companion disapproved of his impetuousness. But after all, the air was fresh and the drinks were good and he was a man who enjoyed a party. 'We will resume our business in the morning,' he said. 'And now—'

But he was cut off by a tremendous whooping. For the bride and her groom were retreating into the hut that had been prepared for them.

It was Bela's mother who presented Ntsina with the hide of purest white goatskin that was to be his love mat, and he who laid it on the floor as Bela secured the hut's door behind them. Lanterns had been lit. They were both sweaty from dancing. He went to her, but she raised her hand. She brought the tip of her small finger to her thumb, holding the palm downwards. It was the sign for 'virgin', and she made it with an unblemished conscience. It was not a requirement that her husband should be a virgin also, and yet . . . In her deepest self, Bela wished that he was. She had guarded her own virginity zealously. Combined with her beauty, it had made her the focus of many a handsome scoundrel. For the first time all day she felt nervous, as she turned her palm upwards and brought the tip of her forefinger to the tip of her thumb, in the sign for 'two'.

It was a question, and Ntsina understood it, and in his heart he felt the deepest shame for what he had done in Johannesburg with the woman whose jolliness was a sham. He decided to lie, but as he began to nod his head he found he could not continue. To begin his married life with a lie – it was impossible. 'There was one before you. I was at the mines, and very unhappy. I did not know you were in store for me.'

Bela heard the shame in his voice, and Ntsina's sincerity touched her heart. When he said 'I am sorry,' and bowed his head, a feeling rose through her that she had never felt before; it softened her – for men did not often apologize in Gwadana.

It was her smile that told him he was forgiven, and he embraced her. They fitted perfectly – her head beneath his chin, his hand on her neck. He had never held a woman in this way. Neither had she been so held. It opened infinite possibilities to them. He ran his fingers down her neck till they met the scratchy blanket, and with a shrug she loosed it. The sensations unleashed by the scratch of Ntsina's fingers as they made their way down her spine billowed through Bela's whole body. They were the hard hands of a labourer, and their contrast with the gentleness of his touch was exquisite. He kissed her neck and she gasped. His cock was hard and hot through his blanket. When she pressed herself against it she saw his eyes half-close in pleasure.

'Let me wash you, my husband,' she said.

༄

By the fire outside, Sukude accepted his guests' congratulations on his son's marriage with as good a grace as he could muster, but the brandy he had drunk had put his mood on a knife edge. In one direction lay frenzied hilarity; in the other, rage. The two states are closer than many think, and at their foundation was a powerful spur towards oblivion: fear.

As he ate the cow that had not cried, Sukude could hear her timid bleating as he kicked her. He began to feel cold, though he sat by a hot fire. Nosakhe, after all, was a mortal. The ancestors had far greater powers at their command, and could unleash punishments that pursued him into the afterlife. He was not at all as stupid as Nosakhe thought. Rather, years of playing prince consort had taught him to disguise his intelligence and to keep his thoughts to himself – a necessary precaution in a village full of gossips. He set his mind to the contemplation of the omen. Its seriousness was beyond all question; the severity of its judgement quite clear. But what, precisely, had the ancestors judged?

He inched closer to the fire, for strong heat concentrates the mind. His deductive powers darted round the edges of the puzzle, looking for ways into its maze. At length he found one. Perhaps the ancestors did not condemn the part he had played in bringing this wedding about, but the fact of the wedding itself. The *manner in which* Bela had been brought into the clan of the Zinis. He took a sip of brandy. The ancestors, after all, had smiled on his negotiations for Bela and on the preparations he had made for the wedding. It was Nosakhe who had intervened by casting the spell for Ntsina's return. Maybe it was *this* to which the ancestors objected: a woman interfering in a man's plans. This was a much more satisfactory avenue of exploration than any he had yet found, and as he pursued it his rage dwindled and became purposeful. His desire to seek oblivion in frenzied merriment diminished. He barely noticed as Noni's mother stormed past him and through the gate.

He was staring into the flames, deep in his own thoughts, when Lundi stepped out of the crowd of dancers and sat by his side. Lundi knew that Sukude had a whole bottle of brandy. His desire for the fire spirit overcame the usual caution he felt about being seen near Sukude in public. Tonight, after all, anyone might be seen with anyone. 'What have you got for me, my friend?' he said, staring pointedly at the brandy bottle between Sukude's feet.

Sukude looked at him. Lundi knew many *sangomas* in the taverns of King William's Town. He poured him a drink and said: 'Do you agree that the ancestors disapprove of meddling women?'

The question was phrased to elicit only one answer, and Lundi agreed enthusiastically that the ancestors did, indeed, disapprove of women who sought to overturn the true order of things by sliding their tails where they did not belong.

They sat together for some time, pursuing this line of thought. In the course of their discussion the moon began to fade and dawn crept over the sea. The sky turned pink as a benediction. Across the Zinis' compound lay the bodies of sleeping guests, lulled by beer and dagga into taking their rest where they could. Coffee was brought out to greet the dawn, and it fuelled the raspy voices that still sang, and several of the sleepers woke, and took some, and refilled their pipes. By no means was everyone in the village of Gwadana as rich as the Zinis, and there were those among their guests who knew they would not have such treats for many moons. They stumbled to their feet. Practical jokes were played. The old lady who lay by the vegetable patch, snoring loud enough to summon Nomikhonto from the Underworld, was doused in icy water, to much merriment – which woke other slumberers, on whom coffee, and fresh pipes, and more beer were pressed.

His talk with Lundi, and the brandy they had drunk during it, had stilled all Sukude's fears. He was seized by the conviction that it was not he, but his hated mother-in-law, who had dishonoured the ancestors. This summoned a powerful resurgence of the determination that had been building in him for many months: to have his own way.

He stood and splashed his face with fresh water. He always woke with an erection, and this morning was no different. He saw Zandi asleep by the pig sty. She was not as beautiful as her sister, but her thighs were large. He had a vision of himself between them, and this vision excited him, and more blood flowed to his cock.

He glanced from her to the closed hut where Ntsina and Bela were. A bolt of genius struck him. There was no goatskin on display. And no goatskin could mean only one thing: no consummation.

Indeed, no consummation had taken place. While their guests jested and drank, time in the bridal hut had stretched to a delicious eternity. Bela lit a fire and threw on it sprays of lavender and a sweet-smelling plant that was known to heighten desire. She warmed water and when it was the temperature of human blood she took her red blankets and dipped them in it and began to cleanse her husband's body of the rock paste Luvo had so assiduously smeared over it. It was a wife's duty to wash her husband, and the combination of duty with erotic pleasure was intoxicating. She began at his neck, working downwards across his shoulders with their sinewy indentations, down his smooth, hard chest towards the trail of hair, stiffened and white, that ran from his bellybutton. As she rubbed the paste away she released Ntsina's smell and drank it in deeply.

In the cleaning of his body it was necessary to remove his blankets, and when the moment for this came Bela stood back, examining him in the light thrown by the fire. She was delighted with what she saw, and Ntsina was pleased that she was pleased. Their mutual admiration heightened the tenderness of the moment, and the anticipation of what was to come. Ntsina's cock stood straight up, throbbing with the pumping of his heart. It extended to his navel. Bela had never before seen an erect penis, and it was fascinating to her. She was taken by an instinctive desire to do something she had never before contemplated, and which no one had ever described to her. She sank to her knees and put the head of Ntsina's cock into her mouth. She wanted to *taste* him, having smelled him. And the saltiness, the heat, the smell of it made her wet enough to think with anticipation, rather than fear, of Ntsina's cock going where her mother had shown her it must go.

The look on her husband's face made Bela feel well contented with the married state. She continued to wash him, returning now and again to the intimate parts of his body. In her happiness, a tremor of conscience called to mind her older sister, who would perhaps never know what she, a married woman, now knew. And then she stood again, and for the first time they kissed, Ntsina tasting himself on his wife's tongue, holding her tight to him, feeling the yieldings of her rounded body, so much more grace-ful than the stick-thin white ladies with no bottoms he had seen in Johannesburg and King William's Town. At length she stood back from him and said: 'We must be kind to Zandi.'

'I will serve with my life all those whom you love,' said Ntsina.

He leaned to kiss her as a fist slammed on the door, and they heard the shout of his father, soon taken up by other men: 'WHERE IS THE GOATSKIN?'

It made them laugh, for it showed how tardy they had been with each other; and for the first time they noticed the glimmerings of day around the edges of the door. They had been at weddings before where crowds of drunken guests hurried the bridal couple through their paces, demanding the bloodied goatskin that is the proof of marital union and the bride's virginity. They ignored the shouts as they grew louder, and more men joined them, the sleeping guests woken by the commotion. They did not hear the recklessness in the crowd, the mad impulsive energy of a large group bonded by beer. They were too lost in the luxuries of the moment to hear a note of violence intrude into the good cheer. For Sukude had seen his chance, and brandy made him ruthless.

It is an accepted truth according to the law that a father may show his son how to be a man, if the youth does not bring his wife to the love mat in good time. This law was seldom invoked, for there were not many young men in Gwadana who could not work out what to do with a woman.

'Where is the goatskin?!' Sukude cried. He cried three times, for the law says that a son must be given three warnings. And when no goatskin appeared, and the door to the hut did not open, he hurled his weight against it, spurred by the cheers of the watching men.

In her own hut, sleeping fitfully, Nosakhe heard the cries. They intruded on her sleep like the bellowing of a demon; and when she woke she was at first annoyed by the drunkenness of her guests. She had taken off her headdress of white beads, the sacred emblem of a *sangoma*, and afterwards she would sorely repent not putting it on again before venturing outside. It meant that she was bareheaded, her power much reduced, when she emerged to see her grandson hurled from his hut into a group of drunk men, who held him down, only laughing harder as he struggled.

Inside the hut, Bela said: 'I see you, my new father.'

'Keep him back!' cried Sukude. And he closed the door.

Seeing the fear in Bela's eyes, Sukude's sense of grievance knew no bounds. He had not imagined this scene in this way – for her to be afraid of him! It made him angry with her, angry with his mother-in-law who had summoned his son home. He lifted his leopardskin kaross and exposed himself. His cock was as thick as a young puff adder, and it was filling with blood. The horror in Bela's eyes inflamed him.

'I am your father. Obey me. Lie down.'

But Bela would not lie down, and he wasted precious seconds while he chased her round the hut, for she was not drunk, and far swifter than he. But a hut is not a large space, and its door was

158

barred from the outside, and finally he had her, and he pushed her onto the love mat. She fell and cried out. Even in this extreme moment, she remembered her promise to obey the orders of her new father. But she would not obey these orders, and it took all the weight of Sukude's hefty body to prise apart her thighs while he kept one hand at her throat, holding her down.

He rammed his cock into her with no preliminaries. She was so ready for mating that it slid in more easily than he remembered with Ntsina's mother, who had always complained of his size. He felt the hymen burst and thrust deeper, the pain on Bela's beautiful face heightening the urgency of the moment. He thrust and thrust, and when he came it was as if the desire of years drained from him. The world faded. His body began to float. He flooded her. And then he collapsed on her, his face on the breast he had so long dreamed of licking.

He was spent. But she was not. She screamed and kicked and scratched, and he hardly had the energy to defend himself, for the little death that follows ejaculation united with the brandy in his bloodstream to render him as weak as Samson when Delilah cut his hair.

Finally he gathered himself. He hit her, hard, across the head. In the momentary silence he stood and adjusted his kaross. He wished to say something superb, but words failed him. Knowledge of coming consequences settled uneasily on him, for the noises beyond the door had grown wilder and he heard his mother-in-law's voice. His artful arguments began to shimmer, then fell away as lightly as mist. For a moment he wished he might never have to leave this hut, and in the end it was not he who opened the door but his son, from the other side.

Ntsina saw at once that he was too late. He hurled himself at his father, and the watching men grew silent. Then Nosakhe was upon them. It was she who instructed her grandson to stop, and when he did not it was she who told the men to hold him – for it is a grave crime for a son to kill his father.

Ntsina was dragged from the hut. He was as strong as fifteen men in this state of wildness, but there were more than fifteen men to hold him. He saw Bela's eyes, and then the door was closed. There was nowhere to keep him but Sukude's hut, and he was carried there, screaming and writhing. The sound woke Piet Barol, who had been dreaming heavily. He went to his door, rubbing his eyes and feeling happy, invigorated for the new day – for he had drunk a quantity of water before retiring, and this kept his hangover at bay. He was in time to see Ntsina being carried, arms flailing, to the hut by the cliff, and when its door was locked the most fearful racket emanated from within. The noise roused Luvo, too. He also witnessed Ntsina's incarceration, but when Piet found him and asked what was going on, he did not know.

The yard was full of guests, but their laughter was gone. The brandy had made a joke of something that was not a joke, and many of the men who had played a part in the drama were slinking away down the escarpment, bent on the creation of alibis. Nosakhe ran inside for her headdress, for the situation might well call for spells, and the efficacy of these was much reduced without her proper regalia. This meant that she did not see the door of the bridal hut open.

Bela stood at it, quite naked.

She stood so long that all murmurs ceased. Again she was the focus of all eyes, but this time she did not see them. She did not see her mother, emerging from a distant hut, or her sister, with her father, hurrying across the grass. She was conscious only of the call of the morning birds, drawing her towards the cliffs. Blood was running down her leg in a ticklish trickle. The lure of the cliffs acted strongly on her, for no woman would survive a fall onto those rocks. But within Bela was a strong instinctive horror of death, and as she stepped from the hut onto the Zinis' lawn, she knew it was not death she chose.

The birds called. The sun seared the mist and exposed the sea. Nosakhe stood ready to do battle with the Queen of Evil, but the look on Bela's face stilled even her.

With absolute dignity, Bela walked across the grass. The guests stood aside for her. She held all who watched in a spell more powerful than the one she had cast the day before, as a glamorous bride. She crossed the lawn, leaving a train of red that caught the light. 'She is going to the kraal.' Luvo dug his fingers tight into Piet's arm.

He was right.

Bela reached the gate of her in-laws' kraal, the kraal she must not enter until her first son had had his twelfth moon. She was at once numb and throbbing with life. Though later people would say that she was mad, and she herself would wonder, Bela Zini was not mad.

She was angry.

She walked into the kraal.

The birds sang as before. The goats bleated. But nothing in the history of Gwadana Village would ever be the same.

7

Many portents had shown Nosakhe Zini that a battle between things seen and unseen was nearing its climax. She who was accustomed to certainty felt only confusion. Her brain was soggy with it. Her memories of the men who had held her grandson were hazy, made hazy by Atamaraka, who is known for protecting her servants while she has need of them. She could hear his frenzied shouts from his father's locked hut. She gave orders for Sukude to be held too, but these were not obeyed.

And now Sukude took his chance.

'You have offended the ancestors by interfering in the ways of men.' He was not used to speaking up to his mother-in-law, and the very act of it gave him courage. 'They were seven hours alone, and he did not sex her, the boy you took from me, whom you have raised as weak-willed as a woman.'

The remaining guests watched, fascinated by the overthrow of an established order. Sukude, seeing that he held their attention, warmed to his theme. The fear that had seeped into him in the moments after spending in Bela evaporated. 'It is a father's duty to teach his son. For years and years you have kept him from a father's teaching.' As he spoke a genuine sorrow welled in him, for it had cost him dearly, in the moons before, to see his own son, flesh of his own flesh, choose the shelter of another when the thunder growled. 'Three times I asked for the goatskin, three times it was not shown. For the honour of our clan, I mounted her.'

Standing by the door to the kitchen hut, translating for Piet Barol, Luvo was stirred to his core by what he heard. The Rankes had been too tactful ever to suggest that the original occupants of the continent were savages, but the notion was so commonly accepted among the authors of the books that stocked their library that it had seeped, unbidden, into Luvo's consciousness. Now he felt it amply confirmed. 'This is what comes of not knowing God!' he whispered to Piet, and Piet nodded, thinking quickly.

Nosakhe looked at Sukude. The law he had invoked, though rarely used, and meant for quite another set of circumstances, remained the law. He had indeed asked thrice for the bloodied goatskin, and Ntsina had not provided it. Her first thought was for her grandson, who would most certainly do his father an injury if he could. Were this to happen without a council of Elders finding Sukude guilty of any crime, Ntsina himself would face death. The thought was unbearable. So was the fact that her kraal, blessed by the Great Founder himself, had been defiled by Bela's entry into it.

'We must summon the chief,' said Lundi. And this cry was taken up by the crowd, who sent a swift boy running down the hill.

'It is time to liberate our friend,' said Piet.

⁊

The crashes from Sukude's hut had quieted, replaced by a despairing silence. The yard was empty, the remains of the feast abandoned where the guests had been sitting when the drama first unfolded. Piet and Luvo went to Sukude's hut.

'We are coming for you,' called Piet.

'Bring my weapon,' Ntsina shouted from within. But the door, unlike all other doors of Gwadana, was made of steel, not wood; and the padlock that usually closed it from the inside was attached on the outside, and staunch it was.

'Where is the key?'

'With my father.'

'Is there not a spare inside?'

163

'If there is, I cannot find it.'

Piet looked at the hut with a carpenter's eye. The beams protruded over the wall at intervals. It had not been built as a fortress. 'Let us find the scythe,' he said.

They found the scythe at the back of the pig sty, and Piet fetched two brandy crates and climbed them. With a great thwack he sent the scythe through the roof and Ntsina saw daylight.

'I must find my wife,' said Ntsina, ripping the thatch away and hauling himself through the gap.

⌒꙰⌒

In the chief's homestead, a crisis of a different kind had been reached. Since the day of Noni's birth, when Nosakhe had both passed and postponed a sentence of death on her daughter, the attitude of Noni's mother to Nosakhe Zini had been one part gratitude, two parts fear, and seven parts hate. The hate hung heavy upon her, for she was a gentle woman. It grew with every moon that passed without Noni displaying the gift of Farsight, and with Nosakhe's rejection of every promising glimmer of it.

Nosakhe's refusal to lift for ever the threat of a violent death, despite superb evidence that Farsight had come at last, destroyed the last of the gratitude she felt towards her. Now there was only fear and hate, and the greatest of these was hate.

She had kept her husband up all night, first begging him to take a stand against the *sangoma*; then screaming at him, as dawn broke. The chief's domestic life was a peaceful one, as a rule, and his wives took an old-fashioned view of masculine authority and rarely told him what to do. He considered his wife's demands, but he had also made a promise to uphold and defend the settlement that was the Great Founder's legacy, and he could not act against the Founder's granddaughter without violating that sacred bond. No satisfactory conclusion had been reached, and no one had slept, and his stomach was quite vinegary from all the brandy he had drunk, when a boy ran through the gate and told them that

164

doings that required the judgement of a great chief had taken place at the top of the cliffs.

The very phrase set the chief on edge, for he knew that he was not a great chief. He liked people to get along. He did not enjoy adjudicating disputes, because he was too inclined to see things from many different points of view. He had never sentenced anyone to death. 'You say Bela walked into the Zinis' kraal?' he asked, astonished – for it was well known that Bela was the best-brought-up young woman in Gwadana.

'Before all eyes,' said the child.

The chief could not imagine, as he climbed the hill, what might make a girl like Bela enter her husband's kraal. He had never heard of such a thing, much less seen something so outrageous. Having been told that her family had taken her away, he sent the boy to their homestead to enquire after their well-being. He did his best to leave Noni's mother behind, but her fellow wives supported her and all of them made their way up the steep path they had descended just before dawn.

At the top of the hill they were met by Lundi, whose complicity in Sukude's actions had given him a strong interest in the out-come of the chief's deliberations. His briefing horrified the chief, who asked his ancestors to guide him as he passed through the gate and into the remnants of the feast.

In the time it took to summon the authorities, Sukude, seeing himself unchallenged, found his confidence. For years the law had been his mother-in-law's domain, and he had never once object-ed to her interpretation. Now he saw that he had the power to bend precedent too, and by the time he stated his case before his chief, he had established the justice of his actions firmly in his own mind. His son had been lured from him as a boy, deprived of the teachings only a man can give. He, Sukude, had given way, perhaps wrongly, out of respect for the Great Founder, whose granddaughter Nosakhe was. Weakened by this woman, the boy had failed to learn the ways of a man, which had left him unable to perform the duties of a man on his wedding night – even with a bride as beautiful as Bela. He, a caring father, had waited until daylight, and still there was no goatskin. He had asked three times for the goatskin, and three times Ntsina had failed to produce it. And so he, as the senior male Zini, had cemented Bela's union with his clan in a manner hallowed by ancient custom.

As he told this story, he was almost able to forget the way Bela had looked at him; the numb unconcern on her gorgeous face as she walked naked into the kraal. He explained this by saying that Nosakhe had put a curse on the girl, who must not be blamed, he finished piously, for her actions.

The chief had no love for Sukude, but his wife had a burning hatred for Nosakhe Zini, and he knew he would never have a moment's peace if he sided with her. He looked at Nosakhe, half-beseechingly. He was used to being led by her. But at this crucial juncture Nosakhe found that she had lost the power to defend herself. Beneath the vileness of Sukude's lies was a horrible, irrefutable truth – she *had* taken the child from his father, when he was young; she had wanted his love for herself, and had won it, and this left her without her usual faith in the righteousness of her own actions.

Seeing the look on his chief's face, and knowing him to be a poor resource in a crisis, Lundi sidled into the centre of the throng and said: 'We must seek the guidance of another witch doctor.'

The chief seized this opportunity to delegate authority. He did not know that Lundi was thinking of one witch doctor in particular, Fezile Khumalo, who was well known in the taverns of King William's Town. This Fezile was as corruptible as the cuckoo bird, and Lundi began to see that, with his help, he might perform a signal service for Sukude, and win for himself the gratitude of a rich man.

'I am the only witch doctor in this village,' said Nosakhe. But even as she spoke, her voice sounded foreign to her; as weak as if she had been struck in the heart by an assegai – which is exactly how she felt when a lingering guest walked in and said: 'Ntsina has vanished, and so has the Strange One.'

Piet could not catch Ntsina, who sprinted across the fields towards Bela's homestead. He did his best, but he was carrying his pack, full of cash and irreplaceable possessions. Luvo kept up with his friend, and was with him when they found the homestead deserted.

To this point, rage had sustained Ntsina. He had been certain he would find Bela here, and her absence brought upon him a fit of despair. He made a sound the samango monkeys heard, crashing through the canopy of the distant trees. They stopped leaping, drew their loved ones close to them. For it is the gift of every ape to understand the anguish of every other.

He was howling when Piet reached him, and the mice who had been plundering the Jaxas' grain store in their absence had retreated to their holes, afraid of this new beast. A tree snake, bright as the greenest leaf and deadly poisonous, shifted distastefully and slid up the trunk of the tree beneath which Ntsina flung himself – for the adult birds had flown, and their nests were unguarded. As the snake ingested their eggs, one by one, Ntsina said: 'I want to kill him.'

It was her father who led Bela away, and her mother who forbade any return to their home. She could not bear the curiosity of visitors. So they went to the homestead of their aunt Nceba, who was too old to pry.

Zandi watched Bela, and through all the jealousies and cutting words of nineteen years, obliterating them, rose a powerful empathy. Zandi knew what it is like to be discussed in disparaging terms. Now Bela would face such judgements for the rest of her life. Her eyes were glazed, her movements automatic. There was dried blood on her ankle, so Zandi spat on the hem of her own skirt, and wiped it off, and all the while Bela – whose eyes had danced so brightly once – sat motionless.

The effort of preparing coffee tired their aunt, who soon fell into a doze on her straw mat, and Mama Jaxa took this chance to signal to her husband that they must speak. Together they slipped out of the hut and stood behind it, out of sight of the track. Mama Jaxa had a rush of memories of their first meetings, as teenagers, when they had also sheltered from public view. Since then, they had never done anything illicit. They were used to being well known, and to honouring their reputations and their daughters' by seamless conduct in public. 'What can we do?' she said.

'There is nothing we can do. Bela must go back to the Zinis – if they will have her.'

'No!'

'We gave her in marriage.' He began to cry. It was the first time he had cried since the morning of Bela's birth. 'It is Bela who has dishonoured herself. Not they who have dishonoured her. Did you not explain?' By which he meant: Did you not tell her that her husband should sex her?

'Of course I told her!' Mama Jaxa's anguish found an outlet in anger. 'She cannot go back to them.'

'It is for them to decide. And I tell you this: if they have her back, they will certainly demand some cattles with her.'

❧

Piet found a small stream and led the younger men up it. At length they came upon a clearing caused by the toppling of a forest giant, its trunk rent in two by a strike of lightning. He sat Ntsina down and made him drink. He felt great sorrow for the boy – a determination to set him on his feet.

The last few days had been exhausting in the extreme for Luvo. He had been the only sober guest at Ntsina's wedding and worked harder than he ever had in his life, doing justice to Piet Barol's social exuberance. Eventually he had seen that God was training him – for when the Native Congress's delegation reached the English king, they would need to catch everything he said.

As Ntsina began to relive the joys and horrors of the night

before, Piet Barol watched as he listened. How different the Bantu face is, he thought, from the white man's. And yet their suffering is the same. As the sun stretched across the sky and Ntsina cursed, he took up a piece of wood in the first, soft stages of decay, and with a file from his pack began to carve a bust of his friend. He worked almost unconsciously, his attention wholly absorbed in what Ntsina said – for in this forest clearing, out it all came. His mother's death, his father's vicious trickery. Now the theft of the woman he loved.

Luvo was horrified by what he translated. He sank into himself as the Strange One and Ntsina spoke, thinking what a wonderful country South Africa would be if all civilized men had the franchise. To him, the superstitions of the Gwadanans were almost as bad as the thievery of the Afrikaners.

It was the first time Piet had carved a human face. His conscious mind being focused wholly on his friend's story, his hands were free to act on what his eyes saw without the intervention of focus or effort. Ntsina's anguish flowed through Piet's fingers into the wood he carved. He caught the dome of Ntsina's head, the precise ratio between his eyes and his nose and his mouth and his chin. He was thinking that catastrophes make many things possible.

As Ntsina lapsed into silence, having said all he could, and Luvo fell silent also, Piet understood that he would never prevail by charm. In any case, charm took time: a commodity he did not have. It was clear from the way he had been dismissed the night before that the chief would never sell him an Ancestor Tree – whether or not he built his ancestors new shrines. If Piet were to have the wood he needed, he must take it.

'Can you ever again live in your father's homestead?'

'Never.'

'Nor in his village?'

'No.'

'To fetch your wife now, only to live in poverty. Would that do justice to her?'

'It would not.'

'Then you need money.'

'That is so.'

It had grown bitterly cold. Piet thought of how his friend had dressed for his wedding – like a statue, in his paste of white rock. His skin prickled. He would not sway the chief and his councillors by rational argument – but that did not mean they could not be swayed. An idea of swashbuckling originality came to him and he smoothed the curve of Ntsina's nose, capturing it precisely.

'Are you willing to do whatever is needed to rescue your wife, and provide for her?'

'Anything.'

'Then sleep. I must plan.'

Luvo made a fire. None of them ate. The day passed and evening came. The two Xhosa fell asleep and Piet sat in the moonlight, working on his bust. The wood was soft and he carved in the direction of its grain, winning it to him. Ntsina was lying on his back. His dreams troubled him, and his features creased in anger and fright. Piet's files, lying on the ground, caught the light. He moved from the largest to the smallest. He was not conscious of effort, which is the enemy of great art. He was in a state humans rarely reach, but which every spider knows. His conscious intelligence stepped back; he was connected to the deeper rhythms of seeing and moving. His mind emptied of words, of worry, of thoughts for the future. He was wholly in the present – in this forest, in this moonlight, with this wood in his hands.

He worked until daylight woke his companions. 'We must spend some days here.'

'But what of Bela?' asked Ntsina.

'You have one chance to build a life worthy of her. Her parents have her safe and sound. A few days won't matter.'

Piet refused to be drawn further. He slept, and woke, and barely spoke. He worked on the bust, and his silence made the others silent also. Ntsina caught a hare and Luvo skinned it, and they all ate; but Piet took only a few mouthfuls. Inspiration had lifted his hunger. A slow excitement grew within him as he saw the quality of what he was making. The bust was life-size and caught Ntsina to the life – his face contorted in fear and anger. Piet began to worry that a hasty movement would spoil it; but he banished that thought, and his hands led him well.

Periodically Piet asked Ntsina to sit still, and trained his total concentration on his left ear, or the jigsaw of his teeth when his lips were flared. The two Xhosa were spent of words and needed rest. They trusted this strange *mlungu*, whose movements were so purposeful.

It took several days, and then it was done.

At last Piet ate his fill. When the meal was finished, he sat on the trunk of the tree and said: 'Here is what we will do.'

He began by reminding his companions of Percy Shabrill's immense wealth. They both had vivid memories of it. He told them that to win the patronage of this man he must have wood that excelled even that of the Furniture Tree.

When he understood where the narrative was leading, Ntsina began to shake his head – and now it was Luvo who intervened. 'Your ancestors reside in the mansions of Heaven, not in these trees. They never knew Jesus Christ, but I believe St Peter welcomed them at the pearly gates. You must free yourself of savage superstitions. Look what they have resulted in. No Christian father is permitted to take his son's wife.'

Ntsina stopped shaking his head.

Piet was dazzled by the chance, so nearly in his grasp, to take the wood he must have to make great art. 'When Shabrill pays me, I will give each of you three hundred pounds,' he said, impetuously. 'Together we will see to everything, hire the help we need from another village. You will be able to rescue your wife, Ntsina. To keep her in a house with electric lights and comfortable beds. Your children will be educated. But until the money is made you cannot – you must not – return.'

The possibility of this life shimmered before Ntsina. He thought again of the bed the Strange One had slept in at Cradock and looked at Luvo. Perhaps he was right – he had been to school, after all.

'My people will never let us,' he said.

'They need never know,' said Piet. 'Later, when we are rich, we can build them new shrines.'

'They will find out, when they come to make offerings.'

'Not if they never enter the forest.'

⌘

In the cause of finding a new witch doctor, the dearest possession of the chieftaincy of Gwadana was produced: a bicycle. Competition for the riding of it was fierce, and its winner was known to be swift. Lundi watched the young man set off for King William's Town, then went to find Sukude. 'If I bring the girl to you, you will be generous to me. Will you not, my friend?'

Sukude looked at Lundi. He felt invincible after his unexpected success against his mother-in-law. The lordly part of his nature wished to tell Lundi that he had no need of him, that he could get the girl and anything else he wished for. But the shrewder part knew that he and Lundi had reached the stage of intimacy at which allies must either go further, or retreat into enmity. The chief had no great liking for him, and village opinion was inclined to be conservative. It would not serve his cause to have an enemy on the village council, so he put on his warmest face and said: 'I will always be generous to you, Lundi. You are a true friend.' And to prove it, he opened one of the brandy bottles that had lain untouched since the departure of the wedding guests.

Across the village, a sense of unease had spread, intensified by the hangover that is the legacy of brandy and dagga-smoke. Since the rescue of their ancestors by the Great Founder, who had spared them and their cattles by thinking for himself, the Gwadanans had grown accustomed to feeling that they were on the right side of Things Unseen. The evil spirits swarming across the country, turfing families out of their homes in the middle of winter, had for a long time been prevented from crossing the great forest. Now something had happened, and they had come – but few could agree precisely what it was that had happened. Many men swore they had heard Sukude ask thrice for the goatskin, and public opinion did not judge him too harshly for sexing Bela when his boy couldn't. That his boy had not sexed such a beauty, when he had ample time to do so, seemed the first assault on the order of things, and Sukude's denunciation of Nosakhe found supporters, even among those who did not care for him. The matter of the cow who had failed to cry was raised in more than one homestead. Mothers forbade their children to leave home after dark, lest they encounter spirits bent on mischief, and the noise made by the children of Gwadana, thus cooped up, did nothing to improve their parents' mood.

In the village's first household, a tense silence reigned.

The chief had often been envied by other men for the graceful subservience of his wives, and the sudden loss of it annoyed him greatly. Each of her fellow wives sided with Noni's mother, and so did all their children. 'You must force Nosakhe to lift the sentence on Noni,' was the universal cry, and his wives took to repeating it every time the chief addressed a word to them. Sexual favours were withheld, which was a punishment he was not at all used to; and yet he had inner strength, when he could find it, and he knew the oath he had made the Great Founder, and it prevented him from acting against Nosakhe.

'We must wait until an independent *sangoma* comes,' he said. 'That man will fix everything.'

But Noni's mother knew this was not so. On the morning of the third day after the crisis at the Zinis', she was woken by her daughter creeping under her blanket. The little girl understood that dark matters swirled and had lost her appetite. Her mother held her close, feeling how bony she was; so far from the phys- ical ideal that she worried, for the first time, what lay ahead for Noni if her sentence of death was lifted and she was permitted to grow to womanhood. Which man would take her? She ran over the eligible boys of the village and found none to whom she would entrust her darling child. For days she had waited, hoping for action from her husband. Now she acknowledged that there would be no action – and the fault was not her husband's, but her own. By the fire at the Zinis', as Piet Barol spoke, she had promised to make a sacrifice if the Strange One would confirm her daughter's gift of Farsight. He had confirmed it. He had asked, before many witnesses, to buy an Ancestor Tree – using the exact words Noni had predicted. The ancestors had kept their end of the bargain. Now it was time for her to keep hers.

She began to cry, softly. She had been blessed with good health and strong bones. She had little acquaintance with pain. Now that the severing of her own limb was upon her she found it impossible to imagine. She fell to wondering how she might achieve it – she who did not look when a goat was slaughtered, for she hated the sight of blood. In the end, she knew she must seek another's aid; the aid of someone who loved Noni, whose aim was sure and true.

She chose Kagiso.

When she had explained what he must do, Kagiso made no sound. He was distraught for Ntsina and had searched every out-building in the village to find him. 'Why did you make such a promise? She had already prophesied. There was already a witness.'

'I wanted to make sure the prophecy would come true. If I go back on my word, our ancestors will cease to help us.'

There was no disputing this logic. They went behind the kraal and Kagiso fetched the chief's sharpest axe. 'How much did you promise?' She showed him. 'You must tell my father first, so that he does not punish me later.'

When told the rash oath his wife had made, the chief felt more than ever unequal to his destiny. Her sister wives cried for her and interrogated themselves. Pumza, the eldest, knew she would have made the same promise and honoured it. The others were less certain, and each of them looked at her hands, the soft hands that befitted a chief's wife, and gave thanks that her children were safe and healthy, that no such sacrifice was required of them.

The chief felt angry with Noni's mother, but the look on her face as Kagiso picked up the axe softened him. 'It was perhaps unnecessary to make this pact. But you made it with a good heart.'

'I honour it so that the ancestors may give you the courage to do what is right.'

Her barb struck true. The chief stood back. He turned his face away as she laid her delicate, plump hand on the tree trunk where the mealie meal was ground. 'Aim true, and be swift,' she said, and closed her eyes.

The axe flashed. Its blade caught the light. She felt the sunshine on her lids, heard the thud of the axe on the trunk. The tip of her finger leapt from the wooden block, the nail as clean and smooth as it had ever been. First she felt nothing. And then WHOOOSH, the pain was upon her. A pain that engulfed the universe. She started screaming. The blood from her finger poured onto the earth and spattered her dress and her face. She cried so loudly the piglets stopped suckling, and the snake that had slithered to the wood pile in quest of fat mice withdrew, seeking the shelter of the grasses beyond the homestead's wall. Pumza bandaged her finger and held it tight to staunch the flow of blood. But the blood did not cease flowing. It poured from her, soaking the linen bandages that her fellow wives brought. She thought she would die of the pain, she who had never even broken an arm, who had so little pain to guide her. Her husband approached to give her comfort, but she turned away from him, and in her heart she blamed him for being weak and unmanly.

'It is time,' said Bela's father. And her mother did not disagree with him. They dressed Bela in fresh blankets, she not uttering a sound, and Zandi saw to her hair. For three days Bela had not spoken, and at last they had ceased in their efforts to make her speak. The light had gone from her eyes, but her beauty remained. Zandi, who had many times before been asked to dress her sister's hair, took more care than she had ever done, and Bela's back and shoulders were as smooth and elegant as before. The family bade their aunt farewell and made their way back towards the village and the escarpment that lead to the Zinis'.

Their appearance caused a sensation. As always, it was the children who could not maintain a discreet reserve. It was known that Bela had walked into the kraal, and then disappeared, but none of the children knew why, for the adults of Gwadana kept their own counsel. Every child who saw her ran to tell another, and then to tell an adult, and the result was that Bela's passage through the village was observed by many pairs of eyes. Zandi knew they were peered at through windows, from behind cloths. Bela herself seemed oblivious. She, so used to attention, moved through this hidden crowd unseeing.

The look in Bela's eyes fixed her closest friends to the spot. Like every child in Gwadana, these girls had been raised on tales of wicked spirits stealing a person's soul. It was clear from Bela's look that something in her had been taken away, and it made them afraid. They did not move, and Bela did not look at them as she passed by. That night they cursed themselves for their treachery and sought the counsel of their grandmothers, who told them that they had done right.

Up the hill Bela went, and the wind stung sharply and the clouds gathered. Nosakhe was at the top of the cliff, seeking Ma's aid, hurling the bones of the cow who had not cried to discern the Goddess's meaning in the swoop of the gulls who dived for them. Sukude's defiance had shocked her. Her grandson's absence left her weakened and confused. She could see no pattern in the movement of the gulls, hear no message in the eagles' cries. She knew that action was required of her, but what this action was she did not know. For the first time in her life she did not trust her instincts, and without them she was powerless.

Watching from the window of his hut, Sukude could not believe the graciousness of his ancestors, who were returning to him the woman he had spent so long yearning for. In the absence of his son, he had every right to sex the bride Ntsina had not sexed. Sukude had been many years without tenderness, and his hasty, drunken spending in Bela was not at all the way he had wished to take his pleasure. As he watched her climb the hill, he decided he would not force her again. A woman who comes willingly is a better mate than one compelled. He went to the gate and waited, like a great lord, as Bela approached.

⁓

Piet left the forest, light-headed with adrenaline and hunger. He had been up since dawn learning by far the longest speech he had yet attempted. He now knew almost two hundred words of isiXhosa, which gave him a far greater understanding of what he was saying. As he walked through the trees, he thought of the stories he had been told in his youth: of a carpenter in Nazareth who was the son of God and had died on a cross; of the prostitute who had befriended Him, and cared for His abandoned body. Piet had a strong sense of forces unseen, but did not see why this particular narrative was truer than the ones the Xhosa had devised about ancestors who lived in trees, or the ancient Greeks about their pantheon of bickering deities, whose temples now lay in ruins.

At the edge of the trees he stopped, nerving himself against the pain he was shortly to inflict, for he was a man of tender feelings. If Bela and Ntsina were to live happily, their only salvation was money – and he was their only source of it. This truth allowed him to skirt his own compelling interest in the coming events. 'In an hour you must follow me,' he told Luvo, who nodded gravely.

Luvo had bargained a heavy price for his compliance, but now that the moment had come to bear false witness, even in the cause of liberating his people, he hesitated. His keen mind combed his Biblical recollections, and lighted on the injunction to give an eye for an eye, a tooth for a tooth. A lie for a lie. He watched as Piet rolled in the mud at the side of the stream, willingly bruising his body on the rocks, allowing their sharp edges to scratch his hands and face. There was a thorn bush growing nearby and Piet considered running through it, then decided this was unnecessary. It

177

would do him no good to blind himself. He ripped his shirt open and picked up the bust of Ntsina.

Then he ran, screaming, from the forest.

A young woman was the first person to hear him. She was in her family's mealie garden, setting traps for rats. Piet's shrieks made her jump. She turned to see the Strange One fleeing from the wood. She had twice visited King William's Town, and seen Strange Ones conversing, doing business, shouting at their servants. She had never seen one running in terror. It was almost the strangest of the many strange things she had witnessed.

⌒∽

Piet ran through the village. He threw himself onto the beach, covering the mud and blood with sand and rendering himself hideous, deranged. Then he took a deep breath and bellowed: 'Help! There is a monster!'

He screamed so loudly that Nosakhe, standing on the cliffs far above, heard him. A cloud of nesting gulls rose to the heavens and soared away, over the waves, like the retreat of powerful saviours. The chief heard him, and his wives, and Lundi, whose conscience, being blemished, made him fearful. 'Save yourselves!' screamed Piet.

He hoped for a stampede. When no one appeared he thought for an agonizing instant that he would not be believed. He was caught in the no man's land between advance and retreat – but Piet Barol had always advanced. He redoubled his efforts, and now his voice was hoarse and harsh and sounded other-worldly, which gave him confidence. In his mind's eye he saw the Creature he was running from, picked himself up and scrambled on. He passed the hut where, days before, he and Ntsina and Kagiso and Luvo had laid their plans, unified by common purpose. His shouts brought many running. Piet threw himself onto the rough ground beneath the Tree of Justice, and as good fortune would have it his cheek landed on a sharp stone, and the force of his body sent the gash deep, and blood flowed.

Noni heard the sounds and began screaming, and soon every baby in the village was crying, disturbed by their parents' fear. The chief had had a very bad day, and no sleep. He could not believe that further disasters were upon him – he who had always struggled to observe the laws of his ancestors. He was aware that his wives thought less of him than previously, and in any case he was no coward; so he strode forth from his hut, grabbing his leopardskin kaross and discarding his ceremonial spear for a sharper one, made for battle.

Kagiso would have gone first, but he held back for his father. Seeing him speechless before the Strange One, he forgot the obligations of deference and took charge. 'Take the Strange One inside and see to his wounds. Summon everyone in the village. Get them now.'

჻

The crowd that gathered in the King's Place was dishevelled and alarmed. While they assembled, Piet lay hunched on the ground, holding the bust of Ntsina close to him without revealing the face. He did not wish to repeat the performance to come. Nosakhe's entrance caused a sensation, because no one had seen her since the wedding but everyone had gossiped about her. Many were those who avoided her gaze lest she look into their souls and discern what they had said. Only Sukude was not there, since the steel door to his hut had prevented him from hearing Piet's cries.

The chief found his authority and sent for him. After some minutes of confusion Sukude entered boldly, facing his neighbours for the first time.

At last Piet stood and began the speech he had learned that morning.

Shaking and stammering, observing the impact of their own language on those listening, he told how he had followed Ntsina into the forest, to comfort him, how he, Ntsina and Luvo had chosen a bivouac near a stream. And then, settling into himself, aware that he held his audience spellbound, he described in detail

179

the monster that had slithered from the water as dawn broke –
a Creature with the head of a woman, the body of a mermaid,
and the tail of a . . . snake. He spat this word out, emphasizing
the slitheriness of its sibilance, and there was an audible intake of
breath. 'Luvo and I held back. But Ntsina was brave. He went to
kill the monster, to protect this village as his great-great-grand-
father once did.'

Piet stopped speaking. He had told his story so well that there
was a lump in his throat. The pathos of what he described made
tears well in his eyes – a horrifying sight to those who watched,
who had never seen a white man cry.

'Where is he?' said Nosakhe.

Now Piet revealed Ntsina's bust. He was met with absolute
silence. And then, as one, a wailing from the women and girls –
for Ntsina had many friends, and to see him turned to wood was
more than they could bear. The expression on the figure's face
could easily be construed as that of a brave man facing a monster.
Its anguish had the ring of truth. No one saw the rough rendering
of certain details. They looked into the lifeless eyes, saw the nose,
the mouth parted.

And they believed.

Nosakhe heard the wailing of the women, as though from a
far distance. She could not speak. Finally it was Kagiso who said:
'Where is the rest of him?'

This was the last of the answers Piet had prepared, but the exertions of his performance, and the pain of its reception, wiped
his brain clean. He looked at Luvo, who was watching Nosakhe,
stricken. There would be no aid from that quarter. He held the
silence, calming himself, and as he did so the tension in the room
rose in direct proportion to his hesitation. He had sat many ex-
aminations in his life and learned many pieces of music and three
languages. He searched through all this knowledge for the phrase
he had learned that morning, and if he could not have it all, then
for the first word of it; if not that, its first sound. He thought
of Stacey and Arthur, of Ntsina and Bela, of the wood he felt

180

destined to conquer. And then he said: 'Mermaid stream snake wrapped tail dragged.'

But Piet Barol was a perfectionist, and his clumsiness annoyed him. All at once he found the phrase, whole and perfect. 'The mermaid snake wrapped her tail round him and dragged him into her stream.'

⌒∽

The chief's messenger found Fezile the witch doctor just where Lundi had told him to look: in the Sunrise Tavern in King William's Town. The young man had not yet been circumcised, and like other well-brought-up young Gwadanans knew nothing of alcohol save the sips of homemade beer he was allowed on the great festivals. He therefore saw nothing remiss in the way Fezile swayed when his name was called, causing the beads of his headdress to jangle.

Fezile and Lundi had made each other's acquaintance in this same tavern. The riches of the Gwadanan villagers were legendary, and stories of them glowed brighter since the dispossession of the Bantu the preceding winter. The natives of King William's Town were not as badly affected as those in the rest of the country, for the town lay within one of the small parcels of land where natives might still buy and sell property; but the flood of refugees had been a great inconvenience – to everyone but the *sangomas*, to whom desperate individuals turned in their hour of need.

At first, Fezile had done a thriving trade in the provision of amulets and charms against further disaster. But by the time the second and third waves of refugees reached him, they were so poor they had little treasure to offer him. Besides, the casting of so many spells led to the disappointment of as many; and desperate people who have parted with their last goods in exchange for magical assistance are inclined to grow violent when such assistance is not forthcoming. All in all, it suited Fezile very well to absent himself from the scene of his labours for a period. He knew that in Gwadana the grain barns were still full.

Unlike Nosakhe, whose belief in the power of her magic was total, Fezile knew himself for the sham he was. Though he told an elaborate story about being called to the service of the ancestors as a young boy, by a spirit who had beckoned him into the forest, the truth was that he had won the robes of a *sangoma* from a very drunk witch doctor in a game of dice in a brothel at Butterworth. These robes gave him stature. By nature theatrical, he had no difficulty devising showy rituals and incantations, and had found that alcohol was an effective guard against the development of sympathy for those he defrauded.

When the chief's emissary explained the urgency of the crisis at Gwadana, and asked whether they might return by flying carpet, Fezile told him that such a mode of transport was forbidden to uncircumcised boys. He went back to his dwelling place and collected the empty skin of a great lizard, as well as several vials of powders and potions and the preserved embryo of a baby baboon. He packed these and his finest regalia in a bag and gave the bag to the boy to carry, and together they set off towards the Great Forest. They took the shortest possible route, and when the ground was flat the boy rode the bicycle in a standing position and Fezile wobbled on the seat. In the course of their journey, by subtle questioning, he obtained a complete and accurate picture of the complex web of family relationships at Gwadana, and learned of the scandal of Bela's entry into her new husband's kraal. He heard of the cow that had not cried, and of a conflict involving Ntsina Zini and his father, though his young guide was too embarrassed to speak of sex.

It was Fezile's luck to arrive at Gwadana at a moment of great drama, and to intercept the uproar occasioned by Piet Barol's presentation of Ntsina's wooden head.

He heard the wailing of the women as he left the trees. Knowing he would need his wits about him, he had resisted the temptation to bring a bottle of spirits with him. The result was that he felt unusually clear-headed and ready for anything. He flung open the door to the King's Place as Nosakhe, cradling the bust of her

182

grandson, sank to her knees muttering strange incantations. Every man, woman and child in the room jumped, as if the Creature Piet had described so vividly might be upon them.

The chief had never known such relief. He bade the witch doctor welcome and cleared a space for him. In the confusion of weeping and shouting, Lundi sidled up to Fezile and assisted him with removing his cloak of eland hide. He was annoyed that there were so many witnesses to their greeting. 'Make no judgement till we speak. Take only evidence.' And Fezile's spirits rose, for he knew Lundi was a sharp thinker.

Watching Nosakhe, Luvo felt sick with shame. In vain he told himself that he had merely translated the Strange One's lies; he had not told them himself. He had not thought beyond the performance he had helped Piet devise. Confronted by its impact, he knew the pain that lies in store for those who break the eighth commandment. He longed to tell Nosakhe the truth, but he lacked the courage to admit his own guilt before such a multitude. Nevertheless, he could not stand idly by. He went to her and squatted beside her. She was rocking over the bust, muttering. He tried to speak, but his voice was soft and she did not hear him. Finally he shook her, and loudly said: 'You have not seen Ntsina for the last time. The Creature cast a spell, but it can be broken. When it is, he will be flesh again. He may be rescued yet from death.'

Nosakhe looked at him. She heard in the strength of his voice the power of unseen spirits. She was astonished. The meek little boy who had visited her before the feast was incapable of pulling a rabbit by its tail, much less of confronting a monster and living to tell of it. But there was conviction in his face, and for the first time she felt fortified.

Sukude, standing against a wall, felt a stirring of pity for the woman who had made his own son love her – for anguish at the moment of death is the price that must be paid for love. He himself felt no such pain, but neither did he feel joy. Ntsina, after all, was his flesh, born of his loins. He wanted to take the bust, but he feared that some Bad Magic might attend it, and preferred to leave it clasped to Nosakhe's breast.

'I have come to warn you,' shouted Piet above the clamour.

It was only Noni, alone of that troubled multitude, who heard a colour in his voice that was the same colour she saw when she smelled a ripened lemon. It was a colour that connoted satisfaction, and indeed Piet was satisfied – for he had acquitted himself well. Noni began to scream for her father, and the chief went to her and picked her up, holding her close lest a monster take her.

As soon as she was in his arms, she stopped crying. She put her little mouth to his ear, and clung tight about his neck.

'The Strange One is lying,' she whispered.

Proceedings were adjourned for two hours, while Fezile the witch doctor was offered refreshment and water to wash. During this time, in the guise of assisting with his ablutions, Lundi acquainted him with all that had happened in explicit detail.

'But what of this mermaid in the forest?' Fezile did not like the idea of being asked to battle an actual monster. He had no doubt such things existed, and no faith in his chances against one.

'Monsters are best avoided,' said Lundi sagely. He told Fezile exactly what was expected of him, and hinted at the rewards that would flow. But Fezile was too quick to be bought with vague promises. In tight undertones they settled a great price, and it included comfortable accommodations in Gwadana for as long as Fezile might need them. He was in no rush to cross a forest in which a mermaid lurked whose gaze had the power to turn men to wood. 'I will need twenty cattle, and boys to tend them.' He paused, looking at the pleasant beach and thinking how preferable this charming village was to the town he had just left, crammed as it was with stinking refugees. 'And brandy.'

'Fifteen cattles,' said Lundi. Sukude had agreed to a maximum of thirty, and Lundi did not intend to settle for a commission of less than fifty per cent. 'And if you fail I will have you sent to the forest myself. Without,' he added, for he knew his mark well, 'any guide to lead you through the trees.'

Fezile looked at him, and then at the pretty village, and then at the trees in the distance. The sky had darkened and they had turned black.

'Very well,' he said.

⁓

It was done with a great deal of fanfare. Fezile wore his most impressive headdress, decorated with curving horns and the dark feathers of a sakabula. He wore a mantle stitched with cowrie shells and copper scales that he had bought from a theatrical costumier in East London, and a knee-length skirt of black sable skin. He tied the seed rattles of a witch doctor at his ankles and in this way ensured that all fell silent at his approach.

Nosakhe watched him through narrowed lids. She clung tight to the strange prophecy that had come from the mouth of the meek boy Luvo, whose face shone with goodness. It was a talisman that halted her tears, but she had no strength to resist the swift flow of events. Conscious of many eyes upon him, including those of a Strange One, Fezile stood fully erect. He was a tall member of a tribe not known for the height of its men, and he was aware that he cut an impressive figure. He took from his bag a pouch of lambskin, soft as velvet, and emptied it onto the ground. Out fell bones, chips of elephant tusk, cowrie shells and beads. He scooped up the debris and spat twice on the objects in his hands, in imitation of the Strange One gamblers he had observed in King William's Town, who often did this before they threw the dice.

Then he spread the relics on the ground and said: 'There is a woman here who is to blame.'

⁓

Bela had not been present during Piet Barol's presentation of Ntsina's head. She had spent that day, as she had spent every day since her parents returned her to the Zinis, along with fifty of the cattles that Sukude had paid as her bride price, meticulously cleaning every inch of Nosakhe's kitchen hut. She had not spoken one word, nor smiled. When she was awake, she cleaned, and pots that had been black for years now glowed bronze again.

It was Kagiso who came to fetch her, while others ran for her parents. Kagiso had known Bela since their infancy, and was a man who respected fine conduct. She had always pleased him, but her desecration of her husband's kraal left him disgusted. And wary. Possession by an evil spirit seemed the likeliest explanation for Bela's conduct, so brutally discordant with her nature. Before he entered Nosakhe's kitchen hut, he had to draw on deep reserves of courage. The blank gaze Bela turned to him at the mention of her name did nothing to reassure him. He had known those eyes dancing with laughter and merriment. Nothing of that remained, no spark of the life fire that had made people love her.

No one in the three generations of Gwadana's existence had been tried for demonic possession. Two adulterous wives had been branded with hot stones on their thighs before their execution, but there is nothing fearful or potent about an adulterous wife. These women had aroused pity in Kagiso, and scorn for the men who had failed to keep them faithful – for he knew that even the most outwardly modest woman has needs as vital as any man's. He did not feel pity for Bela, only concern for what might happen should the evil spirit within her do him a mischief as they descended the escarpment. He had with him a sharp spear, and was ready to drive it into her throat if necessary – but there was no need of this. At his summons, Bela rose with the grace he remembered, wrapped her blankets about her, and made her way serenely down the cliff path.

The cattles watched her go and lowed mournfully – for cattles have a sympathy many humans lack, and they, who had seen so many slaughters, knew that danger attended the gentle creature who followed the warlike man so meekly.

Under the Tree of Justice, Fezile the witch doctor was in full flow. He had questioned several wedding guests, who had confirmed that the bridal cow had not cried – a bad omen, as anyone knew, and an indication of the gravest displeasure.

'The ancestors always know what is to come.' He approached Nosakhe belligerently. 'Why did you not heed this warning? You, who know better than any here what is the meaning of a cow who does not cry.'

Nosakhe said nothing. She could not refute his logic. In her heart she knew she had failed the sacred obligation of the *sangoma* – to judge without tenderness. She had allowed soft feelings to prevent her from halting the wedding of her beloved grandson. Had she acted properly, nothing that had subsequently happened would have happened. As she understood this, she began to weep.

Consternation ensued. The villagers of Gwadana were accustomed to holding Nosakhe in high regard, and to living in fear of crossing her. This exhibition of human frailty destroyed her authority in their eyes. Sukude stepped forward. 'You stole my son and made him unmanly. Now he is gone!'

At this moment Bela and Kagiso entered the chief's homestead. All eyes turned to them.

'But I did not enter the kraal,' Nosakhe said.

Zandi was in the fields, tending the mealies, when she saw a boy running over the hill. Not a single visitor had come to them since the day of Bela's wedding, and the urgency of his movement told her that something dreadful was afoot. She laid down the scythe and hurried into the kitchen hut. Both her parents sat there, immovable. They had not spoken much since they had returned Bela to her husband's family. They were used to facing the challenges of life together; but to this challenge there was no solution, and this left them silent and despairing. Zandi loved them dearly and did her best to care for them, cooking and cleaning and tending the garden. The cattles had not been taken to graze on the hillside, for no boy had come to take them. She had seen that they were all fed, and that the cows were milked. She had made the milk her parents had not drunk into a soft cheese she had flavoured with thyme. She had found, as she performed these tasks, that her heart was flooded with sorrow for the sister she had once believed she despised.

There was a strength in Zandi, a protective instinct her mother knew. She had not been told what had happened in the bridal hut, but she knew Sukude, and she knew her sister's beauty, and she had seen the blood trickling down Bela's legs. She knew her sister had been sexed against her will. She found that she cared less for public opinion than her parents did, and was consumed by a desire to rescue Bela from the clutches of a man who had raped her. This desire allowed her to contemplate public disgrace without flinching. What she could not do was override her parents, and so she had burned within, and tended to them, and prayed earnestly to her ancestors for their aid.

When the chief's messenger, panting from his run, told them that they must go at once to the King's Place, for Bela was shortly to be questioned beneath the Tree of Justice, she ran as fast as her strong legs would carry her – faster than her parents, who felt sapped of their strength by this news. She arrived to see the Strange One who had danced with her sitting on the grass, covered in blood and mud and sand, and her sister standing in the centre of a large crowd. A *sangoma* she did not recognize was haranguing her, his words whipping the indignation of his audience. She knew him at once for a cruel man, and only the strong training of her youth prevented her from shutting him up with her fists.

Bela stared ahead, unseeing. She had withdrawn to a place deep within, and the accusations of this strange man in his headdress of sakabula feathers were far away – further than the cliffs on which the eagles perched. Her dignity did her no favours. Those who loved her most were most disturbed by the absence in her eyes, and everyone thought of the stories they had grown up on – of vulnerable people hollowed out by evil spirits, turned into zombies, to be used for the furthering of evil ends.

'The cow did not cry because the ancestors knew!' screamed Fezile. 'The cow did not cry because the ancestors knew that if the marriage went ahead you would defile their kraal!' He shook Bela's delicate shoulders, violently. 'I see you, Demon! The great Fezile sees you! Fly out! Be gone!'

Bela's parents arrived, and all their many friends felt sympathy for them – though none for the body of the girl they had loved as Bela. Her mother, whose impeccable conduct was the model for her daughters', threw herself at the witch doctor's feet. He kicked her savagely, his seed bracelets hissing like snakes, and turned to Bela.

'Get out, vile spirit! Out! You who are in league with the monster in the forest! You who have come to destroy the legacy of the Great Founder and the people who thought for themselves! Out! Out!'

From his cloak he removed the head of Ntsina that Piet Barol had carved, and held it inches from Bela's face.

For the first time, Bela's eyes focused. It seemed to those watching that something stirred within her. Horrified, they stared as a recognizable humanity returned to her gaze – a sign they took as confirmation that she had been possessed. Suddenly she was herself again. She began to moan.

'Look what you have done!' Fezile's spit flecked her face. He was beside himself. 'You have lent your body to a wicked spirit. You have defiled your husband's kraal and turned him to wood.' It was a jump of logic, but no one noticed. Piet, watching, steeled himself to intervene. He had not anticipated the presence of another witch doctor, nor the way in which his story would ricochet against Bela herself. *If they try to kill her,* he decided, *I will save her.* But he had no weapon, and there were hundreds of strong men to block his path. He felt very far from the comforting civilities of the Mount Nelson Hotel – a lone white man, at the furthest extent of a great forest, surrounded by savage Kaffirs.

But there was another man in the crowd who had no desire to see Bela dead.

Sukude stepped forward. 'I forgive you. And I will ask my ancestors to do the same.'

It was an act of clemency without precedent in the annals of Gwadana Village, and Sukude Zini had no reputation for being soft-hearted. He turned to Bela's parents. 'You raised your daughters well. It is not Bela's fault that a troublesome spirit has gained possession of her body. Human beings are not gods, and are not equal to them.' He looked at Fezile. 'How can we make this spirit flee?'

Fezile prised Bela's mouth open. 'I will pull you out, Demon!' He thrust his hand deep inside it. But Sukude prized Bela's tiny white teeth and did not want them damaged. He was about to pull Fezile back when Zandi launched herself from the edge of the crowd, her bulk an effective battering ram, and sank her teeth into the *sangoma*'s arm.

Shouts and cries and blood ensued. The chief, aghast, looked instinctively to Nosakhe, to whom he had always gone in times of trouble. She was sitting, back straight, arms outstretched – no use. Kagiso, still smarting from the wound his father's dithering had compelled him to inflict on his stepmother, did his best to keep silent. But as the chief hesitated, and the crowd grew riotous, he found within himself the true calling of a chief and at the top of his voice he roared: 'STILLNESS!'

The sound echoed off the distant cliffs, so loud it was. Everyone stopped. 'You must chase this spirit without hurting her.' His voice was iron. 'Step back.'

Everyone retreated, even his father. Kagiso lifted Zandi to her feet. He moved Fezile away from Bela, who was crouched over Ntsina's head, sobbing. Ntsina's face had drawn her back to herself. For the first time she felt guilt at what she had done. The prohibitions of her youth rose up, and she saw the enormity of her action. For a young wife to enter her husband's kraal! It was a breach so vast she had summoned a monster from its lair, and that

190

monster had slain her life mate. She began wailing, and this sound overcame her friends' fear. They went to her and held her tightly. Bela's smell was the same, and her tears were warm. Her friends' touch unleashed them in a torrent.

Kagiso's intervention made Fezile recover himself. It was clear that wounding this young woman would win him no friends – and less brandy. Instead, he threw dry *mphepho* leaves on the ground and lit them. The sweet smoke called everyone to their senses. He closed his eyes and went into a trance. He was very good at public trances, and soon he was swaying and his eyelids were bubbling. He murmured wild things beneath his breath. Nosakhe watched him. Her intuition, usually so true, was clouded today. She was deceived by his air of authority, her trust in herself profoundly shaken by his accusations – which were just. She looked at little Noni. She should be dust by now, eaten long ago by eagles. She had overturned the law by allowing the child to live. Now she was an easy vessel for any spirit. It was clear that many were abroad. As the *mphepho* smoke struck her nostrils, she attempted to enter a trance herself – but none would come. All she could think of was her foolishness in throwing away the hair and toenail clippings that allowed her to operate on Ntsina at a distance. If his spirit were indeed abroad, she could have used them to call to him – she who had the gift of summoning. She teetered on the edge of hopelessness, and all that kept her from fainting was the sense that she, alone of all who watched, had the power to lead the assault on the forces of darkness.

She looked at Luvo and the Strange One who had followed Ntsina into the forest. Would they be her allies? She was looking at Piet's face, in which she read intense alarm, when a memory of her grandfather surged through her, telling her that pain is the ancestor of courage.

Fezile stood before Bela and opened his eyes, as though re-turned to himself. He had the showman's gift for contrast and lowered his voice to a whisper. 'I have spoken to the ancestors.' All fell quiet. 'The wicked spirit within you yearns to enlist others in Her battle against the forces of light. If we are to preserve your body' – he could not help glancing at Sukude, who looked away – 'then the only way is to ignore your spirit entirely.' He turned to the crowd and raised his voice. 'This woman is to return to the home of her husband. She must toil there, to atone for the sins of her body. No one must speak to her.'

Zandi gasped, and regretted it – because Fezile turned to her and said: 'No one.'

'I will go with her.'

'That is a risky thing.' But Sukude might as well have two young women as one, thought Fezile to himself – even if the second is not so comely as the first. He smiled. 'Very well. But you must swear an oath to abide by my verdict.'

'I swear on your life,' said Zandi, smoothly.

'And what of the forest? And the Creature there?' Kagiso asked.

Now Piet Barol was called on, and Luvo translated. He was questioned minutely about the Creature: the colour of its scales, the length of its hair; where he had seen it. Piet invented freely, and Luvo translated unwillingly.

'The Creature came from the stream that runs beside the grove of your ancestors,' said Piet, to wails from the women.

'How did you escape?' asked Noni's mother.

'I did not look in the Creature's eyes.' Taking in the crowd, holding their attention, Piet delivered the most calculated detail of his story: 'It is her glance that turned Ntsina to wood. The same will happen to any who look upon her, or venture near the Ancestor Grove.'

Fezile had no wish to be asked to eliminate this Creature. Nor did he want to seem afraid. 'No one must enter the forest,' he said, 'on pain of death. Until I have consulted further with the spirits of goodness, any who enter will be possessed, and be drawn to the service of this Creature.'

'But our ancestors?' cried an elderly lady.

'You must worship them in your homes.'

And thus it was decided.

192

The gathering dispersed, exhausted. Parents held their children close to them, wives took their husbands' hands. For some time the Gwadanans had heard tales of great suffering beyond the forest that had been their fortress wall. Now that fortress had been breached, and even the bravest of them were afraid. In homestead after homestead that night, *mphepho* was lit, and prayers were uttered to the ancestors. There were many who knew, in their hearts, that they had neglected the worship of their ancestors, and they redoubled their efforts, fearful of the consequences.

Bela climbed the hill to the Zinis', Zandi beside her. Sukude waited a decent interval before following. He could hardly contain himself. As he was leaving, Piet Barol put his hand on his shoulder and said, in flawless isiXhosa: 'If you sex this woman, the monster will come for you.'

Sukude was astonished to have his innermost thoughts read so plainly. He muttered a curse under his breath and strode away, his leopardskin kaross fluttering behind him.

NOVEMBER, 1914

Two Months Later

8

Stacey Barol sat in the drawing room of the Mount Nelson Hotel wondering whether, in such dangerous times, she might drink a cocktail in public. In her years at the Opéra Comique, she had seen more than one of her friends succumb to the charm of a handsome adventurer, who got her with child only to leave her again. In the months since she had last heard from her husband, her certainty that Piet was not like these men had begun to quiver.

The departure of men of all nationalities from the Colony had left the room full of women.

She thought of her friend, Emilienne de Villeroy – a noted beauty, who had resisted legions of importunate suitors, only to fall at last for a scoundrel. She was now managing a boarding house at Marseilles. The chance that such a fate might befall her, if Piet did not return, had begun to haunt Stacey. So, too, the possibility that he might have died.

Throughout the long summer she had drawn comfort from the smell of Piet's suits, preserved in his closet. When she smelled, she believed. She remembered his devotion to their son, his painstaking attempts to please her, in bed and out of it. She had often been sharp with him, and now regretted it. If he had abandoned her, she would hate him. If he had died – even the thought could make her cry. The not knowing was terrible. She replayed over and over their last conversation, on the day Britain declared war on Germany. He had offered to come home, and she had told him not to. Had she done right?

She had waited so long for a telegram that when it came she found she could not open it. She had told Piet to send anything to the Mount Nelson, in case she should move. Now here it was: an envelope addressed to the Vicomtesse Pierre de Barol. It lay on the silver salver, potent as a sentence of life or death. She ordered another cocktail and drank it quickly. Then she asked for a letter knife, and one was brought. Stacey did not believe in God and went to church only for show; but in this moment, she prayed.

She opened it and burst into tears.

Observing her from the other end of the room, a crowd of ladies who usually feared her felt sympathy for her. The telegrams had started to come from Europe, announcing the deaths of brothers, husbands, sons who had gone home to fight. They thought of Stacey's handsome husband, who had always had a good-natured word for everyone. How terrible war is, they thought.

But the telegram in Stacey's hand read: WOOD READY STOP WORKSHOP BUILT STOP SEND TWO CARVERS AND ALL TOOLS STOP WILL COME FOR YOU WHEN HOUSE IS READY STOP UNDYING LOVE STOP

Sending this telegram from the immaculate post office at Butterworth had given Piet Barol a great deal of pleasure. He had no idea that the others he had sent had not been delivered – for the lines between Butterworth and Cape Town were not well maintained, nor was their improvement a matter of urgency in a country at war. Each had reported a milestone: the discovery of a tree of rare quality; the hiring of men from Idutywa to clear a path from the Ancestor Grove to the road; the chopping and seasoning of eight forest mahoganies. He left the post office, whistling, and called to Luvo, who was reading the newspapers outside the town's general store, ignoring the sharp glances of its white manager.

The wagon was loaded with the best steel scaffolding. From the hardware store Piet collected two chainsaws and eight sharp axes. At last he was ready. He had a route to transport his creations to the outside world. Soon he would have carvers to assist him in giving life to the designs that filled ten notebooks. His native labourers were dependable and hard-working. They were used to white men and answered to the names Blessing, Happiness, Grace, Wisdom and Brightness, since previous employers had found their Xhosa names too effortful. Piet had decreed that there should be no women in his camp, and one bottle of brandy a week between them all.

Their vigorous life, and its strictly limited pleasures, had made them strong and their leader more resilient. Insects still bothered Piet, but they no longer kept him awake. He had lost his fear of spiders, and learned to look carefully when he left their clearing to avoid basking snakes.

Piet had thought long and hard before purchasing a gun. He had done so, finally, when hyenas visited the camp one night. He kept it in a trunk to which he, Luvo and Ntsina had the only keys. Its possession reinforced his ban on women and drunkenness, for he knew the violence unleashed by alcohol and lust.

Luvo drove them home along the track the elephants had first carved. Its potholes were now filled. With strong horses, the journey from the Ancestor Grove to the edge of the forest could be accomplished in hours, not days.

Blessing and Wisdom stopped singing as the wagon drew up, and went to unload the stores Piet had bought. He had purchased chocolate for them and handed it round. They had never encountered a white man like him, and he enjoyed their gratitude.

Luvo supervised the storage of their provisions beneath the hides previously used by the villagers of Gwadana. Piet unwrapped one of the axes and tested its blade. It cut his finger and he was well pleased.

Ntsina watched them from the wood lot. According to Luvo, his ancestors' spirits resided in the heavenly mansions of the Christian God. Apparently Heaven was like a very nice Strange One town, its streets paved with gold, its gates made of pearls. Ntsina had no clear idea what a pearl might be, and Luvo's explanation did not

199

satisfy him. He did not see how anything that grew in a small sea creature could be strong enough to build a gate. Nevertheless, his grandmother had often told him that there are miracles beyond understanding, and perhaps this was one of them. Having come this far, he did his best to believe.

What he could not subdue was his affection for the trees themselves. It troubled him that Piet Barol should want to kill one. He watched as Piet went to the furthest edge of the grove and took off his shirt. The Strange One was strong. His muscles writhed as he swung the axe. Ntsina said two prayers – one to his ancestors, and one to Luvo's God, who was now their host.

A being does not live two thousand years without sound defences. Piet's blade barely scratched the bark. It was hard as granite. He swung again. His aim was better than it had been in his early days in the forest, and he did not swing wide. Nevertheless: nothing. He swung a third time, giving it his all, and the head of the axe cracked.

Ntsina was glad. He roused himself and climbed down from the hide. 'The Furniture Tree will do well for us.' He did his best not to sound gloating, for he did not wish the Strange One to act against the Ancestor Tree in order to prove himself.

But Piet Barol's competitive instincts were already engaged. 'It is because it resists so well that it will make furniture that lasts for centuries. Do not worry, my friend. I have planned for this.'

Blessing and Wisdom were unloading the scaffolding he had bought in town. Piet pointed upwards. The first branches began thirty feet above the forest floor. 'We'll cut those first, and dig up the roots at the same time. Blessing! Fetch Grace and dig some holes for me.'

❧

By the end of the following day, the holes for the foundation of the scaffolding were dug, and the poles inserted in them. Piet looked up at the vast blue sky. To approach it made him feel like a god. He had had a ladder made of pine – light enough to move easily when required. He set the ladder against the scaffolding and climbed to the first platform. 'Brightness! Happiness!' He felt bright and happy. 'Hand me the metal logs.'

They did so, and he fixed them into the ones beneath. The methodical placement of the poles, the careful tightening of the screws, raised his spirits further. He worked carefully, heart soaring. By the time he broke for lunch, the top of the platform was twenty feet above the ground. He climbed down. 'Time to start digging.'

Over his months in the forest, Piet had observed the Ancestor Trees at close quarters and given much thought to how one might be brought down. His experience with the axe had shown him that a straightforward assault on the trunk would not work. After lunch, which they ate together, he set Blessing, Happiness and Grace to digging the roots out. Grace was by far the strongest of them all – a man of sinew and taut, lean flesh whose expertise with a shovel was miraculous. The roots alone were as thick as a yellowwood tree. 'Dig until you reach the earth beneath,' Piet said. 'And dig away from the tree, until you reach the narrowest point of the root.'

The roots were smooth, almost the colour of ebony. He felt sure he could put them to good use – as table legs, perhaps, or the posts of a bed.

By unspoken consent, Ntsina was not asked to participate in any activity related to the toppling of an Ancestor Tree. Luvo did not wish to strain his new convert, just as his descriptions of Heaven were taking hold. Nor did Piet fancy testing the arguments by which he had persuaded Ntsina to permit the desecration of a place so long held sacred by his tribe. Watching them, Ntsina could not quell his conscience, no matter how often he repeated Luvo's assurances to himself. He picked up his spear and went into the forest.

He stayed away until sunset. He had speared two impalas, and dragged their carcasses behind him. He felt listless and sad. Piet had convinced him of the necessity of making money, so that he might rescue his wife and free them both, for ever, from his father's clutches and the scandal that must attend a woman who has entered her husband's kraal. With Piet, he had explored the towns beyond the forest. He knew there were houses natives might buy in Butterworth, which might be made very comfortable with money. He had been a hard master to Blessing, Happiness, Grace, Wisdom and Brightness, and fired without hesitation three early workers who were too slow.

Piet had exacted one promise: that he would make no attempt to return to Gwadana Village before the time to fetch Bela had come. It was a hard bargain but Ntsina saw its necessity. If his people suspected his complicity in the violence done the Ancestor Trees, he would be thrown from the cliffs – and nobody would mourn him. So he bided his time. He worked hard to chop the forest mahoganies and ready the camp for the arrival of the workmen Piet had summoned from Cape Town.

Luvo had told him of Kagiso's intervention and of Piet's warning to his father. Were these enough to protect Bela? He did not know, and his worry never left him. But the more he saw of the refugees who flooded the town, the more he knew that without money her future was hopeless. So he begged his ancestors to care for her, and hers to give her strength. He dragged the impalas into camp, kicking the dust to cover the warm blood that might tempt a leopard after them. He felt in need of consolation and prayed for a sign – any sign. The scaffolding depressed him further. He sat on a rock and put a sharp knife to an antelope's throat. He slit her neck and put his hand into the cavity, as his grandmother had taught him. He closed his eyes and reached sure. The first thing he clasped was her heart, still warm.

It consoled him.

'The day is coming when you will save your wife,' said Piet Barol, cheerfully.

'Make it come sooner.'

Ntsina left the clearing and gave the creature's blood to the stream. His grandmother had taught him many ways to

202

communicate across long distances. He beseeched the Water to take a message to the River that ran through the village, for the River to give it to the Sea, and for the Sea to deliver it where it was needed. A swift downward current brought the blood to a larger tributary, and by the time the impalas were roasting on spits above hot coals, its molecules, invisible to any human eye, were flowing into the lagoon that separated the homestead of Bela's family from the village proper.

Bela stood in the lagoon, cooling her feet in its waters. She had come in search of sponges, which sometimes washed up on the beach. From the cliff above, Sukude watched her. As she bent for a sponge, he stamped on a lizard and killed it. He had still not had her, having promised himself the pleasure of taking her willingly.

Her refusal to acknowledge him was a maddening aphrodisiac.

Bela turned back. Sukude was waiting, a cupful of brandy in his hand. He knew alcohol's power to tempt. But Bela walked past him and into the kitchen hut, where she set the sponges to dry and sat cross-legged before the great cauldron. This object was an heirloom, brought by the wives of the Great Founder on their first journey across the forest. It had been black as pitch for as long as anyone in the Zini family could remember. Now the brass shone like gold, for Bela had made a project of it.

Standing in the sea, Nosakhe saw little Noni playing on the dunes with her brother Kagiso. The child's every breath was a reproach to her. In the aftershock of the news of the Creature in the forest, Fezile the witch doctor had detected a service he might do a grateful chief. Without consulting Nosakhe, he had conducted an arresting ceremony in which he confirmed Noni's gift of Farsight and lifted the threat of execution. Watching the sightless thing run and laugh, Nosakhe cursed herself for her weakness. There were now two possessed women in the village, and her grandson was a prisoner of the mermaid snake.

The stories told to Xhosa children about the malice of dark creatures are vivid, and Nosakhe knew no rest. She had searched every inch of Ntsina's hut for a hair, a nail clipping, anything she might use to summon his soul. Only with his soul at her side might she attempt a reincarnation. But the cleaning before the wedding had been thorough, and there was nothing.

A seabird was flying towards her, white and graceful on this bright day. She expected it to perch on the cliffs with its brethren, but instead it alighted on a rock beside her. She looked at it and it flew on – away from her, towards the forest.

At last! A sign.

She summoned Ata and hoisted her bag of charms on her shoulder. She ran through the village, fleeter of foot than she had been in many years. The white bird alighted, waiting for her to catch up, then went on, towards the forest. Ahead were the trees, green and inviting on this sunny day. She paused, asking Ma for permission to advance.

At that moment, a hawk dropped from the heavens and caught the sea bird and tore it apart in mid-air.

$\backsim$

In the forest, the scaffolding had reached the first branch of the Ancestor Tree. Piet was satisfied with his work and climbed down. Wisdom had filled a black rubber bag with water from the stream and left it in the sun at noon. Piet had stitched this bag with his own hands and added at one end the rose from a watering can and a little valve. It gave him great satisfaction to have found ways of being comfortable in this dark jungle. He took the bag and went through the trees to the spot he had set aside for washing. They had built a wooden fence for modesty and hauled stones from the river bed for the floor. He hooked the sack over a pulley and winched it upwards, till the rose was two inches above his head. Then he took off his clothes, kicked them away, opened the rose and let out a long, relieving sigh.

This was *much* better than a jug and a basin.

The water poured over his shoulders, its temperature delight-ful. He closed the rose and soaped himself, then opened it again and washed. The bag held ten litres of water – more than that and the pulley would not take its weight. He had learned to use every drop. When he was done he was clean from head to toe and in a very good mood. He put his feet into his work boots, to avoid clogging his toes with sand, and walked naked to his quarters.

The European War looked likely to last much longer than expected, and Piet did not care to hurry home to be enmeshed in it. He missed his wife, and yet the efforts he was going to on her behalf soothed his feelings. He had intended, when the idea of living and working in the forest first came to him, to establish Stacey in a house at Butterworth. He still meant to offer her this, and had been careful to hold back enough money to pay for a fine one. But he had built such picturesque accommodations where he was that he was seized by the idea of sharing them with his family. Of being with them always.

Piet had not grown up in comfort, but in his middle twenties he had lived for a time in the most luxurious house in Europe. He had never been a man who mistook expense for quality. Life in the forest had attuned him to many subtle pleasures, and he had built for himself a dwelling he would not have exchanged for many a metropolitan palace. Much less for a trench in France.

The structure was of wood. It faced twenty-six degrees east of true north – which meant it avoided the direct sun on hot summer days like this one, and would be warm when the winter set in. It was set back from the clearing, and Piet had cut down eight trees to make space for it. The sudden percolation of light on the forest floor had cast a powerful spell of fertility. Twenty trees distant he had found a creeper with bright purple flowers in the shape of trumpets, and had transplanted it and trained it over his doorway. Already it had rooted. The air was voluptuous with its scents.

The proportions of his new home were rectilinear, its walls straight. The doors fitted. So did the windows. He had made a floor of mud, ox blood and straw, and had himself stamped it flat and smooth. Its roof was tin, and musical in the rain. At night, as he sketched at a small table to the light of a lantern, the cottage took on the air of an illustration in a fairytale – a house deep in the woods, where magic took place. Wisdom and Happiness were building three more rooms, but this first would be forever his – his workshop of the mind, its walls bedecked with sketches of the masterpieces to come.

He had purchased a double mattress and soft linen in King William's Town, and a handful of other European objects that, to his eye, gave the rustic place great charm. There was a silver jug for flowers, a porcelain basin for shaving, six fine china plates, six tea cups, a set of silver knives and forks he had found in a second-hand shop, whose bends and crookednesses spoke to him of cheery meals. In Cape Town, corrupted by the lordliness of the whites, he had developed messy habits. With servants to pick up one's clothes, what point was there in picking them up for oneself? Here there were no servants. He took care of himself and his own quarters, and discovered that it gave him joy to sweep his little room on a Sunday morning.

Prolonged experience of the Xhosa had led Piet Barol to certain opinions that would have horrified his friends at the Mount Nelson Hotel. He had discovered, first of all, that the Xhosa were no less honest than Europeans, and often more so. He never locked anything away from his companions, except the gun. He had kept up his isiXhosa lessons, at first to ease communication with his men, and more recently because the language had cast its spell on him. Now he understood at least half of what was said around the camp fire, and loved to lose himself in stories of ancient feuds and magical adventures as the sparks leapt and the coals glowed. On the table was the newspaper Luvo had purchased in Butterworth. The horrors it recounted were a world away on this gentle night. He dressed and went outside. The stars were out. The town was far away. With no electric light to compete with, the heavens were infinite. He felt that life was treating him very well.

Piet intended to reward his employees handsomely for the risks they had faced in order to help him, and this stilled his conscience when he thought of the look on Nosakhe's face as he told the story of the mermaid snake. How much happier she would be, he thought, when Ntsina returned to her with the funds to keep her comfortable in old age. He and Luvo had had many conversations, progressively frank, about the political situation in South Africa. He found that he could not fault Luvo's logic, nor find grounds to justify the abolition of black property rights. Piet was moved by the stories of suffering Luvo told him. To throw families out in the dead of winter – it was not right. There was a pleasing symmetry to the fact that the profits he would wring from Percy Shabrill, who had made his money so vilely, would be used to send a petition to the King of England – whose ministers alone possessed the power of veto over this law.

Piet did not have the heart to tell Luvo that the European situation, in which the King of England needed every South African soldier he could lay his hands on, did not auger well for the success of his mission. But he also knew that when nothing is attempted, nothing is gained. He took his own circumstances as eloquent proof of this fact.

When he had gazed long enough at the stars, Piet went back to the clearing. The impalas were ready and the fire sent their shadows huge against the trees. Wisdom was an excellent cook. His mother owned a restaurant at Butterworth, serving the native location, and he had brought some of the flavours of the town to the meats of the forest. Piet was habitualized to the toughness of game. With a little judicious guidance he had brought Wisdom to a stage where he could make a decent meal. Hard work made him hungry and he ate his fill, listening to Blessing tease Happiness about Happiness' sister, who was something of a flirt.

In the matter of women, Piet Barol's conscience was unblemished. He was proud of that fact. He was not used to going so long without sex, having been accustomed to ample opportunities since his earliest manhood. But he had promised Stacey, and watching the white men in Butterworth stumble out of native brothels had robbed an affair of all its glamour. There were, in any case, no attractive white women in Butterworth, and the idea of being with a black one was sufficiently strange to add a further barrier to any action he might repent. He did his best to think of Stacey when he took his pleasures in his own hands, and often did so – though not always, for his past offered a range of beguiling memories. Sometimes he found himself thinking of a woman in Amsterdam, in whose company he had gone from boyhood to manhood. At others, of a music teacher who had initiated him into certain gentle arts. It was pleasant to revisit these adventures, but he was too satisfied by the present to wish a return to the past.

'When will your carvers arrive?' asked Luvo.

'Soon.' Piet stretched. 'And my wife will come soon after.'

Ntsina had learned the English word for 'wife', and hearing Piet use it he asked Luvo to translate. When he had done so, Ntsina said: 'I thought no women were allowed in this camp.'

'That's what the Strange One said, certainly.'

They did not pursue this line of thought, for it ended in the unshiftable truth that Piet was the boss, and he could do what they could not.

Ntsina observed the haunch of impala he held in his hand. He put it down without touching it, and stared at the flames.

⟨∽⟩

In Cape Town, Stacey Barol made a decision. Having found her husband, she would not invite Fate to separate them by failing to follow him. With some of Percy Shabrill's advance she re-hired Ierephaan and Mohammed, the two best Indian carvers in the Colony, whose expertise had won Barol & Co. its reputation for quality. She felt safe in the company of these men, who had always been scrupulously polite to her. 'Indians understand deference,' she sometimes said to her European friends. 'It's why they make such good waiters.'

At the Mount Nelson, she made out she was returning to Europe, but she forbade her friends from making a fuss, or seeing her off at the docks. 'I can't bear scenes like that. You'll make me sob,' she said. And the women looked at her more tenderly than before, and felt less afraid of her and wondered whether, perhaps, she had liked them more than they knew. She dismissed Arthur's nursemaid with a month's wages, and had their possessions put into storage. As she selected which of her dresses to part from, she found she could not contemplate separation from many of them. Besides, she had a handsome husband who would be starved of women. She must do her best for him.

So it was that when they took the train for East London, they had a great deal of luggage. Stacey's last action was to send a telegram herself. ANTICIPATE BUTTERWORTH THREE DAYS STOP HAVE IEREPHAAN MOHAMMED AND ALL TOOLS STOP. She hesitated over how to end. A telegram could not do justice to her feelings towards the man who had honoured his promise to her. She left it there. She knelt down and looked at Arthur. She had washed his hair the night before. He was dressed in an Eton collar and looked terribly smart. 'We are going on a great adventure. To find your papa.'

The child's excitement gave her courage, as she handed Ierephaan and Mohammed their third-class tickets. She felt a speech might be in order, but she had never had her husband's gift for making inferiors love him. 'Do buy yourselves lunch,' she said, instead, and gave them a ten-shilling note.

❧

As his wife fanned herself in a threadbare train carriage, for even the first-class compartments on the East London train placed a strain on the cultured soul, Piet reached the top of the scaffolding and hoisted up the double-ended saw he had bought in Butterworth. He had chosen Grace to help him, and they stood at opposite ends of the platform, the blade poised above the bough. This limb of the tree was much less thick than the trunk, for the Ancestor Trees devoted the bulk of their strength to their wide bases, using their branches only for the support of foliage. At first the saw's teeth made no purchase. But Grace was persistent, and very strong, and after repeated efforts they made an indentation in the bark, which focused attention made a groove. And then they were on their way.

After an hour, Piet's hands and back were so sore he decreed a pause. But Grace's lust for destruction, which lies latent in most human souls, had been brought to the surface by the scale of the challenge. He shrugged when Piet suggested replacing them with Blessing and Brightness, so Piet carried on as best he could, settling into a rhythm, the pain in his body focusing his mind on the grandeur of the undertaking.

The tree had survived seven hundred and eleven fires, one hundred and eighty-six droughts – the severest of which, in the mid-thirteenth century, had lasted eight years. It had repulsed the assaults of legions of beetles and termites. Eight species of bat fed from its fruits. Every bird in the forest sought refuge from snakes on its boughs, for the trunk was so tall that only the hungriest serpents attempted it, and these were too weak to scale it.

The tree had not noticed the pin pricks of Piet's blunt blade. She did notice the attentions of Grace's saw, and sap rushed to heal the wound. But sap is at a disadvantage against steel. The branch almost took the scaffolding with it when it fell. Creatures many trees distant heard the sound. Baboons screamed in alarm. Birds rose into the heavens. The three thousand, six hundred and fifty-eight insects on it clung tight as their world began a terrifying plunge downwards. Piet, watching from below, cheered heartily. Ntsina looked away. He had killed many animals, and chopped many trees. But to kill this tree, the empress of the forest. . . He had no words for it, and did not forgive himself his part in her assassination.

They made an incision in the trunk, where the severed bough had exposed tender wood. The artery carrying nutrients from the forest floor to seventy thousand leaves was severed, and the gash attracted swarms of bees and flies. The tree's siblings, sensing a crisis, diverted stores from their own roots to the aid of their troubled sister.

Over the next days Happiness and Brightness dug deep around

the roots, loosening their ages old connection to the earth. Piet felt a delirious delight as he examined the wood that was to be his material. The outer layer was hard as iron, but the wood within, though strong enough to endure for centuries, was not too hard to take the detail of the carver's gouge.

The tree had never endured such a purposeful assault. She did not know what to make of it. The consciousness of a tree, though profound, is not swift. The price for longevity is paid in speed of movement. Only the insects stayed loyal, able to conceive of no other home. She felt her root connections to other trees begin to sever as the hairless apes dug deeper and deeper. Her roots stretched far, but the apes dug further. And then the training ropes were applied. And thus the mighty tree was felled.

And there she died.

⟡

The crash of the slaughtered tree was heard throughout the forest, and in the village of Gwadana. Kagiso proposed an expedition to investigate the cause of the mighty disturbance, but Fezile the witch doctor, seeing no way to evade participation in such a rash venture, sternly forbade it.

Nosakhe waded into the ocean up to her breasts, imploring the Sea's aid. She looked askance at Bela, who had turned her attention from the cauldron to the fence around the vegetable patch, which had become the straightest, sturdiest fence in the village.

Zandi heard it, and thought of the Strange One, who had bravely ventured into the forest, never to be seen again. She had so enjoyed dancing with him. She wondered if he had evaded the Creature, but she knew she had no powers of divination and made no attempt to discover the truth.

Sukude heard it. The sound struck terror into his soul, for Bela's steadfast refusal to acknowledge him had stirred the anxiety of a man who knows he has done wrong, whatever the law says. He thought of the cow who had not cried. Perhaps his ancestors had looked into his heart, and disapproved of what they found there.

Fear induced a foolhardy daredevilry. If some great punishment awaited him, he might as well seize pleasure while he could.

❧

Deposited at the sleepy provincial station of East London, within sight of a slumbersome sea, Stacey Barol gathered herself and asked in her smartest voice how she might reach Butterworth. She was an instant grandee. Every Bantu who passed averted his gaze, in case this magisterial white woman took offence. Every white man who saw her doffed his hat, and not a few were stirred to chivalry.

There was a public bus that ran along the narrow gorge to Butterworth, but the gentlemen who clustered around Stacey and her cartload of luggage would not hear of her taking such a thing. The whites of East London, conscious of being on the edge of their world, were scrupulous in enforcing the dignity of their race. They would not countenance a white lady taking a native conveyance.

Stacey spent the night at an hotel, while her carvers went to find their own lodgings. By the next day, word of her arrival had reached the mayor himself, who attended her at her hotel and suggested she take a private car and a driver – his car, if she so wished. He had meant, he said, to visit Butterworth for some time. He would gladly take her, and her servants could come on with the trunks – if she trusted them, of course.

'They are devoted to me,' said Stacey.

She had had a fretful night's sleep in an uncomfortable bed, kept awake by her ignorance of her husband's address. She had sent her telegram to the post office, hoping he would find it; but she could not know if he had. The mayor was a terrible bore, and his conversation offered no distraction from her worry. Only Arthur did. Sitting beside her in the seat, he was so clearly his father's child that she felt Piet's presence in his profile, his blue eyes so full of life and optimism.

She put a brave face on things at the Butterworth post office, while the mayor hovered at her side. Having been brought thus far, she wished to be rid of him. 'I am looking for my husband,' she said. 'The Vicomte de Barol.'

The clerk looked at her blankly.

Stacey described Piet as best she could, though modesty prevented her from saying how handsome he was. Absent this telling detail, the clerk could not help her. He had seen many dark-haired European men in their thirties, for many came to this out-of-the-way town to evade their responsibilities elsewhere. None of his customers was sufficiently well dressed to be imagined as a consort of this extraordinarily fine lady, and he said as much. It was the worst compliment Stacey had ever been paid.

She stumbled out of the post office and got rid of the mayor. He was most unwilling to leave her alone, and she was compelled to be quite harsh with him. There was a single hotel at Butterworth, the Travellers' Rest, and she permitted him to escort her there. She tried to take a suite, but they had no such thing as suites at the Travellers' Rest. She settled for their best room, and was very haughty with the proprietress. As she reached the turn in the stairs, she caught the mayor looking up at her and nodded in farewell. The worry on his pink face pushed her own nerves to the brink of collapse. They collapsed entirely when the clerk opened the door to room 312, which was plunged in darkness, and lit a gas lamp. It had clearly been unoccupied for a long time. The cockroaches, used to untrammelled freedom, dashed for cover as the light exposed them – but not fast enough to escape detection. The clerk affected not to notice them. Stacey dismissed him, sat on the bed and drew Arthur to her so that he would not see she was in tears.

'Don't worry, Mama.' The little boy squeezed her tightly. 'I will take care of you.'

His courage destroyed the last of Stacey's equilibrium. She had a good relieving cry, at the end of which, doing her best to smile, she said: 'We have come on an adventure. Daddy will join us soon.'

She lay awake that night. She had left the lights on, to deter the cockroaches. She was in the grip of a wild fear. The lies she had told in Cape Town made it impossible for her to return there. Confident of her good fortune, she had lived well in the city and now the edge of her finances was uncomfortably in view again, as she had promised herself it would never be. With her dwindling capital she must house and feed herself, her son, her Indian servants. What if the money ran out before Piet . . . ? But she could not pursue that thought.

A voice in her head reminded her that Piet had not summoned her. Perhaps he was still making preparations for her reception. It seemed foolish to have crossed the country on a whim, and she saw that fear had been her motivation. Fear that if she did not find him he would disappear. Stacey knew that fear is seldom a wise spur to action, and this knowledge heightened the unpleasantness of the room with its velveteen drapes and plush cushions. A room that belonged in a bordello, not an hotel. Finally she exercised the emotional self-control she had developed over twenty years of wandering, and locked her feelings securely within her. She closed her eyes and tried to sleep. When she opened them again, cockroaches and ants had reclaimed their former haunts, and several enormous spiders were hunting them. She got up, and got dressed, and stormed downstairs, demanding to see the owner.

While Stacey was shouting at the fat Afrikaans lady who owned the Travellers' Rest, Sukude left his hut and made his way to the edge of the cliff. The sunrise was spectacular, but he had not come to look at it. He knew that Bela waited to clean his hut until she could be sure he was not in it. He stepped further away, his back to the homestead, every nerve on full alert. He heard the creak of a hinge as she left the kitchen hut. With studious unconcern he picked up a stick and pretended to look at it closely. This allowed him a glimpse of her form as she hurried past the vegetable patch. She opened his door gently. She had greased its hinges with sheep fat, not wishing to alert him to her presence in a room with a lock. Once she was inside, he hurried back. Outside the door, he collected himself. He wished for tenderness, and had washed attentively that morning.

He opened the door and went in.

Bela was sweeping. She did not look up as he entered, but the animal in him sensed her sudden tensing. She swept meticulously, and gathered the ashes from the fire in a fold of her cleaning blanket. The Zinis' three buckets had disappeared during the wedding feast, purloined by guests unable to resist their temptation.

Sukude had not courted a woman for many years. He felt clumsy and uncertain. 'You are a very good cleaner,' he said.

He had spoken to her three times before. She had not once replied. Nor did she now. She worked more quickly, sitting on her haunches as she used a small brush to get into the cracks in the mud floor.

'A very good cleaner,' he repeated.

He went to her. Her neck was so soft, so graceful in its curve. He stroked it and felt her stiffen. He had been so dazzled by her physical presence he had forgotten to take the precaution of locking the door. He remedied this now, and when the lock clicked Bela worked faster still.

'Sit down.' And then, when she made no answer: 'Rest, sister. Take a moment from your labours.' He reached for the brandy bottle and poured for them both. 'Drink this. It is good for you.'

Bela swept on.

'Drink it.' he said again, more firmly. And then, crouching to his knees so his face was level with hers: 'It is time you were with child. The future of our house depends on it.'

With the speed of a striking cobra, Bela ricocheted up from the floor. The force of her movement knocked him over and the dust in her apron filled his nostrils, making him sneeze. He grabbed her ankle. With the power of a thoroughbred horse, she kicked his hand away. Her foot connected with his skull and his head hit the hard floor.

She has the power of a demon, thought Sukude. He looked at her closely. There was a violence in her eyes that shook him. He knew he was stronger than any woman, but demonic strength is another matter entirely. A seagull had landed on the roof of the hut. It sensed a stand-off between two hairless apes and flew away, cawing.

'It can be easy,' he said, assuming a softer tone. 'I am not your enemy.' But as he got to his feet and approached her, he saw that every muscle in her was ready for violence. He might have her, but he would not escape without his own injuries. He looked into her eyes, and his nerve failed him.

'Get out of my hut, you unnatural bitch,' he said.

They had taken care that the great tree should fall away from the centre of the grove, and it broke the canopy for two hundred feet. Piet walked its length, unable to contain his joy. Every spore and seed in the vicinity was woken from its long slumber in darkness. There were nutrients aplenty on the forest floor, sent down from the canopy by the trees themselves, for it was they who breathed out the water that fell as rain. What had been missing for uncounted years was light. At its magic touch tendrils sprouted, nosing their way through the leaf litter. Some seeds had lain waiting since Piet Barol's grandmother was a girl. Now they sprang into action, germinating with all their might. No human saw this race, for few hairless apes have the gift of subtle sight, but the insects knew. They came in their swarms to feed on hopeful new shoots, to lay their eggs beside plants that would nourish their offspring. The race towards the light was vicious and fraught with danger. Only the hardiest, and the luckiest, would survive.

But at the outset, every living thing had a chance.

A day's acquaintance did not improve Stacey's opinion of Butterworth. Neither did the fact that she had been compelled to ask strangers, many strangers, if they had seen her husband. She knew it made her look like an abandoned wife. There were hours when she was able to feel certain Piet would come for her. But her enquiries revealed a worrying fact: Piet, always at the centre of things, a man people remembered, had made no impression on anyone here.

The exception was the owner of the general store, who knew exactly whom Stacey was talking about when she described Piet. But this gentleman obeyed an iron code of confidentiality – especially where wives were concerned. He had abandoned two himself, and seven children who now lived at Port St Johns. He had no inclination to betray a fellow rake, so he told Stacey vaguely that he had many European customers, most of whom had dark hair. 'I never look at the eye colour of any man,' he said.

Stacey asked about other nearby places, but her nerve failed her. If she went to King William's Town in search of Piet, and he happened to visit the post office at Butterworth in her absence, she would miss him – perhaps for ever. She made the clerk promise to send a boy to fetch her if anyone answering Piet's description should come. Twice she was summoned, and the disappointments were shaming.

Stacey had left the United States at the invitation of a French aristocrat who had promised to marry her after an expert seduction. She had arrived in France to read in the newspapers that he had married a Belgian railway heiress. This experience began to poison her dreams and then her waking hours. She had been brought up in a respectable Chicago family. She thought of her parents, her brother Fred. Where were they now? Did they mourn her? Would anyone, if she died in this ghastly hole?

The answer to this question was bleak. When Ierephaan and Mohammed asked when the master would come for them, the knowledge that no one in the world knew where she and Arthur were began to press on her like a rock. On the afternoon of her second day, having rushed to the post office at the summons of the clerk, only to find an elderly Belgian in a cheap suit, she stepped out into the hot sun and had an attack of panic. Her heart began to beat much faster than usual. Her adrenaline levels skyrocketed. This induced a paralysis she had never felt before. She found she could not take a further step. She could barely reach the bench on the post office veranda. She could not unfurl her parasol, nor hold it to shield her complexion from the vicious sun. Arthur was at the Travellers' Rest, in the care of its receptionist. Even the thought of him could not induce movement. She felt she could not move until she had told someone where they were – but past lies blocked every possibility.

Her Cape Town friends believed her to be in Europe. She had ceased corresponding with her own family almost a decade earlier. What could she say to them? The sun, passing the midpoint of the heavens, began to cast long shadows and the street emptied. Darkies who until now had averted their gaze stared at her frankly, for she sat still as a statue. She could not move until she had thought of one single friend, but the urgency of her need inhibited inspiration. At last the sun's reflection on a polished weather vane hit her eyes directly. The sparkle of silver triggered the memory of a platinum stake, set with emeralds, and then the aquiline perfection of Louisa Vermeulen-Sickerts-Longchamp's profile. A friend of her husband's youth. A rich woman. Someone who would help her.

The post office was closing. She forced herself to her feet and staggered in, holding her hand up. Holland was not at war. If something were to happen to her, if Piet never came . . . Perhaps this woman . . .

She took a slip of telegraph paper and examined her purse. It still held Louisa's card. In pencil she wrote PIET MISSING STOP. She hesitated. Then: PRESUMED DEAD STOP. She was a proud woman and never asked directly for aid. But the lady on whose mercy she now threw herself was a world away, and desperation lessened the tingle of shame. FUNDS LOW STOP PLEASE HELP STOP. And she gave the address of the Travellers' Rest, Butterworth.

The clerk was privy to all the town's secrets. He could not wait to get home to tell his wife what had occurred. With indecent haste he tapped out the telegram and charged Stacey for it.

⌒

The next day, at the height of the noon heat, Piet's wagon nosed the crest of the hill and began its descent to Butterworth. He was hot and sticky and unshaven. The bathing facilities at his camp made shaving laborious, and he was looking forward to the attentions of a barber. At Idutywa he sponged his neck and armpits and changed his shirt, his only concession to European sensibilities. Then he pressed on to the town, hoping that his carvers had arrived.

Sitting on the veranda of the Travellers' Rest, Arthur saw him. He began shrieking and waving his arms. But false alarms had hardened Stacey, and she rose unwillingly. All she saw was the back of a covered wagon.

'Daddy's come for us!'

'He will come for us.' She sat down again and continued fanning herself. There were even more flies at the Travellers' Rest than there were cockroaches, and the assault of insect life put her in a bad temper. She had spent the night before chasing mosquitoes around their room, maddened by their whine. It requires great alertness to kill a mosquito. By the time she had hunted them all, she was too wakeful for slumber. A little breeze rose up, and sleep beckoned. 'Do be quiet, darling.'

But Arthur Barol would not be quiet. He was a dutiful little boy, and scrupulous about holding hands while crossing streets. '*Be quiet!*' she said, and even this did not silence him.

'I know it was Daddy! I know it. I know itIknowitIknowitI know—'

She opened her eyes. Sleep would be impossible. Again.

'If we miss him, how will we ever find him?'

This articulation of her innermost fear roused Stacey. She allowed herself to be led down the stairs to the street. The wagon had drawn up at the post office, and Arthur slipped his hand from hers and charged towards it. She had no intention of running – not in this heat, not when she was the object of such provincial curiosity. Besides, her shoes were high heeled and too tight. Her feet had swollen in the hot weather.

Standing at the post office counter, scribbling a telegram to his wife, Piet thought the sound of his son's voice screaming 'Dad-dddeeeeee!!' must be a symptom of sunstroke. A fury of blonde curls, pummelling his thighs, showed him otherwise. There, in the flesh, jumping up and down, shouting at the top of his voice, was Arthur.

Their joy at being reunited moved the entire post office. The clerk, whose wife was sentimental, stored every detail to recount to her later. Piet hugged Arthur so tightly he feared he might bruise him. 'Where's Mummy?' he asked, his heart soaring.

'In the street! We came to find you!'

Stacey saw Arthur dash into the post office. Knowing he would be safe there, she slowed her pace. The post office's walls were thick stone, and she heard nothing of the commotion within. It is often at the moment when hope is truly abandoned that a cherished wish is granted. So it was in Stacey's case. As she gathered herself to face the ignominy of another unsuccessful interview with the post office clerk, a man bounded out, carrying Arthur on his shoulders.

Piet looked so different that for a moment she thought she was dreaming. His appearance had the contorted logic of a dream – he was himself, but not himself. He had three weeks of dark beard, and the sunburned face of a farmer. His hair was long and uncut, unbrushed. His smell— it was richer, deeper, more intense than it had ever been – the smell of a man used to arduous physical labour. The contrast between them was arresting. Everyone on the street watched as Piet put the little boy down and picked up the haughty woman in the embroidered gown, lifting her as lightly as if she were weightless, and swung her round and round on the pavement as she screamed.

They remembered themselves sufficiently not to kiss in public. But as soon as they reached the Travellers' Rest they had to have each other. Piet greeted Ierephaan and Mohammed, who were greatly relieved to see him, and gave Arthur half a crown to spend on sweets. This inducement had no effect at all. Arthur only wanted to be near his father, to touch his newly strange, bearded face, chattering at the top of his voice. For half an hour Piet listened, and Stacey, watching him, felt the knowledge of who he was return to her – a hundred times stronger than it had ever been. Finally, she said: 'Your papa is terribly in need of a rest. When he's had it, we will come for you.'

'Let me rest with him!'

'It's a grown-up kind of rest,' said Piet, looking at his wife.

Room 312 of the Travellers' Rest, Butterworth, had witnessed many exuberant couplings, though rarely between a husband and a wife. Nothing in their history prepared the velveteen drapes for what they witnessed, nor the mattress for the pounding it got. Stacey, impeccably correct in public, was no prude in the bedroom. Her husband's new strangeness enthralled her. The squishy fat she had come to accept in Cape Town had gone. Everywhere she touched was muscle and sinew. His calloused hands sent ripples across her skin, his new strength augmenting his old gentleness.

They were not gentle for long.

Months apart from each other made them frantic, and Piet's new smell aroused in Stacey a response that lay deep in the core of her being, aeons beneath the layers of civilization. As he entered her, she buried her nose in his arm pit, and all the worry of weeks gone by was obliterated.

He came in her, and was instantly hard again. The banging of the headboard sent the cockroaches scuttling into dark recesses, from which they did not dare emerge. Six spiders watched them, and a mosquito clung tight as he sank his proboscis into Piet's right shoulder. The surge of blood was too much for him, and he withdrew, gorged, and flew too close to a spider web. The spider saw her chance and feasted as she watched the merriment below.

'I like your beard,' said Stacey, when they were done.

'Then I shall keep it.' He turned on his side and looked at her. 'What made you come? I hadn't sent for you.'

'I wanted to see you.' She suppressed another, smaller voice that whispered: 'I had begun to doubt you.'

'How has Bumble Jug been?'

'He has missed his papa terribly.'

'I can't tell you how happy I am to see him – and you, my darling.'

She put her arms round his neck and kissed him deeply, but as she felt him stiffen she pulled tantalizingly away. 'I must share you with him now,' she said.

'He's the only one you need ever share me with.'

9

Piet stayed in Butterworth that night, and put Arthur to bed with tales of the forest that was to be their home. In his descriptions of the trees, the animals, the fire they sat round every evening, he got carried away and made the boy afraid. He had forgotten his son was barely six years old.

Arthur, raised on European fairytales, knew that witches live in forests, in gingerbread houses, and lure children to unspeakable fates. 'Is it like the forest Hansel and Gretel were lost in?' he asked, his lower lip trembling.

'It is quite a different sort of forest altogether. And besides, I shall be with you always. No witches will touch you while I am there.'

The boy curled tightly against him. His trust brought a lump to Piet's throat. All the discomforts he had endured, of which sucking up to Percy Shabrill was by far the worst, were more than repaid by Arthur's confidence. What a splendid boyhood lay ahead of him! He would be a man who knew the wild, who could take care of himself beyond the drawing room. He sat quite still as Arthur's breathing slowed, and his little body grew heavy. Piet looked up to see Stacey watching them. The tenderness in her face made the moment perfect.

'We have made a little angel,' he said.

'Looks can be deceiving.' She smiled and kissed his head. 'He won't wake till morning, unless he has a nightmare. Let's have a bath.'

There was only one bath at the Travellers' Rest, but it was long and deep. When Piet ordered the hot water for it with a series of strange clicks and fizzes, Stacey observed the impact an instruction in his own language made on their waiter, who had been sluggish for her, and felt the wisdom of her impulsive choice of husband. When they were alone, she stepped out of her dress and undid the buttons of Piet's shirt. 'The profile of an aristocrat, the body of a farm hand. What an excellent combination.'

They got in, facing each other, their legs in a tangle. 'About that,' said Piet.

'What?'

'The Vicomte de Barol. I'm rather sick of him.'

'Are you?'

'Aren't you?'

'Well we can't escape him now.'

'Here we can. No one knows us. Let's just be ourselves.'

She sensed an implicit criticism, since it was she who had suggested the advantages of assuming an aristocratic title. He saw that he had irked her, and kissed her knee. 'He did well for us in Cape Town. We can always return to him if we wish. But now we're here, and the war's on, we needn't do anything we don't want to.' He smiled. 'Besides, I rather like the ring of Mr and Mrs Barol. And since Holland is not fighting, no one will think it strange that I'm not getting myself blown to bits in France.'

'That alone is an excellent reason to stop being French.'

He told her most of what had happened since his arrival at Gwadana.

'Wherever did you get the idea of the mermaid snake?'

'It's rather jolly inventing a monster.'

He described his discovery of a sumptuous tree, his flight from the forest with the bust he had carved of his friend Ntsina.

'You mean Percy Shabrill's garden boy?'

It was strange for Piet to consider Ntsina thus. 'The very one. He is much more than a garden boy.'

'Clearly.'

Piet omitted certain unpleasant details: the rape of Ntsina's bride on her wedding day; the look on Nosakhe's face as she saw her grandson's severed head. Already the incidents were finding the shape they would assume as anecdotes. Whoever won the war, he felt sure the Mount Nelson's bar would remain unchanged.

'Have you made any furniture?'

'Not yet. I needed carvers and tools, and you've brought them. I came here to find the finest wood in the world, and get it cheap.' He brushed an intimate place on her body with his big toe, and she drew breath sharply. 'I think I've done rather well, all things considered.'

His toe probed deeper and she sank into the water, pushing herself against him.

'Very well, darling.'

'Shall I get you a house in town?'

'*This town*? I don't think so.'

'Will you follow me into my forest?'

'I'd follow you anywhere, Piet Barol.'

❧

'You cannot waste your life here, my sister,' said Bela to Zandi. They were in the hut Ntsina had been born in, the one in which his mother's body had been laid after the puff adder's bite. Bela was standing on a table, furiously scrubbing the beam. It was black with the soot of ten thousand fires.

'I will never leave you,' said Zandi.

Bela stopped scrubbing. In the days when she had been the most popular girl in Gwadana, Zandi had been the recipient of all the nastiness she could not express elsewhere. Now it was her sweetness that had nowhere to go. She stopped scrubbing and got down from the chair. 'I have been cruel to you, my sister. I am sorry.'

Zandi considered these words, which were true enough. She found that none of it mattered anymore. 'I will never desert you,' she said.

'But you have a future.' Bela took her hand. 'You will never find a husband while you live here. They will think the evil spirit within me has possessed you too. If you do not marry there are many joys you will never know. You and I will be the last of our father's line. He and mother will have no descendants to worship them.' She began to cry now, she who had always taken pride in her father's pride.

The prospect of their parents' spirits wandering, homeless, after their deaths, with no one to worship them, was enough to bring tears to Zandi's eyes too.

'He will get me soon enough, whether you are here or not. The evil spirit has made me weak.'

'There is no evil spirit in you, Bela.'

Bela went to the shrine she had made at the opposite side of the hut. 'I think Sukude put the demon within me the night my husband left.' She thought of the semen Sukude's straining cock had flooded her with. 'I do not know how to get it out.' She kissed the bust of Ntsina's head, and began to sob. 'He was a good man, my husband. He was gentle to me.'

'His spirit lives. Luvo told us so.'

Bela began to wail. The gulls had grown used to the wailing of this hairless ape woman and did not stir from the roof of the hut. When she stopped, she was angry. 'They are cowards in this village. They have mounted no rescue party. That *sangoma* should lead us forth to battle. I believe he is afraid.'

Zandi embraced her. She had no words of comfort, for all Bela said was true.

'You must find a husband. For yourself,' said Bela. 'For our parents. You must have a child. Your presence here does not lessen my disgrace, but with each day your reputation grows less. I cannot bear it.'

'And I cannot bear the thought of leaving you alone.'

'Then please bear that. For me. I mean this, Zandi.'

Bela stepped back from her sister. She was present behind her eyes, in a way she rarely was. 'To know that you are happy, that our parents' line will continue. That will give me strength I sorely lack.'

The waves crashed on the cliffs far below. 'Is this the demon speaking? Or is it you, Bela?'

'It is me, my sister.'

'Then tell me something only you and I know.'

Bela hesitated. The sisters' rivalry meant she had to rummage in the distant past for a shard of intimacy that might persuade Zandi. At last she found one. 'When I was little, and Aunt Nonkosi visited, I was afraid of her headdress. You stole it in the night, and burned it, and she never knew what became of it.'

Despite herself, Zandi smiled. Aunt Nonkosi had been proud of that headdress. 'I will do as you say, dear sister. But on one condition.'

'What is it?'

'That if you need me you will summon me.'

'I will surely do that.'

'And what of him?' They both knew whom she meant.

'That is a battle I must fight alone.'

❧

As Zandi packed to leave, all that Bela had said rang true – and more besides. No man had asked to be Zandi's husband when she was the eldest daughter of a respectable family with a large grain store. How much less likely that anyone would ask now – when she had lived in a bewitched homestead, with a sister possessed by a demon. Years without being chosen had hardened Zandi to love. A husband, in any case, would take her from her parents – and she had no wish to leave them. What she had not considered until this day was the loneliness of her parents' spirits without descendants to care for them. She had reached the age at which children see the sacrifices that went into rearing them. That her parents' spirits should roam the Underworld for all eternity, lonely and forsaken! The prospect was not to be borne. And yet, how could she prevent it?

She sat down on her blanket and blinked back tears. Tears would not bring them descendants. She made a mental inventory of every man in Gwadana. None was brave enough to risk the Bad Magic that would linger round her name after her departure from the Zinis'. Might one be bought? Her family was rich now, even after returning half of Bela's bride price.

But Zandi had pride, and it forbade the purchasing of a husband.

She had heard that the mother of the Strange One's god had conceived a baby without the aid of any man. Might that be possible in her case? She did not trust Fezile the witchdoctor to undertake such a spell. Nosakhe might once have accomplished it, but she was now a shadow of herself. It seemed that an immaculate conception would be difficult to accomplish. This returned her to the mental search for a husband – and again her analysis yielded no candidates.

It took her an hour to see that the answer to her problem was close at hand, and that with one sacrifice she might achieve many good things. Her heart started to race. She had almost abandoned herself to a life without sex. Deprived of Bela's outward advantages, she had learned to seek her pleasures alone, but her successes had heightened, not lessened, her yearning for a partner. She stood up and smoothed her hair.

Then she went to the door of Sukude's hut and knocked.

When he opened it, she said: 'If I give myself willingly, will you swear on your ancestors to leave my sister alone?'

The Barols set out early the next morning. Only under protest did Stacey leave her two largest trunks in the care of the Travellers' Rest.

'You won't need gloves and hats where we're going.' Piet kissed her neck. 'You are beautiful to me without all this clutter.'

'It's myself I dress for,' said Stacey. Nevertheless, she was the same woman who had followed a charming Frenchman to Paris when she was seventeen. She had courage and a sense of adventure. As the wagon trundled off she felt like one of the wives who conquered the Wild West – a prospecting pioneeress. She was wearing her prettiest day dress and the post office clerk, watching them go, was moved by this image of requited love.

At the Travellers' Rest, the proprietress, to whom Stacey had been very disagreeable, sent for the trunks and had them opened. She was far too fat to profit from any of the gowns, but the accessories would do nicely; and she had a married daughter at King William's Town whom some of the looser things might fit. Before Stacey had reached Idutywa, her remaining possessions had been neatly parcelled and sent on their way.

'If they ever come back, tell them there was a fire,' said the proprietress to the receptionist.

❧

Nosakhe lay awake in the dark hour before dawn, beseeching Ma for a sign. She knew that her battle with Atamaraka was near at hand, and she had never felt weaker. Her mind was confused. She had expected to have Ntsina at her side, and perhaps the Strange One too. For what other reason had Ma sent him to her? Many years of unquestioned authority had left Nosakhe without the resources to deal with self-doubt. It was plain that her own conduct had been imperfect, and she bitterly repented her many failings. Chief among these was the way she had tossed into the Sea all she needed to summon Ntsina home. She lay awake, fretting and useless. And then she heard the unmistakable bleat of a billy goat.

She got out of bed. She was cross, and opened the door of her hut to find that the goat she had bartered for honey before Ntsina's wedding, the goat that had ruined her fence in his desire for her she-goats, had returned and was attempting the same tricks. She ran at him, but he did not flee.

This billy goat had expended great resources, intellectual and physical, on the problem of how to escape from the goat pen of the Mhaga family, to whom Nosakhe had sold him. This family kept cattles, not goats, and he had been alone. He was not made for solitude, nor for the deprivation of female company at the height of his studly powers. It had taken weeks of surreptitious digging to undermine the Mhagas' fence, and his journey through the dog-filled village had frightened him. He did not intend to be defeated by one old woman, and instead of running away he put down his head, faced her with his horns, and charged.

To his great satisfaction, the old woman stepped out of the way and made no attempt to follow him into the nanny goats' enclosure. He was warmly greeted by his lady friends, who had felt his absence keenly and knew no jealousies. Soon he had forgotten all about the ape woman, and had he turned to look at her he would have been astonished to see joy in her face.

Ntsina had cared for this billy goat, born in midwinter to a mother who had died before she could suckle him. He had fed him milk from a sheepskin gourd and slept with him until he was old enough to face the cold alone. Nosakhe knew that humans and animals can bond beyond the reach of understanding.

The Great Goddess had sent her the assistant she needed at last.

⤬

'When I first came,' said Piet, 'there was no track. We had to walk.'

'I hope you don't expect me to do that.'

'Of course not, darling. Welcome to the road I made.'

Like a showman, he pulled back the screen of fronds and debris that hid the entrance to the elephant avenue his workmen had enlarged. Arthur, looking at the dark forest, began to cry.

'Cheer up, Bumble Jug.' Piet got onto the box beside him and cuddled him. 'Jog on.' He cracked the whip, and the horses moved forward.

From ten trees away, an adolescent baboon on his first solitary patrol screeched a woo-woo bark. Every ape within a thousand trees heard him, and the strongest males leapt at once into the trees. The presence of hairless apes in the forest was a development of the greatest interest to its baboon residents. Over generations, they had become accustomed to occasional incursions of the hairless apes, but the sudden residency of a band was a different thing altogether. Five troops of baboons lived in the forest, and a brutal war eight years previously, during which three alpha males had been killed and seventeen babies had their heads bitten off, had left them inclined to stick to their own territories. The hairless apes obeyed no such protocol.

This baboon had had a fortunate upbringing. His mother was a high-ranking female, playful and affectionate with her children. His older brother had taught him to climb, and stamp his feet, and throw rocks: everything he would need for successful dominance displays. Thanks to these advantages, he had begun asserting himself early, and by the age of nine had already dominated each of the fifteen females in the troop.

Watching the hairless apes pass so close, aware that other males of his own kind would soon be along, he was seized by a strong desire to steal something from the strangers. A trophy, to show he feared nothing and no one. He would not risk an assault on the fully grown male, but there was a baby hairless ape, whose fur was a very strange colour. This baby was holding a bright orange sphere, which became instantly attractive. He jumped through six trees in succession. He was above the wagon now, and the little hairless ape was looking at him. He nerved himself for the most daring act of his life.

'There's a monkey in the tree, Daddy! Look! A monkey!'

Arthur had spent many hours at the Cape Town Zoo, staring through the bars of the monkey enclosure and weeping. His mother had stopped taking him, because the imprisoned creatures' plight distressed him so. In vain Stacey had assured him that baboons had no feelings. They wouldn't mind being shut in cages.

'How would you like it if someone locked you in a cage?' was Arthur's irrefutable reply. The prospect of monkeys made him see the forest in a very different light. 'Stop, Daddy! Do stop!'

'Not now, darling. We've a long way to go.' Piet was aware

of the look on his wife's face and laid a comforting hand on her knee. 'We're quite safe. They give us humans a wide birth.' The wagon jolted forward, and the baboon's opportunity for daredevilry slipped past him. He stamped his foot in a paroxysm of regret. To his astonishment, the baby hairless ape turned its strange head and uttered several cries in its own tongue. The baboon watched, perplexed, then leapt down to the ground to catch what the baby had thrown.

It was the bright orange sphere he had intended to steal. He watched the hairless apes disappear. The thing in his hand smelled delicious. He sank his teeth into it and knew earthly bliss. He had eaten half of it when the male members of his troop arrived. He refused to acknowledge the other males, but handed the alpha half the orange. In a complex succession of leaps and barks, he conveyed a glorious tale of how he had dominated a hairless ape and taken this prey from him.

The troop's leader looked at him quizzically. Here was an alpha in the making. Perhaps he should kill him. He took a taste of the strange fruit, but it made him too happy for violence against his own kind. Instead, he let the young baboon groom him as he considered the future.

❧

The casting of a spell of Reincarnation is a mighty undertaking, not to be lightly attempted, for the only way to rescue a soul from the Underworld is to seek him in the realm of Death. Nosakhe had attempted the spell once before, at the age of twenty-two, in the weeks after her grandfather's journey to the spirit realm.

The Great Founder had greatly enjoyed life as the undisputed chief of a grateful village. Though he had left a stable settlement in case his granddaughter should fail, he had asked her to come for him. Nosakhe had nearly died in the attempt, which can only be made once. Today, as she lit the *mphepho*, she went over the reasons for her earlier failure: Pride and Inexperience. The greatest of these was Pride, and she vowed not to fail her grandson similarly.

At twenty-two, full of the certainty of youth, she had gone after her grandfather's soul alone and unaided. True, she had been the only *sangoma* in the village, and circumstances were not conducive to seeking aid from beyond the forest. This was no longer the case, and she gave thanks to Ma for sending another wizard to assist her. She was aware that securing the co-operation of this wizard would require humility, a quality of which her share was not abundant, but her purpose shone so brightly she was able to contemplate the self-abasement required.

She washed methodically and put on her headdress. The hut was full of sweet *mphepho* smoke, and her trance came easily. She emerged from it calmer than she had been since the morning of Ntsina's wedding feast, and ate a hearty breakfast before descending the escarpment, Ata at her heels.

⁓

Fezile the witch doctor had wisely declined the hospitality of the chief's family. He did not relish intimate observation, and had asked if perhaps there was an empty hut he might use. There was not, and Lundi had offered to take him in while one was prepared. Long weeks in close proximity had not endeared them to each other, and Fezile had started threatening Dark Magic on the men who were building him his own hut – for builders at Gwadana are not more punctual than builders in any other place.

When Nosakhe knocked at his door, he was in a particularly bad mood. He had not had a stiff drink in weeks, and the quantities of homemade beer he had drunk made him gassy.

'What do you want?' he said.

'I have come to seek the aid of a great wizard,' said Nosakhe.

Lundi, sitting on the floor of the pig pen with his ear clamped to a crack in the mud wall, felt a twitching of fear. He had every respect for Nosakhe's powers. The possibility of Ntsina returning from the dead to wreak vengeance on his wife's defiler, and those who had aided her defilement, was alarming. Which said . . . The dangers of the spell of Reincarnation were proverbial. The prospect of Nosakhe Zini securely shut away in the Underworld was very appealing.

Lundi had not slept well since summoning Fezile, partly because intimate experience of Fezile's habits had made him doubt that he would long sustain his reputation as a man of magic. Partly, also, because he feared Nosakhe. Her withdrawal to her homestead had unnerved him. He had often looked at her smoking fire, wondering what charms she was casting and whether any of them were aimed in his direction.

Fezile had a good poker face, and was compelled to use every trick he had learned at the gaming tables of King William's Town to disguise his astonishment at Nosakhe's request. He furrowed his brow in sympathy, raised his head, then inclined it, like a puppeteer manipulating himself with invisible strings while his mind went elsewhere.

On no account did he wish to be drawn into an encounter with the Queen of Evil. Nor still did he wish to be exposed as a coward. His builders had assured him that his own homestead would be ready before the next moon, and he was enjoying life in this peaceful village, whose inhabitants were so eager to extend him credit. He had refused to cast any spells on the grounds that he was saving his energies to battle the Creature in the forest, and this meant that public opinion of his powers remained undimmed.

'Please,' said Nosakhe, concluding the speech she had prepared.

'Which part of the operation would be my responsibility?' asked Fezile, and swallowed.

'I would like you to control the Sea.'

⌒⌒

Ierephaan and Mohammed, sitting in the back of the wagon with their tools, hoped that they had done right in accepting this eccentric offer of employment. They were the two finest furniture makers in the Cape Colony, and in other circumstances would have had many opportunities. The Empire's call for every able-bodied man to lay down his life for the honour of squabbling sovereigns, all related to each other, had given them a strong reason to venture beyond the reach of the recruiting sergeant.

They had plenty of experience of the feuds that can ravage an extended family, and knew that the wisest keep clear. Their great-grandparents had come to the Cape as indentured labourers, and they had known each other since they could crawl. Their parents lived on the same cobbled street in the colourful neighbourhood of Cape Town known as the Bo-Kaap where Indians lived in houses with roofs and windows and, in some cases, indoor lavatories – palaces compared to the quarters of the Colony's blacks. They had been to the same highly competitive school, and for years had disputed the class medal between them.

Ierephaan was the jollier of the two. Mohammed was tall and thin and had little time for human beings. He lived for wood and stone, and the miracles he could achieve with them. They treated one another with an excessive politeness that masked a fundamental wariness – for each wished to be the *best* cabinetmaker, and knew that the other was his strongest rival.

'By the grace of Allah, may we have done the right thing,' said Ierephaan, breaking the silence that had lasted since their departure from Butterworth. He was a social fellow, and found Mohammed's long silences trying.

'Only Allah knows,' said Mohammed. And then, reaching the end of a long interior argument, he unconsciously voiced its conclusion: 'It is better than dying in a field of mud.'

Ierephaan made a comfortable resting place for himself between the packing cases, trunks, and crates of fruit and vegetables that Piet had bought. He lay down, closed his eyes, and thought of his wife and seven children. He had left them with enough money for three months, but that was the totality of their savings. He swore by Allah and all that is Holy that he would work harder, and better, than he had ever worked before. He opened his eyes. 'We should be . . . allies, you and me,' he said. 'We are the only True Believers and the only civilized people in a hundred miles.'

235

It was a delicate way of suggesting that they bury the enmities of the past.

'I have no need of allies,' said Mohammed, 'when Allah is my guardian.'

⌒

When they were three hundred yards from the Ancestor Grove, Piet got down from the box and went on ahead. He had not finished his preparations for his wife's arrival and knew the slovenliness of men.

He had never been more grateful for Luvo.

In Piet's absence, Luvo had taken it upon himself to conduct a spring cleaning of the camp. The vast corpse of the Ancestor Tree still lay where it had fallen, but the ground around it had been swept and cleared. A fire pit had been dug, and logs for the evening bonfires neatly stacked. Luvo had supervised the completion of the cooking shed and personally washed every one of the tin plates and cups. He had seen to the roofing of Piet's new rooms, and washed the glass in their windows. He was laying the evening bonfire, taking great pleasure in the symmetrical crisscross of the logs, when he turned to see Piet Barol behind him.

'Where's everyone?' asked Piet.

'They've gone hunting. It is time to make biltong.'

Piet poked his head into the cooking shed and saw the gleaming crockery. 'It looks marvellous. Thank you.'

Luvo glowed. The Strange One had become much more observant of the trouble others went to on his behalf during their sojourn in the forest. His gratitude alleviated for Luvo the otherwise considerable burdens of the experience – the insects, the exclusive company of men, the fear of wild animals.

'I found my wife and child in Butterworth,' said Piet. 'They came to find me.'

'I am looking forward to making their acquaintance,' said Luvo, though in fact he was alarmed.

'Then I'll get the wagon.'

236

As she entered the grove, Stacey Barol could not stifle a gasp of wonder at the majesty of the trees. Luvo's quiet good manners were reassuring in this strange place, as was the camp's perfect order. The fear that had built within her during the drive began to lift.

'Were you really the man who mixed the Shabrills' cocktails?' She smiled at him. 'How lucky we are to have tempted you from them!'

Luvo's recollections of Stacey did not all accord with the impression she now made on him. In her pretty striped dress, her hair about her shoulders, she looked very fetching against the backdrop of the trees. Her smile made her look friendly.

'I'm afraid you'll find things rather primitive,' he said.

'It's only dirt I object to.' She nerved herself to peek into the kitchen. 'And I can see you have kept things splendidly.'

The word 'splendid' had often been applied to Luvo's school-work. To hear it again was immensely reassuring.

'Our labourers do try, but Bantu men are not well trained in the domestic arts. I do my best to keep them in order.'

'And a very good job you do.'

Watching his wife with his friend, Piet Barol experienced an explosive surge of love for her, and gratitude for being rid of all they had left behind. In Cape Town, she had mocked people – often for his benefit. This had amused him, but somehow the joke had grown stale. 'You two will be great friends, I can see.' He lifted Arthur down from the wagon. 'Arthur. Meet your uncle Luvo.'

❧

'I think "uncle" was rather over-egging it, don't you darling?' asked Stacey, as he showed her where the latrines were. They looked back at their son, who was talking rapturously about the monkey he had seen on the way.

'Luvo is a sound fellow. As educated as you or I.'

She looked at him, as though about to say something. Then she smiled. 'Show me more.'

'Let me see to our Indians.'

Piet showed Ierephaan and Mohammed to the accommodations that had been prepared for them. Then he took his wife's hand and said: 'Welcome to your new home. *Our* new home.'

He led her across the clearing and through the line of trees. Their room was in perfect order, the silver cutlery gleaming. Luvo had placed a vase of flowering branches on the table, beside the lantern Piet now lit against the dark.

'I know you're used to finer things.'

'It won't be for long.'

He showed her the room that was to be their sitting room, and then the one that was for her alone. They were clean and inviting, their walls painted white. He badly wanted her to be delighted, and she was conscious of failing him. She made various polite exclamations, but it was only when she saw Piet's sketchbooks that she gave way to pure excitement.

She sat at the table, leafing through pages of chairs and chests and tables and bookcases, astonished by Piet's exuberance. He had copied none of the fashions of the world they had come from. Elephant trunks curved graciously round the backs of chairs. Antelope legs supported tables. Percy's library shelves showed creepers and trumpet flowers growing through the books. 'You're a marvel,' she said.

'It's the wood that's the marvel. Come and see.'

He took her over every inch of the trunk they had felled, and described in great detail how they had vanquished the tree. Stacey knew how much fine wood cost. To have this much, so cheaply! It began to compensate for the rustic discomfort. She nuzzled against him, banishing thoughts of the latrines. 'You are clever,' she said.

It made him happy to have impressed her at last. The huntsmen were far off and would not return that night. The two Indians joined the Barols and Luvo at a table by the fire. Stacey went to get a shawl before dinner, and when she returned the strangeness of the scene caught her short. There they were – two brown men, a black one, a white man and a white child, who was making everyone laugh. In the town she would have found something repulsive in this overthrow of the social order. Out here, beneath these trees, as the insects roared and the bats swooped and the stars shone, she wondered, for the first time, whether perhaps notions of one race's superiority were rather silly. Politics had never interested her, and she did not pursue this thought. But she did cross the clearing towards them feeling light of heart, and when she reached the table every man stood for her, and she sank to her seat as graciously as at the grandest dinner.

Twelve baboons watched them. The light of the hairless apes' lanterns caught their imagination. The one to whom Arthur Barol had given an orange, unable to contain himself, screeched in excitement. The alpha hit him – to silence him rather than hurt him. He made a succession of low grunts that meant: 'It is better to watch and be ready, than to rush and be found wanting.'

As the hairless apes laughed, the baboons began dozing off. They were early risers. Only the youngster watched on, which meant that it was only he who saw what lay beyond the door of the kitchen hut: a crate piled high with oranges.

All the Barols slept in the same bed that night, since Arthur's had not yet been made. The boy was euphoric to have both his parents so close. He chattered until he abruptly fell asleep, and when he had, Stacey shifted and put her head on Piet's chest. She could feel his beard scratching her face. Together they looked up at the ceiling and listened to the symphony of the forest.

'You've gone native.' She tried to sound light-hearted.

'Don't worry. I still know how to wear a dinner jacket.'

She turned and looked at him seriously. 'You won't forget, will you?'

'Forget what?'

'The world out there. Our world.'

'The one where all the men are killing each other? I won't forget it, my darling.' He cupped her face in his hands and kissed her. 'I intend to conquer it.'

Ntsina, returning from the forest with a kudu the next day, was astonished to be met by a little blonde Strange One. His thoughts ran at once to magic. It was the blonde Strange Ones who were said to be half-man, half-plant – but in truth this one did not closely resemble a head of corn. His face was too round, too much like— and then he saw, as Arthur laughed, that he was Piet's son.

'There's a monkey! A monkey!' cried Arthur, pointing.

Blessing, Wisdom, Brightness, Grace and Happiness, who had been hunting with Ntsina, were shy in the presence of a female Strange One. They had seen them before, of course, but only in Butterworth – where the female Strange Ones were nastier than the males. They were taken aback when Stacey said 'Good morning', and then 'Pleased' in their own tongue. She had taken herself in hand and decided to prevail by charm. Being friendly was putting her in good spirits. The beast Ntsina had killed impressed her. Piet had told her he was more than a garden boy – it seemed this was so. She made the hunters coffee while they washed the blood from their hands and bodies. She served it at the table, and set out oranges – one for each of them.

Ntsina ate his, an inscrutable expression on his face. Inside, he was seething with rage. That the Strange One should have a woman when he prevented all the Bantu men from doing similarly! He thought of Bela – gorgeous Bela, so much lovelier than this skinny Strange One with her simpering smile.

Stacey had judged, correctly, that Ierephaan was the more sociable of the Indian carvers, and was asking him questions about his family. She thought well of herself for showing interest. Ntsina did not for one moment believe that she would be so sweet if there were other Strange Ones to observe her – or if she did not need him and these other men as much as she did.

In the world outside, the Strange Ones ruled. They had the guns and the automobiles – the machines that gave them their unfair advantage. In the forest, the Bantu was king. Without his hunting skills, they would not eat. Without Grace's strength they would never have got that tree down – a tree he had once worshipped. Her fallen corpse was a perpetual complaint against him. He turned his eye from it, and his gaze fell on the Strange One child.

For the first time since his return, his heart softened.

'Come here, my little man,' he said to Arthur, in isiXhosa. The child looked at him, alert for meaning. He was not afraid. He had not yet learned the Strange Ones' vileness to the Bantu.

'He is very keen on monkeys,' said Luvo.

'Tell him I will show him some.'

This was all the inducement Arthur needed. He allowed himself to be lifted on to Ntsina's shoulders, and Piet placed a hand on Stacey's to silence her objections.

Ntsina took Arthur to a fig tree that lay beyond the stream. He had seen before he left that its fruits were hours away from perfection. Arthur began to jiggle up and down. The tree was full of samango monkeys – agile and dexterous, with comical beards that delighted the child. Ntsina approached as close as the monkeys would allow, but the fruit was a strong inducement to them to remain where they were.

To see his favourite creatures on a tree in a forest, gorging happily; to know that there are monkeys in the world who are freed from their cages at the zoo, made Arthur reverential with happiness. They stood in silence, man and boy absorbed in contemplation of these beasts who looked so much more like they did than any other beasts of the forest, and yet were not like them at all. The sugar in the figs sent tidal surges of energy through the monkeys, who began leaping and shrieking.

It was only when they started copulating that Ntsina took the child away.

$\backsim$

The spell of Reincarnation is first and foremost a spell of opening. Nosakhe's grandfather had taught it to her painstakingly, and she knew that having found her ally she must choose her element. Would she meet Death in Fire, Air or Water? She chose Water, for she had always trusted the Sea. The spell's trickiness is partly due to the fact that it is many spells: one to open a gate between the realms of the living and the dead; another to summon the soul of the person to be reincarnated. In this case, adding to the difficulty, she would also need to break the magic of the Creature who had turned Ntsina to wood.

Nosakhe had decided against slaughtering the billy goat and using his heart. Ntsina had loved that goat, and this made her feel tenderly towards him also. Besides, Life is a potent ally in the battle against Death. She cut the hairs from his chin and plaited them tightly into a bracelet. It was a white bracelet, and white is the colour of the *sangoma*. She took this as a sign that she had found the path she must follow.

Nosakhe told no one but Fezile of her intentions, and was unaware that the breaking of the sacred bond of secrecy between *sangomas* did not trouble him, and that Lundi also knew. Lundi told Sukude, who steered clear of Nosakhe in case she read this knowledge in his eyes. He was in an agony of anticipation. What a chance! To be rid of his mother-in-law through no action of his own! With Nosakhe's death, the wealth of the Zinis would come to him. All of it. So would an undisputed right to the body of Bela, whatever he had promised her sister. Watching Nosakhe make her way to the beach, Piet Barol's warning that the snake would come for him if he sexed her seemed absurd. How could a Strange One know such a thing?

He thought of Zandi. She had taken his sexing greedily, almost as if she hungered for it. She had made him spend three times in her, and his back still bore the marks of her fingernails. Why not take her as a second wife?

He was humming to himself as Nosakhe dipped out of sight.

Fezile was on the beach, waiting to command the waves. On his assistance all depended, for it was in the Sea that Nosakhe would enter the Realm of the Dead. This would not

242

be so very hard, since she did not know how to swim. Once she had found Ntsina's spirit, it would be Fezile who calmed the waves and allowed her to breathe again, and so breathe life into her grandson too. She was wearing her heaviest robes, weighted with cowrie shells. Fezile, who was not often moved, found that a painful lump had come to his throat at this image of loving sacrifice. It stilled some of the panic he had felt since waking.

'Is all as you would wish it, my brother?' asked Nosakhe.

He was wearing his second-best robes, in case he should be compelled to wade into the water. 'Everything is ready,' he said.

'Then let us begin.'

Fezile watched her. For his services on this day, he had bargained another twenty-five cattle from Sukude. He need never worry about money or women again, with such a herd. He swallowed as Nosakhe began to draw strange markings in the sand and offered her cowrie shells to the Sea. When she opened the Gate to the Underworld, who could tell what other spirits lay beyond it – perhaps even Atamaraka herself. Should any of them escape, he would be their first victim. He began to feel more content with his lot as it currently was. His homestead would soon be ready. He had enough cattles to live comfortably, if not magnificently. Nosakhe extended her hand towards him. He thought of running from her. But riches are a powerful lure, and he did not. He took her hand and stepped into the circle she had drawn.

'Oh Ma, Great Goddess. I present my ally in this undertaking.'

Fezile was trembling, but Nosakhe held him firm. She begged the Great Goddess for Her aid and thanked Her for Her goodness. She entreated their ancestors to send Ntsina's soul to the Sea Gate of the Underworld. She shook her arms, waving the goat-hair bracelet to attract the attention of Ntsina's spirit. Her certainty in herself had returned. She was not foolhardy. Nor was she proud. She did not underestimate the dangers ahead, as she had as a girl. Her voice rose, clear and strong, and Fezile joined in, making up his incantation as he went along. The wind carried the sound out to sea, and then, changing direction, back over the homesteads of Gwadana.

Noni heard them.

Noni was an early riser, and the fear that had settled on the village had seeped into her soul. Her dreams were disturbing and in the daylight she heard sadness and unease all around her. The discovery that the tip of her mother's little finger was missing had confirmed her sense of unknown evils. Her mother refused to tell her what had become of it, and Noni was certain that a monster had escaped from her dreams and bitten it off. She had been bewildered by the ceremony Fezile conducted, confirming in her the gift of Farsight – but when it was all explained she had felt proud of herself. Today she heard something greasy and untrustworthy in his voice, quite different from the blazing lies of the Strange One who had disappeared.

Nosakhe's voice, soaring over the ocean, was a bright, bottomless blue. Noni could not hear the words, and would not have understood them if she had – for Nosakhe was using an ancient tongue, given by Marimba to the First People and preserved in the traditions of the Zinis. What Noni did grasp was the sincerity and courage in Nosakhe's voice. She went to the furthest extent of her homestead and sat on a rock, listening. She heard Fezile singing a song that twisted round Nosakhe's words. He was afraid, and trying not to show it. His voice was like the muck that gathers at the bottom of a pig's trough. She frowned.

The sea at Gwadana is powerful and cold. Noni heard Nosakhe's cry as the water slapped her breasts. She heard that the blue, true voice was moving away from her. She could not understand it. No Xhosa brought up in the strictest tradition, as Nosakhe was, knows how to swim. Noni listened as Fezile's song grew stronger, gliding over Nosakhe's voice, smothering it. Until Nosakhe's voice ceased altogether.

Noni began to be afraid.

This was nothing by comparison with how Fezile felt. He

had known many charlatan *sangomas*, and never feared them. Nosakhe's conviction made his hands clammy. He stood where he was until her head went under. It was imperative she believed in his allegiance. He waited, teeth chattering, on the edge of the surf. The tide had not yet taken all Nosakhe's cowrie shells and he glanced round him, then knelt and began to rescue them from the water. As if angered, the waves grew rougher and the sky darkened. He retreated, fearful of being dragged into them to share Nosakhe's fate. Beside him on the beach, Ata the dog sat motionless, ears cocked, listening.

As her head went below the waters, and the Sea's currents welcomed her, Nosakhe was blessed with a jolt of fierce energy. Her grandfather had warned her long ago to prepare to meet Atamaraka. She had trained diligently, learned the secrets of natural things and animals, suffered through thirsts and starvations and held the power of life or death, which alone can send a soul mad. At this crucial hour, her fear of Death was wholly lifted from her – the first sign that the spell was working. The water numbed her body. She lost sensation in her limbs. There is a strong current at Gwadana Bay, and soon she was in its grasp. Her brain clouded, and a deathly peace began to creep over her. She clung to consciousness with all her might.

The Sea hurled her, dragging her downwards, tumbling her this way and that. The blood in her head began to thud insistently. She steeled herself against the need for air, drawing on every privation she had ever endured. At the brink of unconsciousness she opened her eyes. It was murky down here, but the sun's light penetrated from above. Her eyes stung, but she could see. Ahead of her, where there should only be water, was a dark mass. The Sea drew her closer, and the mass turned pink. It was covered in gaping holes – smaller than she had imagined, but large enough for a spirit to escape through. She touched the reef, praying with all her might that Ntsina's soul was there, and could cling to her hand. Then she gave one mighty kick, her feet connecting with the coral. It was the last of her energy, but it was enough. Her body hurtled upwards, towards the light. Her head broke the surface of the water.

'Fezile! Now!'

On the beach, Fezile had calmed down. He was about to desert his post when he saw Nosakhe's head rise up through the waves. She was much further down the beach, but closer to shore than he had expected. The Gate to the Underworld must be open, which meant that Atamaraka was close at hand.

With a shriek that made the cattles low and the goats bleat and the gulls rise cawing from the cliffs, Fezile ran up the beach, away from the Sea. He ran as fast as he had run as a boy. He ran and ran and did not stop. A pain rose in his side and spread to his arm, and still he did not stop. Pure fear gave him the energy of a god. He ran and ran, his wizened heart pumping faster. He ran up the dunes, and onto level ground. He ran past homesteads and fences. The pain in his arm became excruciating, and still he ran. He ran until his straining heart shuddered its last. He saw Lundi's homestead, and Lundi himself, standing at the door. But already his blood had stopped carrying oxygen to his brain, and the last thing he saw was Lundi's horrified face.

And then he died.

❧

Noni heard Nosakhe's shout. And then Fezile's scream. She heard Fezile run up the beach, away from the sea, and Ata the dog start barking. Nosakhe called again. Her blue had faded. The sincerity remained, but its strength was failing. Noni was a kind-hearted little girl. At once she understood that Nosakhe had gone where Xhosa children are told never to venture.

She ran into her homestead, screaming. Her family were at breakfast, their usual good humour stifled by a new atmosphere of sullen reproach.

'Nosakhe Zini is in the sea!'

Confusion reigned. The chief got his spear and hurried to the door. But Kagiso charged past him, for he knew what use a spear is against the waters. Nosakhe had treated him kindly and often fed him deliciously as a child. He ran onto the beach. The sea was empty. He stopped, panting.

'There's no one here.'

'She's there! In the waves!'

'There is no one there.' Kagiso turned back.

The frustration of not being believed at this critical hour was more than Noni could bear. She remembered the ceremony Fezile had conducted, and the attention the adults had paid it. In a voice that was no longer the voice of a little girl, she said: 'Nosakhe Zini is in the sea. I, who have the gift of Farsight, command you to save her.'

Her father and his wives gathered behind her. They had never heard her use this voice, and they were wondering what to do when Nosakhe's head appeared above the waves, and they heard her faint cry: 'Feziiiiilllleeee!'

Kagiso charged down the beach. The tide was rising, surging towards the sand and bringing Nosakhe with it. He ran on the shingle at the water's edge, where the purchase of feet is best. When he was level with her, he plunged into the sea and waded towards her. He waded until his feet could no longer touch the bottom, and there was a moment when he might have retreated. But he was a brave man, and he trusted his sister's protection. So he launched himself into the depths, splashing his hands to keep afloat, and one of his hands connected with the heavy robes Nosakhe wore, and he pulled with all his might. Now his father was in the sea, and the chief waded out on the sand shelf to its edge, and his first wife Pumza followed.

When the chief reached the edge of the shelf, Pumza was holding one of his hands, her solid bulk a useful weight against the tides. His hand found Kagiso's, and the turning tide rose up and a huge wave sent Nosakhe's body towards the shore. She was lifeless and very heavy. The chief and Kagiso and Pumza dragged her to the beach. She lay crumpled on the sand, and each of those watching prayed to their ancestors for help. But it was Noni who pushed Nosakhe's body onto her side and gave her back a great clap.

It was this clap that jolted the last of Nosakhe's reflexes to life. Her body contracted, every muscle straining, and her stomach expelled a great quantity of sea water. As it did, her lungs rejoiced in the air once more, and her heart gave a great leap.

She started to breathe.

10

Piet Barol set Ierephaan and Mohammed up in a large, open-sided workshop. He was aware that each wished to outshine the other, and was judicious with his compliments. He had decided to complete Shabrill's commission room by room, starting with Percy's study. The desk was supported on elegant gazelle legs, the chairs inspired by bush buck. Where Chippendale had favoured meaningless curls and curlicues, Piet's designs caught the symmetry of the sable antelope's horns, while supporting the lumbar spine. Percy's chair had a back inspired by the majestic revolutions of the horns of the bull kudu, miraculously reduced to two dimensions. Piet set Brightness and Blessing to study the work of the Indian masters, and drew Ntsina to one side.

'Would you like to learn a skill?' He did not wish Ntsina to have no options save menial service when his earnings from this commission ran out. 'When you live in the city, you might have need of one.'

'I will not cut an Ancestor Tree.'

'You needn't. We have so much work to do with the forest mahogany. You have such a knowledge of animals, I thought you might—'

'If you wish.' Ntsina spoke gruffly because he wanted Piet to ask him what was wrong. He was ready to answer this question in no uncertain terms. But Piet was too cheerful to notice his partner's low spirits, and as soon as he had shown Ntsina how to use a gouge, he was on his way again.

Conscious of his wife's scrutiny, he took care to get everyone busy before he began to work himself. He had not slept all night, knowing that his encounter with an Ancestor Tree was upon him. He was uncontainably excited. With Grace and Wisdom, he began sawing the outlines of the bed. The wood gave way, once stripped of its bark. Its colour was delicate, lighter than mahogany, perfect for the bright sun of the Rand. He set his assistants to hollow out the space between the base and the posts and the canopy, and went into the forest with Happiness and an axe.

Over the days it took his assistants to prepare the rough block, Piet cut down twenty-eight small trees, testing the wood of each for resistance, quality and colour. His nerves were alive. He was in a state that only artists ever know – when their minds are as impressionable as clay. He drank in the atmosphere of the forest and filled a notebook with what he saw – the twisting of a vine on a trunk, the mischievous grin of a squirrel. When he came home at night, he was so happy that Stacey found herself better able to rise above the inconveniences of her accommodations.

Piet's explorations accumulated a pile of treasures – woods of different hues and grains, some pale and soft, capable of taking detail as fine as the veins of a leaf, some dark and hard. After days of searching he found a lime tree, which is ideal for the carving of flowers, and that night he fucked Stacey till dawn and the sound of rising men stopped them.

Ntsina, sitting up late by the fire, heard them and felt very bitter. Every mark of affection between the Barols fuelled his indignation. He tried to concentrate on his carpentry lessons, but the Indians were proud and did not believe that a Bantu could rise to the challenges of their art. This made Ntsina much less inclined to try. Besides, he was a man made for the outdoors, for the exhilaration of the chase and merrymaking with his friends. The concentration required of the fine carver bored him and gave him headaches – he who had never sat at a desk, nor wished to.

Luvo, trying to help, favoured him with long lectures on the importance of acquiring a trade. These had quite the opposite effect from the one intended. After one of them, Ntsina got so cross he carried Luvo to the stream for a good dunking. Luvo clung tight to Ntsina's neck, his hands meeting behind it, his face buried against his friend's hard chest. When Ntsina deposited him in a pool, Luvo dragged him in and they thrashed in the clear water, their bodies locked against each other.

And Ntsina found thereafter that Luvo's behavior grew more provocative, not less.

In Johannesburg, Percy Shabrill said to Dorothy: 'What the devil's become of that wretched Frenchman?' The world war had created many opportunities for influential men to dine together. That his house should not be ready to advertise his prominence made Percy irascible. The garden had taken root and looked much older than it was. The mauve hangings had been taken down. The table at which the Barols had eaten remained in the dining room, and the staff quarters were still packed with refugees, but Percy Shabrill was not a man who did things by halves, and he objected to making do in the vast rooms constructed to show off everything of the best. He and Dorothy continued to live in the house in which Esmé had been born, which was pleasant enough. But it was not the setting for a future Member of Parliament.

'I have heard from his wife this morning,' said Dorothy, putting down her toast and handing Percy an envelope. 'She writes to say they have found a first-class wood, of a kind no one else has.'

Percy scanned the letter. Stacey had enclosed Piet's latest sketches. He rather liked the idea that he had sent his man off into the hinterland, to find the best trees in all the forests of South Africa. It was a picturesque explanation for the empty house, but it did not compensate for its emptiness. He looked at his wife. He had a confession to make.

'That furniture we ordered from England . . .'

'Yes. We sent it back.'

Percy smiled. He had deceived her, but in a good cause. He looked at her roguishly. 'You didn't really think we could send it all back, not after it had been crated up and put on a ship, did you, darling? You women have the funniest ideas.'

Dorothy put down her tea cup.

'It's been sitting in a shed in Potchefstroom. I rather think we should get it out and use it till Barol sends the new stuff.'

Dorothy's hands began to tremble. The expense of this furniture had haunted her. Only Percy's steadfast assurance that they had got their money back had stilled her conscience. Having grown up in a vicarage, she knew the value of money.

After a pause, she said: 'You lied to me.'

Percy guffawed, but he did so nervously. 'Hardly a lie, my little wifey. I didn't like to trouble your conscience.'

'Well, you rather have.'

To his great surprise, he saw that Dorothy was angry. He said no more about it, because he considered it undignified for a man to mind too much about his wife's moods. But he loved Dorothy dearly, and as his chauffeur drove him to his office he grew quite cross at the long delay that had compelled him to bring to her attention a matter he had always intended to keep from her. By the time he reached his place of business, he was indignant. He had an agent in Cape Town, and telegraphed him instructions to visit Barol & Co. in person, to find someone for him to shout at.

When Percy got home, Dorothy saw at once that something had disturbed him. It made her regretful of the morning's scene. 'What's wrong, my little man?' She crossed the drawing room and put her arm through his.

'I've had some rather alarming news.'

Dorothy knew, both from the Bible and from the works of Regency-themed fiction that were her favourite refuges from the heat of the Rand, that ruin can strike even the most prosperous of men. The prospect of losing their station in life, of being freed from the obligations of the ruling class, raised her spirits. How happy they would be in an English cottage! Only guilt composed her face in a suitable expression.

'Barol's shop no longer exists. It's become a bank. The word at the Mount Nelson is that he went off to fight in France.'

She absorbed this in silence.

'If that scoundrel has stolen my money, I'll make sure he doesn't live to boast of it.'

❧

Stacey Barol's graciousness to her husband's Bantu employees did not thrive in the forest heat. To a certain kind of mosquito, the blood of the hairless ape woman is far sweeter than her mate's, and Stacey was soon a celebrity among the forest's invertebrates. By day and by night they assaulted her. Every time her hand lay still, a fly settled on it. Every time she tried to sleep, the whine of a legion of blood-sucking insects disturbed her. Her husband's physical attentions were some compensation, but the nights were hot and sticky and she was aware of the other men's close proximity. The way Ntsina looked at her after a night of adventurous delirium made her sizzle with rage.

Stacey did not discipline Ntsina, but she stopped going out of her way to be agreeable to him. She was no cook, and the only domestic contribution she could make was the washing of dishes – an odious practice to a lady of aristocratic tastes.

Twelve people eating three times a day generates a quantity of dishes, and the cleaning of them in a forest is no simple matter. Water had to be fetched from the stream, which required venturing from the clearing alone. This water had to be heated on a fire that had to be laid and lit. If she did not handle the disbursement of hot and cold judiciously, she was left with a basin of greasy suds too cool to dissolve the animal fat.

Luvo took pleasure in the rituals of cleanliness, and when Stacey volunteered to assist him he was a patient instructor. But he prized diligence in a student, and in the matter of grease scraping Stacey was not diligent. At first he let her alone, not wishing to criticize. But a succession of meals eaten off slippery plates compelled him to intervene. Stacey was secretly relieved to have these duties taken from her, but she found the indolence that followed hard to bear.

All the men were working happily. With nothing else to do, she turned her total attention to the education of her child. She spent each morning doing Arthur's lessons, but the boy was so enchanted by the forest she could not keep him long at a desk, learning European capitals. Arthur still cuddled her, and could not sleep without a story from her, but she knew that in his waking hours he would rather be elsewhere than with her. For the first time in his life, she was no longer the person he preferred above all others – and her demotion grieved her.

∽

Arthur Barol had a child's natural adaptability and did not notice the mosquitoes or the flies. He was afraid only of the spiders, and some of those in Gwadana were fearsome to behold. Stacey later came to regret that at her first encounter with a huge, hairy arachnid she had screamed for Ntsina to remove it.

Ntsina knew that it is not the ugly spiders that are dangerous, but the beautiful ones. He lifted the creature gently in cupped hands and took it outside, ignoring Stacey's sharp instructions to kill it.

This single act earned him Arthur Barol's total adoration.

Christmas came and went, chairs and desks and tables took form, and the friendship of Arthur Barol and Ntsina Zini flourished. The child's fear of the forest, derived from fairytales, vanished when his little hand was clasped in Ntsina's big one. His uncontained admiration made Ntsina feel better about the shapeless lumps of wood that were all that resulted from his lessons with the Indians. He found his resentment of Arthur's parents burdensome.

In their first months in the forest he had felt very close to Piet, and grateful for his assistance. Piet's decision to permit a woman in the camp sounded the first note of discord between them, but because Piet did not trouble himself to delve into Ntsina's feelings, he was entirely unaware of this. In the New Year, at Stacey's insistence, Piet stopped eating with the other men. He and his wife took their meals in their own quarters, where they ate off china, rather than tin. In subtle ways, the inequity of the outside world stole into the clearing of the Ancestor Grove, and a suffocating rage infiltrated Ntsina's soul.

Only with Arthur was he free of it. He taught him the isiXhosa words for tree and leaf and stream and spider and frog and fruit and monkey. The boy's wonder fed his spirit, and lifted the film of habituation from Ntsina's view of the glories all around him.

'Our child is forgetting which race he belongs to,' said Stacey one morning, watching Arthur gambol into the forest, holding Ntsina's hand. She tried to sound unconcerned, but there was a tightness in her throat.

'It's good for him to be among men.' Piet kissed her neck. 'To learn how to hunt and take care of himself.'

She did not answer. But as the summer heat intensified she did complain of many things about which he could do nothing: the temperature, the flies, the mosquitoes, the spiders. Stacey did not mention her loneliness, and had she done so he might have heard her complaints more tenderly. Instead he shielded himself from them; and as the hot weeks passed, and her bickering grew tiresome, he began to channel his love for her towards an idealized, abstract vision, which lived in his own head and could not be contaminated by the fault she found with everything.

In the forest, Ntsina taught Arthur the mating call of the female Lula bird. Many a male arrived in the clearing, plumage fluffed, to find disappointment awaiting him. The boy was at an age when learning anything is possible, if the heart is engaged. The rituals of English spelling could not compete with the thrill of summoning a wild creature. As Ntsina's pupil he began to hear the sound of each bird and insect distinctly, and to follow the conversations of different species in the forest's continual chatter. His brain, so ripe for languages, caught the curls and razor edges of isiXhosa, and Ntsina's delight at his proficiency spurred him to heights of concentration he rarely displayed in the hot little shack in which his mother taught him how to count in French.

One morning, escaping the quiet industry of the camp to see what they could see, they found their portion of the forest mysteriously empty. They were looking for the baboons, but none were to be found. No other monkeys leapt through the trees. No deer grazed by the side of the streams. The emptiness puzzled Ntsina, and then made him grin. 'Come, I will show you a something,' he said. 'But it is a long way off, and I cannot carry you. When a human tastes a Blessing for the first time, he must stand on his own two feet.'

The Blessing is a particular bush that fruits only once in every hundred moons. There were five such bushes in the forest of Gwadana, and finding them was one of the first lessons of Nosakhe Zini. As a boy Ntsina had known their rhythms. Working in the mines had broken this bond. Now he sensed that a Blessing had fruited, because news of the Blessing's fruiting travels swiftly in those parts.

They were led by the spoor of the bushbuck.

As Arthur emerged from the trees into the clearing where the Blessing grew, Ntsina placed a hand on his shoulder. Ahead was a huge bush, two hundred years old and as tall as a tree. Impalas and bushbuck stood at its base, plucking the sweet leaves and sweeter fruit. Above them, five bands of monkeys each had their own spot. The baboons were at the top, babies clinging to their mothers' backs. Birds of all hues and none sat in the branches, singing and eating. Eyes downcast, Ntsina moved towards the tree. His movements were smooth and unruffled. Watching from above, the monkeys saw that this hairless ape understood the laws of the forest, and they did not attack as they would have done had

Ntsina come brandishing a stick. The fruiting of a Blessing is an occasion for truce. Even the impalas, usually so skittish, restrained their impulse to flee.

The fruits at Arthur's level were the property of the antelope, but Ntsina reached for a branch still heavy with them. He gave one to Arthur, and watched the child's face as he bit it. Arthur's cheeks turned pink. Ntsina lowered the branch for him, and he stretched on tiptoes to take one for himself.

From twenty trees away, the leopard who had stolen Piet Barol's biltong heard the sounds of creatures feasting and felt sad. There were too many eyes on a Blessing to permit the clandestine attack that was his only hope. Birds and monkeys watched sharply, and the buck did not forget to twitch their noses for the scent of a predator. Good fortune had placed in the leopard's way the carcass of a female bush pig, one of the lucky beings in that forest to have died of natural causes. By the time he found her, she was half consumed by maggots, but he had eaten her in any case, and digested a quantity of the maggots too; and now he had an uneasy sense that creatures were moving inside him. He lay down in the shade of a bush. He yearned for the company of a leopardess. He no longer thought so much of mounting, as of being nuzzled by one. It was a long time since any leopard had licked his ears, or the fur under his muzzle that his own tongue could not reach. He avoided catching sight of his reflection in the forest's pools, because he had once been proud of his looks and knew that he had not groomed properly in too long.

One other creature shared this glade with him: the young baboon tormented by dreams of greatness. This baboon was in an extremely bad mood. In the months since the Barols' arrival, he had begun his campaign to dominate the other males in his troop – begun too early, because at ten years of age he was nowhere near the size and weight of the adult males. Self-confidence, bestowed on him by a doting mother and attentive older siblings, had inspired over-reaching. Now other males sensed the ambitions of an alpha on the make and united against him. Twice he had been thrown from the top of a tree. On one of these occasions he had broken his shoulder. His right hand now trailed weakly on the ground and made him burn with shame.

His mother, and all his siblings, were at the Blessing; but there were limits to their protection. The most he could hope for was that one would save him a fruit – but he knew that a single taste of the fruit of the Blessing is worse than no taste at all, for the yearning it ignites is terrible. He sat in the tree, muttering to himself. When he saw the baby hairless ape pass by, he felt doubly ashamed that this baby should eat what he could not. His thoughts turned to the hairless apes. They had a special stick that made a bright sound. This stick, wielded by Piet, had killed two baboons, and the decree had gone out that the hairless apes were to be left undisturbed. The forest, after all, had more in it than any baboon could possibly eat.

What it did not have were oranges.

Sitting in the tree, so close to the fruit he could not have, the young warrior's thoughts turned to this other fruit that had been denied him. He was wholly caught up in the unfairness of it all. Using his good arm, he swung down to the forest floor and walked away from the Blessing, following the path the hairless apes had used. He could smell their traces on branches Ntsina had moved, see their footprints on wet mud. As he went, his anger dimmed, replaced by fascination. There had been much private speculation among the baboons about the ways and habits of these strange apes, and about the special sticks they had. Their leader's edict forbidding all contact had heightened the mystery.

The baboon stopped out of sight of the hairless ape colony, disturbed by low sounds. He saw, to his surprise, that two pale brown hairless apes had left the camp and were kneeling by the stream, bowing their heads and murmuring to themselves. He tiptoed past them, to the last of the trees. The colony seemed deserted. No sound came from the shelters where the apes beat wood day in, day out. He saw the door through which he had glimpsed oranges many moons before. His heart pumped faster and despite himself he did a little dance, grinning with daring. There was a small patch of open ground between the last tree and the entrance to the wooden cave. He thought of his leader's prohibition, but his leader was not here to enforce it.

Adrenaline levels rising, the baboon left the trees and approached the wooden cave. The door was closed, but he had seen how the hairless apes opened it. He touched the knob of metal on the door. It was hot. He sprang away, but found his courage again. This time, using the hand that looked so like the hand of the hairless apes, he twisted it.

It opened.

The kitchen of a hairless ape is to a baboon a paradise of earthly delights. Contemplating its treasures, the intrepid explorer felt a surge of his true nature bubbling from within – the nature of a baboon destined to be an alpha, jealous rivals be damned. Those rivals, after all, were sitting in a tree with a single fruit, feeling proud to have kept him off it. When in fact they had done him a favour! Now he had all this! He could not contain himself. Before he sampled anything he began to dance, for caution was not his gift. He danced and waved his hands and found that the saucepans made a most delightful crash as they fell to the floor. So too the tin plates. There were nuts and dried papaya in glass tins, and syrups of many colours. He pawed uselessly at their lids, then found they smashed quite prettily. There were no oranges, but there was a jam made of them and he gorged himself on it, dazzled by his victory. The ingestion of so much sugar, as much as two hundred figs might bear, made him feel invincible. He opened the door of the cave and ventured forth, no longer afraid of the hairless apes with their noisy sticks.

There stood a female hairless ape.

The provision of a female to dominate was the crowning glory of this memorable day. He flung himself at Stacey, leaping and baring his fangs. He threw her to the ground and stamped on her, banging his feet on the earth, looking for rocks to throw. There weren't any to hand, but he remembered the strange implements in the cave, and fetched a saucepan. He would have smashed her on the head with it, so great was his delirium, had Mohammed and Ierephaan, returning from afternoon prayer, not entered the camp at this minute and charged him. He put up a good display, showing his teeth and screeching, and during this Stacey got to her feet, dusty and bruised, and ran for the chest in which Piet kept his gun. It was locked. She shook the padlock uselessly, and rifled his drawers for the key. She watched Ierephaan chase the baboon into the jungle, and stood in the mean little hut in which her husband had left her, shaking with fear.

And then anger.

Piet and his Bantu workers were hauling a forest mahogany back to camp. He had left the Indians and Luvo to guard his wife, though he had not told them this was their duty. The Indians had gone to pray, Luvo had taken a book to a shady pool, with the result that Stacey had indeed been left alone and defenceless. Piet returned to a barrage of hysterical recrimination. He was overcome by remorse and made no attempt to defend himself, but the inconveniences of camp life had built within Stacey for months. She wanted an adversary and was exasperated by Piet's humility.

Listening to the white woman shouting at the white man, Ierephaan, who had begun to miss his wife, was reminded that female company brings its own inconveniences. His wife had a terrific temper, which absence from one another had dimmed the memory of. 'She's a wild one, this infidel,' he said to Mohammed.

'It's this place that is wild. I cannot wait to leave it.' Mohammed went back to the workshop and continued the sanding of a magnificent console, made of forest mahogany with garlands of flowers in lime wood tumbling over its back and sides.

Piet returned to work, chastened. He hoped Stacey's mood would cool, and in another room, at another temperature, it might have done. Not in this room, on this blazing day. She washed. The monkey hadn't hurt her, but he had frightened her terribly.

When a mother is frightened, she thinks at once of her children, and now her anxiety transferred itself to Arthur – sent off into the forest by his father, in the company of a garden boy. What was to prevent Ntsina from kidnapping their child? Selling him to a childless couple in want of a beautiful son? With no one to answer her frantic questions, they assumed the quality of truths. She tried to read, but could not. She put her book down, drummed her fingers on the table. An enormous spider was watching her from the roof. She saw it and fetched a broom. Chasing the terrified creature relieved some of her anguish, as did the satisfying way its abdomen burst when the handle of her broom found it. She sat down again, anger and fear turning to acid within her. The sky turned scarlet. Dusk was coming. She began to pace in a panic that Arthur would not return.

At the Blessing, Ntsina saw that he and Arthur had lingered too late. They were queasy from all the fruit they had eaten, and their pace home was sluggish. Ntsina carried a collection of the fruits carefully in his lambskin pouch. He had decided to share them with the Bantu workers and perhaps, if they were polite, with the Indians; not with the adult Strange Ones. Arthur had discovered the call of the howler monkey, and his renditions were arrest-ingly good. Ntsina did his best to hurry him as the light faded, but the little boy had eaten a great deal, and gone a long dis-tance, and in the end he hoisted him to his shoulders and jogged the rest of the way, so that they would not be in the forest at night.

They arrived in the camp as the last of the light died, and were met by Stacey hurling abuse. Ntsina's shoulders ached with the weight of Arthur. He did not understand all the words the Strange One used, but her tone made her meaning plain enough. She seized the boy from him and his heart contracted at Arthur's despairing backward glance. He stood patiently, while the white woman screamed. He was aware that the workers were watching him. So was Piet, struck dumb by his wife. Ntsina knew that if he listened too well he might hit Stacey, and that hitting a white woman could not end well for a Bantu. Besides, he had never hit a woman yet. He would not let this witch provoke him.

So he lowered his head and trained his eyes on a worm struggling across the dust. Luvo came up and put a hand on his shoulder.

But fear had ruptured Stacey's self-control. In full flight, she said: 'I hate living in this wretched place. I hate it I hate it.' She could see it hurt her husband to have his foolish romantic dream shattered. In the city, it had given her pain to wound him. Now fear and discomfort and the accumulation of countless irritations made her impervious. 'I hate this shack you make me live in. I hate not being able to wash my hair.' And then, spurred by Piet's wide blue eyes and Ntsina's smell after an hour's run with Arthur: 'I hate these stinking Kaffirs.'

Ntsina recognized 'Kaffir'. It lit the wick of his own anger, so long unexpressed. Without a word he went into his hide and took a clean shirt. He went off in the direction of the river, her shouts following him, and washed. He had decided to break a solemn vow, and wanted to look his best for it.

In the camp, Stacey said: 'I don't want that gun locked up. What use is it if I can't get to it?'

∽

Ntsina slipped through the trees, sleek as a panther, following the stream. It is dangerous to be in a forest at night, but the full moon showed him his way in the water. He was too angry to be afraid of wild creatures. He knew, in his heart, that he would have to go back to Piet. He could not be seen in Gwadana. They would throw him from the cliffs, if they knew he had helped a Strange One kill an Ancestor Tree. Nevertheless . . . His turbulent thoughts carried him all the way to the place where the stream widens into the lagoon. He stopped, thinking of the countless times he had trodden this watery path.

Ahead was the village. On moonlit nights in his youth, his friends had sneaked to the edges of their homesteads, young men had courted young women. They had met and smoked and talked. Tonight, though the air was fair, no one was abroad. Every gate was tightly locked.

Ntsina knew it was Piet's lie that kept his people indoors on this gorgeous night. He thought of his father and his rage found a target. It pulled him from the shelter of the trees. He passed a homestead and heard its occupants snoring. The dogs began barking. He started to run, his feet sure on the path he knew so well. He had no clear idea what he would do when he reached his home, but he felt he must see the people he loved or he would never sleep again.

The Zini compound had always been tidy, but there was a new perfection in its order. The fence was as straight as the horizon, the lawn beyond immaculate. The sweet smoke of *mphepho* was coming from the kitchen hut.

Inside, Nosakhe was in a deep trance – one so deep she had tumbled over the cliff of consciousness into sleep, where her dreams were vague and troubled. Ntsina crept to the window. To have told his beloved grandmother he had died! It was an abomination. He had with him ten fruits of the Blessing. He put five of them on the window ledge, and crept on. Ata smelled him and thumped her tail. She did not bark. No sound save the crashing of the waves disturbed the silence.

The tapping of a finger at the door of her hut drove Bela bolt awake. She had driven a hook into the mud wall, and tied the door handle with a rope made of goat hair. It was the best lock she could devise, but it would be no match for a man of Sukude's strength. She got up from her grass mat, and lit a lamp. She could not bear to be forced in the dark. She heard the tap again. She had many times thought of bringing a knife, but the idea of blood and retribution had stopped her. Better to turn it on herself. She thought of the great effort she had put into her life – of what sweetness and modesty had cost her. How envied she had been, and yet it had all come to this: alone, on a dark night, with a wicked man at her door.

Ntsina saw the light. Softly, he said: 'It is I.'

263

The lantern moved.

'Who is there?' called Bela, and there was wonder as well as terror in her voice.

'It is I, your husband.'

Bela took the rope off its hook and shut her eyes tight in prayer. She had never prayed so fervently. Then she summoned all her courage and opened the door.

Ntsina stood there, as tangible as if he were alive. She drew back from him. Nosakhe had told her of the failure of her spell of Reincarnation and the sadder news that it could not be repeated. With it had died her final hope. Yet here he was.

'Ntsina?'

'It is I, beloved one.'

She began to cry. She could not move. He slipped past her, into the room, and closed the door behind him. Bela put her hand out and touched Ntsina's chest. It was solid and warm.

'Praise be. The spell worked,' she said.

'Which spell?'

'Your grandmother went into the Sea to fetch you from the Gate to the Underworld.'

'Is she unharmed?'

'By the grace of her ancestors. And yours.'

He put his hands on her shoulders, but she stepped away. 'Where have you been?'

The moment of truth had come, and Ntsina found that he was not equal to it. Nor could he lie. 'I have seen many dark things,' he said.

'Will you stay in this world?'

'No. But I will come back. I will visit you and protect you, and one day when I have all we need for a good life I will come for you. I promise you. And then I will be with you for ever.'

Relief so powerful it made her giddy rose through her. He went to her, and this time she did not resist. He embraced her gently. He took one of the fruits of the Blessing and bit it, and kissed her. The sweetness of the Blessing's juice twisted round their tongues as they found each other. The suffering and anguish and abstinence of half a year lifted from them, returned them to that moment, months before, when they had stood in this very hut while their friends feasted outside.

Time accelerated. It sped by in a delirious confusion of hands and lips and tongues. Bela smelled salty, of the sea water she used for bathing. Beneath its taste was something sweeter, a scent uniquely her own. It grew stronger as their bodies collided. The stars began to retreat, and Bela, who knew that daylight changes everything, pushed Ntsina on his back. She chose the angle of his entry and his speed, instinctive forces inspiring her. Only the rays of the rising sun striking the hut's walls brought Ntsina to his senses, and still he could not bear to stop. It took a superhuman effort to pull away from her.

'Come with me.'

They emerged from the hut, dishevelled and joyful. Ntsina led them to his father's hut. 'Knock, sweet one, and make him admit you.'

Bela knocked, and they heard Sukude get to his feet, the scrape of his key in his lock. When he opened the door, only Bela was visible. 'I have come to clean,' she said.

Sukude drew back. She knelt to sweep the coals from the fire, and he watched her. He had woken with an erection. Under its influence the vow he had made to Zandi lost its force, as did Piet Barol's warnings of the Creature. There are men in whom sexual desire can blunt all protestations of conscience, and Sukude Zini was one of them. He looked at Bela's blanket, which swung tantalizingly. He could see the outlines of a bottom he had long lusted over. The death of Fezile the witchdoctor had shaken him to his core, but the weeks that had passed since, with no spirit visitations, had begun to leave him feeling grateful rather than otherwise: one of the two men who knew his secrets was now dead. He stood up and took the key and went to the door. He was about to lock it when it opened.

'Vengeance is the headiest mead in creation.' So say the

guardians of the laws. The look on his father's face compensated Ntsina for many hardships he had endured. He stepped into the room. Sukude shrank from him. So it was Ntsina's ghost who had slain Fezile! Sukude's was the courage of brute strength, strongest in the presence of weakness. It deserted him completely now. He began to wail. 'I have not sexed her! I have not sexed her!'

Ntsina strode towards him, and Sukude flinched. Ntsina touched Bela's head. 'Arise, my wife.' She stood. 'By the powers of the Goddess Ma, I grant you sanctity and protection. The first man to harm you will find himself summoned to a hideous fate in the Underworld.'

He turned to his father. His face was fearsome.

'I am sorry!' cried Sukude. 'Forgive me, my son. Fruit of my loins.'

'It is not I whose forgiveness you should seek.'

Ntsina pointed at Bela. It was a rare thing indeed for a man to apologize to a woman in Gwadana; rarer still for the apology to be offered on his knees.

Ntsina presided over a most satisfying scene.

'I beg your forgiveness.' Sukude muttered it at first, but at a kick from Ntsina he found his voice. Ntsina kicked him again, and again, and each time Sukude's pleas reached a new pitch of sincerity. Bela's eyes danced. If a dark spirit had possessed her once, Ntsina now banished it for good. She felt a surging up of her old self – but she had changed, too. She was no longer a pliant maiden. She was a woman, a wife. And she spat on Sukude's head with joy.

This is the first of your punishments,' said Ntsina. 'The second is this: you shall cook and sweep and clean. If you shirk any task I will revisit you. If I do, I will bring creatures from the dark places.'

It was bright daylight outside. He knew he could not stay. He kissed his wife lingeringly, opened the door and bounded down the hillside.

Piet Barol did his best to take no action on those rare occasions when he lost his temper. To Stacey all he said was: 'I think you had better rest until you are calmer.'

She stormed off to their hut and he left her there. He consulted Luvo, who predicted that Ntsina would return once he had calmed down; but darkness came and Ntsina did not return, and all through the night Piet worried for him.

What if Stacey had driven him into the path of a wild creature?

When Ntsina did not appear the next morning, his worry intensified. He was about to take Grace and Blessing on a search party when the object of their anxiety stepped out of the line of trees. He was whistling. He did not mention his absence, or apologize for it. 'It is time to make some money,' was all he said.

Ntsina went into the shed. The Indians were there, who were used to being his masters. He did not greet them. He was done with their patronizing ways. What need had he, Ntsina Zini, great-grandson of the Great Founder, for the trick of making a piece of wood look like an elephant tusk? Let other men do that – he would hunt, and make love, and torment evil-doers. He had begun to see possibilities in his new role at Gwadana. He ignored Ierephaan's protests as he reached over him to measure the width of a table. When he was done, he went to Piet and said: 'It will take three trips in our wagon to get the furniture that is now finished to Butterworth. What happens next?'

'It must go to Johannesburg.'

Stacey overheard this. Her heart leapt. 'I'll go with it. Make sure everything's placed to its best advantage. I can find us new clients.'

A day before, Piet would have entreated her to stay. Now he said: 'That's an excellent idea, my darling,' and his voice was tight with grievance.

'I'll take Arthur with me. He can go to school.'

The look on Piet's face made the watching men retreat, aware that a lightning storm was brewing between these two Strange Ones.

'You'll do no such thing.'

'I will indeed.'

'What good will six weeks at school do him?'

'There are excellent boarding schools. We could leave him there while you finish this . . . business.'

'Absolutely not.'

'I must insist. He needs to learn how to be a gentleman.'

'He's six years old.'

She tried to smile. But she was too angry to skirt a confrontation. 'He's my son. I will decide what's best for him.'

It was a misstep. Piet looked at her. He was truly shocked. 'You mean to say you would take him away from me?'

'For his own good.'

'Are you quite sure?' His voice was dangerously calm.

'Quite sure.'

He leaned close to her, and when he spoke his voice was so cold she was caught off guard. Rage would have spurred her, but this new voice made her afraid. 'I am his father,' said Piet. 'You will never take him from me.' And then, aware that this card could not be trumped: 'Do not think you can treat me like a black man. I have the law on my side.'

Piet spent that night on the floor of their cabin, while Stacey took the bed. The next morning he woke early and gave Luvo and Ntsina fifteen pounds each. He told them it was an advance on the sums owed them, but in fact it was a wordless apology for his wife's behaviour. They accepted it with as much nonchalance as they could muster; but as soon as Piet had gone they gave way to the excitement young men feel when given disposable cash.

It was a greater sum than either had had occasion to handle before.

Arthur clung to Stacey as she said goodbye, but bravely refused to cry. His restraint made his mother ache. She covered his face in kisses and promised to return as soon as she could. Then she got onto the box of the wagon, ignoring Piet's hand outstretched to help her.

The vehicle was heavily laden with tables and chairs. Having errands to run in Butterworth, Ntsina and Luvo came too. They lay in the back, avoiding the solid silence between the Barols. Piet was aware of powerfully conflicting emotions. He loved Stacey. He did not doubt that. But the events of the previous day smarted worse than any disagreement they had had before. Her vileness to Ntsina, without whom they would have no fortune, was deeply objectionable. Her willingness to deprive him of Arthur stifled his urge to miss her.

They stood together in the lobby of the Travellers' Rest. Stacey rang the bell. She waited until Piet had gone to unload the cart before asking whether anything had come for her. The reception-ist, in a panic about Stacey's trunks, handed her a telegram. She opened it. PRAYING FOR HIS RETURN STOP PLEASE ACCEPT SMALL GIFT STOP LOUISA STOP. And with it was a banker's order for three hundred pounds.

'What's that?' asked Piet, coming in.

'A telegram from Percy. It's a good job I'm going. He's very indignant you're so late.'

He took her up to the room they had made such frenzied love in three months before. Today, neither of them wished to, and this made him sad. 'I'm sorry you've had such inconveniences,' he said.

'Thank you for being sorry.'

They looked at one another. The telegram in her pocket had lifted Stacey's spirits. She gave her husband the secret half-smile that was their indication of a truce. He returned it, and tenderness twisted through their anger.

'We'll be back in the city soon enough.' Piet kissed her fore-head. 'And we'll never be poor again. Don't be too cross.'

She put her hands around his waist and drew him to her. 'I have one favour to ask.'

'Anything.'

'Control your perfectionism. Don't spend too long on that bed. It is already finer than anything Johannesburg has ever seen. What matters now is pace. We need to ramp up production.'

'Yes.'

'Promise me.'

'I promise.'

But as he bounded down the steps of the Travellers' Rest, Piet Barol had no intention of keeping his word.

11

Luvo had just sent his money to his parents, and was glowing with the virtue of not having spent any of it on himself. Ntsina was coming out of the general store, with a large parcel.

'What on earth's that?' asked Piet.

'Nails for Ierephaan and Mohammed.' Ntsina loaded it carefully and sat on the box beside Piet. Luvo lay in the back and closed his eyes. Piet jerked the reins. The wagon trundled up the hill towards Idutywa. At length Piet gathered all the isiXhosa of which he was master and said: 'I'm sorry, my friend.'

'For what?'

'For the way my she spoke wife you to.'

His word order made Ntsina grin, despite himself. It was always amusing to see a Strange One grapple with challenges he could not rise to.

'You promised there would be no women,' he said.

It had never occurred to Piet that this prohibition would extend to his own wife. He saw, quite abruptly, as if an artfully placed mirror had altered his perspective, that from Ntsina's point of view things had not perhaps seemed very fair. Piet had the great gift of being able to apologize when he was wrong. He did so now, without attempting to justify himself.

Ntsina had not expected penitence. It threw him. He had prepared many angry statements on this subject, but Piet's apology, and the money he had just dispensed, made them all dissolve. For a moment his mood swayed on the precipice of resentment, deprived of the release of further conflict. But the raptures of the night before still lingered.

'I forgive you,' he said. 'But if you're not careful, the men will invite their own beauties to the camp. Like her, for instance.' He nodded at the woman who had come to her gate with water buckets for their horses. Piet had never looked at her before. With the exception of the men who worked for him, whom long familiarity had rendered specific, he did not trouble much to distinguish one Bantu from another, and avoided looking too lingeringly at their women – because he knew his own nature well and did not court temptation. Now he did look and saw a stout, large-breasted woman, with huge undulating buttocks. She looked up at this moment and her glance intercepted his. She smiled the smile of a woman used to the attention of men. There was nothing ingratiating or servile in it, quite the reverse.

'Well they'd better not,' he said.

⁓

The parcel Ntsina Zini had bought in the general store did not contain nails. It contained a wind-up radio – the last of its kind in the province, the man had told him. It was an old model and had stood in the shop for three years. Its owner was anxious to be rid of it, and would have taken substantially less than the advertised price.

Ntsina had not haggled. It had given him pleasure to pay for what he wanted in the manner of a customer for whom financial considerations count little. The knowledge of his possession lit a pleasant fuse of anticipation. He had already squared his conscience about the breaking of his vow to the Strange One, and Piet's apology, though appreciated, did not give him pause. The Strange One had not forsaken his family, and neither would he. What mattered was not that he should remain in the forest, but that no one from the village should enter it.

As they drove into the trees, all three men, for different reasons, felt their moods improve. 'Helpful been you, so,' said Piet, in isiXhosa. 'Grateful I am. Very.'

'He is not such a bad man,' thought Ntsina to himself. Aloud he said: 'You can cook dinner tonight, for a change.'

Piet did cook dinner. He had bought two bottles of brandy in town and they had something of a feast. The presence of a lady is an inhibiting weight on a group of men, and in Stacey's absence the brandy reignited a spirit of camaraderie. Arthur sat up late with them and begged for some but was denied it. He sat between his father and Ntsina, and though he missed his mama, he did not cry over her absence. Secretly he hoped there would be no more spelling of capital cities until she returned.

The gun lay on the table and Piet shot two hares with it, who had wandered too close. 'To our work!' he cried, raising his glass. 'It will make us immortal!'

⌒

As she lowered herself into the Travellers' Rest's deep bath, Stacey Barol thought of Arthur. She worried for him in the forest, and yet . . . She knew in her deepest soul that Piet could be relied upon to care for him. There was time enough, she supposed, to teach the boy drawing-room manners.

Her husband's penitence had touched her. With an effort of will she focused on the life they would have soon enough – in a proper house, with well-trained servants and ceiling fans and crisp sheets. She washed her hair. Even this horrid room was an improvement on the forest glade she had left behind, and ahead were the delights of a proper hotel. It made her feel secure to have money of her own. That it should have come from a beauty of Piet's past made its possession all the more delicious. Louisa's gift had greatly reduced the pain of learning that a fire had destroyed the possessions she had left behind. A shopping trip would now be in order, and few things soothed Stacey's soul like new clothes.

She had wired the Shabrills, but promised herself she would refuse their offer of hospitality. She had lived long enough among strangers. In Johannesburg she would do as she pleased.

It took her three days to get the furniture to East London, and a further two for the train to reach the Rand. She went at once to the Carlton Hotel, where Monsieur Etellin received her with the perfect admixture of warmth and deference that is the mark of the first rate hotelier. She booked a large suite in the name of the Vicomtesse Pierre de Barol. To be reunited with her title! It was a great pleasure. So was the fact that she might shop with a clear conscience.

She had come to Johannesburg with a mission she intended to execute, and it required panache and haute couture. She had the concierge call ahead for her, and three of the most expensive dress shops in the city opened their private salons, usually reserved for the wives and mistresses of the mining magnates. The European War had stopped the shipment of clothes from Paris, but Johannesburg was a melting pot of nationalities, and many French seamstresses had installed themselves long before the outbreak of hostilities.

One advantage of life in the forest was that Stacey had never been thinner, and it did her self-esteem no end of good to compare herself with the fat matrons of Johannesburg. She sent postcards to Arthur every morning and bought, off the rack, three day gowns, two tea gowns, four evening dresses, six pairs of gloves (to cover the insect bites on her arms), three hats, and two complete sets of silk lingerie. From Madame Chataignier, the couturier of the day, she ordered a further three ball gowns and two day dresses. Some ladies in the city still favoured corsets, but Stacey had no need of such uncomfortable aids to the silhouette. Even the fashions seemed calculated to please her. The dresses clung beautifully. She who had been compelled to put up with the assaults of insects and the unpleasantness of sweaty muslin, could now move in sheaths of rustling silk.

After a week of shopping and massage, she had recovered herself sufficiently to embark on her assault of the Shabrills, and the pocketbooks of their friends.

The months of March, April and May, 1915, would be remembered by Ntsina Zini for the rest of his days, and with good reason. For the first time in his life he had real money, and the prospect of more. He set himself to study Luvo's work in bookkeeping, rather than the laborious efforts of the pompous Indians, and found that it was quite easy to add up the sums Luvo entered on his ledger.

Luvo kept scrupulous accounts, and Ntsina's new dedication was very agreeable to him. Ntsina spent his days hunting with Arthur, which meant that their lessons took place at night, lit by the romantic glow of a lantern. They sat close to each other, and sometimes Luvo took Ntsina's hand under his, and guided him in the drawing of the numbers. These evenings, for Luvo, were filled with a wordless, exquisite pleasure.

On one of them, as he contemplated his future possession of three hundred pounds, Ntsina said: 'Do you think the Strange One would ever cheat us?'

Luvo thought this over. 'I don't think he would. She's the one I worry about.'

Ntsina frowned. He was not a violent man, but he had a vivid memory of Stacey Barol and decided to make sure he knew where the gun was – in case he should be compelled to assert his rights. The decision helped still his unease. So did Piet's friendliness.

And so did sex, wonderful sex.

Ntsina had intended at first . . . He did not know quite what he had intended. Certainly he had not intended to deceive Bela. But he found that the rapture she experienced in the arms of a spirit was so sweet for them both he had no wish to alter it. With the exception of the lady with the rash behind her knees, he had never sampled the joys of the love mat. To do so now, with a woman who loved him, whom he loved in return, supported by the knowledge that every day was leading them closer to a dream few Bantu could realize – a house, with electric light, and comfortable beds; clothes for her; schooling for their children – made

Ntsina disinclined to tell the harsh, glaring truth. What need had they for it? When he had his money, he would return in the flesh, reincarnated by the spell his grandmother had run such risks to cast for him.

Two moons passed, and still he had the radio in its box in the hide where formerly the Zinis had worshipped their ancestors. Nosakhe was not an innocent like Bela. She was a true *sangoma*, a seer of deep things. He did not trust himself to lie to her convincingly, and the thought of being found out . . .

He preferred not to think of it, and did not think of it. Instead, he and Bela tasted raptures with each other – first twice a week, then three times, the minutes ticking by so slowly in the intervals between their couplings that by the time they met they could hardly breathe. They met ten trees from the village, just beyond sight of the homesteads of Gwadana. From here he led her to the forest's secret places. They bathed in the pool behind the waterfall of the purple rocks and cooked in the cave that none but Nosakhe knew, a cave adorned with paintings of the First People, chasing game. He showed Bela where the trees with the widest branches and the best views were, and together they climbed them. Two months after the Blessing fruited, another offered itself, and this time he did not show it to Arthur. He took Bela to the glade of this second Blessing and fed her the delicious sweet fruits. She showed Ntsina how to touch her just so, and he did, reverently, for long hours as the sun turned the sky from blue to gold.

This glade became their place. It was close to water, and large enough for a fire to be built. They made many happy memories in it. At the conclusion of a particularly blissful afternoon, Bela stopped at the forest edge as he escorted her home. 'It is not for me to decide the ways of men and spirits, but in my happiness I must tell you something that is true.'

'Anything, my love.'

'Your grandmother will die of grief unless she knows she has set you free from the monster's clutches. I have been tempted many times to tell her, but in the first place you made me promise to keep this secret, and in the second, I do not think she will believe a young girl like me.' She almost added: 'She does not think much of me.'

The words landed on Ntsina's chest with the weight of rocks. He said nothing, and Bela kissed him.

'If you cannot, you cannot. But if you did, you would do her honour.'

✺

The aftermath of the casting of the spell of Reincarnation had left Nosakhe Zini deeply bewildered. That she had succeeded, at least in part, was obvious. She had found the Sea Gate to the Underworld, and freed a spirit powerful enough to chase and kill an experienced *sangoma*. The expression on Fezile's face at the moment of his death had hardened with *rigor mortis* into a most disquieting mask. It was clear that he had seen something so terrifying he had lost his wits, but what it was no one knew. Noni's role in her rescue added further to the puzzle. It seemed, after all, that Nosakhe had been right to spare her.

Since the death of her grandfather, Nosakhe had not apologized to anybody for anything. The manner in which she sought the forgiveness of the chief's family for her harshness towards their daughter went a long way to restoring happy relations at Gwadana.

For many days the village waited on tenterhooks for Ntsina's return, but as time passed Nosakhe came to see that in this, the greatest part of the spell, she had failed. And because she knew that it is better for a spell to fail completely than for certain parts to work on their own, she was greatly anxious. A spirit roamed abroad, whom she had released from the places of darkness. When would it reappear? To what purpose?

To the chief's infinite satisfaction, Nosakhe made Noni her pupil. She knew that certain children have strengths that adults lack. She began by showing Noni her magical relics and rare potions, and was reassured by the little girl's ability to find anything,

277

unseeing though she was, after once being shown its place. The child was extremely respectful, and Ata the dog loved her. Nosakhe took this as proof of her ultimate goodness, and hoped she would be ready to fight at her side when the moment to confront the Dark Goddess came.

A moon and a half after her rescue from the Sea, Nosakhe began to notice other strange signs. Chief among them was Sukude's behaviour. He had guarded the family's cattles and chased mischievous boys when they tried to steal her chickens' eggs: these were the domestic duties of the Xhosa male, and he had performed them acceptably. He had never lifted a finger in the performance of a woman's work. Nor had she expected him to.

The morning she first caught him on his knees with a dusting brush in his hand, Nosakhe felt so light-headed she had to sit down. She feigned obliviousness, but Sukude made no effort to keep his new activities secret. She said nothing as he swept the yard and emptied the mess from the chicken hutches and the pig sty. She watched him heat water from the stream and squat in the washing place, to do justice to a pot in which Bela had burned mealie meal, which stuck like a demon to its bottom. It was only when he approached her, later that evening, and asked if she might be good enough to teach him how to cook that she said: 'What on earth has come over you?'

She said it half jokingly, but the look in his eyes when he raised them to hers sent a chill down her spine.

Sukude was afraid.

She led him into the kitchen hut. 'What have you seen?'

'Nothing, Mama.' He had not addressed her so respectfully since the morning of Ntsina's wedding.

'Since when have you liked to cook or to clean?'

'I am trying only to be helpful, Mama.'

On this same day, she caught Bela sitting on the edge of the sea, chewing a stalk of sweet grass and gazing dreamily out over the ocean. The child looked *happy*. It was most bizarre. That night, over mealies Sukude had boiled, drinking homemade beer from tin cups he had washed, she looked closely at Bela and saw that, though she was as silent as ever, something had returned to her face that had not been there for too long. So long she had almost forgotten it. At first she was furious. It seemed that Sukude had finally seduced her – perhaps all this cleaning was his way of making nice to her. The idea was disgusting, and filled Nosakhe with impotent rage. She could do nothing to stop it. Sukude was perfectly within his rights to take his daughter-in-law for himself, now that her husband had gone for ever.

But Nosakhe, though it was many, many moons since any man had taken her to the love mat, remembered what intimacy was, and saw that there was none of it between Bela and Sukude; nor less any fear on her side. The fear seemed to be wholly on his.

She could not address these questions to Noni, for little girls should not be brought to knowledge of the love mat before their menses have started. Deprived of Fezile's counsel, she was obliged to ponder this strange evidence herself, and her brain could neither find a solution to the puzzle nor let it alone. The repetitive weighing of what she had seen, the endless searching for an elusive key that would decode the pattern behind her observations, carved deep neural pathways in Nosakhe – so deep that she lost the capacity to direct her thoughts in other directions. Her sleep grew troubled. Her dreams were vague and alarming. She read the entrails of two seabirds, and butchered the Zinis' best pig – but the gore that resulted was shapeless and held no meaning.

One night, waking from troubled slumber, she felt so thirsty she decided to brave the inconvenience of a trip to the water bucket. She put on a blanket, muttering to herself, and went out into the yard. The night was black as pitch. But beneath the kitchen door a low light burned. She was instantly awake. She clicked her fingers and her dog trotted to her side. Ata was a dependable guard dog. She could be relied on to leap for the throat of a malevolent intruder. But tonight she was not snarling. She was whimpering, and her tail wagged uncontrollably.

Nosakhe had learned her lesson. Before advancing she went back to her hut and put on her headdress. She took the most potent of her magic sticks, the one that had led the Great Founder across the forest, in the days before humans knew any such paths. As she crossed the yard, her heart began to beat irregularly. She was not a coward, but she felt weakened by the uncertainty and exertions of the last moons.

She stopped outside the door to her kitchen, and said a wordless prayer to her ancestors. A sensation of calm settled on her shoulders, like a soft blanket on a cold night. She opened the door.

On the floor, by the best cooking pot, was a large wooden box with several dials on it.

Beside it stood the reincarnated form of her grandson, Ntsina.

In the forest that same night, Luvo lay awake. Ntsina's question about the Strange One's reliability in the matter of honouring their bargain had begun to gnaw at him. He had reassured Ntsina as best he could, but deep within he knew that Stacey would never countenance the payment of large sums to Piet's Bantu partners. Across the country, Bantu fortunate enough to have employment were earning twenty-four pounds a year if they were lucky. She would say that the fifteen pounds they had already been given was more than enough for a few months' labour in a forest.

He tried to reassure himself, and failed. There was no contract, no document that could be presented to a court of law – even had there been a court in the country that would find in a Bantu's favour against a white man. He and Ntsina had already provided the services without which none of Piet's furniture would have been possible. He himself had even taught the Strange One enough isiXhosa to replace them both. Piet could continue with new men unhampered by the barrier of language. Against these fears, he tried to place his knowledge of Piet's goodness, his kindness. But he had also seen his weakness, and suspected he might not stand up to his wife if a choice were offered between her and their black workers.

He got up. He could not sleep. He went to the door of the hide and looked into the clearing. One Ancestor Tree had not satisfied Piet Barol. He had killed three more, without apology, and created ugly gashes in the canopy. The scaffolding had been used effectively, and the clearing was scarred with the holes that had been dug for it as it moved from tree to tree. Wide trenches gaped where roots had been ripped from the ground. There was a light coming from the workshop, and he went towards it, in need of company. To his surprise, he found the object of his thoughts sitting on a long bench, an expression of blissful concentration on his face.

Luvo did not find white men desirable, as a rule. He could appreciate the fineness of a Strange One's face, having been taught to look for it in the masterpieces of western art, but the sharpness of the Strange Ones' noses was off-putting. Tonight, watching Piet, whose face was lit by the warm glow of paraffin, whose lashes were long, whose concentration was so childlike in its purity, he had a flash of what it would be like to be loved by such a man. If he were his wife, he would not nag him as Stacey did.

Piet was working on a garland of flowers and fruits he intended to attach to the northeastern post of the bed. The garland was made of eight different woods. The flowers were of lime, but other woods, whose names he had invented for himself, made the twisting vines, the face of a squirrel that peeked between the leaves. Piet was carving from the back of the objects, a long line of tools glinting at his side. When Luvo tapped the wall to announce his presence, Piet jumped as violently as if he had been stabbed. He had been in a realm beyond consciousness. Luvo's tap wrenched him back to this world. He looked at the plant in his hand. He had done no damage. Relief made him laugh.

'You fright give me, my friend.'

'You gave me a fright.' Luvo could not help correcting him.

'You gave me a fright, my friend. What are you doing awake?'

Luvo went to him. He felt he could not last another day with-out reassurance. 'I was thinking about you,' he said, in English.

'Really?'

'And about your promise to pay me and Ntsina three hundred pounds each, as soon as Mr Shabrill has received his furniture. I know it is now two hundred and eighty-five, after the advance you gave us.'

A quick, downward deflection of Piet's glance was like a cold hand clutching his heart.

'Oh, that.' Piet imagined what Stacey would say when he told her he had promised to share half Shabrill's money with two Bantu.

'Your wife will return from Johannesburg with the money, will she not?'

'She very well may.'

'I should like to make my arrangements. You will soon have no need of a translator. If you do need one, I can hire one for you. My mission to King George the Fifth cannot be much longer delayed. It will soon be two years since the Natives Land Act was passed, and still the commission appointed to look into it has not reported. Once it does, it will be very hard to undo the legislation.'

Piet hesitated. It seemed that this was an opportunity for hon-esty. 'It will be very hard to undo in any case. You must know that.'

The timbers creaked. The trees of the forest rose up in unison, stirred by the wind. The dream of championing his people had become a talisman for Luvo, an assurance that his sacrifices in the forest, moral and physical, were worthy of the high principles on which he had been raised.

He said nothing.

'The world is caught up in a hideous war,' Piet went on, gently. 'The statesmen of Europe have far graver things on their minds than injustice done to the natives of South Africa.'

'There is nothing graver than injustice.'

'Well, there are injustices closer to home for your King George the Fifth. The British need the soldiers of South Africa, and above all the gold. The Afrikaners control both. They are not likely to offend them.'

When Luvo was seven, Frau Ranke had taken it upon herself to disabuse him of the existence of Father Christmas. Up to this point, he had believed in the existence of a man who flew in a sleigh, delivering presents to deserving children, as ardently as he believed that a carpenter in Nazareth had been conceived by a virgin. On that occasion he had cried in front of her. He felt a similar desire to cry now, at the destruction of his hopes.

Piet saw that he had wounded Luvo and touched his arm. 'I do not say you should not try. And I will ensure you have the money for a third-class ticket to Europe, and some more to spend in London, which is an expensive city. I just want you to be realistic, my dear fellow, so that disappointment when it comes is not too painful to bear.'

'You promised me three hundred pounds. Not a third-class ticket. I have many uses for it.'

'Very good.' Piet looked down at his work and picked up a chisel, as though their conversation had reached a natural end.

This enigmatic response brought of a note of panic into Luvo's voice. 'You would not cheat us.'

'Of course not. I will do the best I can.'

But doing the best he could was not the promise Piet had made, and they both knew it.

⟨⟩

Nosakhe Zini could not speak. She stopped breathing. Everything in the universe ceased to exist but Ntsina's face, the cleft in his chin, his sizeable nose – undiminished by his sojourn in the Underworld. Her grandfather had told her many times that she would rise one day to accomplish great things – greater than anyone else in the village. She had never doubted these assurances, but neither had they ever assumed such a concrete shape. Confronted by the evidence of her gifts, her faculties deserted her. In her youth she would have sizzled with self-satisfaction. Even a few months before, such a triumph would have doused her, almost drowned her, in pride. But she was old enough to know that she had accomplished nothing on her own. Without the Sea's aid, without the bravery of Fezile, without Noni, without the billy goat Ntsina had loved, she could never have brought her grandson back from the dead.

There was an animal-hide stool by the washing pot and she tottered towards it. She was conscious of a strong desire to sit down. Ntsina watched her, eyes wide. It was the expression he had worn as a child, when he had done something naughty and knew that punishment awaited him. She supposed it must be awkward to encounter a living person when one has spent many moons as a spirit. She opened her mouth several times. No words would come. Her voice seemed to have died. She wondered whether she would ever speak again. Perhaps her gift of language was one of the prices she had yet to pay for the miracle she had wrought. But this was not so. At length, she said: 'I see you, my grandson.'

The sound of her voice dissolved all Ntsina's nerves. He flung himself at her feet, squeezing her knees as tightly as he had as a child. He lost consciousness of the many things he had done that she might disown him for. All he knew was Love. It made him sob and as the tears flowed he choked. 'I see you, my grandmother.' His voice was as high and true as a little boy's.

'What is this?' Nosakhe regarded the wooden chest with shrewd interest.

'It is a present I have brought. To thank you for your courage.' He stood up and wound it, then switched it on, hoping for a jolly song. But all he heard was the chatter of the airwaves. He fiddled with every dial. Nothing but brutal whisperings. Ntsina did not know how music found its way to a radio, and so could not understand why this one did not play. They were far too far from the radio masts at King William's Town to catch any of the patriotic programs beamed into the heavens. He began to feel foolish, and angry with the man who had sold it to him. The anti-climax was devastating.

But Nosakhe approached the dial reverently, and twisted it. She felt only wonder. There are unseen spirits all around us, and they speak in their own tongues. She had never heard their tongues so clearly before.

'Have you returned for good?'

'No, Mama. I must go back tonight.'

'To the Creature?'

'To the forest. I have escaped the Creature. It was you who rescued me. But I have an undertaking to accomplish that cannot be spoken of. No one must enter the forest until I have completed it. When I am finished, I will come again.'

She nodded. Then she touched him. She had expected, per-haps, the cold solidity of wood – but he felt warm and strong. Stronger and healthier than he had been on his wedding day. He was fuller in the chest, more of a man. 'Was it dreadful?'

'Yes, Mama.'

'Will you tell me of it?'

'No. There are some things mortals can never know.'

She accepted this answer without question, and he saw that he would not be interrogated. Relief made him euphoric. 'Let me taste your sheep fat, before I go.'

She made it for him. She felt joyful but uncertain. The dog went immediately to Ntsina and nuzzled him as Nosakhe would have done had she not . . . She knew one must be reverent with a spirit, and did not wish to take liberties. Ntsina ate a whole loaf of bread and all the sheep fat she had left. She had not been a diligent cook in the moons since his departure.

When he was finished, he said: 'Do you know what my father did to my wife?'

'I know,' said Nosakhe.

'Then you know what must happen.'

'A man cannot kill his own father, no matter what he has done.'

'Then I shall not kill him.' He embraced her. Her smell was

unchanging. For a moment he wished to be a little boy again. Then he came to his senses. A boy cannot have a wife, and he would not exchange his woman for anything in the world. 'But die he must.'

When he had gone, Nosakhe sat, listening to the supernatural whispers of the wooden box he had left behind. To be a mortal who hears the spirits! She accepted it as the great privilege it was. When she had sat for some time, she switched off the radio and blew out the lantern. She crossed the yard and went to the hut where she did her magic. Among her many possessions was a padlock. She had bartered it from a traveller in the year of Ntsina's birth. It had no key, but it was open. What it locked it would lock for ever, and she had saved it carefully, wondering why Ma had sent it.

Now she knew.

She went to Sukude's hut and slipped the padlock into the bolt. Then she closed it, tested it, and found its resistance was total. She smiled. For many years Sukude had thought he had the only lock in the whole of Gwadana.

She went to her own hut, in which a brazier still smoked. She folded her best blanket several times and put two coals in it. Immediately the blanket began to singe. She hurried across the yard. Sukude's snores came balefully through his door. She thanked Ma for her assistance, and threw the coals onto his roof.

Nosakhe sat on the sheep trough as the coals found resting places in the dry thatch. The wind caressed them. Smoke twisted towards the stars. She watched intently, urging them to action. Flames began to creep between the stalks of the thatch, and the air was sweet with its scent.

Sukude's snoring stopped. For the time it takes a wave to break there was silence. Then terrible screams broke it. She heard a key scraping in a lock, then desperate bangs on the door. Her padlock held true. The burning of the hut was magnificent. Even from the opposite side of the yard, sweat ran down Nosakhe's face, so hot it was. She sat, back straight. There was fury in the screams as well

as terror. She heard her own name, and bowed in acknowledgement of her authority. The noise brought Bela to her door. At
the collapse of the central joist of the roof there was one mighty
scream, then no more.

Nosakhe shifted along the sheep trough, and patted the space
beside her. Her granddaughter-in-law sat down.

'It is time for us to start afresh,' said Nosakhe Zini.

12

In Johannesburg, Stacey Barol was behaving like a woman with a substantial private income, and good God she loved it. Having no pressing need to charm Percy Shabrill allowed her to be commanding with him. This was just the right line for a stylish woman to take. The furniture was a magnificent success. Even Percy, who had prepared many speeches on this subject, stopped spluttering about how long it had taken to make – especially when Stacey told him that Piet had fought gloriously in France, and been injured and invalided home to supervise its creation.

'Capital, capital,' said Percy, who had no intention of going anywhere to fight.

In the vast, spare rooms Herbert Baker had designed, the furniture Piet had made added enchantment and originality. Each piece, conceived in the melting lava of an artist's inspiration and fashioned by gifted, highly competitive craftsmen, had the stature an object of beauty acquires on its own terms. Added to which, how *comfortable* they were! In the months of waiting Dorothy had grown anxious over the eccentric designs she had approved. She knew that whatever was delivered she must live with for the rest of her life. There could be no pretence of sending it back.

She had rifled through Percy's desk one morning and found the bill of sale. Such a sum could not be wasted – it was many times higher than the original Hepplewhite's bill, and they had chosen the best of everything at Hepplewhite's. She had feared that the chairs would be as uncomfortable as the splendid pieces in the hall of Warrington Manor, the residence of the man who had given her father his living. She had been obliged to spend many hours on those chairs as a child. She could still feel the ache in her buttocks. Piet's chairs – what a revelation they were. As soon as she sat she was welcomed by the lines of the wood. They did not permit slouching. One could not sit in them in any attitude that was not as elegant and graceful as they were – but they made the preservation of an upright posture a pleasure, not an imposition.

Stacey arranged the furniture wonderfully. She had brought the contents of Percy's study, the dining room, and everything in the library save the bookcases. 'The bookcases you are going to *adore*,' she said. 'I am not going to tell you a word about them.'

Stacey and Dorothy went shopping together, and filled the Shabrills' Packard to the brim on each occasion. After twelve weeks in a forest, bombarded by every kind of inconvenience, human and animal, nothing could be more amusing than shopping for silk lampshades, china, eiderdowns of goose feathers, cashmere blankets, satin for curtains – and then dresses. There was a sweetness in Dorothy Shabrill that Stacey Barol's megawatt charm brought out. Dorothy was so ready to play the lesser role, so eager to give way to Stacey on every question of style, so happy to pay any bill Stacey considered necessary, that Stacey's affectionate nature was engaged. She missed her son and had lived too long without a woman friend. To have one again was marvellous. She determined to give Dorothy and Percy a house beyond their imaginings – and as it took shape she remembered why she loved her husband.

She cabled to Piet, instructing him to chop down more of the wonderful trees that were making such an impression. When Percy learned that the Barols intended to sell this wood to other men, his competitive spirit was roused and Stacey made great use of it. She agreed not to sell any pieces in Ancestor wood for twelve months, so that Percy might have full boasting rights. The night she struck this deal, which involved the payment of a considerable sum, she drank a whole bottle of champagne in her bath at the Carlton Hotel. Percy's boastfulness was better than any sales force. She encouraged him to give a party. The drawing-room furniture not having arrived, she filled this room with divans and silk cushions, and called it the Grand Vizier's Chamber. No one in Johannesburg had ever heard of a Grand Vizier's Chamber, nor seen a room furnished with such theatrical panache. It was a hit. Under the pretext of praising Percy's marvellous taste, she drew attention to the subtleties of her husband's.

The next day, she received six telegrams and three telephone calls: new clients, with new houses to furnish. Her promise to Percy not to sell the Ancestor Tree to anyone else had the unintended consequence of creating a waiting list. The mere existence of a waiting list provoked a further nine telegrams that afternoon, and the next morning when she returned to the Carlton after a delightful few hours at the couturier's with Dorothy, she found that twelve women had telephoned her, and eight men.

Her experiences in Cape Town had taught Stacey that verbal agreements count for nothing. She engaged a lawyer. This man drew up contracts, and anyone who wished to be on the waiting list had to sign one. The contracts committed them to the upfront payment of a third of the total commission, and to swift settling of the rest upon receipt of the furniture. Tardiness in paying the bill led to extravagant rates of interest, and she made these clear to her new clients. They were all flush with money pouring from the ground in this time of great demand for ammunitions and gold, so fortuitously facilitated by limitless Bantu labour that cost, in real terms, per person, rather less than the first white settlers had had to spend on the upkeep of their slaves.

A booming economy, a sense of unspeakable horrors across the sea, fused with glorious weather to put white Johannesburg in party spirits. These spirits chimed so well with Stacey's that she found herself with invitations to dine or dance every night of the week. This required, of course, more clothes, and now she had so much cash that she abandoned all attempts at moderation.

She had never had real jewels. None save the single diamond on the ring Piet had given her on their engagement. She had always thought that those who spent money on gems were foolish, since convincing replicas could be had at a fraction of the cost. Now, under the influence of certain velvet-voiced salesmen, she began to see that precious stones were an excellent investment in view of the, ahem, uncertainty of the international situation. They were easy to transport, easy to sell. The salesmen assured her they would never lose their value. Impulsively, she bought a necklace of brilliant cut pink diamonds, and earrings to match. These gave her the confidence to demand ever more exorbitant prices. The swagger with which she did so persuaded many clients to accept them.

The ancient Greeks might have told Stacey Barol what the Xhosa also know: that it is when one is soaring at the heights that a sharp shock is coming. She had done so well in Johannesburg, was so buoyed up on the currents of her own audacity, that her drastic error, when it came, caught her quite unawares.

∽

Stacey had bought a gorgeous desk set of green alligator skin for Percy's study, and had taken it back to the Carlton. She could not resist arranging it on the writing table in her suite, and found its impact so alluring that she wrote a love letter to her husband. In this letter, she described her many victories over Percy Shabrill. She blotted the letter and took a bath and went out, telling her maid to pack the set and send it round to its owners. Percy opened it at his new desk, in his comfortable new chair, feeling on top of the world. He was surprised to find the blotter had been used, and his eye was drawn to a series of shapes that was clearly his own name in mirror writing. He took the page to the mirror above the fireplace, and, holding it up, read the unfortunate phrase: 'Percy Shabrill – what a booby!'

It was a long time since anyone had articulated his greatest fear to Percy. Assiduous cultivation of contacts, and a useful patent, had allowed him to make the sums of money that shield a man from unpopularity. As more people had reason to make nice to him, he had begun to lose the social anxieties of his boyhood. Now they returned, in full force. He had cried bitterly in the boot room at his minor public school, when cleverer boys who were better at games had made him feel less than them. He had learned to cover his unease with bluster. This bluster had sustained him on a three-week voyage to South Africa, sharing a cabin with a man as endowed with natural advantages as Piet Barol. Dorothy's love had calmed him, and his brutality to the middle managers in his cooling concern allowed him to feel powerful. Reading Stacey Barol's opinion of him sent him hurtling back to the boot rooms of his youth.

Except this time he did not feel sad.

He was angry.

The ladies arrived half an hour later, gossiping and laughing, and when she saw the desk set, Stacey had an inkling of what had happened and felt a pricking of panic. Her eyes sought Percy's, and when his did not meet hers she knew deep within that one of the unflattering things she had written about him had come to his attention. The suspicion was confirmed when Percy, who until now had thrived on her attention, did not ask her to stay to lunch. When Dorothy did, she excused herself and hurried away. On her way out she popped into the study and saw that the top sheet of the blotter had gone.

That afternoon, she received a short note at her hotel. 'If I do not have my furniture, every last stick of it, within a month, I will cancel the order and return it all. In such circumstances a full refund will be required and pursued. Shabrill.'

The first Piet knew of this was a telegram announcing that Stacey had engaged twelve cabinetmakers and that they were already on the train to East London. With them was coming the equipment of a furniture manufactory Stacey had found that was closing down, as well as its foreman. Piet made his way thoughtfully back to the wagon and spurred his horses to a quick trot. He knew he should be happy, but he was not.

In the weeks since Stacey's departure, Piet had known the happiness of the artist who at last has everything he needs to make good work. The quietness of his forest life, the companionability of his men, the way they had grown used to one another: all this had combined to put Piet in a state of heightened, energetic tranquillity. He had set himself up in a corner of the workshop, and thrown himself into exploring the mysteries of the woods he had found in Gwadana. He had learned, and come to love, their eccentricities – the pliability of lime wood, the resistance of another Ntsina called *luyolo*, the differences in their grains and inclinations. With each passing day, his designs for the Shabrills' bed grew more elaborate. He had come to understand that nothing short of an enchanted bower would suffice, a woodland glade in which magic happened. He had worked on the single block of Ancestor wood, fashioning posts and a canopy, but had cast aside the model of the European four poster. His posts curved sinuously, reached the canopy at different heights, created when one lay on the base – how much better this effect would be when there was a mattress and fine linen! – the sensation of having entered a world apart.

He had intended to carve the wood of the Ancestor Tree, but it was too hard to take extra-fine detailing, and he was fearful of making a mistake and spoiling the whole. Instead, he embellished it with many different woods, each the right one for the object it represented, and these were discreetly nailed into the main frame. It was these embellishments that took infinite time, for he took infinite pains with them. He had thrown away half a tree's worth of lime wood, because the trumpet-shaped flowers he made with it had not come out quite right. Now the foliage was nearly complete, and he was adding the dramas of forest life – frogs climbing the tendrils of a vine, on the lookout for mates; monkeys scrapping in the leaves. It had a mischievous atmosphere, this bed, and Piet took care to make the creatures friendly, not frightening. Ierephaan and Mohammed made the rest of the furniture, he spent his days and most of his nights with this bed, while Arthur roamed the forest with Ntsina and learned the ways of the wild.

To have his little boy with him, to have him close but to be freed of his constant presence so he could work, was perfection for Piet Barol. He spent an hour every day with Arthur when he returned from the forest, and bathed him and listened with total attention to the child's tales of what he had seen. Piet's own father had been gruff with him. He could not remember a single hug, much less a cuddle, and he took his inspiration from the way his mother had loved him. The boy was daily more fluent in isiXhosa and the calls of forest creatures. It delighted Piet that his son could summon a Lula bird, or make a howler monkey appear in the trees. He delegated the teaching of counting and writing to Luvo, who was a strict but gentle master, and when Arthur got all his sums right he was allowed to stay up with the men by the fire. This was a far more powerful incentive than the sweeties the Barols had bribed Arthur with in Cape Town.

In Stacey's absence, Piet's anger with her cooled and he began to miss her. But the prospect of having his purposeful life disturbed by the arrival of a crowd of strangers nevertheless depressed him. He could see no way to resist. They had come to Gwadana to make money. Stacey had gone to Johannesburg to win orders. She had done so. It was now his duty to fulfil them.

Having collected her telegram, he stopped to water his horses in Idutywa and noticed that the woman with the direct gaze was not there. Instead a child, perhaps eight years old, was standing by the roadside with a pail, his hands outstretched for a coin. Piet got down from the box, and said: 'Good day. My name is Piet Barol. What's yours?'

The child, whose name was Zuko, had gathered every last ounce of his courage to approach a Strange One in this manner. He had not known what to expect from this mythical animal. Certainly it was not to be spoken to in his own tongue. Without a word, without even remembering to take a coin, he dashed away from Piet and into the house, where he sent his mother to deal with the creature outside.

'You have a fine son,' said Piet to this lady, as the horses drank.

'So do you,' she said. 'I've seen him.'

'We are lucky.'

'Where is his mother?'

'In Johannesburg. She will return shortly.' Piet had never seen a man here. 'Where is his father?'

'At the mines. He may never return.' She shrugged as she said this, as though it would not cause her much hardship if she never saw him again.

'May he come back safe and sound.' Piet got onto the wagon, paid her, and drove off up the hill towards the forest. He could not afterwards explain to himself quite why he turned just before the bend in the road, but he did turn.

And she was watching him.

∿

'She is coming back,' said Luvo to Ntsina, 'and bringing more workmen.' The night was chilly. He edged closer to the fire. At dinner, Piet had made everyone roar with laughter describing certain misadventures of his youth.

'Now we will know the truth,' said Ntsina.

Luvo had the uncomfortable sensation of believing many things at once, not all of which could be true. The man he had dined with that night, who understood the injustice of the Natives Land Act, who had made him laugh, and rescued him from the employ of Percy Shabrill: he liked him. He could not deny it. He made friends rarely, but when he did he kept them. He only liked honourable men. He liked Piet. Therefore . . . But no matter how many times he ran the equation in his head, it produced the same, jarring answer. 'He would be honourable to us on his own,' he said. 'But she won't let him. And he won't stand up to her for us.'

It made Luvo feel worse to say it, as though the articulation of this thought made it more likely to be true. 'I could be wrong,' he added.

'You are not wrong, my brother.'

They gazed at the coals.

'He will certainly give us something. Probably enough to set us up.'

'He owes us three hundred pounds each. Without us, none of this would have happened.'

They talked on, reinforcing each other's sense of grievance.

'So what do you propose?' said Ntsina, some time later. His voice was cold with anger.

'I do not know.'

'I know.'

'Tell me, brother.'

'If it is justly ours, then taking it cannot be thieving.'

Stacey Barol had no intention of confessing the mistake she had made with Percy Shabrill, but this did not reduce her mortification. Her return to East London, which should have been triumphant, was spoiled by self-recrimination. She had learned a great deal from the way the leading ladies of the Opéra Comique handled their patrons. To puncture a man's vanity is rarely wise. When he is rich, it is catastrophic. Her subtle mind examined the situation from every angle. She knew she had lost Percy's future patronage. This would not be fatal, as long as they got him his furniture on time and he paid what he owed. She had enough orders to keep Barol & Co. in production for months. But she feared Percy's vengeance. Would he campaign against them in her absence? She could not be sure, and dozed fitfully as she tried to convince herself that he wouldn't. Turning against the Barols would require disowning his furniture, which would undermine his new status as a connoisseur. Surely Percy wouldn't do that?

In East London, she bought a truck and paid in cash, hoping to

God she was right. She had left her fine gowns in Johannesburg for safe-keeping, and was back in her old clothes. Their shabby grandeur depressed her. She had taken the precaution of hiring white craftsmen who spoke English, and allowed their foreman, whose name was Frank Albemarle, to drive them. They roared through Butterworth in a cloud of dust.

Every night as she had gone to sleep in her suite at the Carlton Hotel, Stacey had whispered, as though he could hear her: 'I love you, Piet Barol.' And yet, as the truck left Butterworth, passed the village of Idutywa, and wound up a dirt track towards the forest, a little voice reminded her that the man she loved had been a man of fashion, the handsomest gentleman at a party; a man whose looks and charm were proverbial. She had found his beard arousing before she had known the life it represented. Now she knew, and her long weeks of luxury made the coming squalor oppressive.

The track ended and a barricade of trees and vines blocked their path. Frank Albemarle stopped the truck. He had had a chequered career in Johannesburg and had just decided to sign up for the navy when Stacey discovered him. He rather thought they might have a love affair. He was in the mood for one, and had chosen passion over fighting the Germans. He had no faith in the female sense of direction, and wondered how on earth they would get to where they were going with no maps. 'Are you sure this is the way?'

Stacey's look silenced him. She got down from the cab and inspected the trees, looking for the elephant track. She made Albemarle's men pull back a fallen log and masses of ferns. Ahead was a road, just wide enough for the lorry. She got back in and said: 'Drive on.'

The arrival of a motorized lorry in the forest of Gwadana was a seismic event. Snakes reared as the ground shook, and raced for their burrows. Spiders clung tight to their webs. Impalas fled in terror from this fast and violent beast. Baboons gathered their babies close to them, and Lula birds dashed for the heavens. The

297

sound of the lorry's engine penetrated the cold sleep of starvation that had come to claim the leopard who had stolen Piet's biltong many moons before. It was heard long before it was seen in the clearing that had once housed a grove of Ancestor Trees, and Piet looked at his band and their workshop, storing them in his mind.

He knew how all this must seem to a woman who has grown used to the Carlton Hotel. And yet he also knew that there was beauty here, and happiness. He thought that of all the places he had lived, this was the one he most preferred. If only Stacey could see its loveliness . . .

He closed his eyes, found his tone, and went to meet his wife.

⌒

To his surprise, Stacey had brought with her a man quite clearly taken by her charms. He greeted this individual without enthusiasm and kissed Stacey passionately, aware of their audience.

Frank Albemarle was annoyed by the fervour of their embrace. He took his temper out on the darkies Stacey had told him to whip into shape. One of them spoke English, and Frank berated him at length. He demanded an instant checking of the inventory, and on being told there wasn't one he began shouting at the top of his voice.

'Who on earth is that?' said Piet, as he and Stacey reached their little house.

'We need someone to hurry things along. You'll be glad I brought him.'

Albemarle waited for Piet to close his door. Then he claimed the largest hide for himself. It had, until now, been occupied by Ntsina, who returned from the forest with two impalas to find that his few possessions were scattered on the ground in front of it. He asked why and was met by a torrent of English words.

It was so long since a Strange One had shouted at him that Ntsina had the awful sensation that he was waking from a dream, returned to a reality he had forgotten while he slept. He collected his things and put them in Luvo's hide. They sat without speaking

298

as Albemarle's men invaded the clearing. They had brought three cases of gin, and their first action was to fashion a door for one of the hides, and equip it with a lock.

'You can't trust Kaffirs with alcohol,' said Albemarle, whacking back a stiff one.

Arthur had come back from the forest with Ntsina. He was overjoyed to see his mama but did not like these new arrivals at all. Stacey made him shake hands with them, and the way they crushed his little hand in their large ones made him aggrieved. He followed his mother into her room when she went to wash, and said: 'Why have you brought these horrid men here?'

'To work, darling. We need to get out of this ghastly forest.' Stacey opened the cabinet by her bed and shrieked. An enormous spider was within. 'Piet!' She did not intend to ask Ntsina to assist her again. She was horrified to see Arthur scoop the frightened creature up, very gently, in both hands.

'These spiders only bite if you hurt them, mother. Don't be afraid.' And he took the creature outside and put him on a bush.

Dinner was fraught. The white men drank too much and the black men, until recently as entertained as they were entertaining, sat in silence.

'We will use these visitors to get the furniture finished,' said Piet to Luvo, once Stacey had gone to bed. 'Think of them as a temporary inconvenience.'

'That man cannot call us Kaffirs. Tell him.'

'I will. I promise.'

That night, as Piet kissed her tender places, Stacey tried to relax but found that she could not. He was used to giving her pleasure and persisted. When he knew he had failed he pulled away and lay on his back, staring at the ceiling. In the past, pleasure had always soothed their disagreements. Without it, there was only the deafening roar of insects.

'I'm sorry you do not care for this place,' he said.

'I don't care for our son going native. That's what I don't care for.'

'He's becoming a man. Can't you see?'

She said nothing. Outside, Arthur's high voice floated over the growls of the men by the campfire. Instinctively, she listened to what he was saying, and found she could not understand it.

'He's speaking like a Kaffir.'

'Don't use that word.'

'Why ever not?'

'It isn't polite.'

'Our son is speaking like a native, then.'

'There are millions of natives in this country. The white man who can speak to them in their own tongue will be at a huge advantage.'

'In what possible way?'

'He won't be cheated, for one thing.'

She turned away from him and said, 'Tickle my back.' He did so, sending ripples across her skin. At length she whispered, rather timidly: 'Did you miss me?'

'Terribly.'

But they did not make love.

~

Ntsina had been up till dawn the day before, in raptures with his wife, and though he and Luvo had many things to discuss he could not keep his eyes open. Luvo watched him, and felt afraid of the future. What Piet had said about the likely priorities of King George the Fifth had the ring of truth. This demolished his last defence against despair. To live in a country where no Bantu might own land! It was not to be borne. His parents could not live with the Rankes for ever, yet what alternative did they have? He thought of his sister. Anna had suffered doubly: the Xhosa did not educate their women, and now the whites would not let her work as anything but a servant girl. She was cleverer than him, with a natural quickness he had often envied. Thoughts of her brought the knowledge of the way his nephew had died. He could hear the white men carousing by the fire. Who would tell

300

them that in this place the Bantu were treated respectfully?

It was May, and very cold. He thought of all that had happened since Ntsina had asked him to translate for the Strange One in the Shabrills' rose garden. Like Piet, who was also lying awake, he understood that something had ended for good: a way of life they had made for themselves. Now it was over, he regretted not enjoying himself more. He had been annoyed by the inconveniences of forest life, by the endless amounts of washing up. He had grown too used to being treated as an equal, and the prospect of a return to servitude was unbearable.

He did his best to believe that Piet would pay him what he had promised, whatever Stacey said. The effort made him sleepy, and then sentimental. He looked at Ntsina's sleeping form. How many more nights would they have together? What would happen to him? He grew angry on Ntsina's behalf. By helping Piet he had betrayed his people. No sum of money could compensate him for that.

Luvo lay down on his blanket. He was freezing, and he pacified his conscience by reminding himself that it is natural for animals to seek one another's warmth when they are cold. He lay right against his friend, closer than he ever had before. The solidity of Ntsina's body was reassuring. He allowed his nose to touch the back of his friend's neck, and drank in his smell, praying to God for His protection.

When Piet woke the next morning, Frank Albemarle had already had half the contents of the workshop laid out in the clearing and was shouting at Ierephaan and Mohammed. He had authorized his men to conduct a search of their sleeping place and they had discovered two chisels and a gouge.

'Barol! Perhaps you can help. This coolie is trying to say that the tools we found hidden in his bag belong to him. Is that so?'

Piet examined them.

'It is so.'

'Well lucky for you this time,' said Albemarle to Ierephaan. To Piet he said: 'This camp wants order. You won't keep darkies on the straight and narrow without it. Boy! Coffee for your master.'

The individual thus addressed was Luvo, who made coffee for everyone every morning, as a politeness.

'Now, Boy,' said Albemarle. 'I take four sugars. You go ask the other baas men how they like their tea, their coffee, their gin. And don't you forget what they tell you.'

Luvo looked at Piet.

'A word if you please, Mr Albemarle.'

Piet took Frank Albemarle to the furthest recess of the workshop, where they would not be overheard. 'Welcome to this forest,' he said.

'Much obliged to assist you, I'm sure. You leave everything to me. I've been in South Africa twenty years. Know how to get the best out of darkies.'

'In this camp, we don't refer to anyone as a darkie. Or a Kaffir.'

Albemarle looked at him. His eyes narrowed.

'The Bantu who work for me have made many sacrifices and shown themselves loyal and dependable. And very good fellows. I don't want you to address fully grown men as "Boy", and I don't want you to suggest that people have been stealing unless you have clear and abundant proof.'

Piet did not enjoy giving these orders, and Frank Albemarle did not enjoy receiving them.

'Kaffir lover are you?' he said. 'Well, you'll learn the hard way.'

❧

There is nothing like the observation of an attractive woman to sharpen a man's work ethic. On the train from Johannesburg, Stacey Barol had told Frank Albemarle plainly what must be accomplished. She had not been disloyal about her husband, and had praised Piet's genius as a designer; but she had made it quite plain that he was too soft-hearted to get the best out of his men.

Spurred by her approving glances, Albemarle set about getting results. He observed a strict hierarchy of labour: heavy unskilled work for the blacks; carving for the Indians and the whites. He himself was no furniture maker, but he knew a thing or two about production lines. He had another workshop built, twice as large as the first, and put his twelve craftsmen in it. He put Grace in charge of the black crew and sent them on an orgy of destruction through the forest. Within a week, ten further mahoganies had been felled and brought to the clearing. This was enough for the carvers to be getting on with and he turned his attention to the Ancestor Trees. Fifteen had once grown in this hallowed place. There were twelve standing when Albemarle arrived. Within six weeks, only the greatest of them was left.

The strength of the Ancestor Trees had derived, always, from their unity. Their fused roots, deep in the ground, were an anchor that kept them steady in the fiercest winds. When fire or disease ravaged one, her sisters sent nutrients to her aid, as well as a particular toxin that no bacterium had yet been able to stand for long. In this period of crisis, their leaves filled with this toxin. Ants ate the leaves, and tree frogs ate the ants, and became very poisonous. One of Albemarle's men, who fancied himself a naturalist, caught one of these frogs and made the mistake of not washing his hands. He was in bed for six days, writhing in agony.

'We should take him to a hospital,' said Piet.

'No such shakes,' said Albemarle. 'Food poisoning and too much gin. No one leaves this clearing till the last of these trees is down.'

His swagger made Stacey feel safe, and she tended the ailing man herself, and after a time he got well.

With the felling of each tree, the job of slaughtering the others grew easier. Few men crossed the clearing any longer. It was scarred by deep trenches where the roots had been dug out. Each severed root weakened the trees that still stood. The scaffolding was put to punishing use, and soon it was the tallest object still standing.

It is a sad truth that once a sacred rule is broken, it is rarely

adhered to again. Ntsina was powerless to hold Piet to his promise that one tree would suffice. When only one still stood, Luvo
found him at dawn by the stream.

'Do you promise me, my brother, that my ancestors are safe
with your Christian God?'

'I promise,' said Luvo. 'And once the furniture has gone the
Strange One will pay for new shrines, closer to the village, where
you may pray for their souls.'

'Do you believe that?'

'I do,' said Luvo, trying to.

And that day, the last tree came down.

No one at Gwadana mourned Sukude Zini, or objected when his
body was weighted with rocks and offered to the Sea. When the
chief ventured that perhaps lightning had struck his roof, and set
the fire, Nosakhe merely said: 'It was time for him to meet the
Goddess.'

For many moons the villagers had avoided the homestead at
the top of the hill, so much closer to the heavens than theirs,
but once word got out that Nosakhe had a box that allowed her
to hear the spirits, curiosity got the better of fear – as it so often
will. The children went first, and knocked on Nosakhe's kitchen
door, offering their services, eyes peeled for evidence of this magic
box. Once they had confirmed its existence, many adults found a
reason to climb the escarpment.

In these worrying months, the displeasure of their ancestors,
made so alarmingly plain, had caused many an interrogation of
personal piety at Gwadana. Few failed to find themselves wanting. Twenty-eight white goats had lost their lives to the cause of
winning ancestral forgiveness, and the death of Fezile the witch
doctor left people feeling exposed. The possibility of finding out,
once and for all, where they stood, gave them the courage to brave
Nosakhe's piercing gaze, and her kitchen filled with all manner of
good things.

Nosakhe had no need of a spirit box to tell her that her neighbours had gossiped about her, but the success of her spell of Reincarnation had left her in a forgiving mood. Why should a woman with power over Death itself to worry about the unkindness of mortals? She received them more gently than they expected. The spirit box was placed at the centre of her magic hut, but it was not Nosakhe who set its dials to the correct frequency.

It was Noni, whose gift of Farsight became plainer with each passing day.

The elevation of Noni to chief operator of the magic box was her mother's crowning happiness. She found it possible to forgive her husband for his weakness. Perhaps the flowering of Noni's gift had required the fertilizer of a mother's sacrifice. She was by nature a contented, gentle person, and satisfaction so profound made her very obliging on the love mat. Happiness reigned once more in the chief's household, and again Kagiso proposed a mission to the forest to rescue his friend. This time Nosakhe forbade it, though she blessed the young man's courage. She told him Ntsina was fighting a war only spirits can wage. 'When the time comes for you to play your part, you may be sure he will send for you. And in the meantime, dear boy, savour life as it deserves and put away your fears.'

Noni's pronouncements were not always so reassuring. Her light footsteps and uncanny ability to navigate the village even on the blackest nights had left her with a treasure trove of information about Gwadana's residents. The attention she received when she used these nuggets went to her head, and she developed the impressive trick of running up the escarpment as quickly as her legs would carry her, despite the narrowness of the cliff path. She was not unkind, and there were things she knew that she never spoke of, as befits a great seer. But in the matter of husbands who hit their wives, or took young girls who were not their wives to the love mat, she was unforgiving.

Many a man left Nosakhe's magic hut chilled to his core, and determined to do better.

On a windswept day, when the waves danced, Bela's father came. Zandi was with child, and he wished to know the father. Noni listened intently to the box, and told him to come back the following day. As soon as he had gone, she went to Bela's hut and told her of her father's visit.

That her father should visit without greeting her punctured Bela's great happiness. She spent her days praying to Ntsina's shrine, and three nights a week worshipping the manly form his spirit had taken. The sweetness in her nature, intensified by isolation, found a happy recipient in Noni, who had never had a big sister. They were inseparable, and when Noni told her of her father's enquiries, Bela was glad. So what if her sister had not married! She had tasted the joys of the love mat, and that was wonderful. 'You must tell my father his ancestors have sent Zandi a child, so that he and my mother will have someone to worship their spirits when they have crossed to the world beyond.'

The following day Bela's father returned, and Noni told him. His relief was so potent she could feel it in the close little room, though she could not see him. 'Before you smile much longer,' she said, 'there is something else your ancestors wish to say.' Noni's habit of referring to facial expressions she could not see was unnerving. It tempered Litha's smile.

'I am listening, little mother.'

Noni wound the set and switched it on. There was a knob that raised the volume, and she turned it as far as it would go to emphasize her point. 'Your ancestors are angry with you, as you can hear.' She drew herself to her full height. 'They have sent you an heir, yet you do not visit your own daughter.'

It had cost Bela's father dearly to obey the witch doctor Fezile's injunction that Bela was not to be spoken to, for her own good.

'But what of the evil spirit?'

'That spirit has been chased from her. And even if it were still there, no child can be injured by a parent's love.'

☙

It was time, Nosakhe said, to show the world that Bela was under the protection of Good Magic once again. She was surprised by her granddaughter-in-law's resistance. Bela was not at all sure how she felt about the friends who had abandoned her, and found that she had no desire to resume her girlish pursuits. Having been elevated to commune with spirits, she was in no hurry to rush back to the low gossip of village life.

Nevertheless, the thought of seeing her parents was a powerful temptation. She fixed her hair and donned her best blanket for her walk through the village. She went hand in hand with Nosakhe, and the chief himself came to his homestead gate to greet her. Those watching saw that the Bela they had known had gone for ever. Her eyes were no longer glazed, but neither did they sparkle with mischief and innuendo. She had serenity now, and it gave her beauty a dignity that made them hesitate to approach her, conscious of their own weakness.

When Mama Jaxa saw her daughter, she dropped the mealies she was carrying and threw herself at Bela. Their separation had been the sternest trial she had yet endured. Zandi's return, at Bela's request, had heightened her worry. So had Zandi's sudden swelling, which seemed a further cause of shame. She had almost beaten her to extract a confession of the baby's paternity. But Zandi had kept her own counsel, and now her mother understood that the child had been sent by the ancestors themselves.

Oh the merrymaking in the Jaxa homestead that night!

Bela's father slaughtered his finest cow, and Mama Jaxa produced the special spirit she distilled from the leaves of the aloe plant. It was at this feast, more truly than at the wedding of Ntsina and Bela, that the two families became one. 'A very great battle is under way,' Nosakhe told them, accepting a drink. 'I hope Light will prevail over Darkness, though one can never be sure.'

'I am sure,' said Noni.

Two days later, Bela and Ntsina met in the clearing of the second Blessing. She could not wait to share the news of the child her ancestors had sent Zandi.

The Blessing had withdrawn into itself, conserving its sweetness for another hundred moons. Ntsina lay down on the blanket Bela had brought, and when she joined him his face sought the squishy comfort of her breasts. He often reposed himself thus after they had put the love mat to good use. Today he seemed to have no strength for love making.

'Are you injured, my dear one?' She stroked his cheek. 'Is the battle hard?'

Ntsina did not reply. A strange sound found them – a thudding, regular beat. Frank Albemarle had devised a shift system, so that production need never stop. Far away, his men were dismembering an Ancestor Tree, and the wind reminded Ntsina of all he had done. He closed his eyes and held his wife tight. He was consumed by regret for permitting the destruction of these trees, and by rage at the possibility that he might not get paid for his pains.

'Is the battle hard?'

He had told her many fanciful stories. 'Very hard,' he said.

'Does it tire you, to take human shape for me?'

'I do it gladly.'

'We can meet less often, if you need it so.'

He raised himself on his elbows. 'I couldn't fight this war without you.'

This pleased her, and she kissed him. 'Does it go well?'

'Not as well as formerly.'

'Why not?'

There was so much he wanted to tell her. In the end what he said was: 'There are new forces in the forest.'

'Tell me of them.'

He contemplated the many truths he could never share with her. At last he said: 'A wicked queen has come. She has brought with her twelve fiends, who do as she commands. Their

308

leader is called Albamaah. He is a dark, dark wizard.'

'What of the Strange One? Does he aid you?' She knew she should not pry, and yet it is hard for a human to resist the temptation to question a spirit. 'Tell me of the Strange One. What became of him?'

Ntsina sat up and turned away. 'He used to be my friend.'

'And now?'

'He is bewitched by the wicked queen. He cannot remember the promises he once made.'

'What promises?'

'To do well by the Bantu.'

'What of Luvo?'

'He fights for goodness still.' Ntsina turned to her. 'If Luvo escapes the Creature and makes it to Gwadana Village, you are to treat him with all honour. Care for him if he is wounded. Succour him if he is distressed. Feed him, clothe him. Hide him if Strange Ones come searching for him.'

'Might he come to us?'

'It is hard to say what might happen.'

✑

Under Albemarle's supervision, many feelings were hurt but three Shabrill bedrooms, the drawing room, the smoking room, the billiard room and Dorothy's boudoir were completed in record time. Albemarle's craftsmen did not work to the standard set by Ierephaan and Mohammed, who hardly slept, doing their best to elevate uncaring workmanship. Piet was not satisfied, and forbade the dispatch of the furniture; but when he protested Stacey nodded in the direction of their hut.

He followed her with a heavy heart.

'My darling,' she said, when they were alone. 'Pour me a cocktail.' She had decided to be conciliatory.

There were now glasses and a decanter where before had been a vase filled with forest flowers. Piet mixed them stiff gins, and turned them pink with Angostura bitters.

'God, I'm going to enjoy a cold drink when we're back where we belong.'

Piet looked at her warily. 'You liked it here in the beginning.'

'I liked being with you.'

'Did you never find any charm in living in the wild?'

She looked around the sparse little room. 'I thought it charming that you would make such sacrifices for us.'

'I could happily spend the rest of the war here.'

'Without me?'

'If you don't care for it, you could live in town. Take a house. I could visit.'

'For that matter, you could have a workshop in town.'

'I'd rather live here than in Butterworth.'

'What about Johannesburg?' This was Mr Albemarle's suggestion, and seemed eminently sensible.

'Have you forgotten I'm meant to be fighting in France? I can't show myself in Johannesburg.'

'I told Percy you were invalided home. You'd need to walk with a limp for a few weeks, that's all. Everyone will soon forget.' But she could see this was not a fruitful line of discussion and changed tack. 'Remind me, my angel, what got us into this scrape to begin with.'

'What scrape?' Piet was looking out of the window. His eyes focused on a pile of autumn leaves. Something was not quite right about them. 'You mean us having no money?'

'Exactly.'

Piet had learned something of a forest's deceptive powers. He took a sip of gin, his eyes trained on the leaves. They shifted. They were not leaves at all, but a Gaboon viper, coiled in the patch of sunlight caused by the felling of a tree. His pulse rate rose.

'We had a successful business in Cape Town. We nearly went bankrupt for two reasons. First, you did not pursue our debtors. Second, you spent too long fussing over every piece you made. I don't say this to goad you, or to blame you. You have genius, and genius must be nurtured. That is why you must leave all the business side of things to me.' She rose and went to him. Piet's face, usually so animated, was as still as a photograph. She didn't touch him. 'The next shipment is ready. It may not be perfect, but I know our market in Johannesburg and our clients will be bowled over. We have made a splash. The worst thing we could possibly do is take so long with a second delivery that everyone forgets us. You know how fickle people are.'

'Take it then.'

'I need to take the bed.'

'Not that.'

She took a deep breath to suppress the frustration in her voice. The realities of Johannesburg were hard to summon here, and yet she knew them to be true. 'It's your masterpiece, my darling. People must see it. Let it go with this shipment. The other things can follow.'

'Only three of its posts are finished.'

'Have Ierephaan and Mohammed knock up some vines and stick them on the empty one. That's all that's needed.'

'No one touches that bed but me.'

'Then you make the vines.'

'That post is to have jasmine. It's tricky.'

'I'm afraid I'm going to overrule you.'

But Piet would not have this. His stubbornness so infuriated her that she forgot her good resolutions and said: 'Why can't you be more like Percy Shabrill?'

It takes a great deal to disturb the repose of a Gaboon viper, but the raised voices of the hairless apes were sufficient to make this one twitch. He was a male in his prime. Three days before, he had lain in wait for a baby bush pig, and caught him. His venom had made the pig bleed from every orifice. As his meal lay dying, a puff adder had chanced to pass. With dazzling effrontery, this puff adder had taken the pig's haunches in his jaws. The viper had taken the head. They had ingested him together, moving steadily towards one another, neither giving way. But it was the viper who had sprung his jaws extra wide and locked them over the head of his rival – whose body, consumed whole, now lay within him, taxing his digestive capacities most pleasantly.

This contented viper felt the shudder of the earth as a door slammed. Still he slept on, quite happily. He would have done better not to, because the person slamming the door was Piet Barol, and he was in a white temper.

Stacey sat in their shack, alarmed by the mood she had provoked. Piet crossed the clearing, leaping over the wider trenches, and went into the toolshed. Frank Albemarle was there. His wife's trust in this odious man was a daily provocation. Piet took a pitchfork that hung on the wall and went back towards his house.

The viper felt the tread of the hairless ape and lay insolently where he was. It was not until a sharp piece of iron pierced the skin above his skull and went right through his brain that he grasped the ape's malevolent intent. His body thrashed, his venom glands filled, but the rupture of his brain destroyed his higher faculties.

Stacey watched from the window. The spectacle solidified her resolve to leave this place by any means necessary.

When the snake was quite dead, Piet lifted the fork and flung his body far beyond their clearing, to become a feast for the ants. Then he went back inside. His anger made him fearless. 'Since we are having a frank chat, I have something to tell you.'

Stacey had locked her awareness of Frank Albemarle's admiration far away from her conscious thoughts. Now it seeped from its confinement, bringing with it the knowledge that her husband must have had many opportunities for infidelity. What a time to confess them! She sat down. She could not breathe.

'It concerns Ntsina and Luvo.'

Oh the relief! It was all she could do to keep her tone business-like. 'Ah yes. I wanted to speak of them also. It's time we let them go.'

'Is it?'

'Ntsina can't carve for toffee and you speak Kaffir quite well

312

enough now. We don't require a translator. Besides—' and this was Stacey's real objection, 'there is something uppity about those two.'

'I have promised them each three hundred pounds as soon as Shabrill pays us.'

'I beg your pardon?'

'It's thanks to them we have this wood at all. I've also promised to build new shrines for their ancestors, closer to the village.'

'Pay them twice what Shabrill paid them, then.' She saw the look on her husband's face. 'Three times, if you like. But the shrines must be their affair.'

'I promised them three hundred pounds, and new shrines. They used to worship their ancestors in this grove.'

'That's quite out of the question.'

'They have families to support. You must have seen how hard things are for the Bantu in this country.'

'It can't cost much to build a mud hut and buy some cows. Nor still a wooden shrine.'

'I have promised them better than that. Electric light and beds, education for their children. And the shrine must be a proper Christian chapel. Everything comes at a price.'

This observation enraged her.

'Finally! It takes the plight of two insolent Kaffirs to teach you that everything comes at a price! So do *our* house and *our* clothes and *our* son's education. Or would you rather Arthur grew up a piccaninny, knowing nothing but the call of wild birds?'

'Arthur will be leagues ahead of the other boys when he goes to school. Luvo has taught him his times tables already.' Now that he had said what he had promised himself to say, Piet felt calmer. He went to Stacey and took her hand. 'You've done splendidly. I am grateful, believe me. I'll make the furniture more quickly. I'll even put up with that foreman you brought, who can't keep his eyes off you.'

This was a little too close to the mark. 'Without Mr Albemarle, we'd be miles behind.'

'If I grant you that, will you let me keep my word to our Bantu partners?'

They looked at one another. Piet's anger was spent, and he gave her his most winning smile. It was the smile that so often got him what he wanted. He kissed her on the lips, felt an answering tremor in her body and stepped closer. But this proximity was too much. Stacey stood back. She had a flash of intense memory – of the first time she had seen this smile. He had been wearing evening dress that night, sitting by the stage in the first-class nightclub of a glorious ship. Now the liner's gilt and velvet had been replaced by a squalid shack in a forest teeming with snakes, the waiters by insolent Kaffirs. 'What have you become?' she asked.

'I am the man I always was.'

'That you are not.'

'A better man, then.'

'What if I forbid it?'

'Then I will overrule you. For a change.'

The air was thick with unsayable things. Abruptly Stacey sat down. She felt she could not stand this dress, this heat, this place a moment longer. Her relief at being spared one kind of betrayal intensified the pain of learning of this other, quite unexpected piece of treachery. To give six hundred pounds to Kaffirs!

Piet could not read her silence. As it endured, he felt his own resolve creaking. 'I will finish the bed. Give me two more weeks with it. Then you may have it.'

She said nothing.

'One week then. After that I will let you strike all our bargains for us.' Eight spiders were watching them intently. They could sense that a battle was taking place between these hairless apes, and feared for their webs. 'Are we square, my darling?'

Stacey had a gift for strategy. It told her now to defer the making of a decision until they were in a civilized place, where logic might prevail. 'Do me the favour of allowing me to think about it. Let's get this shipment off to Percy. We'll pay everyone their standard wages. When we know what's left, we can decide.'

It was more than Piet had hoped for. 'Thank you, my love.' He sank to his knees and kissed her.

'Pour me another drink,' she said.

⤸

The axes heaved that day, and long into the night. The electric motors of the chainsaws roared, and in Gwadana people heard the sounds, and knew that the great battle was taking place at last. Lundi sat alone in his darkened homestead. The deaths of Fezile the witch doctor and Sukude had convinced him that his own would not be long in coming. How he repented the day he had taken Sukude's first bribe!

Nosakhe, Bela and Noni gathered in the Zinis' magic hut and prayed with all their might. 'Oh, but this is a powerful monster,' said Nosakhe. She switched on the magic box and asked Noni to tell what she heard. To a child with a vivid imagination, the sound of a chainsaw conjures horrifying explanations, and the shrieking of the box intensified them. Bela had told Noni that Ntsina had appeared to her in a dream and told her that a wicked queen had come to the forest to aid the Creature, and brought with her twelve fiends and a dark wizard named Albamaah; that the queen had bewitched the Strange One and made him a traitor to his friends. Noni fused this information into a chilling narrative.

Nosakhe leapt up to join the fight, but the child restrained her. 'No, Mama. This is a war of the spirits. The ancestors are in the forest with them. Stay here, so that you may heal your grandson and his brave friend when they have vanquished the monsters.'

So Nosakhe stayed, and cast spell after spell, and hurled them over the forest.

The sun set and the noises went on. Now a further strange phenomenon was observed: a huge glow, half a day's walk away, in the Ancestor Grove itself. It was visible only from the escarpment of the Zinis, and Nosakhe thought it must be fire. But fires dance, and this light glowed still.

It was electric light, great banks of bulbs running off a generator

315

that contributed to the clamour. Frank Albemarle had bought the kit in Butterworth, to keep his men productive beyond the hours of daylight. He had listened with satisfaction to the Barols' shouting match, and suspected that the man who removed Stacey from this hateful forest would win much acclaim in her eyes.

He had not felt adequately compensated at the furniture manufactory whose production lines he had supervised in Johannesburg, and the wood of the Ancestor Trees ignited a blinding greed. He was sharp enough to acknowledge the brilliance of Piet's designs. That same sharpness told him that with this wood, and those designs, he could set up a profitable concern on his own – with no need to make nice to a Kaffir lover. Albemarle's own opinion of himself had taken a few sharp knocks in recent years, and the chance to restore himself in his own eyes, by snatching opportunities (and perhaps a woman) that Fate had sent his way was a strong spur. While Piet worked on his bed, oblivious to all around him, Albemarle had the Ancestor wood chopped and planed into long planks. With Stacey's permission, he loaded the lorry, which made the first of many return trips to Butterworth.

At length, Noni told Nosakhe and Bela to sleep. They would be useless without their strength. She sat up late, listening to the savagery, and woke at daybreak to find that the sounds continued. For three days they went on, Albemarle's men sleeping in relays. In those days, Piet's feelings, too complex to articulate, flowed through him, were released by his fingers as a creeper of jasmine, so lifelike he could almost smell it.

'I tell you,' said Ntsina, 'they were fighting about us.'

'Do you think so?'

'I know it. See how she won't speak a word to us, not even to tell you to make her coffee.'

Luvo said nothing.

'It always comes to this with Strange Ones. You give them a lake, they want a sea. You give them a sea, they must have an ocean. So much for one tree.' Behind them were great piles of wood. All around were the smaller branches of the Ancestor Trees, their leaves still turned to the sun, hopelessly resisting their fate.

'So what do we do?' Luvo asked the question with a heavy heart.

'It is time to make sure we have the gun, not them.'

This was more easily achieved than Ntsina had anticipated. Most of Albemarle's men were working furiously. Those who were not were sleeping. When Stacey went to wash, Ntsina stole into her shack. Blessing saw him, but made no sound. Ntsina still had a key to the gun chest, given him by Piet long ago. He opened it. There was no weapon in it, but there were two shiny pink stones. He took them without hesitation and continued his search. He found the gun in the cabinet by Stacey's bed, where she could get at it easily. He had never used a gun before, but he had seen a gun's impact. He put it in his lambskin pouch and felt better. Back in the hide, Luvo said: 'You must make sure not to kill anyone.'

But the weapon was already exerting its Dark Magic on Ntsina, who said: 'Then they must not resist too hard.' He sat down. He was conscious of the two glittering stones, and of a strong impulse to keep them both for Bela. How well they would look in her ears. But he had already betrayed one set of sacred obligations, and the thought of cheating his friend was insupportable. He produced the stones. 'One for you, one for me.'

Luvo leaned back from them, as if they were poisoned. 'Those are diamonds,' he said.

'Pulled from the ground by our poor toiling brothers.'

'We cannot take them.'

Ntsina put his hands on Luvo's shoulders. 'If you had let me steal some riches in Johannesburg, we would have saved ourselves much trouble. And this forest much destruction. She wishes to cheat us of money that is rightfully ours. Think of this as a fine for bad behaviour.'

Luvo looked at the jewels. 'The minute you try to sell them, you will be arrested.'

I have no intention of selling mine.'

'You must give them back.'

'Don't "must" me.'

Now a daring possibility struck Luvo, and he seized what might be his last chance. He threw himself at Ntsina and pulled him to the floor, grappling for the diamonds. His friend, taken unawares, fell on top of him. The hide creaked with their exertions. Luvo would not let go. As he fought for the jewels his legs twisted around his friend's, their cheeks touched, they rolled on the hard floor, bruising each other and themselves. And finally, for one glorious moment, Luvo was on top of Ntsina, holding him in his arms, staring down at his face.

Lula birds, crows, bou bous and mouse birds were dotted around the clearing, feasting on the grubs and worms exposed by the destruction of the Ancestor Trees. They took flight as the hairless apes fought, but as soon as the creaking in the hide stopped they flew to earth again, and resumed their excavations.

Luvo's determination to prevent the breaking of a commandment allowed him to enjoy this fight to the full, without conscience or regret. He got Ntsina in a tight hold and tried to prise his fingers open. He dug his elbow into Ntsina's ribs. It had not occurred to him that his friend might be ticklish, but he was. Squeals of laughter ensued, and as he laughed Ntsina lost his strength and his fingers flew open and one of the diamonds was flung onto the floor of the hide. It rolled as far as a small hole, bored long ago by beetles, and fell through that hole. In the course of its descent to the forest floor, the light flashed from it and caught the attention of several birds. The bravest of these, a crow, risked the proximity of the hairless apes and swooped low. The crows of Gwadana are larger than the crows in a city garden, and this crow's wingspan barely fitted between the wooden supports of the hide. It required nifty aerobatics to navigate them, but she was known for her mastery of the air. With an elegant dip her beak found the sharp shining fruit and she soared into the air with it, shouting a song of daring and jubilation.

When the forest fell silent, Bela was seized by a painful foreboding, worse than any she had known. While the battle still raged, she knew that Ntsina lived and was fighting. The ominous calm spoke of finality. One side or another had won, and no matter which way she worked the odds, she could not satisfy herself that victory was Ntsina's. She shared her fears with Noni, but not with Nosakhe, for she knew that a spell of Reincarnation cannot be repeated. If Ntsina had died again, his grandmother could never rescue him. What point was there in troubling her?

Noni tried to reassure her, but she heard no peace in the radio waves and could not refute Bela's logic. In the end she fell silent, her first silence in days, and though she tried very hard to stay awake, sleep abruptly claimed her. Bela looked at her prostrate form and sensed Dark Magic. She carried Noni down the hillside, to the shelter of her mother's arms, the child strapped to her back. The chief's wife saw at once that something was wrong, and invited Bela in. When they had laid Noni on the mat, she said: 'I am acquainted with sorrow, my sister. Tell me what ails you.'

Out it all came. Bela told her of Ntsina's miraculous appearance, of their trysts in the forest, of the battle that had raged for three days, and of the fear that silence had brought with it. This account made sense of many things to the chief's wife. 'What do you fear?' she asked, when Bela was finished.

'That he is dead. Or gravely injured. Lying somewhere in the trees with no one to care for him.'

Her confidante nodded. This seemed likely. She hesitated. She had a secret of her own, known to no one outside her immediate family. At last she said: 'There is one thing more powerful than Death.'

'What is that, sister?'

'Love.'

The chief's wife told Bela the circumstances of Noni's prophesy on the night of her wedding. As she did so, both women realized that Noni had been right about the Strange One from the beginning. She had ordered his execution. Had she been obeyed, the wicked queen could never have enslaved him, or made him turn against his friends.

Bela stood up. She could not sit still a moment longer. A tingling, fiery energy took hold of her. She paced up and down the ample hut.

'I made a pact that night with my ancestors,' said the chief's wife. 'They demanded a final sacrifice before the gift of Farsight was confirmed.'

'What was it?'

The older woman raised her pretty right hand. The tip of her little finger was missing. She usually kept this hand in a fist, or in the folds of her eland hide skirts. Bela stopped pacing.

'Should I cut mine?'

'I do not advise it. The pain is quite terrible. My point is only that Ntsina may need you, and if he does nothing will heal him better than your love.'

'How can I prove it? What should I do? Guide me, sister.'

'I know what I would do if my husband lay injured on the field of battle.'

'What is that?'

'I would find him.'

13

Once, in his final year at the mission school, Luvo had given way to the pleas of the boys in his dormitory and taken from the kitchen the provisions for a midnight feast. He had hidden them in his trunk, and all through that day had known a terrible fear of discovery. That was nothing by comparison with how he felt as he waited for Stacey Barol to discover that her diamond earrings were missing and that Ntsina had her gun.

He spent the day in prayer, while Albemarle's men loaded wood onto the trucks. Only the morning-room sofas, a writing desk, and the great bed remained in the workshop. God answered Luvo's prayer and Stacey did not discover the absence of her jewels or her weapon. When the lorry was packed, Albemarle said: 'Time for a holiday, boys.' He was a great believer in alcohol and women to reward a man's endeavour, and had promised his team plenty of both if they saw to things in double quick time. He handed round bottles of brandy – one for the whites, one for the Bantu. Blessing, Wisdom, Grace, Brightness and Happiness drank swiftly, grateful for the abrupt change in the baas man's mood. 'Give me a cheque and I'll pay them,' said Albemarle to Stacey.

Piet could not find it in himself to utter a word of thanks to the white men. He went to his Bantu band and compelled himself to go through the niceties. In isiXhosa he said: 'I am sorry this man has badly so treated you. Large bonuses shall have you. Promise I.'

He did not know that Albemarle intended to dismiss every one of his black workers once they reached Butterworth. For this reason, he did not say goodbye to any of them.

'Perhaps he means to pay us,' said Luvo to Ntsina. 'Let us at least give him that chance.'

Ntsina hesitated. It seemed unwise to resort to violence when he was so outnumbered. 'Very well,' he said. 'But I will take the gun.'

༄

Being a beauty with a naturally pleasing disposition, the triumphs of youth had come easily to Bela. She had taken trouble, of course, had bathed her skin in the milk of pregnant cows and learned to cast beguiling glances at handsome boys. She had kept the secrets of her girlfriends and honoured her parents. But she had not suffered to acquire her position as the most popular girl in the village. Her suffering had begun on her wedding night, and in the months since she had acquired an inner steel that only hardship can bring. As she prepared herself to enter the forest, she did not feel afraid. Nor did she seek anyone's permission. She did not want Noni or Nosakhe to try to dissuade her; or, worse, to join her and so risk all their lives in a dangerous undertaking. When she got Ntsina back to the village, he would need his grandmother at her fullest powers to complete his recovery. She did not imagine that she, so newly acquainted with the magical arts, could cure him. But she did believe what the chief's wife had told her about Love, and she knew that her own was strong enough to prevail.

She considered taking Kagiso with her, as guide and protector. But there was a part of Bela, a proud part, that imagined her return to Gwadana with Ntsina – a return that would answer all those who still gossiped about her demonic possession. The intrusion of a third party into this scene, and the necessary sharing of her glory, was not pleasing to her. It is known that a woman's hair holds great power, and she went to Zandi to dress it. Zandi was

322

swollen now, and Bela itched to ask who the father of this child was. There was a new ease between the sisters, but when Zandi did not offer this information Bela did not pry. Zandi dressed her hair in two peaks, as she had worn it as a bride, but when Bela saw herself in the reflection of the rainwater trough she shook her head. 'I look like the girl I was, sister. But I am a woman now.' Privately she added: 'A warrior.'

So Zandi devised a new hairstyle, combing Bela's hair up and out, setting it fast with lemon juice. It was magnificent. Bela embraced her. 'When I was alone and forsaken, Zandi, you stayed with me. Whether I live or die, my spirit will watch over you. And your child.'

It was an enigmatic choice of words, and Zandi opened her mouth to question it, but Bela silenced her with a kiss. She kissed her parents, and her cat. She had intended to ascend the escarpment once more, and bid farewell to Nosakhe, but the day was moving on, the resetting of her hair had taken precious time, and she did not wish to be further delayed. Instead, she blew a kiss to a gull, and asked him to deliver her greetings.

Then she turned, and made for the forest.

She went first to the tree where Ntsina usually waited for her, hoping against hope she might find him there. She did not. She closed her eyes and begged her ancestors to lead her to him. The forest was vast, but she did not doubt that she would meet him. The strange, constant light had told her where to look: the grove of the Ancestor Trees, the site of the mighty battle.

In Butterworth, Luvo and Ntsina waited outside the bank with Albemarle's men and the other Bantu. A white lady crossed the road to avoid the crowd of black men. 'What shall we bet on this?' said Ntsina.

Luvo didn't reply.

Albemarle emerged from the bank and handed envelopes to each of the men. Luvo knew at once from the secretive way the whites looked into theirs that they had been paid more than the Bantu, though he and his kind had worked so much longer in the forest. 'Thank you, Boy. Thank you, Boy.' Albemarle went down the line of his black workers, handing them envelopes. It made Luvo burn with shame to see how these men, who had done such fine work, bent their knees and said 'Thank you, Master,' with eyes downcast.

'Train for Jo'burg leaves in four days, by which time I expect you to be shaved and sober,' said Albemarle to his white crew. 'We'll be getting premises in the city. No more Kaffir living for us.' He wondered, as he spoke, whether this gamble would pay off. Stacey had told him to find a place in Butterworth, not Johannesburg. Still, the greater part of the wood was in his possession . . . Once it was on its way, closer to the customers, he felt sure he could persuade her to join it. Not so much her husband, but then Albemarle had no great desire to see her husband again. He had in his trunk ten of Piet's notebooks, full of original drawings. Quite enough to keep his gang occupied. 'You can come with us if you like. Your choice,' he said to the Indians. 'You're hard workers. I'll give you that.' To the Bantu he said: 'Thank you for your services. Good luck to you.'

From the thinness of his envelope, Luvo knew that it did not hold two hundred and eighty-five pounds. He did not wish to open it, since opening it would destroy a fairytale more precious to him than the one about Father Christmas: that Bantu and Strange One could make bargains on honourable terms, and stick to them.

He opened it.

There was five pounds in it.

'Mrs Barol is giving you two something extra,' said Albemarle, drawing Luvo and Ntsina to one side. 'Now don't spend this all on liquor.'

He handed them each a one-pound note.

The effrontery of this gesture made Ntsina so angry he almost drew the gun in this public place. Only the thought of Bela stayed his hand. A husband in jail would be no use to her. 'We will return to the forest tomorrow and make Piet do as he has promised,' he said to Luvo, in an undertone. 'Meanwhile, let me put this to good use.'

And he boldly entered the gentleman's outfitters.

⟡

Bela had made many pilgrimages to the Ancestor Grove, and knew her way there. As she walked through the trees, her feet following the path laid down by three generations of Gwadanans, she looked for signs of magical conflict. She could not detect any. Wariness of the monster rose within her, but suffering had made her brave. Outside the forest, it was cold. Within, the trees kept the wind at bay and the light filtered through their leaves as she remembered. She had brought mealie pap for her lunch and ate it with her fingers, sitting on the trunk of a charred Mopani, which had been severed by lightning. She checked for snakes, and finding none she lingered a while there. The sounds of the forest were soothing. This trail was full of memories – of her parents, when she was little; more recently of her husband, and the wonders he had shown her. She had expected to feel afraid, but the rustling of the trees bestowed a deep calm on her, and she rose from her luncheon feeling happy. She knew that Love is a powerful shield.

Two thousand trees distant, Piet lifted a spray of jasmine and nailed it to the post of the bed he had made. He stepped back, took off his shoes, and crept onto the base. Above and around him, all was nearly as he had wished. There was drama in the foliage and sweetness in the flowers – a happy drama. The creatures were playing and flirting, not killing one another. He had been tempted, for the sake of verisimilitude, to include a serpent slithering on a branch, and congratulated himself on resisting this impulse. The base was hard and unforgiving. A delightful idea came to him. He got up, put his shoes on and crossed the clearing.

325

Stacey was at her table, testing Arthur on his sums. She had hoped to find fault with Luvo's instruction, but Arthur knew all his times tables from 1 x 1 to 20 x 20. These prodigious feats contributed to a softening in Stacey's mood. So did the absence of all others save her family.

Piet was relieved to detect this improvement. She glanced up at him, and gave him their secret half-smile. He returned it, and a great contentment rose through him. 'The bed is almost finished. Bumble Jug, do these sums for me, and if you get them all right you may stay up late and see the stars.' Deprived of Ntsina's company, the forest was less beguiling than usual, and Arthur accepted this inducement without remark. Piet flipped towards the end of the text book, looking for a tricky page. He wanted his son busy long enough for his parents to release all their anger. When Arthur was settled, Piet took an armful of blankets and pillows and said to Stacey: 'I'll come for you in five minutes.'

He laid the blankets on the bed, three deep. They were not as soft as a mattress, but they would do. He put a sheet over them, and another over that one. He plumped the pillows as vigorously as any maid at a grand hotel. The afternoon was growing languid, the light beginning to fade. He went to fetch Stacey, and on an impulse flung her over his shoulder and carried her across the clearing. It was some time since she had permitted such playful impudence, and despite herself she laughed. There was no one to see them, after all.

He put her down in the workshop. He was standing very close to her. Their smells reached places deep within them, beyond anger. When he kissed her neck, she did not resist. He closed the workshop door. It was dark, all at once, and he lit two lamps. The dancing light brought out the enchantments of the bed, and Stacey crawled into it with a feeling approaching wonder. Piet took off his shirt. He was much more attractive than Frank Albemarle, and she was glad not to have given that gentleman any reason to hope for more than her sincere thanks.

'The forest has made you strong,' she said.

'It's made me happy.'

He took off his trousers and went to her. Her dress opened at the front and he undid the buttons slowly, kissing as he went. She had the delightful sensation that many hours stretched ahead of them and raised her hips as he slid the muslin over them.

'When you said you had something to tell me . . .' She smiled, shyly. 'I thought perhaps you had taken a lover while I was away.'

'Never, my darling.'

She hugged him tightly. 'Most handsome men are rascals.'

'Not me.'

She put her nose in the space between his neck and his shoulder, where his smell was sweetest. It connected her with the happiest moments of her past. He felt the tension drain from her. Her body became heavy and malleable in his arms. He unloosed her brassiere and pulled it off. He ran his tongue towards her left nipple, and her skin puckered. He felt that the moment had come to ask a great favour.

'Will you forgive me for honouring my promise to my Bantu friends? It is your money as much as mine. I should have consulted you. I'm sorry.' He ran his lips over her nipple and she gasped. He pulled away and looked deep into her eyes. 'But if I break my word to them . . . I will not be able to think well of myself.'

She said nothing. He moved downwards, his beard sending ripples over her stomach. He did not take her underthings off, but slid his tongue round them. When he found his object, a sensation was unleashed in Stacey that banished all thoughts of the future.

'Say you will.' Piet was grinning mischievously. 'If you do, I will show you how much better I am than Percy Shabrill, in so many ways.'

She could not help herself. The yearning to be free of her resentment of him was powerful. She did the sums in her head. He had been foolish, certainly, and impulsive. But with the orders she already had, and the free supply of excellent wood, and the new efficiencies of Frank Albemarle, they would hardly be destitute. Quite the reverse. 'Very well,' she said. 'On one condition.'

'Anything.'

'The cheques you write them are the last you ever write. After that, all expenditure goes through me.'

'I give you my word.'

He pulled her drawers off.

'Pour me a cocktail before you begin.'

The effort it cost him to stop was very pleasing to her. 'Mint and lemon?'

'Yes please.'

He got up, dressed, and went outside.

ᴄᴏ

The leopard lay in the shade of a lime tree, conscious of the vultures. How undignified. That they should circle him, waiting for starvation to do its grisly work! He, who had once been lord of a thousand trees. He thought of the bats. They would be leaving their cave soon. The sun was already long past the midpoint of the heavens. It might not be so very hard to catch one. He had long since learned to bear the humiliation of such humble meals and glanced at the rock face across the river. The effort to climb it seemed insuperable. Even the thought of blood could not inspire him to attempt it. He thought of the many vicious battles he had won against other leopards. Too late he understood that the only fitting fate for an alpha is to die in conflict. His hips ached. Arthritis had long made leaping dangerous. His old injury sent a quiver of pain through his left hind leg. There was an anthill not far distant. He knew there were creatures, quite large creatures, who lived off ants. Could he . . . But no. He had a shard of dignity still, and besides the ants stung. He raised himself gingerly and padded to the stream. He drank his fill – because a stomach filled with water is better than an empty one. He washed his face in the water, then stopped, rigid.

A creature was walking towards him, singing.

The song Bela sang was the song all Gwadanan children learn – a song extolling the feats of the Great Founder and the people who thought for themselves. It is a song of praise and she drew courage from it, but as she came closer to the Ancestor Grove she fell silent. The light had been golden and romantic. Now it was sinking. The world was on the cusp of night. She thought of the noises she had heard, and the light she had seen, and she began to doubt the wisdom of setting off alone on this mission so fraught with perils. She repented her failure to confide her plans in her grandmother-in-law, whose spells of protection were so potent.

There was a stream running by the path, and she went to it, and prayed earnestly that the water should carry news of her to Nosakhe. She put these wishes on a leaf, and placed it in the stream, and the current bore it quickly away, towards her home.

She advanced. A hundred trees from the grove, she began to see evidence of heavenly violence. Trees were missing – hacked away at their stumps, used as spears, perhaps, for giants. She left the path and began to wander through the wood. Albemarle's men had not been tidy, and Bela found all manner of strange things that have no place in a forest: tins with serrated edges decorated with pictures of smiling Strange Ones, a match box and several sheets of newspaper. She did not touch them, for she knew that the most innocent objects can have powerful magic. Her heart beat painfully fast.

The grove of the Ancestor Trees was a shady place, but all Bela could see ahead was the golden light of sunset. She sank to her knees behind a bush and peered through its branches. She heard a twitching in the undergrowth and turned, terrified that the Creature might have found her. But there was nothing there. She left the bush and crept forward, to another, larger one. Peering through its leaves, she could not credit her own eyes.

The Ancestor Grove had disappeared.

She looked for the tree where her ancestors lived. She was not there. Nor were her sister trees. She said a prayer to her ancestors. Where were they? She dashed across a piece of empty ground and hid behind a termite mound on the edge of the clearing. From here nothing was hidden. The earth was gashed and wounded. The hides she knew were still there – the only detail that confirmed she was in the right place. She looked for Ntsina – for anybody. The clearing was empty. She waited, in case dark creatures were resting in one of the gashes of the earth. Nothing stirred. She considered running back to the village, getting help – but this would waste too much time, and it was clear that Ntsina's need of her was urgent.

Nothing in Bela's cosseted life had prepared her for the courage it required to walk onto the battlefield. As she rose to her full height and took the fifteen steps from where she hid to the grove, she crossed the threshold from youth to maturity. For some, this takes years. For others, it happens in one significant moment. Bela was one of these. She walked into the grove, as if consciously entering a nightmare. All around were signs of terrible violence. To see the limbs of the trees, left in the clearing, untended! She picked up a branch, and caressed it. There were strange new structures dotted among the hides. They were as odd as if they came from another world, with none of the gracious curves of the Xhosa hut.

She knew that the Ancestor Trees are descendants of the Tree of Life, born of His mating with a mortal tree. For a moment she had the wild hope that they had not been vanquished. Perhaps they had retreated, gone to another place in the forest, taking their roots with them. But the quantity of small branches on the ground cast doubt on that hope, as did the sap that oozed from them. They were bleeding, and ants were feasting on their carcasses.

The loss of the trees caused her such anguish that she forgot to be terrified of the monster, or the wicked queen, or the wizard Albamaah. She jumped across a trench, and made her way into the centre of the clearing. Every nerve was sparking, and when she heard the clack of wood on wood she jumped half out of her skin.

The Strange One was there.

They looked at one another.

Piet Barol did not look as Bela remembered him. He had a beard, and was pale no longer. There was a wildness about him. She could well believe that Dark Magic had taken hold of him. Where was the queen? Where were her fiends?

'Bela,' said Piet. 'Welcome.'

But his tone did not support the greeting.

'You've walked a long way,' he said.

Something was very wrong. It took Bela a moment to identify what it was: the Strange One was speaking to her in her own tongue. There could be no clearer evidence that he was in the control of a dark witch. He smiled at her, and the baring of his teeth was terrifying.

'Where is Ntsina?'

'He's not far. Would you like to wait for him?' The Strange One moved towards her. A wide trench lay between them. His blue eyes were mesmerizing. He was focused wholly on her. Bela felt herself lulled by those eyes, by that smile. It is well known that when demons possess a human being they have ways of sending others into a trance. She forced herself to look away.

'Where are the trees?' She picked up a branch, weighted with foliage. 'Stop where you are.'

The Strange One did not stop. 'Would you like a drink? You must be thirsty.'

'Where are the trees?'

Their eyes met, and she read fear in his. At this moment, he leapt across the trench. Bela screamed and stepped back. The earth gave way and she fell. She scrambled to her feet.

'Don't be afraid,' the Strange One was saying. 'I am your friend.'

Now she ran. She tore across the clearing, leaping the trenches, clinging tight to the branch of the Ancestor Tree. She would need this evidence to rouse the village. Piet thought quickly. He had no truck, no wagon, no means of escaping with his wife and child. No way to take the bed until Albemarle came back. Habituation had made him used to the destruction of the Sacred Grove. Now he saw it as Bela must see it, and its savage aspect struck him forcefully. He thought of the chief, of the big men in the village. If they knew . . .

For the first time he realized he might lose his life in this undertaking, and the lives of those he loved. 'Come back!' he shouted. 'Ntsina is freed from his spell. He asks you to wait for him!'

But she could hear desperation in his voice, and it made her run faster.

Many moons living at the top of a steep escarpment had made an athlete of Bela, whose youth had been as indolent as a Xhosa's can be. Fear now deepened her resources. Her senses sharpened. Her eyes saw the ruts in the path, the jutting roots. Her feet leapt over them and landed surely. She became conscious of nothing but the beating of blood in her head and the need to run as fast as she could – towards the village and its reinforcements.

Piet faced a choice between retreat and advance. He did his calculations. If Bela outpaced him, he might have eight hours before the men she summoned arrived. This was nowhere near long enough to get Stacey and Arthur out of the forest. He must make her wait for Ntsina to return. They would find some story she would believe.

He began to run, powered by the thought of all he held dear: his wife and child, defenceless in the clearing; the life that lay ahead of them, in the world beyond. He thought of the bed. He could not abandon it.

The sound of the chase of the hairless apes caught the curiosity of the forest. The thud of their feet cleared the snakes that lay ahead, emerging from their burrows as the sun sank. The hyenas and jackals, the leopards and vultures, stopped what they were doing and listened closely. The activation of his deepest instincts

332

overrode the weakness of malnourishment in the leopard who had stolen Piet's biltong. His ears slicked back. He lost consciousness of the pain in his gammy leg as he lowered himself to the ground, moving with the sleekness of old. The apes were getting closer.

Piet accelerated. Bela might have greater endurance, but his legs were longer. Stride for stride he must beat her. He broke into a sprint. He was not wearing shoes, and the soles of his feet were not toughened as hers were, but adrenaline anaesthetized the pain of the rocks and sharp twigs. It did not prevent their punctures from wounding, nor the wounds from bleeding, and now the smell of the blood of a hairless ape began to twist deliciously through the air of the forest.

Eighty trees' distant, a family of hyenas were grooming one another. The youngest female had an acute sense of smell. It was she who first caught the tempting notes of blood, and at once her siblings and parents stopped their licking and lifted their noses, twitching, to the breeze.

Piet gained on Bela. He threw into his pursuit every ounce of physical power he possessed. He had no clear idea what he would do when he reached her; only that he must detain her until Ntsina returned. But his work in the forest had made him strong, not swift. He was not gaining quickly enough, and he could not sustain this burst of speed for long. As he ran, he ransacked his memory for any detail that might help him.

Words had always been Piet Barol's way. He thought of the stories he had listened to at the campfire. He saw Bela's face in the clearing, her horror at the devastation; heard her ask the unanswerable question: 'Where are the trees?' Now a memory came to him, of his first morning in the grove, and what Ntsina had told him. He stopped running. He needed his breath for the loudest shout of his life. 'The Tree of Life wounded is. The Ancestor Trees tending their father they are.' He bellowed it. He knew the word order wasn't right, and panic took him deeper than before into the intricacies of the language. 'They need you. They have given me the gift of your tongue to tell you.' The words ricocheted down the avenue of trees.

Bela stopped.

'The future of your village depends on you!'

She turned. He was at a safe distance. She was bent double, her lungs clamouring for air.

Piet stayed still, lest a sudden movement set her off again. 'The Creature has wounded the Tree of Life. Ntsina is with Him, and His children, the trees of your ancestors—' He saw he had her attention. 'They need— He needs— The Tree of Life will die without— a woman's care.'

Bela was looking at him intently, trying to discern the nature of the Magic in his eyes. She knew from her own experience that wicked demons can be beaten. The Strange One had been her husband's friend. Had Nosakhe been right, after all, to spare him?

'Please believe me.' Piet spoke with total sincerity.

When the female hairless ape bent low, showing him the back of her neck, the hair on the leopard's spine stood erect. His tail twitched. He had delayed once before with these strange beasts, and lost his chance of a good meal.

'If the Goddess speaks through you, tell me the name of my grandfather,' said Bela.

As she spoke, her eyes trained on Piet, conscious of nothing but his eyes, the leopard leapt. His force knocked her sideways, onto the ground. He weighed barely half what he had weighed in his prime, but it was enough to knock his prey off balance. Bela's scream made the hyenas run faster. The youngest could not resist a whine of victory. Like a benediction, the leopard brought his front paw over Bela's face and sliced through her right eyeball. With his other paw, he cut through her skirt of eland hide. He had long since abandoned all hope that one day, just once before he died, he would know the thrill of his claws driving through ripe, living flesh. He, for whom bats had become a delicacy, who must be grateful for the cast-offs of other kills, the anuses and front hoofs, knew again the delirium of slaughter. Bela's buttocks

334

were exquisitely tender. Much larger and fatter than the haunches of an impala, with none of the hairs that got stuck in his teeth. He tore them open, and the blood flowed warm and fragrant. His left paw moved to her breasts. His claws sliced through this flesh, even softer than her rump. His prey was wriggling and screaming, heightening his ecstasy.

'Help me!! Help me, Strange One!'

Bela was still strong. With a mighty kick she knocked the leopard away from her. 'Help me!'

Piet watched. The leopard was old and mangy. He charged him, clapping his hands. The leopard looked up. Their eyes met. The beast bared his fangs. Piet stopped. If he had a gun . . . or even a stick . . . But the only stick to hand was the branch of the Ancestor Tree Bela had been holding, and it was very close to the leopard, too close to be reached with safety. The instant became infinite. Piet's eyes scanned the forest for a weapon. But as they did a small, insistent voice noted the severity of Bela's wounds, the likelihood that she would die even if he risked his life to save her. And then, more faintly still, the fact that her death would dissolve a great threat to all he held dear.

The leopard turned away from Piet and bit hard into Bela's face. His teeth punctured her jaw and her chin and met again through her tongue.

Piet watched as Bela turned to him, blood pouring from her right eye and her cheek, from her breasts and her buttocks. She was screaming, but she could no longer form words. Only one eye could see, and this eye connected with his, and he saw that she saw that he was standing still.

The leopard's next bite was to her throat, and now her scream became a gurgle, blood frothing as the air left her lungs. She was wriggling frantically, and her attacker – who had not had a piece of prey worth playing with in longer than he could remember – was loath to let her die. Only the scent of the hyenas spurred him to action. He did not wish them to doubt his capacity to

335

finish off a hairless ape on his own. In the joy of the struggle he had resisted the early training of all leopards – to break the prey's neck swiftly. A hairless ape with a broken neck could not struggle, and her efforts to save herself were fuel to his vanity. In his younger days, he had played for hours with injured gazelles and bush pigs, for the pumping blood of a living creature is sweeter than the pooled blood of a dead one. At length, and regretfully, he bit the nape of Bela's neck, in the place Ntsina had most loved to kiss it, and snapped the vertebrae at the top of her spine. She was still alive, but this stopped her struggling. He took a mouthful of flesh from the top of her collarbone, exposing the white shining bone. The blood gushed, the hyenas approached, Bela's eye found Piet's again, and in its gaze was a question.

❧

Stacey stretched, luxuriantly. This was a most magnificent bed. Her husband's touch had left her body in a very pleasant state. She decided to prolong it while she waited for him. She lay back on the pillows. As she took in the subtle details of Piet's craftsmanship, she felt the lifting of her anger as a physical lightening. It left her better able to see things from his point of view. Piet was not a scoundrel. She loved his good nature, and if it led him occasionally to impulsive, foolish generosity, that was a fault she could live with – as long as she held the purse strings. She had concluded a satisfactory negotiation in that regard, and this pleased her too. There would no longer be any friction between them over money. She stroked herself gently, heightening her anticipation for Piet's return.

But Piet did not return.

She brought herself to the brink of climax and waited for him. Kept herself there, and waited some more. And now a certain irritation crept through her. No woman, ready for love, appreciates being made to wait too long.

She called for him, and heard nothing but the echo of her own voice. Eventually she got out of bed. She was loath to put on her dirty, sweaty dress – but she did. She opened the door. It had been glorious afternoon when Piet closed it. She was shocked to find that now it was pitch dark. She took a lantern and made her way back across the clearing. Arthur had lit a paraffin lamp, and was still doing sums. Luvo had taught him that numbers are our friends, and he took pleasure in leading them in their dances. At the sight of his mother, he looked up and smiled and said: 'I'm hungry, Mummy.'

'Where's Papa?'

'With you, I thought.'

He went back to his exercises. She did not wish to alarm him. Now that Arthur mentioned it, she was hungry too. She opened her mouth to call Luvo – but of course he was not there. Neither was anyone else. 'I'll see to some dinner for us,' she said, repressing her body's frustration at being denied the conclusion of its pleasures. 'And find your papa.'

She took a lamp. The clearing was riddled with trenches and dangerous in the dark. She crossed it gingerly, fearful of breaking her ankle. She called Piet's name, but no answer came save the roar of insects. A bat swooped and she ducked and the lantern fell to the ground and went out. There were lanterns in the kitchen, and she made her way forward. The sensation of lowering your foot into a black hole in the centre of a forest clearing is disquieting. She was compelled to do it several times before she reached the kitchen hut. She had no idea where the matches were, and touched every place she could think of with no luck. Her fingers alighted eventually on a bunch of bananas, and more groping yielded the bread tin and a pot of jam. She put the banana and the jam into the tin and went outside.

On moonless nights at Gwadana the stars are bright enough to light a person's way – when they are visible. But a low cloud had crept in. All she had to guide her was the glow from Arthur's lantern, a long way off, and she shouted for her husband at the top of her voice.

Had a leopard found Piet? Or a snake? She listened. The wild mint grew close to the clearing. If he was injured, he would be nearby. She felt sure he would be shouting for her. But the insects' cacophony grew louder, and a million leaves rustled, and she could hear no human voice but her own.

Now she began to be afraid. Were beasts feasting on Piet in the darkness? The thought was unbearable. She fought against her fear. She must rescue him. But for that she needed light and a gun. She moved faster, scrambling across the trenches, banging the ground with her feet to send the snakes away, as she had been told to do. There were two vipers in the clearing, and Stacey's stamping had the desired effect. They slithered away, down a forest track, and one of them smelled human blood.

∽

Many creatures were tempted by Bela's screams – and her silence was more tempting still. The leopard left her heart for last, and as her blood frothed her remaining eye never left Piet. It was still trained on him when the hyenas appeared. He was paralysed by adrenaline and the judgement of that eye. A battle was brewing around the carcass. The hyenas formed a circle, not daring to defy the leopard in his newly invigorated state. But now other leopards came – two leopardesses and a male. One of them wrenched Bela's hip out of its socket and pulled her leg some distance off, burying her muzzle in the delicious blood. Her growl deterred the male, who set himself at Bela's belly and began tearing great chunks of meat from her rib cage. Bela's entrails were spectrally white – as white as her brain, which was the favoured delicacy of the second leopardess, who had sophisticated tastes.

Bela was so plump and well-rounded that no creature, for the moment, thought of troubling herself with the male hairless ape. It is part of the etiquette of the forest that when one gazelle is taken, the others are allowed to flee. None of the fearsome beasts intervened to stop Piet as he edged away. He knew not to expose the nape of his neck and went backwards, terrified of stumbling on a root.

Night now cast its curtain between him and this drama of life and death. He began shaking so violently he could not walk. He dragged himself some distance off the path. He heard growls, then scuffling, and then an almighty fight broke out, the hyenas shrieking. Some distance into the wood he found a log, and sat on it. Bela's eye pursued him. He told himself he had risked his life for her, charged a leopard for her sake. But the insistent voice that had whispered the convenience of her death now turned on him, and told him the price he must pay for that convenience.

It was a terrible price.

He rocked to and fro, trying to be quiet but whimpering despite himself. His teeth were chattering. Why had Bela come into the forest? A fire of rage kindled in him. Had the witch doctor not decreed that no one was to venture beyond the village? He did his best to cling to his anger, but the ice water of guilt doused its comforting flames.

The necessity of finding his own family, and the shelter of his wife's arms, helped him to stand. He went in the direction of the path, but with every step a leaf cracked or a twig snapped, and now he became conscious of the fact that his feet were bleeding. His heart raced, his eyes watered, his adrenaline levels spiralled again, took him beyond heightened responsiveness into a state of near-total immobility. He now knew at first hand what it is to be eaten by a wild animal. He tried to run, but the undergrowth was too thick. Where the path should have been there was only thorny bush, which ripped his clothes and scratched his skin.

A sense of direction had never been one of Piet's gifts, and the vastness of the wood and the darkness of the night drastically heightened the challenge of finding his way home. He called Stacey's name, but something rustled in the grass beside him and he stopped. Deep impulses warned against advertising his distress too widely in a forest at night. He took five steps in one direction, then thought better of it and tried another; then doubted his choice and struck off a third way.

Soon he was utterly lost.

Life had presented Piet Barol with many challenges, and he had risen to most of them. None of them had prepared him for this one. In the wild, in the dark, all his past successes counted for nothing. He did his best to focus his thoughts, but panic blurred them. Bela's eye followed him. He cursed the absence of the stars, but the more he railed at the clouds the less inclined they seemed to budge. At length, deep instinct prevailed and told him to hide. He weighed the merits of earth or tree and decided on a tree. Snakes and leopards were the only tree prowlers who alarmed him, and most snakes are shy. The risk was disturbing one if he chose the wrong branch. He crept from trunk to trunk, looking for one to climb. Gradually, his eyes grew better accustomed to the darkness. He was able to discern the shapes of things. All around him were twitchings and rustlings, and every one stopped him dead.

Finally, he found a tree with a thick, sturdy bush growing close beside it. Using the bush as support, he could perhaps make it into the branches of the tree. He shook himself. His limbs felt rubbery. He made two attempts, and failed. He lacked the strength to haul himself up. He hit himself hard in the face. Twice. He had seen men do this to women in films, when the ladies were having hysterics. It worked. He pulled himself together and got into the tree. The pain of the bark on his hands restored him to himself. He banged the branch, to send off any snakes that might be sleeping on it. The bright green boomslang is extremely poisonous, and the possibility of encountering one made him start shaking again. He hit himself a third time, as hard as he could, and pressed on. He tried to ignore an uncomfortable fact: that there are snakes who cannot be chased off by the rattling of a branch, and who welcome the chance to take prey as large, or larger, than themselves.

At length Piet found a branch wide enough to sit on. He did his best to stay awake, but weariness crept over him like a shroud. After the horrors of the day, his body's strong impulse was to sleep. Twice he nearly fell off, and each time he glimpsed Bela's wedding in a dream, and woke to the appalling truth that the woman whose marriage he had witnessed, who had conducted herself with such perfection, the wife of his dear friend, the man whose sacrifices had made his own fortune, had been *eaten by a leopard*. In 1915! This was not, after all, the Stone Age. He regretted bitterly not throwing himself at that animal. The quiet voice of honesty in his head reminded him that the beast had looked frail. The pain of these thoughts was so extreme that Piet's body, against its better interests, sent sleep to anaesthetize him. He began to see that it would not be possible to stay awake all night, and now he faced a choice between wearing his clothes to guard against the cold, or using them as a safety harness.

He chose safety.

He took off his trousers and his shirt, and tied them together, wishing he had paid more attention to the mysteries of knots. He had quite forgotten the lessons of his childhood. He did as well as he could and wrapped the rope around the branch and knotted it tightly over his waist. He lay down, and locked his hands under the branch.

The naked, sweaty flesh of the legs, chest, arms, face and feet of a hairless ape summoned insects from far and wide. The blood on his feet welcomed them, and set them the delightful challenge of keeping his wounds open. It was now very, very cold, and fear no longer blocked his awareness of the temperature. Self-pity twisted through his other feelings, but he was honest enough to banish it. The sounds of the insects, the sensation of being feasted on, kept him awake for half a tortured hour.

Then he fell dead asleep.

⌒

Stacey did not sleep. Not one wink.

She had locked the door and looked for the gun.

It was missing.

She put Arthur to bed, and told him his daddy was working and not to be disturbed. She went to the window. Her imagination populated the clearing with murderous beasts – or, worse, murderous darkies. She had heard tales of whites in outlying places being punished for the superiority of their race. Her mind ran over many moments with their Bantu workers when she had been rather less than charming. She thought of Luvo – surely he would not? No. He wouldn't. But Ntsina? She knew Ntsina had no love for her. She thought of Blessing, Wisdom, Grace, Happiness, Brightness. She could not imagine any of them having the nerve to enter her shack and steal her gun. But Ntsina . . . She had often caught him looking at her with hatred. She flew to the gun box, hoping against hope that Piet had returned the weapon there.

It was empty.

Her diamonds were gone too! Now she suspected a plot. The darkies had robbed her, kidnapped Piet. They would return for her . . . She found she could easily imagine Ntsina stealing both the gun and her jewels. Perhaps he was in Butterworth, already celebrating with the proceeds of his theft. Or, worse, lurking in the forest, waiting for her to sleep.

Her worry for Piet reacted with fear to intensify her anger. Her grievances against her husband, so recently lifted from her, returned in full force. She found that the possibility that he was dead, or lying injured, did not neutralize her rage at him for bringing them to this hellish place, exposing her and Arthur to such danger.

It took an eternity for the sky to brighten. When it was light enough to make sure there were no snakes on the ground, she went out into the clearing and called her husband's name. She went right to its edge and shouted. She screamed until she was hoarse and her throat ached. She screamed and screamed and Arthur woke, and started crying.

Piet heard her. He would have fallen had he not tied himself to the trunk. He could not make sense of where he was, why there were leaves above him, and ants—There were ants all over his chest. He sat up, scrambling to untie the knot in his shirt. The ants were in warlike spirits and stung him as he swatted them.

The branch was eight feet from the ground and he jumped, frantically trying to trace the direction of Stacey's screams. He didn't land well on his bare feet. He made strange animal noises as he batted the ants away, their venom causing red welts and fierce pain. They clung to his arms, to his hands. They were used to clinging on in a storm. He looked wildly around, saw a pool and threw himself in it. It was unbelievably cold. The water brought him to full consciousness, and instead of lifting, the nightmare around him assumed a solid shape.

He was in the forest because he had chased Bela. He had seen her being eaten by a leopard. He had not saved her. He had lost his way. He picked up his shirt and trousers and hurried towards the sound of Stacey's voice – just as she stopped.

He waited, praying she would call him again. He called her name, but a wind rose up and the leaves drowned his voice. He shouted until he could shout no more, but nothing came back. He looked about him. He had none of Ntsina's subtle observation, and could not distinguish the glade in which he stood from any other in the forest. There were trees, a stream, two termite mounds, two fallen logs, creepers, birds, ants. He began to walk in the direction he thought her voice had come from, and called again, but only a cracked, dry sound emerged. By day, the forest was not as frightening as it was in the dark, but it was still full of snakes and wild beasts. He reached a vast thicket of ferns and plunged into it. Here he could not see where he was putting his feet, and the possibility of cobras came vividly to him. He pressed on.

He made it through the ferns and into another glade. Again

there was a stream, this time a solitary anthill, leaves, ants, two Lula birds in a tree, who rose, squawking, at his approach. He began to mumble incoherently – half in encouragement to himself, half as a prayer to any deity who might hear. Piet had not troubled God much in his life, and did not imagine that He would be much interested in saving him. Still less so after . . . He tried to put the horrors of the night before out of his mind, but Bela's eye would not be banished.

14

Frank Albemarle had set out at dawn, to get most of the driving done before it got too hot. The truck's radiator was inclined to overheat, and there was no point wasting good money on fixing it. 'You've got to do two more trips, my lovely,' he said. 'Then I'm going to find you a nice new owner.'

Like many of the ladies to whom Frank Albemarle addressed endearments, the lorry did not respond. She just got on with the job.

As he drove through the forest, a conflict arose within Frank Albemarle – the same conflict he experienced at the roulette table, when tempted to put all his winnings on a single number. If the gamble came off, his rewards would be exponentially amplified. If it did not, he would lose what he'd already won. He had most of the wood in Butterworth, ready for transport to Johannesburg, and more than enough of Piet's designs to keep him in business for years. He had the carvers he needed, and had got rid of the Bantu whose loyalty to a Kaffir lover could not be shaken. A sensible man would have taken the Barols' cheque book and left at once for the city, and a part of Frank Albemarle found fault with himself for not having done so. And yet . . .

He was naturally inclined to place all his winnings on a single large bet. The many occasions on which this had proved to be a foolish course of action heightened his desire for risk, rather than reduced it. He was mighty fond of a well-turned ankle, and Stacey

Barol had exceptionally fine ankles. His animal nature told him she was aware of his admiration, and her failure to censure him for it struck him as significant. His gambler's sense told him that his chances of coming between the Barols were worth a flutter. He had heard them shouting, and knew from his own experience that a woman who uses such a tone as Stacey had used can be induced to take drastic action. A lady like her did not belong in a forest, surrounded by Kaffirs. Rescuing her from such a predicament would make the joy of riches much keener.

So he drove on, with two objectives in mind: the wood and the woman. He would try for both. If she would not come, he would take the wood alone. He had brought the six least hung-over members of his gang to help.

Frank Albemarle's star had often let him down. He had grown so accustomed to disappointment that he could barely credit the sight that met his arrival. Stacey was alone in the clearing, having hysterics. The joy on her face when she saw the truck, and him in it, was unmistakable and greatly gratifying. He leapt down and took her in his arms, muttering soothing words as she clung to him.

The comfort of another human being after all she had been through was deeply relieving, and Stacey prolonged Albemarle's hug longer than she should have. So long that Piet, who had begun to run in the direction of the lorry's engine, entered the clearing in time to see his wife and her foreman locked in a fervent embrace.

He had expected many sights. Not this one. Jealousy was an emotion he was unaccustomed to, having never been condemned to it. Now it cauterized his wounds, sealed his anguish deep within him.

'I am sorry to disturb you,' he said.

They sprang apart, and in the quickness of that leap Piet read, quite correctly, Stacey's guilt at clinging a little too tightly to Mr Albemarle. To be caught at a disadvantage, when it was she who had been abandoned, made Stacey furious.

'Where on earth have you been?' She wanted to hit him, and also to be hugged by him. These contradictory impulses kept her where she was. She took in Piet's near nakedness, and the welts all over his body where the ants had bitten him. 'What's happened to you?'

'I was lost in the dark. There were leopards and hyenas . . .'

As Piet spoke a great weariness came over him, and a desire to see his son. He walked past his wife and Albemarle and went into their little house. Arthur's delight was so soothing he clung to the little boy, soaking in his love.

'I did all your sums, Daddy. And the ones on the next page.'

'Show me.'

Piet sat at the table, haggard and bitten. Albemarle saw him through the window and knew what he should say. He went to Stacey, careful to keep a respectful distance. 'There are insects in this forest whose bite can send a man mad. Think of rabid dogs. He is clearly not himself.'

This was true enough.

'It is most important that you get yourself and your son to a place of safety. Act quickly and do as I say,' said Albemarle.

To be provided with an explanation focused Stacey's attention. She went into the hut and packed Arthur's few clothes while he sat at the table, his attention keeping his father calm. Outside, Albemarle and his crew loaded the last of the wood into the truck – all save three planks. Piet saw them carry the bed. It took seven men to lift it. He did not protest. They loaded it into the truck, and left behind two sofas and a desk. Then Albemarle went to the hut and knocked. He was ready for the trickiest part of his plan.

'We've got the rest of the furniture loaded, Barol.' He tried to keep all exultation from his voice. 'We'll get it off to town, and leave you here to finish the last three pieces.'

Piet looked up. He nodded.

'You need to see a doctor, my darling.' Stacey went to him. She could not help herself. She touched his welts, and Piet

347

winced. The ant bites were very painful. He became aware of the suitcase.

'Why are you packing?'

'This is not a place for a woman and a child.'

He had no answer to this. Nor the energy to make his wife believe in the charming fantasy of a forest life. He opened his mouth. If he could just tell her what had happened, what he had done to save them . . . But words could not do justice to the spectacle of a woman being eaten alive. 'You belong in town,' he said. 'I see that.'

'Thank you.' And then, in a little voice, a voice which overrode her fear and her anger, Stacey said: 'We belong with you. Come with us.'

Kindness was more than Piet could bear. He teetered on the brink of tears, but Albemarle's presence kept him in check. 'Very well,' he said.

To his great irritation, Albemarle could see no way of leaving Piet behind.

✿

They left the clearing and set out along the track that Piet had followed so often, and so happily. Zuko, the little boy whose mother watered the Strange One's horses, had waited all morning for the truck to return. He was fascinated by this outrageous beast – and by the beings who had tamed it. The sight of Arthur made him frantic with curiosity. A baby *mlungu*! He had not thought to see such a thing. He remained staring after the lorry long after it had disappeared, and traced the dust cloud it left behind.

In Butterworth, Stacey put a fresh shirt on Piet and took him at once to the doctor. This gentleman gave him a stiff brandy and some calamine lotion. The lotion did little to diminish Piet's pain, but the brandy opened a promising door to oblivion. He bought two bottles at the general store, while Albemarle and his men unloaded the lorry. Albemarle had confided his decision to

348

send the wood to the city, and Stacey found she approved of it wholeheartedly.

'Will you come with us to Johannesburg? Please, darling.'

'"Us"? "Johannesburg"?'

'I must place everything correctly in Shabrill's house.' She looked at him. 'You know Arthur can't stay in that forest.'

Piet sat down. The weight of these words was crushing. He found he could not bear the absence of his child, nor the removal of Arthur's innocent faith in his goodness. He tried to think of a reason to keep him. At length he said: 'Please don't take him from me.'

The meekness in his voice neutralized the last of Stacey's anger. She took his hand and kissed it. 'Come with us. We have all the wood. We can make the last things in Johannesburg. If you walk with a limp, no one will question you.'

'I can't tell any more lies,' said Piet.

⌒〜⌒

Ntsina took very happily to the spending of money. He purchased a suit from the outfitters patronized by the best Strange Ones, and washed well in a rain tub, whose middle-aged lady owner was happy to lend such an obliging young man her water, and happier still to receive a shilling for her pains. Once dressed, he went to the jeweller's and bought a gold chain. He was wise enough not to show any white person the pink diamond he intended to give his wife, but Luvo agreed that it looked well on the chain.

Luvo's own spirits were muted as he waited for his friend. It seemed, indeed, that violence would be called for if the terms of Piet's contract with them were to be honoured, and he abhorred violence. He had never imagined a situation in which he might be a party to the breaking of the most important commandment: Thou Shalt Not Kill. It gave the day the aura of a strange dream, and this was heightened by Ntsina's transformation.

Luvo had been brought up to value polished shoes and neat

349

ties. Seeing Ntsina in them made the clothes of the Strange Ones, for the first time, seem foolish and constricting. 'I preferred you in your eland hide,' he said, when Ntsina stood proudly before him.

'Yes. But no one in Gwadana has a suit like this.'

The possession of a gun gave Ntsina total faith in his own destiny. He knew he was prepared to use it. He imagined his return in splendour to Gwadana. For the first time he began to see that he might get away with all he had done. He had invented a gripping account of his battle with the Creature that ended, most sadly, in her escape. The idea that a monster roamed their forest would keep enquiring minds away from it. No one need ever see what had happened to the Ancestor Grove.

He shut his troubled conscience deep inside him. His ancestors were safe with the Christian God – Luvo had told him so, and Luvo knew about such things. They would soon have new shrines, whether or not Piet paid for them. He would see to them himself, if necessary. It was a shame that the trees had died, but in these days it was essential to have money, and he knew that his ancestors did not wish him to earn it by drinking in the evil dust of the Rand and its mines. Besides, the destruction of the trees made his friend's mission to the English king possible. He was convinced that Luvo would be successful, and saw that he himself might play a role in the liberation of his people – by getting Luvo the money he had earned.

He put a deposit down on a brass bed and a feather mattress. Then he took off his brand new clothes and put them in a bag – for he did not wish to dirty them. 'It is time to find the Strange One,' he said.

სა

'I have to finish his furniture, or Shabrill won't pay us. I must go back to the forest – at least for a few days.' Piet's logic was absolute, but so was his resistance to the company of any human being save his son. Only loneliness and grief and work could soothe him.

350

The most tender part of Stacey's being was wounded by her husband's refusal to stay with her. But she had not slept, and the terrors of the night before remained, and she would not beg him. 'The train leaves on Wednesday. We'll wait for you,' she said.

'I'll do my best to finish.'

'Are you alright, darling?'

'No.'

'Why not?'

But he could not answer. Instead he said, remembering the leopard: 'Where is the gun?'

'Someone's taken it.'

'From the box?'

'From the cabinet by my bed. I kept it there . . . In case I needed it.'

'That was stupid.'

He had never been insolent to her before – angry, sometimes, but never rude. He felt he was detonating the bridge by which he might return to his old self. It seemed right, since he could never be that person again.

He kissed her goodbye and went into the general store, where he purchased a rifle and cartridges for it. Then he went into the bank, and withdrew eight hundred pounds. It was almost all the cash in the branch, and the teller looked at him curiously. Piet's eyes warned her not to question him.

Observing the strained parting of husband and wife, Albemarle felt giddy with elation. He could see the sorrow in Stacey's face, and reminded himself not to act abruptly. He did not have the physical charms to prevail against a lady's conscience. Only by feeding her sense of grievance, and doing that subtly, might he prevail. He waited until Piet had squeezed his little boy half to death and climbed back into the lorry. Then he went across the street and said: 'May I escort you to the hotel?'

⁓

351

To have exchanged his wife and child for the company of two bottles of brandy seemed, on reflection, to have been a sensible decision. Piet had never been an enthusiastic drinker. He took another swig, and another, and began to understand why other men drank. The world edged away from him. The noise in his head grew fainter. It was a glorious day. He was reminded of his first sight of the forest, when he and Luvo had angered Ntsina's ancestors. That scene belonged to another lifetime.

Ntsina and Luvo were on the road and heard Piet's truck long before it reached them. Ntsina said a prayer to his ancestors and remembered how they had foiled his earlier attempt to rob this white man. How right they had been! He would have got a few pounds that night, and probably been caught. The situation now was very different.

'Go into the road and make him stop,' he said.

Luvo hesitated. He had been an observer of much immorality, but he had never been its prime mover. He heard the words of St Paul to the Christians at Rome: 'Shall we go on sinning, so that grace may increase? By no means!' He turned to his friend. 'I cannot.'

The lorry crested the hill and came into sight. 'You stop him,' said Ntsina. 'I will search the truck for money. Go.'

'I will not.'

'For the sake of our people.'

'He may not have money with him.'

'He has the means to get money. If you ever wish to meet the English king, do as I say.'

The lorry approached. Ntsina's nerves were at breaking point. He thought of little Arthur, of how much he loved his daddy. He felt an urge to put the gun down, but he banished this weakness. 'If you don't stop him, I'll shoot him through the windshield.'

Luvo stepped into the road and waved his hands. Piet was thinking so intently of his Xhosa partners that when he saw Luvo up ahead, he felt no astonishment. He slowed.

'Go to the other side and keep him talking,' said Ntsina.

Luvo was not suited by temperament to criminal undertakings. His quick mind turned sluggish when deception was required. He found he could not speak as Piet stopped. He remembered his first sight of Piet on the Shabrills' terrace, the friendliness in his tone. No white man had ever spoken to him in this way save Herr Ranke, whom he knew would abhor the waylaying of anyone to rob them, on any grounds whatsoever.

'What's wrong?' Piet got down.

'I do not feel well.' This was true enough.

Piet put the back of his hand to Luvo's forehead. 'You don't have a fever. Have you had enough water? I have some.' He turned to the cab but Luvo put his hand on his arm.

'I don't need water.'

On the other side of the truck, Ntsina stood on the step and looked over the door. The seat was empty. The strange power of a weapon exerted its heady hold on him. He went round to the front.

The appearance of Ntsina with a gun, his gun, the gun they had bought together in happier times, seemed somehow fitting. Time slowed. Piet's eyes travelled from the gun to Ntsina's face, took in the nose and the chin he knew so well, remembered the many nights of laughter they had shared, their first entry to the Ancestor Grove, his wonder then, the mushrooms they had eaten together. For a moment he thought Ntsina knew. The Bantu had powerful magic, after all.

'You have not been true to us,' said Ntsina, gruffly.

This was so precisely the truth that Piet sat down on the step of the truck. It was the look on Luvo's face that made him say: 'It is dangerous, in these times, to kill a white man.' And he took from his pocket a wad of notes.

Luvo's joy at this moment was so overpowering he could not stop himself from executing a little dance in the road. The Strange One had proved himself worthy of their trust! He knocked the gun from Ntsina's hand and instantly regretted it – what if the thing went off? But it did not go off. It lay on the road between them, like an abandoned grievance.

Piet counted the notes. Four hundred for Luvo. Four hundred for Ntsina. It was more than he had promised them, and Luvo pointed this out. 'You have earned it,' said Piet. 'And there will be more for new shrines.'

Ntsina felt humbled and regretful. 'You are a good man. You are not like the others.'

Piet would have chosen a bullet over Ntsina's gratitude. To Luvo he said: 'I wish you luck in your mission. Do not be discouraged by what I have said.' He smiled. '"In a great undertaking one must leave no anthill unopened." Is that not correct?'

They parted, with mutual expressions of esteem. Both Piet and Ntsina had weights on their conscience, but only Ntsina shared his. As he shook Piet's hand he said: 'I have stolen something to give my wife, but that was wrong. I am sorry.' He took from his pocket a pink diamond on a gold chain.

To the astonishment of the two Xhosas, the white man began to cry. Soon he was sobbing so violently he could not stand.

'Forgive me, Piet,' said Ntsina. 'Take it back.'

But Piet would not. He bade them farewell and climbed into the truck. As its engine came to life, Ntsina turned to Luvo. 'The Strange Ones are very strange after all,' he said.

To Zuko's delight, the beast stopped outside his own homestead. The lorry's radiator needed water. Zuko watched, fascinated, as the Strange One got down from the cab. Up close, he looked stranger even than usual. There were bites all over his face. Zuko recognized those bites, and knew how painful they were. He ran to his mother.

Zuko's mother was Lindiwe. She gave the Strange One the water he asked for, and dawdled a while at the gate. He was a handsome Strange One, and he looked sad. Lindiwe's own husband was a violent man, who had left few happy memories behind him after his departure for the mines. For a year she had neither heard from him, nor seen any money. She was a woman of strong appetites, but village gossip had deterred her from seeking her pleasures. The sorrow in the Strange One's face was beguiling.

'Were you sleeping in the path of the Matabele ants?' she asked. 'That is a very strange thing to do.' There was something insolent and sexy in the challenge of her eyes.

'I was tired. I did not wake.'

'You should not leave their bites unattended. If you do not draw the poison out they will fester.'

'They are already itchy. I went to the doctor.'

She flicked her head, indicating her opinion of Strange One medicine men. 'Has he made you feel better?'

'No.'

She smiled. 'The forest offers cures for all its injuries, if only you know where to look.'

'I most definitely do not know where to look.'

The presence of a woman who had no idea who he was, whom he had once been, what he had just done, began to awaken a part of Piet's nature that the events of the last day had suppressed.

'I know,' she said.

To Zuko's great satisfaction, his mother invited the Strange One into the hut. He saw her go to the garden where she grew her medicine, and cut several leaves. He took great pleasure in watching his mother make her potions, as a rule, but today a more glorious adventure beckoned. He had seen mechanized beasts in Butterworth, but never had the opportunity to peek into one. He sat on the wall, looking very innocent, until his mother went inside.

'They bit me all over my body,' said Piet.

'Then take off your shirt,' said Lindiwe.

'What about your son?'

355

'He knows not to enter when the door is closed.' She closed it.

Piet took off his shirt. Lindiwe had milked several leaves of the aloe plant and ground into the foul-tasting juice a secret recipe of seeds and flowers. She took a silvery green leaf and began applying her ointment to the ants' bites. 'First this will heighten your pain. Then it will ease it. Sometimes the only way to fight poison is with poison.'

She was standing very close to him. He did not look at her as she touched his chest. The ointment stung. He winced.

'Be a man, Strange One.' But she smiled. He smiled back. She was as unlike Stacey as any woman could be. His body now remembered his last friendly encounter with his wife.

'Did they bite your legs?' she asked.

'Yes.'

'Then take off your trousers.'

✌

While this was taking place, Zuko approached the dark green beast. It was dusty from the road, but its body gleamed beneath the dust. He stroked it, relishing the brightness beneath. He looked behind him. The door to his mother's hut was closed. His heart sped up. He was a well-brought-up child, and rejoiced in the absence of his father, who had twice hit his mother in front of him. She often told him he was the man of their homestead. This inspired a powerful sense of duty. He knew she would be cross with him for playing with the Strange One's beast, and yet the temptation to do so was powerful. Too powerful. He stood on the step and tried the handle. He pulled down on it as hard as he could and the door swung open.

Zuko was met at once by the scent of leather and oil and petrol. It was intoxicating. The bench creaked as he sat on it. Ahead was a wheel and beyond that many circles with numbers on them. He knew what a Strange One number was, though Strange One letters made no sense. Zuko placed his hands on the wheel. It was moulded to receive his fingers. He turned it, and it moved! He began turning it right and left, throwing his full power into it. He could tell from the crunching on the road that the wheels were moving. Oh the joy! There was a large stick, and he moved that too from side to side, delighting in its resistance.

To Zuko's left was a lever with a button on it. He felt compelled to touch this button. When he did, the lever responded. He pushed it down as far as it would go.

The lorry began to move. Backwards.

This gave Zuko a terrible shock, and reminded the law-abiding part of his nature of the magnitude of his transgression. Cattle thieves were not sympathetically treated by the village council of Idutywa. How much worse to be caught stealing a beast like this. The lorry continued to roll. He wanted to leave it, but what if it went off by itself? He knew he would be blamed.

It took a great deal of courage to touch the lever again. He wondered what to do. But it is in the nature of a lever to be pulled, and he pulled it. There was a loud, scratching sound, and the vehicle stopped.

Zuko felt immensely powerful.

He got down from the cab and closed the door. Then he went round to the back. He had often asked himself what mysteries were housed in the body of this beast. He lifted a flap of the tarpaulin and peered into the gloom. It was a little room. He climbed onto the step and let the tarpaulin fall behind him. There were treasures in here – crates and a bucket, soft blankets.

To his consternation, he heard the Strange One and his mother bid farewell to one another.

Then the beast started to roar.

⌒

Ntsina bought a horse in Idutywa for a generous price and disdained the offer of a bridle. 'Would you like to come with me?'

he asked Luvo. 'You can rest up for the journey ahead.'

But Luvo shook his head. He could barely wait to take this money to his parents, to liberate the Rankes from the burden of caring for them, and purchase his ticket to England. He felt powerfully rewarded by God for tempering Ntsina's murderous instincts.

They embraced one another.

'When you are back from the Great King, you must visit us,' Ntsina said. 'Promise me.'

'I will do my best, brother.' Luvo was careful not to promise. He preferred to leave his friend like this, at the height of their glory, and to nurse his memories of him in secret, than to see him happy in the arms of another.

'The destiny of our people is in safe hands with you,' said Ntsina.

'I will do my best to be worthy.'

Luvo set off down the hill towards Butterworth, denying himself the bittersweet pleasure of a backwards glance.

Ntsina leapt on his horse. The animal knew at once that a man with experience sat upon his back, a man with strength who was also kind. He had not had a happy life at Idutywa, and relished the prospect of freedom. Ntsina's heels had only to touch him lightly for him to break into a canter, and then a gallop. As they climbed towards the forest, Ntsina saw Piet in the distance, moving aside the barrier of ferns that hid the elephant track. He did not wish to spook his horse by following a lorry and turned to the left. There were many entry points to the forest, and another path would do just as well. The air was close. The humidity was rising. It was pleasant to feel the warm breeze against his cheeks, and the energy of a willing animal beneath him.

As they entered the wood, the temperature dropped. It was deliciously cool. In this part of the forest, there was no trace of the destruction Piet's band had wrought. He leaned down and kissed his horse's neck. 'I will show you such a happy life,' he said.

Ntsina took the animal as fast as he could. He did not approach the Ancestor Grove. He had decided not to think of it again, and happiness is a potent aid to the suppression of unhappy memories. He skirted it with care, then joined the track that led directly to Gwadana. He felt uncontainably joyful. So joyful that when he saw a dead leopard ahead, maggots already festering in his wounds, he got down from his horse. He saw at once that a larger creature had been killed and suspected that this old leopard had lost his life in the jousting that follows a kill. It did not seem dignified to leave him in the road. He bent down and pulled him by his leg into some bushes. There was a gash in the foliage where the larger kill had been dragged and he did not pursue it, in case those who had feasted were sleeping there. He said a prayer for the leopard, for it is known that certain noble creatures can enter the realm of the hallowed dead.

Then he got back on his horse and galloped for home.

❧

The mechanical beast took Zuko a long way in the dark, over rough ground. He clung to the side and watched the earth shoot by where the tarpaulin was strapped to the chassis. He was excited, but also afraid. As the journey continued, and the ground got rougher, and the scratch of trees told him they had entered the forest, fear began to prevail over excitement. He began to worry for his mother, who would miss him. He had never been further from her than the village, and the beast was taking him an incalculable distance from home.

In the cab, Piet felt many contradictory things. The ant bites were sharp little pricks that chafed him when he moved. Carnal pleasure had soothed his pain, physical and mental. But as it lifted, his mood plummeted. He had now broken his first promise to his wife, a promise it had cost him dearly to keep for seven years. He tried to tell himself that Stacey had broken their bond of fidelity first, but he knew in his heart that there

359

was no equivalence between her furtive embrace of Frank Albemarle and the frenzied coupling that had taken place in Lindiwe's hut. The taste of another woman on his lips made him sad. And beyond that sadness was Ntsina's delight as he handed over the money.

He drove into the clearing grateful for one thing only: solitude. He got out of the truck. The grove, usually full of working men, was eerie in its emptiness. He reached for the brandy.

He could not bear to go back to his house. It held too many painfully unrealized hopes. He wanted to work but had drunk too much to carve with precision. He went into the workshop. The absence of the bed depressed him. He might have christened it with his wife, and sent it into the world with pride. The fact that his masterpiece should be owned by Percy Shabrill – Percy Shabrill! – was galling. So galling he was able to forget, for a few blessed moments, the horrors of the day before.

It was Bela's eye that reminded him of them. The eye of the woman whose sister he had danced with. Whose husband even now was racing home to give her a diamond.

He went out into the clearing. Only one thing still stood in this vast open space: the scaffolding from which the branches of the last Ancestor Tree had been felled. The last tree to die had been the largest. The scaffolding was much the tallest thing in the vicinity, for the trees that grew around the grove had been too deferential to attempt the height of the giants.

Piet hated all this evidence of destruction. He took the brandy bottles and went to the wooden ladder. He wished to be consoled by the nearness of the sky and the view of healthy trees. The rungs of the ladder were far apart. It was not easy to climb with two bottles of brandy. He went into the workshop and found the knapsack he had brought from Cape Town. He put the bottles into it and slung it around his neck and climbed towards the heavens.

He climbed to the height of the standing trees, and climbed on, leaving them behind. He reached the level where the eagles glide. The clouds were white, the sky blue. It was possible to believe in redemption.

He reached the small platform at the top and sat down. The structure swayed in the wind, and made him afraid. But the view was irresistible. It has been an adventure after all, he thought, and opened the brandy. He drank it straight from the bottle. It burned his throat, and made him retch. But he drank on, till half the bottle was in him.

He had never before drunk like this, and the knowledge that he now belonged to that hopeless race who seek oblivion in alcohol came to him painfully. For several minutes, nothing happened. But alcohol is drawn to water, and it raced through the expansive walls of his small intestine and into his bloodstream. The ground below swayed. He held the rail for support. The turbulent flow of his feelings was dampened. Bela's eye still watched him, but it was further away. He was distracted by the sudden movement of the earth, the spinning of the trees.

He did not know how long he sat there. But while he sat dark clouds began to drift in from the sea. The rising heat of the forest drew them towards itself. The pressure in the atmosphere mounted. Piet grew conscious of the clamminess of his skin, the drip of sweat down his back. The pain of the ant bites lifted, as Lindiwe had said it would. He thought of her – the vastness of her curves, her smell. Her tightness in the midst of all that undulating flesh.

A plump raindrop landed on his cheek.

He looked up. The darkening sky lent a majesty to the scene. He thought how beautiful forests are, in any weather. Large drops began to fall, zinging on the hot metal, evaporating instantly, leaving dark traces.

In the lorry, Zuko heard these raindrops too. He was a brave boy, but one thing made him mortally afraid: thunder. He heard a rumble of it, and then another. He knew it was coming closer. He sat in the lorry, his knees hunched under his chin. In a dark place

361

in a forest it is easy to imagine that the thunder might find you. What then? He started to rock back and forth. The Strange One would be angry with him, no doubt. But he was a strong Strange One. An adult. He would know what to do.

As the first fork of lightning jabbed between two great clouds, a thousand trees distant, Zuko found the courage to get out of the lorry. He had expected trees, having driven through so many, but none were here. He had never seen such a landscape. Its devastation undermined the last of his courage. He looked frantically for the Strange One. He was nowhere to be found.

At the top of the scaffolding, Piet tilted his head back and let the rain wash his face. The drops were coming faster now, the water a benediction. He remembered being taught, as a child, that a baptism in water cleanses sins. He held fast to this thought and closed his eyes, and let the rain run over his lids. With his eyes closed, the earth's instability increased. When he opened them, the trees below were lurching crazily. He was now very drunk, and for the first time it occurred to him that he should perhaps seek shelter. A *crack* of thunder made him jump. The storm was hurling itself towards him.

Zuko saw him. He felt an overpowering urge to seek the comfort and protection of another human being. He ran across the clearing, leaping the trenches. The ladder stretched above him, dauntingly. He was not a tall boy. He began shouting, but still the Strange One did not see him. He banged the ladder. The sound was drowned by thunder. He pulled it with all his might. It lifted away from the scaffolding and clanged back into place. Zuko pulled the ladder again. Piet saw that the ladder was leaping about, of its own accord. His fuddled brain struggled to comprehend why this might be. He looked over the edge and saw a child – but he was not Arthur. He was a Xhosa child. He felt sure he had seen him before. Who was he?

Their eyes met. There was something glazed and terrifying in the Strange One's gaze. Zuko clung tighter to the ladder. As it drifted from the platform, approaching the vertical, Piet reached for it. But his reflexes, usually so fast, were blunted by brandy. In the time it took his brain to process the information relayed by his eyes, the ladder had moved further away. He grabbed for it, and his knuckles connected with it – but not his fingers. This final push sent the ladder upright. It swayed, awaiting the instruction of the wind.

And the wind blew it away from Piet Barol.

Zuko leapt aside as the ladder hit the forest floor. It made a dead, violent sound that disturbed six nearby snakes. The storm was upon them.

'Shed into go!' cried Piet. 'There safer!'

He shouted with such authority that the boy obeyed him. Zuko ran into the open workshop and sat on one of the sofas intended for Percy Shabrill's morning room. He waited as the wind became a tempest. Rain lashed the tin roof, and then the darkness was banished by a light that was brighter than day. Not half a second later came the loudest bellow of thunder Zuko had ever heard.

The storm was right above them.

It is said in many tongues that Nature will have her vengeance on those who injure her. The lightning bolt that illuminated the workshop as Zuko sat on Percy Shabrill's sofa, biting his lip till it bled, reached a temperature of twenty-seven thousand degrees Celsius. It was five times hotter than the surface of the sun.

The clouds could not contain such energy, nor dispute it among themselves while a flash channel of steel was at hand. The electricity leapt from the heavens, found the steel scaffolding, and shot down to the earth – and up through the water and brandy in Piet's body. The first flash burned the linings of his lungs. One hundred and eighty-two capillaries ruptured. The second came swiftly. It struck Piet's head directly, which was the tallest object for miles around. The lightning entered through his eyes, nose, mouth and ears and converged on his brainstem – and then his heart. The damage to his central nervous system was so acute that he lost for ever the power to breathe.

And in Gwadana, Nosakhe Zini watched the storm, and knew that the Great Goddess had joined the battle at last.

POSTSCRIPT

Luvo Yako returned too late to Johannesburg to participate in the delegation sent by the Native National Congress to plead their case in London. A member of this congress, Sol Plaatje, left a remarkable account of it in a book called *Native Life in South Africa*. Despite widespread support from South African missionaries in Britain, and the British public and press, the delegation achieved nothing. The Colonial Secretary, the Right Honourable L. Harcourt, informed the House of Commons that 'The day the deputation saw me the period of twelve months during which that Act could be disallowed on my recommendation had already expired.' At a meeting in Downing Street, he assured the deputation that he had the 'assurance of General Botha, the Prime Minister of South Africa, that the Natives have too much land already.'

The Natives Land Act remained law in South Africa until 1994. Less than ten per cent of the land confiscated in 1913 has been returned to the descendants of its original owners.

ॐ

Ntsina Zini never found Bela's body, and never married again.

When the villagers of Gwadana were compelled to abandon their homesteads in the forced removals of the 1970s, he was eighty-two years old. For several years he worked as a security guard in the hotel built at the top of the escarpment, where the view of the bay is still the best. During this time he lost his health

365

and his wits and on the morning of March 21st, 1983, he walked into the Sea.

ഏ

When Piet Barol failed to arrive in Butterworth in time for the Johannesburg train, Stacey returned to Gwadana to search for him. She drove into the forest with Albemarle and found a distraught child hiding in the workshop.

The ladder lay on the ground at the centre of the clearing, but there was no trace of Piet, whose body lay at the top of the scaffolding. Fearing that he would be blamed, Zuko kept his knowledge of events to himself. Albemarle gave him the hiding of his life, but this failed to elicit any information.

Stacey took Zuko to Butterworth, where his mother eventually found him. She waited a week in the town, then left word at the Travellers' Rest that Piet should follow her to Johannesburg. Two months later she returned to Butterworth alone. No one had seen her husband. She waited a full year, fighting against the knowledge that he had abandoned her.

Six months later, in a rage, she married Frank Albemarle.

Pieces of Albemarle furniture, inspired by the beauties of an African forest, remain some of the finest objects South Africa has ever produced.

ഏ

The forest of Gwadana endures. It is now a fraction of its former size, and shrinks each year as human beings chop the trees at its perimeter. To this day, no Xhosa will venture far into it. When asked why, they will tell you that a Creature lives there, in a stream, with the face of a woman and the body of a snake.

A Creature whose glance can kill.

HOW THIS BOOK WAS MADE

On a hot, dusty day in 2007, I got on a bus in rural South Africa. With me were Nonkazimlo Tom and Onwaba Nkayi, without whom I could never have written this book.

They are Xhosa. I'm a white South African of English and Dutch descent. We were friends despite the vast separations of culture and language. Together, we spent a freezing night on the bus and got off in Butterworth, a ramshackle Colonial town in the Eastern Cape. I knew I wanted to write a book about the powerful magic of forests, and about a European adventurer who had come into my head – a man named Piet Barol.

In Butterworth, I asked the first man I met to tell me of a forest. 'You must go to Gwadana,' he said, and hurried away.

The forest of Gwadana occupies a mythical place in the Xhosa imagination. Every Xhosa has heard of it. Many don't know it actually exists. Most believe it to be a place of dark magic. As far as I know, no human being has spent a whole night in it in living memory.

Nonkazimlo was sceptical about my desire to sleep in such a place. She insisted I seek the permission of the chief of the village. I did, and he granted it – though, again, with the same uneasiness the man in Butterworth had shown.

The village witchdoctor led us to the edge of the trees, and cast spells of protection over us. Gwadana is a primordial forest, just a few acres large now – a remnant of the ancient past. I went in alone. In a few steps, I was not only out of the modern world, but out of all time.

That night, many of the villagers visited the makeshift camp we had set up above the treeline. They were curious to know who on earth would seek out Gwadana, much less spend the night in it. Through them, I made the acquaintance of a man named Mr Mbiko, who was 100 years old.

I asked him *why* no one entered the forest of Gwadana.

'There is a mermaid there,' he told me, 'who lives in a stream under the ground. She has the face of a woman and the body of a snake. Her look turns you to stone.'

I asked him how, if this were the case, anyone knew of the mermaid.

He considered a moment. Then he said: 'When I was a boy, the white men came. They erected structures in the forest. They told me about this creature.'

I thought to myself: I bet there's no mermaid. Those white men had reasons of their own to keep the Xhosas out of their own forest.

And thus a book was born.

I knew who Piet Barol was, and wrote a book about his youth in Holland called *History of a Pleasure Seeker*. I knew from the beginning how he died. But as a white South African, I wasn't able to write richly three dimensional black characters. Apartheid had kept our rainbow nation's many cultures apart very effectively. I knew that if I were to tell this story, I would need to go in quest of lived experience.

I decided against visiting the Eastern Cape as a passive observer. I felt that any black family would feel obliged to behave graciously in the presence of a guest. In a forest in the Tunga Valley, staying up late with Onwaba and Nonkazimlo by the fire, it came to me that I should give something of myself – my time, my money, my energies. That by doing so, wholeheartedly, I would somehow have whatever experience I needed to tell this story with warmth, but no sentimentality.

With Onwaba, Nonkazimlo, the Community of Mthwaku, and a team of others, I helped found Project Lulutho – a place where people can learn green business skills. I recruited an intrepid band of Xhosas, Zulus, French, Americans, English, Germans, and white South Africans. We lived under canvas for a year, and turned a desiccated hillside into a forest of a thousand trees.

The experience was fabulous and appalling and hilarious and miserable, in approximately equal measure. I ended up meeting Cebisa Zono, a young man who had written his own first novel in isiXhosa by the age of 21 – which I had done, in English. A year before our arrival in the Eastern Cape, Cebisa's ancestors appeared to him in a dream and told him that a group of *mlungus* would set up camp on the opposite side of the valley, and that when we arrived he should join us. He became my collaborator. I told him the story I was making, and he told me what a Xhosa might be thinking when certain things occurred.

I am a great believer in the power of fiction to tell the truth. The fact that this book exists is thanks to many people – far too many to name here. My gratitude to them is profound and life-long. They include: Nonkazimlo Tom; Onwaba Nkayi; Cebisa Zono; Benjamin Morse; Jane and Tony Mason; Lunga Dyantyi; Litha Dyantyi; Tim and Anne Wigley; Wendy Sanderson-Smith; Sibusiso Mntambo; Natasha 'Flash' Dyer; Jens Bayer; Anna Henkel; Nathalie Gros; Gary Grabli; Jean-Francois Soleri; Rachel Docherty; Chief Morris Mkhatshane and the entire village of Tunga, who welcomed me so warmly, especially Nosakhe and Albertina, Mntukanti, Zibonele, Zimasile, Thembinkosi, Busisa, Bayanda, Nkosiyabo, Lubabalo, and Landu. Thanks also to Kathleen Anderson, my 'necessary angel', and Patrick Walsh; and to Kirsty Dunseath and Victoria Wilson – two of the best editors a man could hope for.

To learn about the strange things that happened while I wrote this book, search Richard Mason on Youtube.com.

blog and newsletter

For literary discussion, author insight,
book news, exclusive content,
recipes and giveaways, visit the
Weidenfeld & Nicolson blog and
sign up for the newsletter at:

www.wnblog.co.uk

For breaking news, reviews and exclusive competitions
Follow us 🐦 @wnbooks
Find us 🅕 facebook.com/WNfiction